MADDOC

D1527506

A novel by Bertil C. Nelson

First published by Dog Ear Publishing
4011 Vincennes Road
Indianapolis, IN 46268
www.dogearpublishing.net

ISBN: 978-1-4575-3239-9

Library of Congress Control Number: has been applied for

This book is printed on acid-free paper.

This book is a work of fiction. Places, events, and situations in this book are purely fictional and any resemblance to actual persons, living or dead, is coincidental.

Printed in the United States of America

Acknowledgments

E very writer brings his experience to writing, and every writer relies on the knowledge and experience of others. In this writing I have relied on a number of extraordinary individuals who were kind enough to read through the text and provide thoughtful suggestions. I am grateful to each of the following individuals:

Dr. James Espinosa's advice on trauma spared the life of a major character whose role impacts irrevocably on the denouement.

Alan Robinson's lifetime experience in police science and public safety guided me at key points in the text.

Tim Snoha, an extraordinary young man whose life experiences are a beacon to anyone who has experienced cerebral palsy, contributed above and beyond any expectation. His thoughtful reading of the complete text and keen insight resulted in observations that brought clarity, improved organization and maintained flow.

Among the readers who brought darkness into light as I struggled through the writing, Nelson Antonio Denis, J.D., Dr. Scott Farah, Robert J. Boxwell Jr., Ellen Nichols, and Jonathan Nelson provided encouragement and keen insights to the characters and situations found in the pages of Maddoc. Finally, I would be remiss if I did not acknowledge Portsmouth's Deputy Police Chief (Ret.) Leonard DiSessa, a friend of many years, who through conversation and observation, gave me a deep appreciation of the people, the joy and the anomalies that are New Hampshire.

Prologue

I don't like you Sgt. Maddoc, but that's not the point. We need a simple map of the enemy's supply dumps with coordinates. You're the man for the job. Come back with the goods or don't come back at all. Now get your ass out of my office.

*   *   *

Once in enemy territory, 180K southeast of Hanoi, Maddoc concealed his gear and moved around, ranging six or seven miles each day. Fourteen days passed, and he missed his rendezvous.

Twenty-seven weeks to the day. One hundred and eighty-nine days of hunting and killing. The NV would fight to the last man, and they were looking for him. They found his cache and stopped looking, certain the jungle got him.

3:48 PM: April 7, 1972

He was a snake. The grass and dirt that made up his cocoon was an earthy membrane leaving him unseen and deadly. He heard the enemy moving his way.

The first to come into view had his arms tied in front of him, a spiked bamboo pole running through the crook of each arm and across his naked back. Each time his arms dropped, the spikes dug in and he yelped. Charley laughed. Six regulars sauntered behind him.

Maddoc waited twenty seconds and rose silently from the hummock shaking off the grass and twigs for the jungle to rearrange. He came up behind the Cong in minutes, his rhythm attuned exactly to theirs. They sensed no presence but the birds flying away as they passed. A nine inch stiletto killed the first one, its razor edge entering between the ribs, severing his aorta. There was no break in the rhythm and no sound from the victim. Maddoc eased the body into high grass and resumed his place in line.

The five remaining heard nothing but the cacophony of jungle noises. Maddoc, bereft of feeling, floated behind them, untouched by the grace of his surroundings.

The second one died less neatly. He turned toward Maddoc asking for a cigarette and found the stiletto driven up under his chin and into his brain as Maddoc clamped his victim's mouth shut and answered softly using the local patois. He hoisted the body to his shoulder and moved off path to release it. He wiped the blade on the man's shirt and swung back into line.

Maddoc exploited their confidence. Nothing disturbed the rhythm of these last moments. Charley number three, a good eight inches shorter than Maddoc, experienced the garrote. Looping it over his head, Maddoc snapped it tight, lifting him and walking forward as his last heart beats pumped crimson curds into the dust.

The remaining three were too close to each other when the prisoner tripped. As he pulled his arms forward instinctively to break his fall, the spikes dug into his back. He screamed. His captor's rhythm was broken, and Maddoc became a killing machine. Two died from swiftly severed spinal cords. The last one met death just as he kicked the fallen airman. He died with a song, emitting moans and bloody gurgles through a slashed trachea. Maddoc had the airman's ropes cut and the man on his feet before his assailant stopped singing.

He had to leave the jungle. He both loved and despised its permanence, but he was losing his grip. He carried the airman through enemy lines to safety.

CHAPTER 1

September 30, 1974

A s a young man, Anthony Maddoc entered the military with a Bible in his hand. He came home with it dog-eared and blood-stained. He slept in a dark room, often under the bed, and frightened his family with nightmarish outbursts. He seldom spoke and was brusque if asked about Viet Nam. He refused medication, claiming he needed to remain alert. He spent quiet time with his wife and daughter and went to church. The latter helped.

Time heals, and so it did with Anthony Maddoc. He came to enjoy society as he worked in his father's shop speaking with customers. Many knew him as a boy. They enjoyed his smile and demeanor and did not ask about Nam. He laughed and liked his work yet announced one evening he had joined the NYPD. He and Marie had their first argument. Marie wanted to drop it but couldn't. She busied herself with breakfast, carried her silence over from the previous evening.

"Your father is hurt; I know it," she blurted. "Why must you be a policeman? It's dangerous."

Maddoc did not respond. There was no changing his mind, but Marie had to try. "I worried when you were away. Do I have to worry about you on the streets? Your father's wants you to have the store."

He left no room for discussion. "In Sicily my father worked in a market, and came to America to work his trade. He never questioned his duty. My father understands. Defending others is my trade. I need no handout to care for my family."

Each morning, Marie walked three blocks to the church to pray for him.

*   *   *

1

It might have been Maddoc's last day given the turn it took. The recruits were into their third week. Anthony Maddoc remained largely aside, not inclined to engage in the banter. When the other 'cruits ragged on each other, Maddoc listened. Each day's activities were like military training but, without the rigor common to boot camp. The sounds drifting in off East 20th Street, a cacophony of horns, rattles, sirens, shouts, yells and bangs breaching the walls and maintaining their own rhythm. In them he detected both the steadiness and unpredictability of a river's flow, reminding him of Smetana.

The academy had seen better days. The architecture was confused, a miscarriage of time. He lamented the floors, once terrazzo perfectly installed by Italian craftsmen, but now covered with asphalt tiles. What might have been beauty in stone was ugliness, as dreary and unredeemable as the muck from which it was drawn.

Their first two weeks included orientation, strength and fitness tests. Many of the recruits came from a long line of police families. Most worked hard, but some coasted. Those who came because fathers and fathers' fathers wore the blue worked the hardest. They had traditions.

Maddoc's family had traditions. His father's market sold meat, vegetables, and homemade pasta to the old Italians who trusted only those who spoke their dialect. Maddoc's grandfather and uncle, transfers from Calabria, were tied to the Gambardella family. Police officers and wise guys drifted in and out of his young life. As he grew older, their differences were clear yet less distinct.

His joining the NYPD incensed Uncle Carlo who claimed, "Antonio, when you become a man you become part of the family. I give you your own crew."

Maddoc's father, three years older, responded, "He be only in this familia. We need no more bums."

Carlo glared but didn't say a word. The elders, Elio and Mafalda Madduccino, who lived a few doors away, never questioned Sylvio. His word was law. He had papers.

Jobs were scarce. His closest friend, Caleb Abranos, invited him to join his business, but Maddoc denied him. Caleb's activities seemed not much different from Carlo's.

Old stories and new rumors accompanied self-defense training. The Nam vets said nothing. The self-proclaimed hard-asses made claims. Big muscular men, some reminded Maddoc of his comrades in Nam, many of whom came home in body bags.

They lined up quickly on the inside wall of a gymnasium-like hall. Three men in blue fatigues entered. The big man, Lieutenant Eldridge "Jack" Neary, rumored to be a sadistic son of a bitch, led the way.

"At ease, men," Neary commanded. "Today we begin the most important part of your training, defending yourselves on the street. Those who cannot handle it will wash out. I may kick the shit out of some of you. It's not personal. I will kick ass because no matter how tough you think you are, the streets are tougher. When your gun fails, when your stick is not enough and you are down to your last act of desperation, what you learn this week may save your ass. I'm what the boys in the hood call one mean motha. By the end of this training you'll know why."

The men around Maddoc stirred.

Neary pointed to a black cadet half a head above his companions. "Step out here, son." The recruit stepped forward and saluted. "What's your name, niggah?"

"George Kennedy Roosevelt Jones, Sir," refusing to be baited.

"George Kennedy Roosevelt Jones, you are one big-ass niggah," Neary taunted, drawing out each word. "Are you a bad ass, George Kennedy Roosevelt Jones?" The man did not flinch.

Five inches above six feet, taller than Neary, he had proved himself as a defensive end at Syracuse until compressed vertebrae ended his career. He spoke clearly.

"No, sir, people leave me at peace."

"On the streets, Mr. Jones, you will be tested every day. Every punk looking to make his name by killing a niggah cop will come at you. If we put you in El Barrio, you will be uninsurable. The first one you meet will seem friendly enough."

With this, Neary stepped toward Jones, his hands down and smiling. As he came within range, he raised his left hand. As Jones turned toward it, Neary's right leg kicked out viciously, catching Jones in the groin, and doubling him over. Neary stepped forward and brought his knee up into the man's face. Jones went down on one knee; but as he came up, Neary struck him with another kick, knocking him unconscious. Without taking a breath, he turned to the others and said, "Get the picture?" He paused, waiting for a response. "Do I have to answer for you?"

Scattered replies of "No, sir" drifted from the ranks.

Neary stomped his foot. "I want to hear every damn voice! Do you get the picture?"

Almost every voice rang out. He turned to a subordinate and pointed to Jones. "Get this pansy out of here. Those who think you're tough guys will take the same road. If you get through the next few weeks, you'll have some good cops depending on you. If you can't get past me, you'll be a two-bit rent-a-cop."

He paused, looked out at the recruits; some were angry. Jones had made friends. "Hate me if you like. It'll get worse before it gets better."

"We have vets in our ranks. Those who chickened out fall out and sit." In less than a minute, nine veterans stood before the lieutenant. Maddoc was in the middle next to Tommy Byrne, a tough guy from Queens with three tours in Nam; he made his reputation as a tunnel rat. Neary, 40 pounds heavier and five inches taller, called him out. "You ready to try me, young fella?"

"Yes, sir," all Byrne got out just before Neary punched his face and chopped him down with an open hand to the side of his neck. The lieutenant didn't expect much from the smaller man. Neary, hands on hips stood over him in contempt.

Byrne, came up, rage pouring from his eyes. Neary stepped forward and struck him before he got his legs under him. Byrne was up again, stepping back and circling. He snaked off four sharp jabs and caught Neary with a punishing right hook. The lieutenant clinched and got his arms around him, snapping him forward into a bear hug and squeezing relentlessly. Byrne brought his head to the big man's nose, hurting him; but Neary held on. He had Byrne's arms pinned and his feet off the ground denying him leverage. Unable to breathe, Byrne lost consciousness. The lieutenant, shaken and enraged, dropped him and turned away. The little man made a good showing. The lieutenant paused, pointed to Maddoc, and commanded "Clean up this trash."

"Your trash Lieutenant; you clean it up." A collective gasp followed.

Neary failed to understand Maddoc's demeanor. He saw only the challenge and stepped forward as those closest to Maddoc moved aside. He kicked as he had done with Jones. Maddoc caught the kick, moved to his right and gave him a slight push. The lieutenant's failure to make contact left him off balance, and as he spun to his left; one leg hooked with the other and he went down. Laughter followed. He got to his feet, crazy-angry and attacked again.

Maddoc backed away. "Lieutenant, let's forget this happened. No one has to get hurt."

The men watching muttered, "Maddoc's done." "The lieutenant will kill him."

"You want to forget it ever happened?" Neary screamed. "You'll never forget. I'm going to kick your ass out of my academy."

He rushed at Maddoc, stopped just short of him, and faked a kick and duplicated the left hook that buckled Byrne. Maddoc leaned back, the punch passing in front of his face. As he spun with the force of his effort, Maddoc gave him another push, accelerating his movement and again tangling his feet. The lieutenant pulled himself off the floor to laughter and hand-clapping.

"That's enough, Jack," his colleagues injected. "The man doesn't want to fight you."

The lieutenant reached for his sidearm, but came up with a baton. .

Maddoc was emotionless. He was in the Nam jungles facing the enemy.

He held his hands, palm out at head height, a defensive posture Neary mistook for submission. Knowing there was no point; Maddoc offered the man one more chance to back off. "Sir, we can stop this. Let me step away."

"Don't show me your hands. This is not over. Step away? You'll crawl away, you sonuvabitch."

Neary was now cautious. "Well ...you have some tricks up your sleeve," he challenged, "but I'm not one of those slant-eyed bastards in Nam. I'm going to handle you the same way I would handle any thug. With this, the lieutenant stepped forward and pointed his sixteen inch leaded baton. A solid blow could break a bone. He began to circle Maddoc, trying to throw him off stance. Maddoc moved with him, maintaining his position. Neary stepped forward and swung the stick in an arch toward Maddoc's head. Maddoc stepped into the movement, deflecting the swing as his shoulder struck his adversary's elbow. He brought the heel of his hand up under Neary's chin with such force he shattered the lieutenant's jaw and knocked out several teeth. The man was unconscious before he hit the floor.

"Shit," he killed the lieutenant. "He's done." The men stared as Neary's aides called for an ambulance. They muttered. Some of the men applauded lightly. Others smiled. Neary's second, a sergeant, remarked, "This was bound to happen sooner or later."

Maddoc helped Byrne to his feet, and they left the room without looking back.

* * *

Neary's jaw needed reconstruction. Some teeth remained, but he would need dentures. A slight jaw misalignment affected his bite. When the investigation uncovered Neary's earlier assaults, he was reduced to sergeant. He found himself in 103rd Precinct sorting and filing paperwork. Through it all, the pain, recuperation, disfigurement, reprimands, and ignominy, his hatred for Maddoc sustained him. Although his Queens assignment saved his career, his hatred did not abate. He dreamed of destroying Anthony Maddoc. He planned and rehearsed the moments, his rancor a burning coal eating into his soul. As time passed, memories would fade; but the coal never dimmed. There was an inquiry. Maddoc was charged with the assault of a superior officer, but the reviewers reduced the charge to insubordination and issued a verbal reprimand. In the interim, Maddoc and his class graduated to a person, distinguishing themselves under a new deputy superintendent. Ironically, with Neary gone, the superintendent asked Maddoc to conduct the self-defense training.

CHAPTER 2

April 20, 1991 — 7:43 P.M.

...17 years later

The repeatedly ringing bell pulled Marie Maddoc awake. She did not expect anyone. Anthony was on three to eleven. Looking at the bedside clock she saw she had slept for three hours, more than she intended. She was up abruptly, dizzy with anxiety. She never got used to his work, fearing he would be hurt. With her daughter away at school and her husband's odd hours, anxiety was a daily event. Sylvi would graduate in two weeks. Each day since the invitation arrived, she felt better.

Looking through the slats, she had a full view of the entry. It was near dusk. A police officer stood at the door, and her heart sank.

He told her she was never to open the door for anyone she did not know, but it was a policeman. As she unlocked the door, it was pushed open, knocking her down. Two men rushed in; the second one grabbing her by her hair and pulling her to the interior of the house. She passed out. He put a pillow over her face until he believed she was dead.

The men worked methodically turning over bookcases, smashing the glass of a china closet and breaking bric-a-brac. Pictures were pulled from the wall and slammed to the floor. One assailant entered the kitchen and drew a glass of water, knocking a sponge into the sink and failing to turn off the tap. The sink filled as the sponge slid into the drain.

They went room to room. They placed all items of value into a canvas bag. Sylvi's coin collection, cataloged over the years, went in along with jewelry. Anthony Maddoc's service medals went into a trash pail. Marie's small shrine to the Virgin Mary was kicked across the floor. A box cutter destroyed couches, cushions and chairs. They laughed as they broke the legs off tables.

It was dark when they left. The last man out turned back and saw water gathering on the floor but paid no attention. After a few drags, he flipped a cigarette that struck an overhead lamp. The cigarette's ember broke off on impact and landed on a shredded cushion. Having the benefit of darkness, her assailants crossed the street and got into a waiting car. The car moved away slowly.

They did not think things out, but how much thought did murder need? The fire smoldered on the sofa and activated a smoke alarm as it ignited the cotton batting. Light tufts of burning ash floated to the ceiling and became ghostly fireflies dancing across its surface. The flames climbed the curtains to the ceiling.

Marie woke up coughing and crying, "Madre mia help me." Pulling herself to her knees, she crawled, seeking a way out. She reached the kitchen and found a chair. Trying to get up, she slipped and fell against the kitchen table, banging her head and blacking out.

Water and smoke damage were heavy. The fire department arrived within seven minutes, but fire moves quickly. The fire investigator believed the water slowed the spread of the fire; most of it was burning cushions and drapes. It was under control within minutes and cleared within an hour. They discovered Marie's body under a water-soaked tablecloth.

*   *   *

9:07 P.M.

Maddoc, anxious to get home, showered and changed his clothes before feeding Dogbone, an adopted K-9 no one else could handle. A knock on the door snapped the dog to attention. Opening the door, Maddoc was surprised to see a uniformed police officer. The man seemed hesitant. "Sergeant Maddoc?"

"Yes, I'm Anthony Maddoc."

""Sergeant, your home was set on fire earlier today. It was a break-in."

"What about my wife?"

The man's answer terrified him. "Sir, Commissioner Byrne is on his way to the scene."

*   *   *

Wednesday, April 24, 1991

Dozens flanked Anthony Maddoc as he turned from the gravesite. Marie was gone. Sylvi was off campus and could not be reached. It was senior week, the last hurrah before graduation.

All the dean could say was, "We're sorry Sergeant; the seniors are off doing whatever they do after the last exam is written."

He could not picture Sylvi without her mother. Nothing remained for him. As teenagers, he and Marie fell so deeply in love there were no moments when they were not. When Sylvi arrived, she became a part of it. The murder made no sense. Marie survived the cancer. Now, less than four years later, she was gone. Maddoc could not make sense of his world. The things she loved were stolen or destroyed.

There was no wake, and Maddoc asked that the service be open only family and close friends. Nevertheless, a sizeable group of uniformed comrades gathered, including Commissioner Byrne and Inspector Neary. Maddoc could not conceal his grief. No sounds escaped him, but his body shook and tears flowed as the service came to its conclusion to the muted funereal strains of an organ.

Caleb Abranos tried to console him, "Mi amigo, we all loved her. She was a saint. You honor her with your grief. Now you must take care of your daughter. This is what Marie always wanted. Now we tend to your daughter."

Maddoc nodded but was unstrung. He was sad when his father died. He grieved his mother for months, but they both lived full lives and died in their time. This was not Marie's time.

"Caleb, I don't know where to turn. Marie is gone. Once out of Nam, I put killing behind me. Now I have only the urge to kill."

"I understand, my friend. The killing damaged us all, but we were at war. There are no words for this."

Maddoc recalled Maria's words when it seemed the cancer would take her.

"Anthony, we'll keep our faith in the doctors; but should I die you must keep your promise."

Her words echoed.

"There will be time enough to grieve, time to remember me, but you must care for Sylvia. When that is done, you both will understand I remain with you—in mind and in spirit. We have never questioned God's will in our lives, and we cannot question it now."

These were words they shared when she feared the cancer would kill her.

"Why did she open the door, Caleb? It wasn't like her."

"Hombre, she opened the door because she knew who stood on the other side. She would open to a neighbor or to her priest. She might open it to a girl scout selling cookies. She would open it to a policeman."

Maddoc replied. "She beat the cancer, Caleb. When she received Sylvi's graduation announcement, she held it to her heart and cried. She dreamed of Sylvia holding her diploma, achieving what we had not. She was so proud. Who did this Caleb?"

"A policeman or someone dressed as one. Neary perhaps?"

"Neary wouldn't be so clumsy."

"He wouldn't do his own dirty work. The smug bastard relished standing at Marie's graveside."

"He was there?"

"… with his friend, Commissioner Byrne. The scars in Neary's head run deeper than those on his face."

"Byrne is no friend of Neary. You may be a wise man, but Neary is too easy an answer. Besides, I spoke with him shortly after he joined the precinct. I didn't expect much, but he came as close to an apology as he could."

Abranos laughed. "… and gave you a shit assignment. This is payback time."

"He won't come after me."

"You are so dumb. You accepted his authority. The man thinks you're done. Stop thinking! Your daughter is next if he hasn't already got her. We have to find her and then we'll kill this mothafucka."

Maddoc walked to his car.

*   *   *

10

CHAPTER 3

6:33 A.M.: *Thursday April 25, 1991*

Sylvi Maddoc rolled soundlessly from her bed and to the floor, catching herself on her fingertips and toes while trying to learn what awoke her. She looked carefully, her sight adjusting to the gloom.

Jeff slept. A noise drew her attention as someone moved toward the bed. She scampered around and came to her feet with a kick that hammered the left side of the intruder's leg, just above the ankle, tearing tendons and muscle. He cried out and crashed.

As Jeff awoke, a second man came at her from behind and pinned her arms to her side. She slammed her head back against his nose while driving her calloused heel on top of his foot, breaking small bones. He yelled and stumbled forward, falling full weight upon his companion's damaged leg. As he struggled up, she kicked the side of his head, knocking him out.

Jeff's hitting the light switch blinded her. A giant of a man grabbed her throat and punched her midsection, knocking the breath out of her as Jeff rushed him. An open hand sent Jeff across the bed where he fell between the wall and the bed railings. His assailant dropped Sylvi onto the bed and wrapped her tightly in a sheet. She struggled to free herself but was firmly bound. He then walked around the bed. As Jeff attempted to get up, the man hammered him. Jeff was a bag of rags. His assailant dropped him; his body half slipping between the side rail and wall.

Ludim Potter, the second man to go down, was up and limping to the door, moaning and threatening with every step. "I'm gonna kill the bitch. She broke my foot! I'm going to throw her in the sty and let the pigs eat her."

The big man, Maximillian, carried her easily under one arm and spoke up. "You watch what you say, Ludim. Otha wants her. He ain't gonna listen to you, and he better not see you limp. Get Eban. He's hurt bad and needs fixing. If Eban ain't fixed, he ain't no use no more."

Ludim complained. "No one told us she was a wildcat."

Maximillian, usually laconic, responded, "Otha says we bring her back right proper, and you best not mention your foot."

Sylvi, near panic, worked to get free, but failed. She calmed herself.

Ludim's swelling foot pressed against the inside of his boot. The pain was terrible, but it didn't block his thoughts: hurt or not, *Eban's done.*

Maximillian dumped Sylvi onto the truck bed. Sylvi steeled herself against the fall, but gave a small cry when she struck the floor. He then retrieved his friend Eban, who was awake and groaning and gently placed him into the truck with his back against the front passenger's seat. "I'm hurting bad Maximillian."

Maximillian gave him a jug of apple whiskey and then went into the cabin. Jeff seemed dead, and he feared the dead. He backed out, taking nothing, and pulled the door shut.

The big man seldom drove, but no one else could. He placed a cushion between his head and the roof pressing upon it. They soon were moving down an unpaved road with Sylvi bouncing around and Eban complaining.

Maximilian wrapped her well; she couldn't move and relaxed. She listened for Jeff's breathing, having trouble breathing herself. The truck rattled and struggled with engine roaring and wheels slipping. Eban cried with each bump, but quieted as the whiskey dulled his senses. Sylvi dozed.

She awoke as the truck entered a main road. She again listened for Jeff's breathing.

Other than the sheet, she was naked. The dust lifting off the floor choked her. She fought panic and whispered to Jeff but got no response. The hum of the wheels overcame her, and she dropped off.

She came awake as the truck slowed, turned right onto a rough-cut road and bounced, throwing Sylvi against Eban and then back against the wall. Eban awoke screaming she was a whore.

Ludim, in pain himself, yelled over the engine noise, "If you don't stop your caterwauling, I'm gonna leave you on the side of the road for the varmints. Otha sees you like this and he's gonna drop you into the hole." Whatever that meant had an effect. The screaming stopped.

The truck came to its final stop and the two men got out.

Maximilian lifted Eban, who passed out.

Sylvi was dropped to the ground face down. A hum of voices calmed her. They quieted down. She could not see much but knew Jeff was not with her.

Ludim took the end of Sylvi's sheet and unwound her. Pulled to her feet, she stood defiantly with her hands to her sides facing a homespun crowd ogling her. She challenged Ludim, "Where's my friend?"

Ludim laughed. "Your friend is where we left him. Maximillian broke his neck."

Sylvi began to cry. The women, embarrassed by her nudity, grew quiet. They felt her shame without understanding that Sylvi cried for Jeff and was crimson with rage, not shame. The men made crude remarks and adjusted their testicles. She paid scant attention and hugged herself against the coolness.

One bold girl, about seventeen and sexually a veteran in the camp, stepped to Sylvi's side and lifted her breast, giggling as she toyed with the nipple. Sylvi was about to slap her hand away, when a man slapped the girl's face saying, "You bring shame to us before God, Naomi. You will do penance."

At this point a man whose aspect insisted he was in charge stepped forward. He looked Sylvi over and then he turned to Ludim. "From the looks of you and Eban, she is a mite tougher than you expected."

CHAPTER 4

May 2, 1991 – 8:34 P.M.

A curtain of miscellaneous stink settled on curbs and sidewalks between Broadway and 11th and spreading north to 46th and south to 38th, the area host to filth and flatulence. The temperature stood at 74, down 10 degrees from the midday high.

Maddoc returned to work three days after the funeral, unable to sit idle. This was his final shift as a New York City policeman, the last of many weeks undercover. He sat mourning his loss, while watching the parade of riff raff, whores, pimps, drug dealers, itinerant preachers, and scam artists pass by.

He blamed himself. He did not have to take the assignment. Marie was happy with his being on the day shift. Even in winter, he was home before dark. She asked why. Looking back, his explanation seemed foolish. "It's a chance to make a difference, something I haven't done for a long time."

He was stung by her response. "That difference doesn't benefit me."

*   *   *

Inspector Neary waited almost two weeks before summoning Maddoc to his office.

"Sergeant Maddoc, the years have been good to you. They've been good to me, also, and enabled me to put much behind me. I've accepted responsibility for the wrongs I brought upon myself, and I want you to know that bygones are well gone."

Maddoc did not acknowledge his comments. "Sir, you're in charge. What do you require of me?"

14

"Good. We understand each other. I'm taking you off days. You'll be working irregular hours between midday and 1:00 A.M., including overtime."

Maddoc knew the routine.

"You'll follow the usual undercover routine as a homeless person and work several locations but largely on the northwest corner of 8th and 42nd. The mayor's calling for a cleanup, and we need to slow down the pimps and the pushers. You can expect the assignment to last until the cold sets in. Can you do that?"

"Why me, Inspector?"

"There is no better man on the street, and the mayor wants you."

"Fine, have the mayor call me. He'll talk for himself, and I'll listen. I'll let you know what we decide."

He stood and left without another word.

*   *   *

Maddoc's replacement, Hal Pinto, staggered toward him with his cart. Neither acknowledged the other. Undercover officers randomly and unpredictably changed locations.

Maddoc picked up his stuff and turned away, pulling his wagon behind him as Hal shoved another man from the spot. He shuffled down 42nd Street toward the river and turned north on 10th Avenue. Hell's Kitchen seemed normal enough, but the stink remained. The dog followed.

They didn't seem together, yet when Maddoc moved, the dog moved. Near 90 pounds, this mix of lab, standard terrier, and shepherd foraged, seeming skittish except to other dogs.

No one owned him. He and Maddoc shared living space, and Dogbone came and went. He might stay at home when Maddoc was on duty but more commonly showed up. It was a good relationship. Maddoc anticipated the dog's moves, and the dog knew when he was needed. Dogbone was about to be tested.

They were on 10th Avenue, halfway between 44th and 45th, when two young men and their dog turned a corner and ambled toward them. Maddoc saw them earlier on 8th Avenue struggling to control the pit bull.

15

Dogbone watched from across the avenue as they passed Maddoc, giving him wide berth as the dog stretched toward him. Maddoc paid no attention. They walked about twenty-five yards when they stopped, arguing in the local patois.

"That's him. That old bum be getting money on that corner forever. He carries it in the wagon."

"Who says?"

Ernesto's friend. He says we get the money and an extra c-note each if we snuff him. I'm gonna let Guerrero get that old bum. We'll pull him off once the mothafucka stops yelling."

"Yo, that's nuts. This dog sinks his teeth into that bum, and he ain't letting go. He snuff that man."

"…and we get the money, man. Man's nothing to nobody, another scabby old bum dead on the street."

"You spacing, bro. The dog chews him up and the cops be all over it. Can't have no man-killing dog on the streets."

"Shit, who cares?" With this, he released the dog and watched it run toward Maddoc.

Maddoc heard it and thought, *better me; there are the thousands of homeless wandering the streets tonight. Somebody fingered me.* He waited for the right moment.

The moment came, and the wise guys didn't believe it. The dog feared no living creature. Though young, he would fight to the death. He was bearing down on a creature that feared snarling dogs.

At the right moment, Maddoc turned, dropped and roared: STOP! The pit bull stopped ten feet short of Maddoc and snarled. Maddoc attacked. The dog, confused by the dark heavy bulk, jumped back. The creature kept coming. Not trained and following his instincts, the pit bull began to circle.

He ran at Maddoc who yelled again. The dog hesitated and then attacked head-on. Maddoc came to his knees and caught the dog in the air as it went for his throat. He threw the dog off, tossing him ten feet in the air. The dog scrambled to land on his feet; but it was too late.

Dogbone reacted when Maddoc hit the ground. He struck the terrier at full stride, knocking the smaller dog over. Before it could rise to fight, Dogbone clamped his teeth on the underside of a heavily muscled neck and lifted. He shook the animal, crushing his throat and tossing him aside. The dog was dead before it hit the ground. From the moment the dog attacked and Maddoc responded, no more than twenty seconds passed.

The boys were stunned. The owner came running calling "Guerrero, Guerrero." The other, two steps behind him, was waving a small pistol. Dogbone was about to attack when Maddoc gave two short whistles. Dogbone moved to Maddoc's side. On command, Dogbone moved into the street within striking distance of the gunman. Maddoc did not fear for himself. He wore steel under his Kevlar vest. Not by chance, a cruiser pulled up and claimed the gunman's attention. Knowing the drill, he laid the pistol down and pushed it away.

His tearful friend picked up Guerrero and tried to make him stand, unwilling to believe the dog was dead. An officer pulled the boy to his feet, grabbing the dog by its collar and tossing it into the cruiser's open trunk. The boys were cuffed and placed in the back seat. The boy, yelled, "That crazy motha' let the big dog kill my dog. We was just defending ourselves. Arrest that mothafucka."

Maddoc didn't want to kill the dog. The boys were responsible. Early in his career Maddoc tried to turn others like them around. They were ignorant bastards looking for victims to torment and rob without knowing they were victims themselves. These two, however, were on a mission. This was not coincidental.

In his shift between sorrow and rage, rage was taking hold. The attack didn't trigger it. It illuminated it. He needed to sleep and clear his mind. The fight was now joined, and he was beginning to see where it led. He opened the door to the apartment and called Dogbone, but the dog remained outside.

Maddoc threw the bolt, shed down to his skivvies and sat before the TV. He opened a rear window and whistled. Dogbone cleared the sill and walked through the apartment. The incident was more than a message. The cold resolution that drove him in Nam was back. Now he would attend to Sylvi's whereabouts. At forty-three, he was walking away from his career. His pension could wait for him. Sylvi could not.

Unable to sleep, he got up and turned to the late night news, grabbed a beer from the kitchen counter, sat and fell into his thoughts. He awoke to a black and white storm on screen and laughed. He pushed back the recliner and drifted back to sleep.

He was lost in a dream, a dream too real. First the smell. Someone was smoking and jabbering in Vietnamese mixed with crude insults. He heard crying. Everything seemed real, not a dream at all; but only his eyes moved, fluttering, as in a storm.

He hovered above a procession of six regulars and a prisoner and watched himself slaughter them. Then he saw her, Sylvi, naked and tied on a cross. He became a grim reaper.

The last man died as the blood bubbled from a slashed throat. Sylvi lay on the ground somehow free of her bounds but unmoving. He floated down and touched her. She turned her face to him, fear written in her eyes. "Who are you?"

"It's daddy, Sylvi. It's daddy. Don't you know me?"

The dream jarred him awake. His chest heaved as he recalled his last hours behind enemy lines. He took deep breaths and rested. Sylvi was not in the jungles of Nam. The dream was vivid, and the fear in Sylvi's eyes was that of the air man he rescued many years earlier. He was shaken, but his fear faded. In a strange sense, it calmed him. She was not the airman. She was his daughter, tough, resilient and able to manage anywhere.

He caught the early news as he brewed coffee and buttered a raisin bagel. The closing story, with pictures, was pure bathos. He shut it off and finished his breakfast.

Sticking to routine, he held to a regimen no different from the first day he began in his teens. On the streets, his strength was a weapon. His weight remained at 190 on a frame topping six feet. Maddoc, easily able to lift double his weight, was not bulky; but his strength was extraordinary.

His workout finished, Maddoc rewound the answering machine. A flutter ran through him as he sat at the oak block that served as anything at any moment. He heard Sylvi's voice as he played back the messages.

"Dad, it's me. I'm taking a couple of days to hike with some friends. Mom won't be able to reach me, but I'll call her from Franconia Notch. Love you. Give Mom my love. She didn't answer my earlier call. Gotta run."

He played the call back, needing to hear her voice. A knock on the door got Dogbone to his feet; he growled. It was a stranger.

*   *   *

Maddoc closed the door behind Willie.

"Maddoc, I got out yesterday, good behavior. Within hours I learned that Zip Cinto and Mario 'the Mole' Demeola are dead. No one's talking, but they word is they killed your wife on a home break-in. It was a mistake according to the streets, but I don't believe it. Ex-cops don't make such mistakes."

Maddoc, shocked, could not speak. He paused, breathing deeply. "Any ties to Neary?"

"That mothafucka? I don't know. Maybe you'll find out, but we both know you have enemies. Hell, until you saved my ass, I dreamed of killing you myself.

"I didn't save your ass Willy. I just nailed the real killer."

"I'm a reformed man now, no more Willy the Spook. Now it's William Aloysius Battison, handyman."

"Aloysius?"

"Hey man! It ain't easy, but my mom liked it. It keeps me straight"

"So where's the other one?" Two men were in the house. A neighbor reported a car idling. There was a third man, a driver. Any idea that might be?

"Who knows? Maybe Neary drove."

CHAPTER 5

Friday, April 26, 1991

Maddoc arrived on campus expecting to see students walking about, but none were in sight. The Dean's office, sitting just off a pond, was easy to find. She stepped from her office to greet Maddoc.

"Mr. Maddoc, it is a pleasure to meet you. Your daughter is a wonderful member of our community. When I received your call I was sure she would be here when you arrived. Most seniors have returned. She and Jeff Spooner have not."

"Is there a problem?" Maddoc asked.

"This is not uncommon. She'll be here by midday tomorrow. We have accommodations if you wish to stay over."

Maddoc took a deep breath. "Dean Nichols, may we step into your office?"

"Yes, of course. Please forgive me for not asking."

Maddoc nodded. "Dean Nichols, Sylvi's mother was murdered this past week. We buried her yesterday. I need to see Sylvia."

"Oh my lord, oh my lord, that's awful?" She placed her hand on her desk."

Maddoc thought she was about to cry. "I am so sorry for you and Sylvia. We have a grief counselor, if you would like, when you tell her. We'll do all we can to help."

"Dean Nichols, I'm a New York City Police sergeant. I must learn who killed my wife, and the trail gets colder every hour. Please do not tell Sylvia anything. Give me a call when she shows up. I'll come and take her home. It would be helpful to have a counselor when I break the news."

"I understand Sergeant Maddoc. I'll call when she is back on campus."
Maddoc thanked her and left.

Maddoc picked up Route 7 South through Pittsfield to the Mass Turnpike. Once he reached the turnpike, the slap of the wheels seemed to echo moments in their lives.

He thought of Marie and Sylvi. As Sylvi got older, she and her mother seemed more like sisters. Marie and Sylvi shared many campus stories. He saw less of her but stayed abreast of her studies and friends through Marie.

A bittersweet moment pushed him close to tears. It may have been the last 'little girl' moment with Sylvi. The evening before leaving for school Sylvi sat on his lap, all 130 pounds of her, and put her arms around his neck.

"Hey Mom; let's spend a week hiking and camping." It was a thought neither of them believed they would ever hear again.

"It will be fun and give me a chance to see if I remember everything Dad taught me."

Maddoc smiled remembering Marie's response. "I'm game," she lied.

"Sounds like an idea," Maddoc hedged.

Sylvi laughed. "Don't worry Dad. We'll wait a bit. Now that Mom's surgery is over, and the doctors said everything's okay, she'll bounce right back."

"Yes," Maddoc replied, "but it will be weeks before we know for certain."

Marie broke in, "Dr. Purcell said my hair will grow back, although I look pretty good without hair."

"Mom, you're beautiful. I might shave my head when I get on campus."

"You wouldn't," her mother screamed, laughing and throwing her head back.

"Why not? I'll start a new trend. Every independent woman will go along. We'll be known as the Bennington Balds and strut our stuff without hair."

"Sylvi," her mother stammered. "What …what will the boys think?"

"Dad? What will the boys think?"

"It's not your hair the boys see when they're looking at you."

"Anthony, don't put those ideas into your little girl's head."

"She's not a little girl, Marie. She is a woman, in many ways the same woman you were when we married."

"I wasn't the athlete she is."

"That's Dad's doing," Sylvi interjected.

"Well, that may be part of it, but young girls of my day were not so athletic. The boys didn't take to muscular girls."

"Mom, I know what boys want. I'm not going to give it to them. I'll stick with girls."

Maddoc laughed on seeing Marie's reaction. Sylvi laughed. "Don't worry! I like boys, but I'm not ready to get involved. Sometimes I want to kick every boy in the ass."

Marie said, "Sylvi, you wouldn't fight a boy, would you?

"Not unless I had to. Mom, you don't think I'm odd, do you?"

"I wasn't thinking anything bad. You're much your father's daughter, and that's not odd."

"Mom, when I consider having sex, I imagine you as a young girl. Look how young you were when you got married."

Marie blushed. "We were in love …and times were different."

"Mom, you're talking about twenty-odd years ago. Things were not so different. The sexual revolution had come and gone. Bra sales were way down and at every protest women marched topless."

"Maybe," Marie answered, "but they were not first-generation Italian Americans."

"The busty ones were," Sylvi teased, "and those first-generation Italian Americans were no less hot-blooded than their ancestors in the Roman baths."

"Sylvi, where did you learn such things?" Marie laughed.

Maddoc swallowed and caught his breath.

Tears ran down his face distorting the traffic lines.

* * *

Friday, April 26, 1991 — 9:17 P.M.

Maddoc arrived at the precinct and was greeted by the Desk Sergeant, Stan Brosnik. "Hey, you just missed a call from a woman named Dean who wants a call back right away. She left a number."

Maddoc was hopeful. Perhaps Sylvi showed up. Dean Nichols answered immediately.

"Sergeant Maddoc, I spoke to her closest friend, Diane Rasto. Sylvi did not show up at the lodge where they planned to meet. Have you heard anything?"

"Not at all. Please call the state police and ask them to put out an APB. Sylvi can take care of herself, but we can't wait any longer."

"Campus security already called. I'll follow up."

"I need to speak with a state policeman, someone reliable."

"That would be State Police Lieutenant Al Harrington. I'll ask him to call you."

Maddoc confirmed Harrington's contact information and promised to keep her informed.

CHAPTER 6

Friday, July 21, 1989

Jonetta Van Loos fretted, unconscious of the massive brass and glass doors closing behind her. This could be her last week with McDonnell-Paget. Early in her career, she became Gordon Cash's office wife, a risky path but one she negotiated well.

Cash trusted Jonetta and tutored her. It was not about money. She was wealthy, beautiful and haughty. She followed Cash up the ladder and gained enormous influence. Once he retired, it was over. Cash encouraged her, but Jonetta felt naked with all eyes on her.

"I'm going to miss you Van Loos. We spent wonderful evenings together."

"Your wife never suspected, did she?"

"The subject never came up, but she knew. Enough people suspected. Most surmised our globe hopping was not simply business."

Jonetta said, "I'll miss you. You know I love you."

"I know your feelings are as close to love as you can get."

"Perhaps Gordon, but no man will mean as much to me again. What can I expect now?"

"Jonetta, you are a wealthy woman, perhaps wealthier than anyone in this organization. You can retire now if you like, but Lucas has a special interest in you."

"Lucas hates me. What interest other than my head would he have?"

"I am not able to say, and Lucas does not hate you. He admires you. You will be at my farewell soiree next week, I presume?"

"I'm not sure. You and your wife will be feted, and I will not sit with those people who kiss your ass every day. Besides, I cannot go alone."

Cash laughed. "I'm sure you'll have someone on your arm."

Cash's optimism seemed foolish. Yet, she perked up knowing he was no fool.

M. Lucas Chen, the new CEO, had not spoken to her in twenty years. She never liked him. There was too much of the Asian in him. Some years back Chen, the new Chief Operating Officer, tried forcing her out. Cash could not interfere.

Chen chose the wrong fight. Jonetta had solid relationships with Board members, and her own holdings were substantial. Her response to Chen humiliated the C.O.O. Jonetta's attorney detailed the legal grounds upon which his client stood. Chen was not swayed. He then received several calls from Members of the Board. Van Loos had outflanked him. He sent her a brief apology without explaining.

*   *   *

An only child, Jonetta grew up with a concert-flutist mother, Muriel, and an investment-banker father, Pieter, who amassed substantial millions. His estate on the South Shore with its 200 foot beach front and twenty-six room mansion represented a modest part of his wealth.

Pieter spoke early to Jonetta about business. He sent her to Sarah Lawrence to gain intellectual confidence and to the Wharton School where she found herself competing with super stars. She graduated magna cum laude and joined McDonnell-Paget.

Her father failed to see the pathological narcissism she inherited from him.

When he died, he left the entire estate to her with ample provisions for the care of her mother. He gave his closest friend, Milton Halprin, full power as Trustee. This mattered not to Jonetta who at fifteen seduced Halprin; their affair ended when she went off to college.

Jonetta inherited more than three hundred million dollars and all other assets. This was not on her mind when Chen took over McDonnell-Paget. In spite of her wealth she was depressed, sinking into self-doubt. She feared her professional life was over.

Then she received a formal invitation, signed by Chen himself, asking her to join him at the black tie affair hosted by Edward Cesaré Gilletti to honor Gordon Cash. Gilletti was in his final year as McDonnell Paget's Board Chairman. She feared it might be a prank, but a call to Chen's secretary confirmed the invitation and her acceptance.

The day arrived, and she had her hair, nails and makeup done at Garren New York. She dressed, paying careful attention to her undergarments. Only a perfect fit would do. By 7:30 P.M. she was waiting with a glass of warm sherry to calm her.

"Ms. Jonetta," her maid asked, "Are you not a bit nervous to be going out with the company president?"

"No, Anna, I am not. There is not a man in the world I cannot manage."

"I do not understand, Ms. Jonetta."

"It's simple enough. It begins with making him feel wonderful and believing you're infatuated. Once he begins to believe he's got you, you may let him have you. He'll keep coming back. Also you must understand the importance of clean sheets and perfumed pillows."

Anna giggled. "Ms. Jonetta, you are a naughty girl."

The concierge buzzed as the limousine pulled up.

Chen's Bentley arrived promptly at 7:45 p.m. Although she admired the car, she liked to do her own driving. They next picked up Dr. Chen, who stepped through the doors as they pulled up at the company's headquarters. The ride to the Long Island estate took forty minutes during which Chen thanked her, saying, "You will be meeting important people this evening."

"Dr. Chen, let's not be formal. I'm Jonetta and you're Lucas, if that's all right."

"Yes, of course. I'm sorry; I should have suggested so myself. It's Jonetta and Lucas, of course."

"Who are these important people?"

"People whose support I want and you will ensure."

"This is intriguing."

An attendant waved the driver through an iron-gated entryway. They drove about a hundred yards to a house that surprised them as they rounded the last curve. A valet stood ready to park their car. They faced a one story elongated ranch house built on the side of a hill. It seemed small for an estate this size. Jonetta estimated it to be about 6,000 square feet. But what appeared as the main house fronted a downgrade. Once inside, she found herself in a grand foyer with wide circular staircases to the left and right curving down to a large ballroom. A small ensemble played while professional dancers waltzed as guests watched admiringly.

Jonetta was taken aback by the wall hangings realizing she was in the most luxurious home she had ever seen. An assortment of tapestries of varying sizes, none less than six feet wide stunned her. The overlapping panels seemed kaleidoscopic. The largest was a sky line with buildings that she recognized as Hong Kong. She recognized a François Boucher.

Chen escorted her to the top of the stairs. He stood with her for a few moments, waiting to be noticed before descending. Once satisfied he stepped down, each movement paused, giving everyone an opportunity to see the magnificent woman on his arm. Jonetta's bearing answered the moment. Her carriage was regal, each step taken precisely with that of her partner. As they neared the bottom, a contingent of McDonnell-Paget upper management and several board members began a soft cadence of applause, acknowledging their new president and, in doing so, acknowledging Jonetta. She stepped on to the floor and curtsied. She felt wonderful in the knowledge none of them believed she could win over Michael Lucas Chen. Chen smiled as he raised her to full height.

"One drink and one dance Jonetta, and then we must meet some friends in Mr. Gilletti's study." Chen led Jonetta on to the floor and picked up the beat to *In the Mood*. Jonetta was at ease. Chen was a good dancer, not spectacular but competent and improvising a bit as he lead. The dance ended and, with a slight bow, he thanked her. They worked their way back to their table where a dry martini awaited him, a Rob Roy for Jonetta. Chen came to the point.

"Jonetta, you have at least five more good years with McDonnell Paget, more if you like; but I want you to take a five year leave and assume another position, a very important role in which you will be the Chief Operating Officer and Executive Director answerable solely to the President and a board of trustees."

Jonetta was silent. The light mood disappeared, and Chen read her perfectly.

"This comes as a surprise to you, of course; but I want you to consider it. You will meet three people, each a trustee, who will have the final word on my recommendation."

"And if I am not interested, Jonetta said.

"Then you remain with McDonnell-Paget as one of three executive vice-presidents. In either case, you'll be on my team. I have no one inside the company I would trust to do the job I am asking of you."

"Well, I certainly want to support your interests. What is this position?"

You have to allow me some mystery. It is my heritage."

They both chuckled as Chen went on. "You'll have all the details quite soon after which we dine and dance. Ah, Mr. Gilletti is approaching us now."

Seen on the streets, Cesaré Gilletti would not be noticed. His gait was loose, his manner friendly, as though his smile meant something. He was an attorney, a man who honed his mind at Yale. He knew a great deal about Jonetta Van Loos. Chen stood to greet him.

"Lucas, so good to see you. This lovely woman must be Ms. Van Loos."

Jonetta smiled and held out her hand, with practiced charm, said, "Dr. Gilletti, we have not met, but you are a man easily recognized."

"Ms. Van Loos, please call me Cesaré without the title. It is a title American lawyers accept uneasily. Our medical malpractice group would never use it. Of course, were we in England ....?"

Chen broke in. "Enough; I have kept Ms. Van Loos in the dark all evening, and it is time we erase the mystery."

"I agree," Gilletti answered. "Let's adjourn to the study. Your drinks will follow us. Others are waiting."

Chen moved deftly to slide Jonetta's chair from under her.

"Thank you, sir. I sense a mystery unfolding."

"Not much of a mystery Jonetta, but I would appreciate your listening to everything being said. You will be asked only one question; you will have adequate time to consider your response."

Chen and Van Loos followed Gilletti through a double door as a house-man stepped aside. Three people were in the room, a friend, a woman, and, by appearances, an interesting man.

28

The room itself was more than a study. It was a library, a communications center and a board room. The furnishings of bleached mahogany and brushed stainless were flawless.

Jonetta, almost never at a loss for words, was stunned. Everywhere she looked in this house was opulence. She could not contain herself. "This is magnificent! I thought my father's study was beautiful; this is stunning."

Gilletti smiled and spoke, "I knew Pieter Van Loos. He was an extraordinary man who gave me the privilege of settling a number of matters for him during my early years in practice. Until today, I thought his pride in you was exaggerated, but I now see it was not."

Jonetta was hooked. Once Chen read this, he introduced her to the others.

"Jonetta, this is Antonia Gilletti, Cesaré's daughter and a successful attorney in her own right. She made partner in Skaaden Arps before she moved to her dad's firm."

Gilletti broke in, "Of course, she could have joined the firm out of law school, but she insisted on proving herself before she consented to grace our offices."

"Do not believe one word of it Ms. Van Loos. As I recall his words were, 'when I think you're ready, I'll have our HR people contact you,' or some such."

Jonetta, not often gracious with other women, remarked, "You are quite beautiful and an impressive woman. More than one firm recruited you."

"You are right Ms. Van Loos, but once around to it my dad made her an offer I couldn't refuse."

"Please, call me Jonetta. How do wish to be addressed Ms. Gilletti?"

"It's Toni, Jonetta."

Chen interrupted. "Jonetta, this gentleman is Austen Elias Phillips, the current executive director of the Matterlink Foundation. Dr. Phillips joined the foundation with a Rice University Ph.D., and has been hanging around for 30 years."

Dr. Phillips laughed." Please call me Austen, Jonetta. I wasn't hanging around. Largely, I was sleeping while the foundation's assets grew forty-fold."

"Then you were not sleeping, Austen; but you are a young man. Why would you retire?" Jonetta asked.

"It's time for new blood, and I have some books to write, if I have the stamina."

Gilletti scoffed. "Austen, you were born running. Stamina is not your problem."

"Oh, I have a problem?"

"We all have one or two," Jonetta teased.

"Last but not least, Jonetta, this is Milton Halprin, Associate Counsel to the Matterlink Board of Trustees."

"No need to tell Jonetta anything about me. I have known her since she was a wee lass, and I remain Trustee of her father's estate."

"I guess it was my turn to be surprised, Chen said. I presume you are keeping Jonetta's spending down."

"I manage Jonetta's mother's affairs and ensure she remains comfortable. She's approaching 80 but is as sharp as ever. Jonetta, I am sure you know she still practices several hours a day."

"Yes, after which she swims for an hour and then has Harold drive her to her dance class."

"What does she play, Jonetta?"

"Mom graduated from Manhattan as the top flutist in her class, but she always wished she had gone to Julliard and taken up the cello."

"Enough chit chat", Gilletti interrupted. "For your information, Michael, I knew Milton was the Van Loos Estate trustee; but he was surprised when she came into this room. Shall we sit?"

Jonetta sat on Gilletti's left side as the others picked their spots. Gilletti spoke.

"Jonetta, you are here tonight because we wish to have you spend two weeks with Austen before you take over the Matterlink Foundation, assuming, of course, you are interested."

"I know nothing about it."

"Michael, you could have given Jonetta some notice and not leave me to explain."

"Yes, of course, Cesaré, but I knew Ms. Van Loos loves drama."

Gilletti went on. "By way of explanation Jonetta, the Matterlink Foundation grew out of McDonnell-Paget when its founder, Sidney Maratolla, decided to give something back to the community. Since, it has grown spectacularly under Austen's leadership. The foundation's charter requires the McDonnell-Paget CEO to serve as the titular head. It was Dr. Chen's decision to ask you here.

Jonetta, you are an experienced executive in a major organization. What you need to know about this job you will learn quickly as you work with Austen. Michael, please go on."

"Jonetta, we would like you to commit to five years after which, should you not wish to remain in the role, you will return to McDonnell Paget as executive vice-president. Because the company and the foundation are linked, you would attend our executive meetings and would hold the title of senior vice president-at-large with McDonnell-Paget and that of Executive Director and COO of The Matterlink Foundation. You would report on the foundation's activities, but have no votes within the company.

"...but Michael, I already have several thousand votes."

Michael Chen's a bit nonplussed, responded smoothly. "Of course, and Milton is conscious of your wishes when he casts them."

Everyone laughed, blunting Chen's discomposure.

Chen continued. "Your skill in public and corporate relations is well established. You are a fine administrator; your leadership has been evident in every department you managed.

"Your salary will be fixed at $500,000.00 with an annual seven percent increase and a bonus relating to the growth of the foundation's endowment. Over the years, the foundation has never experienced a loss. In addition, you retain your benefits with McDonnell-Paget to which the corporation will add one thousand shares of preferred stock annually, vested upon the completion of your first full term as Executive Director. Do you have any questions?"

"Yes, I do, but I am not going to ask them now. I am intrigued by the opportunity, but I need to digest it all. Details can wait. Right now, I would like to get Michael back on the dance floor."

"Bravo, Toni interjected, and you must tour the estate. There's so much to see."

To this her father responded, "Toni, I would trade it all for the estate Pieter Van Loos built on the south shore. It is the only one I covet."

This brought a laugh as the group pushed away from the table and stood in unison.

"Well Dad, perhaps Jonetta will consider selling it to you if you can afford it."

This elicited a second laugh in which Jonetta joined. She countered, "Perhaps we can trade once it is available; but the furnishings, all the furnishings now here, must remain with this house."

"We have found a wise addition to our inner circle," Gilletti laughed.

*   *   *

Miles away, Anthony Maddoc leaned back on his chair and smiled as Marie and Sylvi fussed about in the kitchen.

"Anthony, are you leaning back on my new dining room chairs?"

He wondered how she knew, but of course she knew. His after-dinner sitting posture never required more than two legs. He sat forward in thought as he waited for the warm apple pie.

Sylvi had narrowed her college choices to Brown, Dartmouth, and Bennington. Her father and mother wanted her to be within driving distance. She decided on Bennington.

*   *   *

CHAPTER 7

Friday, September 6, 1989

After spending $50,000.00 on redecorating and furnishings, Jonetta's office was exactly what she wanted. She preferred modern décor. Austen Phillips's taste was traditional. Many of his furnishings were now worth a small fortune. She suggested he take whatever pieces he liked. The trustees agreed.

During her review of her staff, she took particular interest in Hank Rudinsky, the grant manager for the Perfect Love Adoption Nexus. The program was successful and in the last year of its three-year grant with an option for two more. Rudinsky had proposed one year. He waited in the anteroom while she completed the *Times* puzzle.

Jonetta stepped out and walked him into her office and invited him to sit.

"May I call you Hank?"

"Yes, of course; and how should I address you?"

"What did Dr. Phillips require of the staff?"

"We used first names."

"Being a woman, I am not at ease with that. Unless I take you into my bed, you should refer to me as Ms. Van Loos." She laughed at the expression on his face.

"I'm teasing you. You must call me Jonetta. Tell me about PLAN"

"PLAN is in its final year of a one point five million dollar grant. I am recommending another year at two hundred and fifty thousand. Bram Stephens has done well. PLAN is established in twelve major cities and is expanding."

"In three years?"

"Less! Surprising, isn't it? Stephens absorbed six clinics that couldn't hang on."

"How did he manage that?"

"He looked into communities with needs but inadequate services. He absorbed the community-subsidized programs with a pledge to settle debts and retain qualified staff."

"A bit risky, perhaps?"

"He renegotiated the debt, paying it off at fifty percent and giving local politicians credit for saving the programs. His public relations skills are solid."

"Tell me about the services "

"The agencies counsel couples seeking to adopt. They also assists pregnant women who do not wish to keep their children. Many of the children delivered through the programs are adopted."

"Yet not all."

"No. some mothers decide to keep their babies."

Rudinsky handed a one page document to Jonetta. "As you can see client fees contribute substantially to operations. Surprisingly, income is more than expected. In my view PLAN does not need two more years of funding. While the program is not fully self-sustaining, the one year $250,000 extension will get it there."

"I thought Stephens ask for the two years."

"I told him not to count on it. This gives him an incentive."

"There was a time when I might have thought the same way," Jonetta responded, "but I am not going to sign off. I want Stephens to rework the request and come back for a two year request at $750,000. This is not an issue we should have to visit again. Also, I wish to inspect some of the sites."

Rudinski nodded. "I'll make the changes and arrange dates. Stephens will be pleased."

* * *

CHAPTER 8

5:01 P.M.: Wednesday, July 22, 1991

Maddoc felt born to El Barrio, so like the neighborhood of his youth. The streets, with their smell of the onions, peppers, beans, fish, shrimp, pork, chicken, beef, plantains, and myriad spices, energized him. The atmosphere, the music, the women, and the optimism of the place suggested unmatched sensuality. Saints or whores, the women were vivacious, though somber when in church. Young and sculpted, they challenged the senses. They could blind any man to his vows.

Walking the streets, Maddoc marveled at the array of colors and warm smiling faces belying the daily grind. While largely Puerto Rican, the neighborhoods were a mix of Latin Americans, each with its own sources of pride and great skill in turning common foods into ambrosia. Usually he stuck to a regimen, but in El Barrio he ate for the pleasure of it.

The events of recent days shook his faith. As an altar boy, he had committed himself to God's will in his life. It was a final choice, so fixed that it didn't allow doubts once he put himself in God's hands. He didn't speak of it. He explained to Sylvi when she turned fifteen and was expressing doubts.

"You must have something greater than yourself in your life; something that you believe cannot and will not fail you. You may fail yourself. You may doubt yourself. When you do, you turn to that something inside of you, what I call God's presence, and turn yourself over to it. Somehow it will lead you to right places, and it will give you the strength you need to survive. You've been praying since you were a little girl. Now you're old enough to know why you pray."

He never forgot that conversation, and he believed that she hadn't. It would sustain her and tempered his doubts.

He liked the outdoor play. Children ran at will as the women sitting on the stoops kept the little ones from wandering too far. On a warm evening he saw pockets of men clustered around tables where a game of dominoes was in progress to spectators' hoots and suggestions. There were chess players who mesmerized the watchers with their skill. Stick ball was not as common as it had been – too many cars, but any wall invited a game of handball, and the few tennis courts were always busy, often into the night under the light of the stars and streetlamps. Weeds didn't grow on empty lots, pounded into submission by soccer fanatics who played into the dark of night with fluorescent balls that had to be wiped clean every few minutes. A heavy rain might dampen enthusiasm, but a light rain had no effect.

Young Ivy Leaguers returned. They were street smart and would bring change, but it would take time. Being culturally rich, the neighborhood gave much; but those who returned could not overcome the apathy carried over by many from their early years. Without good schools to support the efforts of church and family the community gained little ground against drugs and sex. Maddoc knew this; yet no matter what his mood, El Barrio, restored him.

He ducked into a non-descript storefront at Lexington Avenue and 119th and was greeted by Caleb "El Gato" Abranos. While Abranos was a good photographer, the store was a front. El Gato produced paper. His documents, from social security cards to green cards to passports, were as good as the genuine article and expensive.

"Hey Cabron! What's with you? I call; you don't call back. We have a plan. "

"More or less."

Abranos shrugged, knowing details would emerge. "Any leads?"

"Dean Nichols set me up with a state police lieutenant named Al Harrington. An APB has been issued. Harrington learned that Sylvi used her credit card at a gas station just off Route 16 near Conway. Two days earlier, a woman was reported to have knocked down two men outside a bar in Portsmouth. "

"What can her Uncle Caleb do?"

36

"I don't think she's lost Caleb. We're checking hospitals. The Portsmouth incident was called in, but the woman left before police arrived."

"You think it was Sylvi?"

"The description fits.

"Can Reuben check her bank records and her credit card?"

"He'll monitor them and know if they are used and where."

"Amigo, I have to believe that Neary is involved. Marie's murder was no accident and his soul still burns with memories of the beating you gave him."

"A lot of years have passed. My gut says there is more to this than simple revenge. I might accept Neary's being behind the break-in. I cannot accept his being involved with Sylvi's disappearance. It's too great a stretch. Besides, he's put those years behind him."

Abranos shook his head. "Most men would, but he is reminded of you every day. He seldom speaks in public. Until his jaw healed up, he never ate in public. His hate is burned into his soul. Until you came along, he was the NYPD's rising star, had any woman with a nod; but now no woman smiles on him."

Maddoc asked. "Do you think everything is about having a woman?"

"All men do."

Neary faced you, and you brought laughter upon him. He would go after your family. His bitterness is that of a forsaken man. Let's not forget that when his wife left, the children and her family fortune went along. I think he was behind the break-in."

"I get it. Can Reuben get into an organization's files?"

Abranos laughed. "Amigo, he makes miracles. Every package I put together is as legitimate as it would be if issued by Uncle Abe and notarized by Jesus Christ. Once he puts them through the system, they're legal. What do you want Reuben to do?"

"I want Neary's financial records. How does he spend his time and money? Who are his friends and confidants? I want his phone messages. How much of that can you do Reuben?"

Reuben, who had been listening, smiled. "Tio Antonio, I do all that now. Give me two days, and I'll tell you all there is to know about him."

"Do you do it legally?"

Abranos interrupted. "Everything Reuben does is legal. Our clients have certain requirements".

Maddoc laughed. "Legal ay? I guess that means legal so long as you don't get caught. Tapping into government files is dangerous, a major felony."

"Oye, compadre. You know that we do no funny business here."

"So be it, Caleb. I trust what you do — unless you're doing it for criminals."

"I do no work for criminales! "Es bastante; it's enough."

"Es justo mi cinismo, mi amigo; nada más."

"Oh, my friend, just your cynicism and nothing more, ay? Well, cynicism is religion for you. Caleb Abranos respects religion."

"Ah, you are now a priest, Father Caleb." Both men laughed.

"In two days," Abranos continued, "Reuben will have so much information for you, you'll need time sorting it out."

Maddoc nodded and said, "If it's good information, we may know all we need to know about Jack Neary.

"You'll know where he was when Marie died"

"Yes. I also want to know where he was when Sylvi dropped from sight."

Reuben interjected, "Hey, Tio, I can tell you what Neary had for lunch yesterday."

Abranos smiled as he spoke, "Amigo, you will never change. You have thought through a hundred possibilities and come up with Neary. I suggest Neary, and you deny me."

Maddoc responded, "Neary is a coward who needs others to do his dirty work. We have little reason to believe Sylvi is in trouble."

"Hah! Again you tell me nothing. The Sylvia Maddoc I know would not miss her last week on campus."

Maddoc said, "Caleb, let's walk and get some sun."

"Good idea, Antonio. You buy me lunch."

Maddoc laughed. They walked to 1st Avenue without speaking until Abranos could no longer remain quiet.

If you're going to tell me something, I would know, would I not?"

"You would know if you listened."

"What have you said? I've been doing all the talking."

"At which you are quite practiced."

"What is it you want, amigo?"

Maddoc then told Caleb what he learned from Harrington. "He's looking north of Conway."

"… and what makes him think that?"

"All towns and suburbs have been canvassed. If she were in a populated area or in trouble, it would be known. All we know is she did not return to Bennington."

"Mi hermano, we go up there and bring Sylvi home."

"That's the plan."

"When were you going to tell me?"

Once you stopped mewing, El Gato. Sylvi is simply a missing person. Without proof of a crime not much is being done. Harrington suggested a request from the Commissioner would get things moving."

"Neary's friend Commissioner Byrne? They stood together at Marie's funeral.

"He and Neary share a history that does not suggest camaraderie."

"What do you want me to do?"

"Contact Star Engstrom, G. K. Jones, and Dave DeCarlo. Harrington thinks we should get underway with our own team."

"Do we know where in hell we're going?"

Harrington wants us to look north, starting in Franconia. The police search ruled out hospitals, hotels and vacation areas."

Caleb said, "Hey my friend, there are many little towns up there."

"So Harrington says."

"And you think Harrington is on track?"

"If he asked that question about Manhattan, would we trust our views."

"I see you point"

"Good! Now you buy lunch."

* * *

39

CHAPTER 9

Otha Gubbin read newspapers daily. He learned white babies were scarce – big demand, small supply. He laughed when he told Erla, the senior of his several wives.

"Imagine. With all the white folks around, you'd think they'd throw off extra chillun. Our women sure throw 'em off fast enough.

Erla got to thinking. "Look what you made off the ones you sold. Their mommas were happy with what you gave'em."

Otha, in thought, nodded. One boy went to a Portsmouth lawyer for $3,000; $50.00 went to the child's mother. The second child, a cameo baby girl, seemed perfect in every way. Otha went back to the lawyer who needed papers. Being the mayor and Erla the registrar, he got a birth certificate with a physician's signature and a signed release. This baby brought $5,000. Otha paid that mother $50.00.

When the lawyer inquired if he might have a third baby, there were none; but for generations Otha's family raised livestock. The parallels were clear, and his baby farm was born. He had everything he needed. Gannett had a small clinic set up when the town had thriving industries. The clinic had little demand once jobs disappeared, but the doctors, both settled in, hung on.

He couldn't rely on community women. Few would give up their babies. He needed a source he could manage. He found his first girl begging on a street in Conway, a pregnant fifteen-year-old thrown out by ascetic parents who drove her to find love wherever she could. Otha kneeled in prayer with her on the street and offered to care for her and her baby. "It is God's will," he proclaimed.

He named her Leah, disregarding her given name. When her baby boy was born she was told it was a child of sin. She loved the baby but Otha's prayers swayed her. "Lord, you brought Leah to me heavy with child, and called upon me to save her. I prayed about it, and you answered. Your message was clear. Leah must put this child in a Christian home to be born again through Jesus Christ and raised in the ways of the Lord."

She cried about it. Otha blessed her for washing away her sins with righteous tears. He said, "God is now within you. You are now his vessel, and ready for the planting of his seed, as he planted his seed in Mary. The Lord will bring unto you Christian men who, as God wills, leave their seed."

She handed the baby boy to Otha. He sold the child for $7,500, but there was no payoff. The $7,500 he pocketed, along with what remained of his previous gains, represented more ready cash than he ever had.

Things fell into place. Otha was able to arrange for Leah to have various men from outside the community. She soon was pregnant. He gave her $25.00 each time she serviced one of them, pin money he called it. His rounds of itinerant preaching brought young street girls easily taken in. These were transported to Gannett for religious retreats and invited to stay. With further indoctrination, many did stay and followed Leah's path. Those refusing were sent to a logging camp for rehabilitation and cohabitation. No one ever found a way out of the camp. Some tried, but Otha's clansmen knew the woods. Town was no paradise, but it was no camp in the woods either. Once pregnant, the women found it easier to go back to Gannett.

Young clansmen brought in women whose situation was no better than those on the streets. After that, mother willing, any clan newborn appearing normal became inventory.

Placements grew and with them cash flow. Otha spoke with his attorney, Faye Knielex. She was comfortable with their arrangement, and he trusted her.

"You know, my folks don't earn much. Sometimes hikers come by, and a family from time to time. We feed them, and they buy things our folks make, but that's it. I'm thinking we should set up something in case the folks drifting in turn out to be revenuers."

"You pay your taxes, don't you?"

"Can't much avoid it, but we don't pay much. We ain't had any property assessment for years. No one's buying or selling. We don't make any real money.

"What about federal tax?"

"I don't pay none," Otha admitted. "Never made enough to bother."

"Now you do."

"Yep, but I don't want to pay taxes."

"You can avoid paying."

"How?"

"You maintain a home for unwed mothers at your own expense. We can set up a foundation, and the money will go to the foundation. You won't pay taxes on any of it except what you pay yourself. We can run it out of my office."

Otha thought for a bit and asked, "Who controls it?"

"You do as Trustee. You need a board of directors and must submit an annual report. I would handle those details. You run the day to day and sign the checks."

Otha, silent for several seconds, said, "I control the money?"

"Better it be someone you trust, a treasurer. We have to have the annual report."

"Okay. That's you. That means you sign the checks?"

"We both sign."

It was clear that Otha had already given this some thought when he announced, "We'll name it The Samuel Haven Trust after my pap, Samuel L. Gubbin who will serve as President."

"I thought he was dead."

"Yep, dead and buried right behind the house, but no one thinks about that."

"It should be in your name."

"No problem. My pap and me have the same name. I grew up being called the otha Sam. The Sam got dropped, and Otha stuck."

*　*　*

42

CHAPTER 10

2:28 P.M. Thursday, April 27, 1991

Gubbin sized up Sylvi. Fine-boned, firm breasts, good hips, a baby maker no doubt, though a mite thin. He believed he saw God's intent in bringing her to him. "God gives us this offering as a blessing on his mission," he announced. She would be cleansed and added to the flock. Sylvi shuddered.

He turned to Naomi, his seventh wife, who was stripped and whipped and doused with cold water by the Elders. Otha did not find her teasing of Sylvi's breast a concern, but he allowed the Elders authority in such matters. This was a common public humiliation and would be repeated as often as necessary until she cried out to God for forgiveness, not just a cry but cries judged by the Enforcers of The Faith to be sincere. She had been punished before, more than once; and the Elders said there was no saving her soul, but Otha liked her spirit. The Elders offered no resistance to Otha's wants.

They were not satisfied with Naomi's cries for forgiveness and were about to take her punishment to the next level when Otha lifted his hand and raised his voice, commanding, "Hold Naomi and bring forth Eban Docker!"

Two men lifted Eban from the ground and dragged him before Gubbin with no concern for his cries as his injured leg bounced along the rough surface.

Gubbin looked at him and spoke. "Thou shalt not covet thy neighbor's house, thou shalt not covet thy neighbor's wife, thou shalt not covet thy neighbor's manservant, not his maidservant, nor his ox, nor his ass, nor anything that is thy neighbor's." The words cracked Eban's will, and Gubbin's maniacal stare made those closest turn away. Icy fear overtook Eban, sending a chill through the watchers. "Thou shalt not commit adultery!" The words boomed and echoed from every wall, tree, and rock. Gubbin's voice fell to a near whisper.

"So sayeth the Lord, our God, who fed the flesh and skull and bones and hands of Jezebel to the dogs when she betrayed God's servants." As quickly as it quieted, it rose to a startling boom delivered with a measured cadence those present knew too well. Eban was doomed.

"And what are we? Sinners, we are sinners; ain't fit to look upon the miracle of God, ain't fit to breathe his name, ain't fit to crawl through the offal of his true servants. God loathes us for our sins. He shows us, brothers, sisters, servants, and children, the meanness of our ways. He asks for pure lives and we fail."

He stopped and looked from one end of the group to the other and screamed with terrifying anger, "and fail we will,…fail we will,…fail we will,…fail we will,…fail we will,…fail we will,…—and God will curse us into a Hell filled with everlasting pain, rivers of blood in which we bathe as sinners, blood that burns our flesh, melts our eyes, enters our entrails and eats away our substance as we lay helpless, awake and screaming with pain, unimaginable pain, fearsome pain, pain that would make us kill our own children as they come forth from the womb for one second free of the pain that is ours forever and forever. We are sinners, and we come together to cleanse our sinful brother Eban and our sinful sister Naomi."

He stood, drawing deep breaths that echoed deathlike in the surrounding silence.

"Bring Naomi Gubbin before me to be judged."

Naomi was brought to a small altar set before Gubbin. She was pushed to a kneeling position and directed to raise her hands to heaven in supplication. Not one word was spoken. Those standing witnessed such displays before. Jubal advanced with a cup and placed it in Gubbin's hands. Gubbin stepped before her and chanted while sprinkling drops of cold water on her head.

"Woman, you kneel before God in your nakedness, the state in which you came into this world as pure as God's chosen lamb. Now you are filth, stained by your wantonness and your lies. You are adulterfied. You betrayed your vows before God and must be cleansed. His head bowed and hands reaching to the heavens, Otha prayed.

He stopped, drawing deep breaths, the sweat, in spite of the coolness, evident on his forehead, plastering his sparse hair to his skull. No one dared breathe. Otha's Elders stood ready to react should anyone stand against him.

Otha's shoulders dropped, a sign of resolution, and he spoke again. "Give praise to God. Give thanks to God. He commands us to scourge our brother and sister for their sins against him. Vengeance is mine, bespeaks the Lord, and we are but instruments fighting Satan for their souls."

Otha waved his arm and a large time-worn galvanized tub was brought into the circle. This was followed by a line of six women, with heads covered by white napkins, carrying buckets of water to fill the trough. They each paraded in silence from a stream-fed pond, more than ten circles each until the trough was filled. A huge man stepped into the center holding a live young deer, its legs trussed, over the trough. Otha stepped forward, chanting in tongues and slit its throat, allowing the hot blood to flow over his hands and into the water. The man held the struggling deer until the flow became drips. Otha removed his hand dripping with blood and splashed the blood on those standing in the circle. He repeated the action until he had circled the full group and anointed all of them with the animal's blood, all the time chanting in polyglot strings of nonsense words believed to be the ancients speaking through him. Once the water was suffused with the animal's blood, the big man handed the deer to the women who wrapped it in a white sheet and laid it on four logs set in a diamond as a rudimentary altar.

Naomi knelt at the altar and raised her arms to heaven in supplication. Erla Gubbin, Otha's first wife and the senior woman of the clan, stepped to her and in one motion pulled her hair straight above her head and, using a knife, cut it almost to the roots, leaving her more naked. She threw the hair overhead and cried out, "O Lord, we cast this sinner's evil to the winds." Otha's chanting continued over a cup of blood red water from the trough. He stood above Naomi, the pitch of his chant rising and then falling to a whisper that quieted those present. They strained to listen but couldn't

45

understand anything he said. He stopped. An eerie silence vacant of the calling of the birds, the whisper of the leaves, and the chirps of crickets remained. Naomi scarcely breathed knowing that to break the silence could be fatal.

Then Otha spoke. "Our Father, who art in heaven, we offer the soul of Sister Naomi, and we baptize her through your grace to bring forgiveness for her sins. We baptize her with blood;" he poured the cup of blood and water on her head. We baptize her with fire."

To Eban's horror, Erla appeared from nowhere with a white hot branding iron of three triangulated sixes and placed it on Naomi's left breast. Naomi's scream cut through the silence.

"We baptize her through the suffering of your faithful as they built your church upon this land."

Naomi, crying with pain and shock, was taken by four of the women and spread-eagled, facing the heavens, across the deer's body. The sheet enclosing it had been unwrapped and served as an altar cloth. Her arms and legs were secured to the deer's legs, and the clan women resumed the fearsome ritual of her earlier beating, maintaining a hypnotic cadence as Gubbin continued chanting, interspersing his gibberish with praise to God as the whips cut furrows across her legs, her arms, her abdomen, her breasts, and her face.

She was beaten for a long period, and was unconscious when Gubbin brought it to a stop. Her face and body forever altered by the bleeding stripes that stole her youth promised ugly scars, the mark of her sins. Once, the jewel of Gubbin's harem, she would never be beautiful again.

Eban was petrified, knowing he could expect nothing less. Otha knew of the plot to assassinate him and would have Eban pleading to die. He watched as the women laid their whips aside and lifted Naomi from the doe's body. They tied her arms together at the wrist and elbows and her legs at the knees and ankles. She remained unconscious as they carried her to the trough. Eban, despite his fear, cried for her. His love for her drove the plot and led to their duping Maximillian. They never again would join in unrestrained sex. Her beauty was gone, and with it the elfin spirit that amused everyone in the camp. The women dropped her into the trough.

The effect was instantaneous. The cold water woke Naomi. The blood in the water hit open wounds, triggering an immediate reaction from an immune system experiencing a blood invasion. Her body was on fire, the deer's blood having the effect of acid. She thrashed, lifting her body but unable to escape the sanguinity burning into her flesh. She was a banshee raising her head above the bloody water and shrieking in pain. Her frenzied attempts to escape, to draw breath weakened. When she dropped below the surface and could no longer scream or raise her head to breathe, the women pulled her from the water.

The women carried her to the stream, throwing her into the deepest washout after cutting her bindings. Two of the women waded into the mountain-cold water to ensure she would not be pulled under. The water cleansed her wounds, and the pain subsided. Within minutes, Naomi, clothed and scarred, stood before Otha's congregation.

Otha approached and pressed her to her knees, praying over her, and pronouncing her cleansed. He raised her to her feet and led her, supported by the women, to a broom placed in a clearing. He positioned her so that her back was to the broom. Standing beside her, he took her hand. He commanded her to jump backward. With help, Naomi backed over the broom. Otha stepped with her. He then declared to all those present that she was no longer his wife.

Otha then walked to Maximilian. He took the big man's hand and led him to the broom. He placed Naomi's hand in his. He turned to the crowd.

"On this day, I give this woman Naomi, who now is as pure as a virgin, to this man Maximilian that they may live together as man and wife.

"Jump!"

With this, Maximilian and Naomi, still assisted, jumped over the broom and, according to clan traditions, became husband and wife. Maximilian cradled Naomi in his arms, and walked to a cabin prepared for the marriage joining. Eban looked on, understanding that Otha held Maximilian guiltless.

Eban was frozen with fear. Otha turned to him and spoke with just enough volume to be heard by all.

"Eban, the Lord has placed upon me the burden of your repentance. He has forgiven you. I have forgiven you, but you are no longer my kin. You are the serpent of Eden, the corrupter of Eve. God made the serpent to crawl on his belly. He commands that you crawl on your belly for the rest of your life. You will be the lowest creature among us. You'll be fed whatever scraps are left by the dogs. You will live wherever you can crawl, and you will never know a woman again. Any woman who goes with you shall become as you are. You can speak to no one, and no one can speak to you, and all men, women and children can relieve themselves upon you."

Eban could not grasp the weight of his words. At this point, the big man, known as Little Jug, came into the clearing carrying two three foot logs. He placed them a foot apart in the circle. Eban was brought to the logs. He was grasped from behind and held in a powerful grip. His body was swung sideways without regard for his damaged leg as he screamed with pain. His good leg, its inner side facing upward, was laid across the logs. He cried for forgiveness, but his cries meant nothing. Dropping to one knee, Little Jug brought his oversized fist across Eban's leg at the knee joint. The joint bent and Eban passed out from the pain of muscle tears and torn ligaments. He was dropped in the dust. No one dared step forward to help.

Sylvi now stood in the square facing Otha. He carried a Bible and spoke of his community as a place for Christians while he ogled her nakedness. Despite the horror of Naomi's beating and torture and Eban's crippling, she had to be calm. His judgment upon them was brutish and insane.

She spoke. "Mr. Gubbin, I'd like to talk to your wife and the other women."

"Why?"

"I do not know why I am here. I believe the women can tell me."

"No!"

"Did you say no? Sir, you are holding me against my will. You are breaking the law. Are you aware you could be jailed?"

"There is no law for you, Jezebel, except the law of my pappy, his pappy, and his pappy's pappy. I am that law as were they."

"Why will you not at least let me talk to my sisters? I'm a Christian."

Otha, shocked, cried out, "Oh, you blasphemer. Oh, you whore of the ages. The women know you. The women see you come here naked with promises of sex doings to take their men."

Sylvi, except for the chill, almost forgot her nakedness. She became anxious as this brutal man condemned her nakedness as he ran his eyes over her body.

"Oh, yes, you're old Beelzebub's whore, all right. We knew you was coming. Me 'n my boys don't fear you none, we don't fear old Beelzebub. We took care of the other whores he sent. They were naked and proud with their pointy tits just like you."

Sylvi was stunned. How could she get this man on her side? Before she could respond, a bag dropped over her head and was pulled down to her ankles. She was knocked off her feet and lifted. Her panicked struggle was met with a kick when her assailants lost their hold and dropped her to the ground. The excruciating pain radiating through her lower back immobilized her and left her gasping and choking. She passed out.

* * *

Eban awoke crying. The thought of Otha's condemnation rushed upon him, and rage replaced pain. Had Little Jug applied full force, the bone would have shattered and the muscle and sinew torn; his legs would have been a weight to pull behind him. His knee and ankle would heal, but both would remain twisted and painful. He would never again walk upright. Knowing he would not be punished further he thought only of the pain, pain that went to his soul; and there was no apple whiskey. His rage was his respite, but he needed relief. Lying about twenty yards from the stream, he pulled himself by pressing his hands against the ground, lifting and tilting forward. Each move gained him more than a foot as he stopped to wait for the pain, growing worse, to ease. It took almost an hour to reach the stream. Once there, further bruised and bleeding from the debris that cut into his arms and torso, he rested to revive his strength. He fell into the sleep that pain calls to ease its burden.

Once he could move around, he would wash, but those who crawl in the dirt must live with the dirt. That itself sustained his rage.

* * *

Three hundred miles south, Anthony Maddoc stood at Marie's grave site crying for his beloved and disheartened by his daughter's absence. He asked God for the wisdom to help Sylvia understand.

49

CHAPTER 11

Wednesday, January 20, 1992

Over the five years of its grant, The Perfect Love Adoption Nexus did well. Van Loos built a solid relationship with Bram Stephens who welcomed her views on PLAN's future.

Two months into PLAN's fiscal year, Hank reported Stephens was experiencing losses. He was underreporting revenues to account for gambling losses

"How bad is it? Jonetta asked.

"It's hard to tell without an audit, but my guess is about $60,000.00."

"How did you come up with that?"

"I compared the cash flow with previous reports. Should we audit?"

"I would prefer we did not. I do not understand why you didn't tip me off sooner. I'll speak with Stephens. On another note, Angela Willimas is leaving the first of the year."

"Really, she always seems so happy with her work."

"She had an offer she couldn't pass up. I want you to replace her."

"I don't have the background for that job."

"You'll catch on. The technical stuff is handled by staff, but I want someone who has a nose for this business, someone with field experience. That means you."

"I don't know."

"I would not expect you to know, but this is a job you will grow into. It puts you on the succession plan. Someday you may have my job."

He didn't know there was a succession plan. The increase alone would jump him five years ahead of his current track, not counting bonuses. He was twenty-nine years old. Rachel was losing patience with his excuses for

50

not getting married. He accepted. "I appreciate this opportunity. I will not let you down."

"If I thought there was any chance of that, we wouldn't be talking."

*   *   *

Nine Weeks later....

Bram Stephens reviewed the previous night's conversation with Jonetta.

"Bram, I have lost confidence in your management. Your gambling, embezzlement, and omitting your arrest from your personnel record require me to replace you."

Bram felt a wave of nausea. She was serious. Her detachment seemed to suggest they had no history. He almost stuttered as he responded.

"The arrest was more than 20 years ago; I was just a boy."

"No, it was nineteen years seven months ago, and you were convicted as an adult."

"It was a college prank, and I did not embezzle. My financial report is valid, and I'm not gambling any longer."

"Relax! I am not going to destroy you. What I am going to do is bring in a business partner, Enzio Rubino, to move PLAN forward."

"The man is a criminal, a Mafioso. I want nothing to do with him."

"Bram, this is not a negotiation, unless of course, you are willing to stand before a judge and face the prospect of finding millions of dollars to reimburse the foundation. Your contract is quite specific on that point."

Bram looked away.

"There's also your Boston office's affiliation in New Hampshire."

"The Samuel Haven Trust is a legitimate organization."

"Legitimate, perhaps, but I've heard that some clients are forced to give up their babies."

"That could not be true."

"Let's hope not. Otherwise, we have a mess to clean up. Your reports show, also, that you are paying Haven too much for their babies."

Stephens did not argue. "While I'm somewhat uncomfortable with the arrangement, I am realistic."

"What do you mean?"

"We inherited a contract."

Jonetta said nothing more. The following Monday she and Bram met with Enzio Rubino. Bram was now a figurehead. He passed on having dinner with Jonetta and went home and drank until he slept.

He avoided Jonetta. Her secretary called asking him to come in review his final report, but he ignored it. He called Hank Rudinski and asked him to call back. Bram's phone rang at 6:57 P.M. It was Jonetta.

"Bram, you are ignoring me."

"It is not possible for me to act like nothing happened."

"I understand, but you still have your office and substantial income. Why did you call Hank today?"

Bram was nimble. "I thought Hank might have some insight as I review my final draft. I don't want any surprises when we meet."

"I do not want him involved. The preliminary draft seems fine. Let's meet tomorrow."

"It has to be late in the day."

"No rush; let's wait until Monday morning, say ten?"

"I'll be there." He hung up without another word.

Hank's call came shortly afterwards. Bram explained the situation and asked what he could do without making things worse.

"That's easy. Call Antonia Gilletti, Cesaré's daughter. Call right now."

Bram glanced at his watch. Less than ten minutes had passed since Jonetta's call. He dialed, surprised that the phone was answered immediately.

"Ken Boucher here."

"Antonia Gilletti, please."

Toni Gilletti answered with the first ring. "This is Toni."

"Miss Gilletti, this is Bram Stephens calling. I wonder if I can see you."

"I'm about to leave. Can it wait?"

"I need to speak to you about Jonetta Van Loos."

"I haven't dined; perhaps you would like to join me at Smith & Wollenski?"

Stephens was waiting when she came in and was seated. He picked up his O'Doul's and walked to her table.

"Bramford Stephens, she asked. You recognized me."

"We were never introduced, but I have seen you at Matterlink. You leave an impression."

"Thank you; I assume that's positive."

"Of course. What else?"

"Sit down and tell me about Jonetta Van Loos. I've ordered the house salad for both of us."

Thank you Ms. Gilletti."

"Bram, call me Toni. We need not be formal."

Bram smiled and relaxed, liking the woman. He went through the entire story, withholding nothing. He was candid about his misappropriation of funds, his criminal record, his gambling problem and, shamefaced, his intimacies with Jonetta. He spoke of Rubino and Jonetta's taking over PLAN leaving him a figurehead.

"That's about it. PLAN is the best thing I have ever done. If I am replaced as its director, so be it, but Rubino can't have control."

Their salads arrived along with a bottle of select white wine.

"The maître d' sends his regards, Madame. Will there be anything else?"

"Not this evening, Henri. Thank Charles for me, but leave it corked."

"Oui, Mademoiselle Toni."

"Your first time here?" Bram teased.

She smiled. "There are several fine restaurants with which the Firm maintains an account. S&W is my first choice. Let's enjoy our dinner and plan to meet with my dad in the morning. He'll clear his calendar. Plan to have breakfast with us at eight."

*　　*　　*

The Gilletti's were waiting when he arrived at 7:55. They sat in a small room that allowed no interference; a light breakfast was served.

"Well, Bram, from what Toni tells me, you are a gentleman and a rogue."

"Bram was composed, hesitating before framing his response. "Miss Gilletti is too kind. I can't claim the former, and it is evident I am the latter."

"That is not something that we have to deal with now," Gilletti answered. "Tell me yourself what you shared with my colleague."

Bram repeated his account. Gilletti waited before he spoke.

"Is there any reason for Van Loos to question the Samuel Haven Foundation?"

"We inherited a contract when we acquired our Boston site. We provide their placements, and have reviewed their previous placements. They are a legitimate foundation. Besides, Jonetta reviewed the contract earlier and bought into it."

"You have never met the top man at Haven?"

"No; I have tried. He is something of a recluse. His attorney handles all business matters."

Gilletti leaned back. "I think we have enough. I want you to avoid Van Loos for the next week or so. Drive down to Wilmington and take a flight to Bermuda. Everything will be arranged."

"I have a Monday morning appointment with Van Loos."

"Cancel it. Call her secretary but do not reschedule. Do not give any reason."

"She'll question it."

"Of course she will. She'll conclude you are afraid to meet with her."

*　　*　　*

Within hours of meeting Stephens, Toni called Jack Neary to her office. Her father sat in, remaining silent.

Toni got to the point without preliminaries. "I want you to fly to Portland to join me for a meeting with Faye Knielex, Samuel Haven Foundation's trustee and attorney.

"I've asked that its chief operating officer, a fellow named Samuel Gubbin, be there. We should not meet resistance. It may become a bit dicey once he learns you plan to check out his operation to see if it is all he claims it to be. If so, remind him of his contract. Meet his people, check the facilities, and get some sense of the organization's legitimacy. If you can't take the time off to do it yourself, assign someone you can rely on."

"I'll do it myself."

Gilletti turned to his daughter. "Toni, I want you to meet alone with Gubbin's attorney. She'll be honest about her dealings with her client.

*　　*　　*

Friday – April 1, 1993

Toni Gilletti called Faye Knielex and announced, "I plan to fly in tomorrow morning to meet with you alone."

"I thought our appointment is on Monday."

"We do have a Monday meeting that includes Mr. Gubbin and Inspector Neary, but I want to speak with you alone. Shall we dine together?"

"Yes, of course. I know just the place."

"I hope you won't mind that I've arranged for an office on Monday with the Rice Rickell firm, our liaison in Portsmouth."

"Not at all; I'll pick you up at the airport. The finest seafood restaurant in New Hampshire is nearby."

"And if I don't like fish?"

"No problem. There's a MacDonald's next door. The maître d' will order in.

Toni laughed as she said good bye, thinking she would like this woman.

*　　*　　*

The two women met and sparred a bit before getting down to business. Toni got to her point. "I want to know all about Mr. Gubbin and his foundation."

Faye Knielex was quite candid. "Otha Gubbin is one of those people who with little formal education but great love of humanity has built the Haven Foundation and refurbished a small local clinic as a healthcare and birthing center. Everything he does is driven by his charity."

"There is nothing about the man that you would question?"

"Not really. He is reclusive and doesn't give out much information, but my dealings with him have been 'by the book'. I had some concerns early, but he addressed them."

"For example?"

"Placement of two babies was delayed because he did not have documentation. Once I explained what he needed, he was able to provide it. He learns as he goes. The problem never recurred."

Toni got a complete picture of Gubbin's taking in homeless, sometimes pregnant, women working the streets. Once they delivered their children, though welcomed to keep them, most of them were put out for adoption.

"One last question Faye. Is there anything odd about this business and your arrangements?"

"There are several things. First, I have not seen his clinic. Second, I have never met any of the mothers. He is secretive, less so with me but in general."

"Does he have something to hide?"

"I don't think so. He does not want anyone nosing around. He set up the foundation upon learning he had to account for the income."

"I hope he understands that Mr. Neary will be inspecting the facilities."

"I informed him. There's not a problem."

"One more question. Do you think he would coerce women into service?"

Faye Knielex hesitated before she answered. "I doubt it, but he once said something that made me uncomfortable."

"What was it?"

Knielex thought for a moment. "I think his exact statement was, 'I met a girl over Dover way who wants to make babies. She's moving to our community. It made no sense. No sane woman would agree to move to the mountains to have babies."

Toni did not question the statement except to say, "Perhaps this one isn't sane."

Toni left satisfied with what she learned.

CHAPTER 12

Toni and Neary met Gubbin in Faye Knielek's office. She thought Gubbin crude. He needed a bath, reason enough to condemn him. Yet he seemed to know what he was doing. She took Neary aside before she left and said," I want to know everything that goes on with these people. I want to know if they are what they claim to be."

"Not to worry; I'll learn everything there is to know."

She had a driver take her back to the city.

*   *   *

Neary regretted accepting the hour and a half drive in Gubbin's truck. The roads were little more than country lanes and unmarked, distinguished only by a farmhouse here, a tilted oak there, ruts and broken stone foundations. He saw groundhogs, but they weren't much as landmarks. He asked what they were. Gubbin replied, "Supper from time to time" and laughed.

He relaxed, loving the atmosphere, so different from the city. The fresh air pleased him. Perhaps he would retire here or have a getaway when the time came. There seemed no better place after a lifetime in New York City.

Once they arrived, he found Gannett had one way in, the same way out and no posted street names. He asked Gubbin the name of the town.

"Has a couple of names. It's old. Did well when the stone and lumber was going. Not much has changed over the years. Some old-timers called it Pierpont; that didn't stick in the townsfolk's minds. I call it Gannett, after my great grand pappy Josiah who kept it together when the jobs got lost. Revenuers call it Gannett. Most of the people call it 'town,' not having much need to use anything else."

"What about street names?"

"Only one street."

Gubbin took Neary to his home, a small cape with a substantial addition in back. They dined on baby back ribs, winter peas, mashed unpeeled potatoes and a side of apple sauce. Apple cider was offered, and lemon meringue pie ended the meal. Neary complimented Erla. "Where did you get these ribs? They're finer than anything in New York." Erla was pleased but did not answer. Gubbin answered questions in his home.

"Not familiar with taciturn New Englanders, Neary spoke to her again. "I imagine Ms. Gubbin that you are quite busy working alongside of your husband."

Gubbin spoke. "She's got her hands full right here in this home, what with the cleaning, the cooking, and the washing."

"Well, she does some fine cooking."

"Inspector, everything you ate came right off my farm, just a mite behind the house."

"Well, you may have another market here, Otha. I bet I could sell every pig you produce for outrageous prices in New York."

"Well Inspector, we produce only for our community, and I'm busy enough without other interests."

"I guess that's so. We didn't see many people outside on this beautiful day."

"Most are working or cooking this time of day. The children are in school. Enough light for us to walk through town a bit. We'll run over to Carter Notch in the morning, and I don't want you missing anything. There's a car rental place near Franconia to get you back to the city."

Neary was disappointed. He planned to allow time to get a feel for things, but he couldn't manage Gubbin's schedule.

As they walked through the village, Gubbin explained that visitors were common during the foliage season and late spring. We got some guest rooms back of the house.

"We're off the beaten track, but we welcome guests. They help us maintain ourselves like when the quarry and a lumber kept us going. Lumber's still good, but machines have cut back on most of the jobs.

58

"Some visitors come to hunt antiques; some are hikers, and some are revisiting their roots. The most common are hunters and fishers looking for guides."

Neary learned the community was self-sufficient, a commune before the term became fashionable. It began to grow in the late 20's when men looking for jobs left their homes and stumbled upon this little town. They were welcomed with a meal and a bed. Gubbin remarked that most drifted on.

"Yep, and some never left; have families born right here in Gannett." When I was a boy there were between 900 and 1000 folks living here. Now there are little more than 300 if we don't count the babes. Some of the folks went off to war and didn't come back. Most killed, I suppose. Some went to college and got jobs you don't find in Gannett. Others got themselves in fixes and are on the run. Most drifted off, but they come back for a sit-down from time to time. Sell you one of the empty houses if you have a mind to settle in these parts."

Neary laughed. He complimented the paved main street with neatly trimmed trees and bushes. The houses on both sides, capes and turn-of-the-century federal colonials, were well maintained.

Yep, folks here take care of the town out of respect for God's love in our lives. They're all churchgoers."

They stopped at the local diner, had coffee and said hello. Everyone deferred to Otha. Neary was not introduced. As they left, the counter girl called, "You come back now, you hear?" Neary laughed to the puzzlement of those watching.

Along with the houses they found a general store, a barber shop, a blacksmith and a church. A late-19th-century school house stood behind the church.

Neary was surprised. "That's got to be the oldest building in town."

"Just about, although the church and some houses are a mite older. Isn't much for looks, but it's heated and has lights. It got redone inside and out in the 1940's. Classes held from eight to three, although we are a bit easy about that. Got two crackerjack teachers."

"For all grades?"

Yep, they're good ones; live right here in town"

There seemed to be narrow streets right off the main street, but they were little more than rutted alleys used as service roads behind the houses. They allowed access to a number of stone structures appearing to be small factories evidencing Gannett's history with its ironworks, maple syrup industry, carriage works, and furniture shop, the latter and the maple cooking house still operating.

At the far end of the main street a cobblestone paved circle boasted a well maintained walkway around its perimeter. A large house with a veranda rose about forty feet from the walk. Built in the 1890's with a mansard roof topping its three stories, it appeared to be something Poe might have used in one of his tales. Fashionable in its day, today it might seem garish to some.

It was built by Otha Gubbin's great grandfather, Josiah Gannett, owner of quarries and lumber mills. He held foresting rights for much of the woodlands that surrounded the community. The Gannett family still held substantial woodlands and a few worked-out quarries.

Gubbin and Neary entered the main house, a clinic with a well-equipped twelve-bed maternity ward. At any time it would have six or more mothers with their babies. The medical staff consisted of four nurses of a sort and two doctors, a man and wife. The doctors lived in a 900 square foot apartment on the top floor. Otha found them holed up in a mountain shack after they escaped custody. He offered them sanctuary, not concerned about their conviction for illicit abortions.

The clinic surprised Neary. The rooms were spotless. The mothers seemed content sharing time with their babies and moving freely. He thought it to be ideal, a stage setting accompanied by coos and smiles. At present there were four ladies in waiting, and three nursing.

They visited the police station last, a structure of stone blocks with oak plank doors screened with heavy steel mesh. The town constable, Jacob Calin, was affable, asking about New York police operations. Neary offered to host Calin in New York. Not realizing that Calin and Otha were cousins, he offered to pay him for information on the goings-on in Gannett.

Five deputies oversaw the three lockups. While everything was nailed down, the cells were more like rooms in a rustic inn than jail cells. Two-men were always on duty, and the cells served to dry out the town drunks.

Neary spent the night as the guest of a couple who never stopped smiling. The housekeeper, Leah, freshened up his bed and told him that she was there to provide whatever services he would require. Suspecting she might be in her teens, Neary, nevertheless, shared his bed with her.

They left the next morning with Leah along for the ride. She rode in front pressed against Neary. There was no conversation. They arrived at Carter Notch, a local lodge on Lake Winnipesaukee. Gubbin spent time scheduling guides through a local contact after which the two men sat at an outside table facing the mountains. The expansive lake replete with boats spread south beyond view. Gubbin exploited Neary's vanity, learning about Von Loos's operation and sharing Leah's story. With Leah's breast still pressing against Neary, he answered the old fox's questions without a thought.

"Inspector, Leah was a good girl when we found her, and she still asks Jesus for forgiveness every morning. Girls like Leah come with nothing but the poor innocents growing inside, gifts from God. They are doing God's work just as you do keeping the streets of New York safe.

"Well, I'm not sure how safe, but there are many such girls to be found in New York.

"Well, Inspector, you might send them girls our way. We'll provide for them and make certain their babes go to good homes if the moms don't keep them."

Neary learned nothing more about the Haven Foundation.

While they were talking a young couple, Sylvi Maddoc and Jeff Spooner, passed walking to the buffet. Sylvi looked familiar to Neary. Impulsively, he called her to Gubbin's attention. "Imagine having a girl like that in your stable."

Gubbin nodded saying, "Maybe I'll get 'er."

Neary gave it no further thought until he learned Sylvia Maddoc was missing.

* * *

CHAPTER 13

7:59 A. M. — *Tuesday, August 17, 1991*

When Monsignor Elio Madduccino entered the room, Cesaré Gilletti, Michael Chen and Milton Halprin rose to greet him. Gilletti spoke first.

"Father Elio, it is good to see you. How was the trip?"

"I slept, Dr. Chen. How is our company doing?"

"McDonnell-Paget is having a good year, as you know."

"Of course. How is the foundation doing?"

Gilletti spoke up. "Elio, Dr. Chen is seldom involved in Matterlink's day-to-day operations. We have a problem."

"That is why I am here Cesaré." Madduccino turned to Milton and spoke.

"Counselor, it has been years since I saw you."

"…and, yet you remember me Monsignor."

"The Church remembers every son of Abraham who gives generously to the Holy See."

"It is a privilege, Monsignor."

The old priest nodded. Gilletti broke in. "Gentlemen, let us get under-way."

Each waited for the monsignor to choose among the chairs circling the table. He spoke as he sat.

"My friends, you are Maratolli Trust. You tell me that Dr. Chen is not very involved, yet he put the Van Loos woman where she is to get her out of his, …our company."

"We shared that decision."

Madduccino waited, and no else one spoke. Seconds passed before he spoke.

"Everything is God's will. I know nothing of this Van Loos woman."

Gilletti thought back to when Jonetta Van Loos became their problem, although no one knew so at the time. It was Chen's coup, a clever scam. He sold her to Matterlink after he failed to remove her from McDonnell Paget. She seemed a perfect fit, intelligent and charming. Gilletti spoke,

"Van Loos's replaced Bram Stephens with Enzio Rubino and reduced Stephens' role to title only.

"It appears they run a legitimate operation, but their practices belie their legitimacy."

"Cesaré I read enough on the plane. What are we to do about this?"

"We fire Van Loos. Rubino is out and knows he is to ignore her."

The old man interrupted, "So you have solved the problem?"

"Elio, we need your approval to deal with Van Loos."

"Why? You put her under contract without me. There is the final solution."

"That is not something a priest should suggest."

"…but it is something you could suggest."

"and only you can approve," Gilletti added.

"Let's review the letter that is to go to her. It will be sent if we have your approval?"

Halprin read.

> Dear Ms. Van Loos,
>
> Be advised that upon receipt of this letter, your contract, in accordance with its terms, is voided. This terminates your service.
>
> Please sign the attached agreement within twenty-one days in exchange for a tax free severance award of $100,000.00 provided by the Foundation. It is suggested you review your Contract of Employment and this letter with your attorney before signing. Failure to respond will be deemed acquiescence.
>
> Your office is sealed. Your personal property will be sent to your home by courier.

Please call my office if you have any questions.
Sincerely yours,

Michael L. Chen
President, Chief Operating Officer & Chairman of the Board
The Matterlink Foundation

"Do you expect her to accept it, Milton?"

"No. She'll try to back us down, but before the letter arrives on Saturday morning her office will be cleaned out and rekeyed. Her belongings will be inventoried, certified and sent to her home. It matters not how she responds."

"When will you send this letter out?"

"With your approval, it will be certified and sent by courier today, Monsignor."

"…and if I agree but she does not?"

She will experience problems that make losing a job seem inconsequential.

"I am a simple priest, but I understand she holds substantial voting stock. She could create problems."

Gilletti broke in, "… but she then subjects herself to criminal charges. We wish to avoid the notoriety."

"Milton, you manage her trust. What's your view?"

"Like many Jonetta Van Loos fails to appreciate the power of discretion. She has told others she has files that will destroy Mr. Chen and expose Matterlink to tax fraud. These are fabrications. Pieter Van Loos was quite explicit when he named me trustee of his estate. She can vote her shares only, which are comparatively few."

Madduccino slammed the report on the table, his ire clear as he spoke.

"It is the devil's work when couples put up their savings to adopt an unborn child, and there is no child. It is the devil's work when innocent girls are impregnated and coerced to give up their babies. The devil rules over of our charity."

"I travel thousands of miles because my friend Cesaré tells me my granddaughter has disappeared. He tells me her mother is murdered. He tells me Enzio Rubino is selling drugs. I feel nothing but heartache, and all you focus on is this woman, a Jezebel. Cesaré, what do you say to me?"

"I am sorry Godfather. We light candles for Marie, and we pray for Sylvia."

The Monsignor continued, "Enzio, a bastard child, is party to this. Cesaré Gilletti, who is as a son to me, did not stop him. How do you explain?"

The others looked at Gilletti. He was uneasy. He did not expect this turn. Content to stay in the background, at his peak Elio Madduccino was the voice of reason and the voice of the church within the New York families. His power, derived from traditions older than America, was not to be challenged. Gilletti spoke,

"Elio, this is why we meet today. We will deal with Van Loos and protect the Foundation. We are equally concerned about Sylvia Maddoc. You have the full story. Is she still in the mountains? Who knows? Was there an accident?" Gilletti lifted his arms and shrugged. We are much troubled. We sleep poorly"

"As do many," the patriarch interrupted; what have you suggested to my grandson?"

"Maddoc wants no part of us. He makes no claims upon the family, but we stay close to him."

The old man nodded. "You keep a file."

"Yes. When necessary we step in, but Anthony does not know."

"Sylvi's disappearance has nothing to do with the foundation."

"No, but Maddoc is family."

"Yes, my grandson's losses are my losses. That is reason enough?"

"But we cannot approach Maddoc. You will see him while you are here?"

"Certainly. I must extend my regrets and ask him about many things. I am tired. So how do we this Van Loos person?"

Gilletti replied, "I have asked Inspector Neary to join us. Perhaps he might assist."

Recalling his grandson's history with Neary, the old man smiled. A few, knowing the story often repeated within the NYPD ranks, laughed when he remarked, "Neary? Was he not Anthony's maestro at the academy?"

"He was Anthony's instructor some years ago. Anthony serves under him now," Gilletti responded.

Another laugh followed. The old man spoke.

"Cesaré, I have known you since you were a boy. Your parents were childhood friends. Did you know that we worked together? Of course you would know. We traveled by cart from Palermo to Marsala and worked sun up to sundown, six days a week picking the grape. Sunday was for church and swimming. What wonderful times. Great food, great vino, great health and sometimes great sex, ...but just a little after the vino,... enough to excuse."

Everyone chuckled but Gilletti seemed struck dumb.

"Why so surprised, Cesaré? I took the collar after I married and had a family. If my Mafalda—God bless her soul, were still alive, your world and my world would be different. Cesaré, you are keeping something from me. Should we speak alone?"

With this simple story, Madduccino reminded Gilletti there could be no disregarding the blood that bound the Gilletti's to Madduccino and his family, and there was *omerta*, the code that kept family business within the family.

"I think we might speak alone."

As though orchestrated, the others left the room. Madduccino gave Gilletti time to arrange his thoughts. Gilletti spoke,

"Godfather, I was negligent. Before Bram Stephens's grant ran out, Van Loos charged him with embezzling. She stepped in and took over with Rubino as a figurehead."

"So where's the negligence?"

"I did not follow up until I learned Stephen's story."

"Oh yes, of course; the blackmail. Now we find ourselves with questions."

"More than questions, Godfather. PLAN activities include extortion, fraud and the heartache of those who have been duped into paying thousands for a child they will never see. It is dirty business. PLAN exploited innocents, and I slept through it."

"I need to hear nothing more. PLAN has put Matterlink's reputation at stake. This is your problem to fix. My confidence in you is a birthright your parents passed on. Those ill-used will be compensated. Amends must be made.

Now we see what this Van Loos person will do. Call the others in."

The meeting reconvened with no one asking but everyone wanting to know what transpired between Madduccino and Gilletti. Gilletti pick up where they left off.

"Milton Halprin has everything in place to take control of Van Loos. Milton, please explain."

Madduccino interrupted. "…in one sentence that I can forget, please."

Milton thought a moment and then spoke, "Within thirty days, Jonetta Van Loos will no longer be a problem of any kind."

Gilletti nodded and said, "Inspector Neary is waiting."

"Cesaré, I see no need for Mr. Neary. We know the man, and we know how he feels about my grandson. Send him off. His face is a painful reminder of my grandson's indiscretion."

Now I must settle in. My bags await me at the hotel?"

"Of course. Monsignor. The staff are pleased you have returned.

CHAPTER 14

Once Toni reported her impressions of Gubbin and his operation, Cesaré Gilletti expected a report from Jack Neary who had returned two days earlier. He asked his secretary to call him.

His private line rang. "I have Inspector Neary on the line, sir."

"Thank you Gerri."

Cesaré was brusque. "Neary, where is your report?"

"I'm writing it now, Mr. Gilletti."

"Stop writing and come to my office. I want to hear it."

Neary arrived, with driver and flashing lights, within minutes. Gerri led him to Gilletti's office.

"Sit down Jack. I hope I wasn't too brusque." Tell me about Gannett.

"As you know, Toni and I met Gubbin in Faye Knielex's office. Gubbin impressed us, but I believe my judgment was hasty.

Gilletti interrupted.

"I met the man during a fishing trip to New Hampshire. Gubbin was our guide. I found him quick of mind and well informed. Bram was along, and there was some discussion of his program, although the details escape me. Gubbin, claiming divine intervention, informed us he had a baby farm some miles north. He was more than I expected, but I did not take him seriously. Who knew it would take this turn? Please go on Inspector."

"Once we arrived in Gannett, I paid attention to everything. Things seemed all right. Gubbin answered my questions."

"Something made you doubt."

"No one spoke to me, only to Gubbin. When I remarked about it, he said they are shy. I know a set up when I see it. It was the same when we toured the clinic. Oddly, new mothers nursing their babies turned away when we came in. They seemed content but did not make eye contact."

"Did you ask Gubbin why?"

"I knew why. The women were afraid."

"Gubbin read my concern and said, 'These women are shy, especially when nursing. They were living on the streets when I found them. They worry that family might come looking for them".

"What did that suggest to you?" Gilletti asked.

"I felt the women didn't want to be there, at least not after their babies were born. I think he's selling their babies and Van Loos and Rubino knew it."

Gilletti was uneasy. "This is hard to believe. Gubbin has a legitimate organization, yet you and Toni don't trust him."

"Toni suspects him?"

"She thinks he's crude and a liar, but she didn't have any idea of what you saw."

"She would have if she were there. There's no fooling her."

"In talking with Gubbin's lawyer, she learned that the woman knew almost nothing about Gubbin's operations. Toni believed that Gubbin concealed information from her, which he has a right to do."

"I don't know what's going on with Stephens and his program," Neary chimed in. "but any involvement with Gubbin has to be trouble."

"Is there anything more I need to know."

"Mr. Gilletti, Gubbin drove to Conway on some business and arranged for Avis to have a car waiting for me. We left near sunrise and stopped at a place named Carter Notch for breakfast. A young woman caught Gubbin's eye. I noticed her but didn't give it any thought. Gubbin admired the girl and remarked,

"That's a fine looking woman. Maybe I'll get her."

"I gave it no thought until I heard Maddoc's daughter is missing."

Gilletti was jarred. "Was it the Maddoc girl?"

"It's been years since I saw the girl. What the hell would she be doing in New Hampshire?"

"What did Gubbin mean with his 'maybe I'll get her'?"

"As I said, I didn't give it a thought."

"But you had to know she is missing! Was it Sylvia Maddoc?"

"I don't believe it was, but Sylvia came to mind when I recalled that she was missing."

"Inspector Neary, I am most concerned. If your life depended on its not being the Maddoc girl, what would you say?"

"I would say she wasn't. What are the odds that we both would be at that place at that moment?"

"Yes, of course, it is highly unlikely. You are a skilled investigator, as was your father, may he rest in peace. You're not mistaken? You are sure?"

"Mr. Gilletti, you have known since I was a boy. You saved my career. I could not be anything but honest with you."

"So how would you address this problem?"

"I should go back to Gannett and find out for myself."

"Let's not be hasty. That old fox is not going to let you into his business. If he has Sylvia Maddoc, unlikely to be sure, we have to find out. I want you to put together a team. Get that big fellow, the one who worked the Soho job. What's his name?"

" Reinholds. He's available and has a team."

"I want you to lead. Get his team together and have them stand by."

"I see no need to be part of this."

"You made a friend of the constable and can walk right in. We're not looking for a war."

"I understand."

"Thank you. I must get on to my business now. I will call you."

Neary nodded and left.

Gilletti was uneasy. Neary would immediately recognize Sylvia Maddoc if her saw her.

*   *   *

Gilletti sat at his desk facing Joseph Reinholds, a man whose wardrobe said Brooks Brothers but whose bulk said WWF. Gilletti was direct.

"Joseph, I cannot be linked to Otha Gubbin. Do you understand what I want?"

"Absolutely! Neary called me. I put together Figueroa, Walsh and Kincher. No one wants Neary but he'll hold his own."

"Five men will be enough?"

"The four of us would be, but Neary gets us in."

"You may be underestimating the odds." Gubbin has a village up there."

"Neary showed us the layout. It will work to our advantage. Security is adequate but adequate won't help them."

Gilletti paused for several seconds before speaking. "Joseph, you worry me. You sound like Neary."

"Sir, I took over Viet Nam villages twice the size of Gannett."

"It couldn't hurt to have more men."

"In ordinary combat situations, yes; but this not combat. In this case we have four veterans. We have the team we need."

"Neary runs the show"

"He made that clear enough, but my men don't like it."

Gilletti smiled. "I am sure that will not become my problem."

"Sir, if Neary is a problem, I'll kill him."

"Do what it takes, but let's not stir up the authorities. Of course, if you're under fire, you must protect yourself."

Reinholds chuckled." You sound like a military man. Neary knows what is expected?"

"He knows all he needs to know. You will have the funds you need to equip and carry out the mission. Why the smile?"

"If it needed only money, you would have bought your way out. It appears to me the old man in charge up there needs killing."

Gilletti paused before he spoke. "I do not want him killed."

Gilletti opened the left-hand drawer in his desk and removed two items, handing both to Joseph. "There's $20,000 as a bonus when the job is done. The envelope contains six copies of a recent picture of Sylvia Maddoc. Each man must be able to recognize her."

"I don't understand."

"If you find the Maddoc girl, bring her back, but I want everything connecting PLAN to Gubbin's operations destroyed. You have a week."

"Sir, once we engage, it will be a matter of hours."

Gilletti walked him to a private exit.

CHAPTER 15

7:14 A.M.: *Sunday, August 15, 1991*

Maddoc dreamed but believed he was awake. He was floating above his bed looking down. Dogbone slept at the closed door. The room was silent. An amorphous cloud drifted into his line of sight as he tried to move downward. He was fixed in place. The shape of a woman hung in front of him. He was asleep, yet he was awake. She spoke, her voice an echo.

"Anthony, Sylvi waits. When you come near; you will know."

Maddoc shook violently waking himself. The cloud faded. Maddoc raised his arms to be sure he was awake and swung his legs to the floor. Groggy, he took a step, then another before his legs were under him. It had been more than a dream. His legs remained heavy. His body seemed dense. He turned on a small lamp, giving enough light to examine the entire room. Everything was in place. He believed Marie had come back for a brief moment. Feeling returned to his body.

A tap announced a visitor. Dogbone looked up from between his paws and moved his tail as Maddoc opened the door to Bernie Van Eyck, Marie's childhood friend and a communications specialist in the commissioner's office, a poet spitting out press releases.

Bernie held the pizza, the usual breakfast when she showed up early. When Marie was ill, Bernie threw herself into helping her. When Marie died, she threw herself into Maddoc.

"I guess you didn't get my phone message."

Maddoc was silent; he had skipped over it.

"Well, are you going to agree with me?"

"I'm not sure yet. I don't see the wisdom in it".

72

"So you've decided not to bring me along?

"I discussed it with Caleb; he thought the mountains would be too hard for a woman."

Bernie stammered, "What the hell is he talking about? You told him he was wrong?"

Maddoc played it out. "Well, what could I say? He has a point. It's not a macho thing. He'll take to the woods looking for Sylvi but doesn't want to care for another woman in the process."

"Where is he? I'll kill him, the little shit. If I need a man to watch out for me, which I do not, Caleb Abranos would not be it. Who the hell … ."

Maddoc stopped her. "I was kidding. Abranos has the team ready, and you're part of it. We leave at the end of the week." Bernie threw a pillow at him.

He laughed and said, "Bernie, I thought of you when I was in Vermont. You became so much a part of Sylvi's life that as I thought of Marie's being gone, I thanked God for you."

She almost cried; he needed her. He continued speaking as much to confirm his thoughts as to inform her.

"We now know enough to narrow our search. Once we begin, we'll have the support of the New Hampshire State Police. Portsmouth's department is already involved. There was an incident at a local bar that may have involved Sylvi. I believe it did. Once I speak to the officer who took the report, I'll know more. That's where we begin."

"Have you clothing and other personal items for her?" Bernie asked.

"What do you think she'll need?" Maddoc asked.

Maddoc's thoughts wandered. How would he react once he came face to face with her? What if she's injured? She could be married. Maddoc dismissed that but realized he was looking for a woman, not his little girl.

He turned to Bernie, asking, "Can you pull some things together for her?"

"I already have," Bernie replied with a grin.

"What do you mean, you have? You just learned about it."

"It's woman's intuition? I read your mind just as easily as I read your moods."

"Good! We'll take your Jeep. She's going to need you. You can bring whatever you think."

Maddoc, in his typical manner generalized, expecting the details to work themselves out."

"Well, thank you."

"Were Marie alive she would be with us. Sylvi didn't much separate you two in her thoughts. Once she learns of her mother's death, she'll need you."

Bernie smiled through her tears and nodded. "I love you and Sylvi; she is mine, too. I bathed her and changed her and loved her before you ever saw her."

She turned away, determined not to have tears flowing down her face.

She waited as he remained silent. She believed he was in his cop world.

She was wrong. His thoughts went back to his early days with Bernie. He trained Bernie when she hoped to be a patrol officer. The intimacy of their workouts was not lost on either of them, recalling as it did their high school days; but they never acted on it.

Maddoc broke off his thoughts and spoke

"Bernie, Sylvi thought she had two mothers for much of her life. I do not know what I can say to her when we find her. You will. You have to be with me. Marie would want it."

New Hampshire authorities were investigating, but Maddoc was impatient. There was no need to wait; He wanted to step in now. Harrington agreed. "Maddoc, your insight to your daughter will help our investigation."

CHAPTER 16

7:31 P.M. Thursday, April 27, 1991

Four women carried the sack holding Sylvi to a cabin set back among trees. It wasn't much of a cabin, more a shed, about eighty square feet, containing no furniture and a dirt floor. The women deposited her on the dirt, using the sack as a ground cloth. Another sack provided scant cover against the chill. The women left in darkness.

Shortly, Otha and Erla carrying a lantern came in with a young man. They directed him to have his way with her before she woke up. Then Erla uncovered her and positioned her so that she was on her back, still naked. Erla told the young man, "You have your little fella fill her with little soldiers. She can't push you away. You do your duty. We expect fine babies from this one."

"Yes, ma'am," he said politely, having learned the price of resistance. He looked at Sylvi. He liked her grit, but standing up to Otha could have got her killed. Otha spoke.

"We'll send in something for cleaning her and helping with the pain. You get her canny to what's gonna happen here. Got a lot of gumption, this one. Once she's with child, she'll quiet down. Minds me of Erla as a young'un. The first time I poked her she fought like an injured doe, but she come to like it."

Erla kicked the young man. "I don't want you mooning. I'll feed your sack to the pigs if you don't do what you're told." With this, they left. Several minutes later, two women came in with a bundle of willow branches, a pail of clean water, a burlap bag stuffed with straw, clean bedclothes and a flower-sack shift. They said nothing and left.

Peter Cohn recalled the day his car ran out of gas. Eban and Ludim stopped, beat him, took his Breitling, hogtied him, put in gas and threw him into the trunk. He'd been held ever since. After a time he stopped trying to keep track of the days. His car was gone and he had few family members left, most living on his father's estate. No one would look for him.

For months he had seen people stand before Otha Gubbin and tremble. This woman had spunk. He would not impregnate her, but he had to fool them into believing he had.

Erla and Otha showed up every day. To fool them, Peter masturbated and left evidence of sperm on Sylvi. The Gubbin's were satisfied. She awoke on the third morning, shocked to find Peter over her.

"What are you doing?

I'm trying to help you."

"Help me? I wake up with all over me, and you claim you're trying to help?" She attempted to get up and fell back in pain.

"Don't try to move. You're bruised, but nothing is broken."

"Where are we?"

"We're prisoners."

"I ache everywhere. Why did that old man get crazy?"

"He is crazy. You stood up to him. He kidnaps women to make babies. He sells the babies and has the women making more."

"He's selling their babies, and the women allow it?"

"They have no choice. If a woman makes too much of a fuss, she disappears."

"That's insane! Why do the people allow it?"

"Everyone benefits from the money Otha brings in. No one questions it. To oppose him is death."

"Did you try?"

"My one attempt to reason with him got me a terrible beating. They have me here to get you pregnant."

"You've been screwing me?"

"They have to believe I have. I leave sperm on you to fool them."

"So you watch me naked and masturbate. That's sick."

"I have no choice. You angered Gubbin. What you saw out there was his worst. I was sure you were next, but something held him back. You didn't fear him, and he needs to be feared. If you don't get pregnant there's no telling… ."

"I won't get pregnant. That is not going to happen."

"I know, but they have to believe you are if you want to survive in this place."

"And how do I do that?"

"How would I know? You're a woman. Figure that out for yourself. Feign morning sickness."

"I guess you know something."

Sylvi had deep bruises. She drank water and chewed willow bark to relieve the pain. Over the next week, Otha and Erla showed up daily. Although repulsed, Sylvi remained silent. Erla examined Peter and was satisfied. Otha remarked, "He's sure enjoying her Erla. She's a good'un."

Erla frowned.

During the days that followed, Peter shared all he knew. She came to trust him and argued that someone would bring help. That was his lost dream. She learned Otha Gubbin believed the Devil was a man who appeared in the body of a woman to seduce men just as the Eve seduced Adam.

Sylvi regained her strength and spent her days planning an escape. She shared none of her thoughts with Peter but hit upon submission as the key to winning over Gubbin.

Peter left after two weeks. Once he was gone, two women came in with a small tub, tepid water, and soap and towels. They removed her shift and bathed her. They left her naked. When she complained, she was told-"you are naked so that you stay put. Once you are of the family, you get duds."

Both Gubbin's came in to see her over the days that followed. She pretended to be asleep. It was easier for her for many reasons, primarily to control the rage she felt when Otha put his hands on her. That stopped when Erla challenged, "you have no need to touch her. You got enough women."

Each time Otha and Erla came in, Erla rolled Sylvi on to her back and positioned her so that her legs were together and arms were at her side, palms upward. Otha would pray over her and read scripture. Erla interposed with Amen! Thank you, Lord; the Lord be praised, and so forth. One time after the praying Erla placed a small round pebble in each of Sylvi's hands and rubbed her abdomen with a vile jelly, not far removed from the smell of a skunk. Sylvi paid close attention.

On the first occasion, her right hand closed involuntarily on the pebble, and Erla got excited. "Look, Pa, she's in the family way, and she's gonna deliver us a little boy. It's the Lord's will."

The next time they came in, they went through the same ritual, but this time she closed her left hand over the pebble. She got no reaction. Otha began to pray and chant. She smelled cinnamon burning. This went on for many minutes.

Erla spoke. "It came to me, Otha. The Lord has revealed himself to me. She's going to have a girl. It's sure a little girl she's bringing to us."

The last time they came in, they surprised her, catching her before she had any chance to assume a lateral position. Otha glanced at her. "She showing yet, Erla?"

"No, it's too early, Pa. She's a big girl, won't show for weeks, although she'll firm up a bit. You lie down missy so that Otha can pray over you and help make certain that God be making that little one inside you grow right."

Sylvi did as told, knowing that she could not soon become pregnant under any circumstances. She had been on the pill for years and without a period in months.

At this point, it didn't make any difference. Even if she ovulated, she and Peter had not coupled. She was grateful for his care and disappointed when he left. He had more to tell her, but she had more immediate concerns. She had ten weeks, more or less, to get away from the madness. She estimated she needed four of those weeks to recover fully and prepare.

Erla gave her instructions, and she complied. She lay back as before. "You just relax, honey. Better if you sleep."

Sylvi listened to the prayers and the chants, finding herself relaxing and falling into a light sleep but conscious to what was going on. Erla laid the stones in her hand once again. This time, she waited awhile before closing both her hands over them.

"Lord!" Erla cried. "Oh Lord! You told us and we didn't see! Otha, look, she gonna have twins, a boy and a girl. The Lord tell us true both times."

Sylvi had to steel herself against laughing. How in hell could they conclude that she was going to have twins, a boy and a girl, when she couldn't be pregnant? Then she realized they wouldn't know. In their simplicity, all their signs said she was pregnant. It was the reason for her being there, and they wanted to believe.

"Thanks be to the Lord," Erla prayed.

"Amen," Otha confirmed. "She is one of the family now, 'another daughter who beat the Devil and will provide pure sweet new babies for our flock. She shall be called Mary, showing her pureness and her agreeing with God's wishes. Let us pray."

At this, Sylvi was pulled to a sitting position and turned so she would be on her knees. Otha and Erla flanked her while Otha went into a drawn-out prayer made up of mixed metaphors, biblical commands, religious diatribe, and nonsensical allusions such as "until that day we shall walk upon the water, driving Satan from the ranks of the godly, cleansed whiter than the fire on the rock," and such Otha had acquired from odd sources. Listening, Sylvi realized he had a prodigious memory and enough basic intelligence to make it work. Her original assessment changed. He was a lecher, but she would not underestimate him.

The prayer ended. Erla picked up a bag she had brought in and left near the door. "Here be your clothes, Mary. Now you may walk among us."

Sylvi was pleased, thanking Erla. She had gained some time in order to plan and make her escape. Except for occasional sharp pains, she was in good health, moving about easily but not able to do anything strenuous. Sylvi was told no one ever escaped; no one could get more than fifteen or twenty minutes out of sight without being missed. Otha's men loved chasing down escapees. They were babes in the woods and instinctively traveled south. It was not much of a contest.

Even if an escapee tried to remain off the trail, strangers to the woods made noise and left signs with every step. The woods were heavy with undergrowth. The woodsmen traveled quietly, often coming upon a victim before he knew anyone was close. If the escapee were a woman, nothing might happen to her, perhaps some fondling. Males were beaten and might be sodomized. The only safety was in being caught by Little Jug, a story in himself. Unless ordered, Little Jug would not assault anyone.

Despite Gubbin's threats, random couplings were common: cousins impregnating cousins, fathers impregnating daughters, brothers with sisters, and so forth. Little Jug had a congenital accident that resulted in an overactive pituitary. Delivered three weeks late, he weighed sixteen pounds. His father may have been one of the hunters who bought his mother's services. His mother died at birth. There was nothing odd in Little Jug's appearance except his size. He was a giant made more fearsome by his massive strength and no understanding of his danger to others.

He grew rapidly, and at sixteen, when he was close to seven feet tall, his growth slowed down settling somewhat over seven and a half feet. The common belief was that he had limited intelligence was false. While he might be termed a moron by some, he had extraordinary skills apparent to anyone who spent time with him in the woods. He was as one with his surroundings. He could travel a path and, on the return, recognize every disturbed leaf or blade of grass. If a fox, a rabbit, wolverine, deer, bear or a man was the source of the disturbance, he usually knew. When he served as tracker, the hunters got what they wanted. When Gubbin served as a hunting guide, he took Little Jug along. No dogs were ever as successful.

No one could hide from him. Escapees didn't get far before Little Jug pulled them out of a tree or crevice, or kicked away the leaves under which they tried to hide. He recognized unnatural changes. Such was the extraordinary power of his recall. Had he been able to read, he might have fixed the Encyclopedia Britannica, Gray's Anatomy and the King James Bible in his head. He might not be able to apply the information, but he would know if a comma were out of place. In the camp, he knew every stick, every scrap, every face and every rock, anything that affected his surroundings. He was fooled only by information coming at him too fast. It was impossible to judge his abilities because from birth there was no effort to teach him to read or write.

Sylvi knew none of this. While still locked in each night, she was luckier than many who preceded her. Erla had taken a special interest in her and made certain she was well fed. With twins coming, she was special. She had a canvas cot with bedding supplied. Some of the food was not to Sylvi's liking, but if she didn't eat what was brought to her, the leftovers were not removed. Until it was gone, no fresh food would arrive. She found a break in the back wall through which she pushed unwanted food. The varmints ate it, and she got fresh food every day.

The diet was well balanced, even without the meat, which she wouldn't eat. She did eat fish. Occasionally, there was a lump of maple sugar. On cold mornings, it might be accompanied by hot tea. Sylvi ate to keep up her strength, but she saved the sugar. Now that she was thought to be pregnant, milk was a regular part of her diet.

She was closely watched. Gubbin had plans for her. Erla was getting up in years, and of his several wives only Esther would be up to the task of being number one. Otha thought this woman superior to Esther and up to anything he would demand of her.

* * *

CHAPTER 17

Ludim sauntered across the yard. He knew the Devil woman had won over Otha and Erla. She was pregnant, and he couldn't touch her. The pain in his broken foot fueled his hatred. It had not been reset and was now ulcerated where the bone pushed against the skin. He walked straight, but the constant pain reminded him every day of Sylvi stomping him. He accepted no fault. He went into a darkened cabin expecting no resistance and suffered since. Only blood would satisfy his hate. Forgetting his earlier experience, he hoped to get close enough for payback.

Otha had Little Jug looking out for Sylvi. As limited as the giant might seem, he sensed Ludim's hatred. It wasn't something he could explain. It was something he felt. When Ludim tried to get close to Sylvi, Little Jug would appear. He watched her cabin late into the night. If warm enough, he slept outside the door. Sylvi was never far from Little Jug's sight.

Ludim worked out a plan. Little Jug was off dealing with hikers who stumbled upon the camp. Otha did not tolerate strangers. Ludim told his peers that Sylvi came on to him because, as he put it, "ain't no one giving her none. She would be happy to see you boys. She sure treated me good. Ain't never had a more wantin' woman." They believed him. He sat behind the tree line as they entered the cabin and went after her. They overpowered and stripped her few garments. Stef Tillis had his pants around his ankles and was trying to get her legs apart. She fought damning the two holding her down.

Ludim moved further into the trees as Little Jug came into view and stepped through the door. Two of the men escaped. Little Jug went for Stef. He didn't quite understand, but Sylvi's fighting was enough. The giant

82

pulled Stef lifted him by his hair and shook him so violently that Stef's pants fell off and his neck broke, killing him. The giant stepped outside and tossed him into the brush. Sylvi feared Gubbin would rage over the killing, but the matter passed.

Erla got the story from Sylvi and passed it on to Otha who remarked, "God was good to Stef. I wouldn't have kilt him so quick."

Sylvi won Erla's confidence. They worked together planting and tending a small garden. Erla fussed over Sylvi's pregnancy as though she were a daughter.

She was left to herself and trusted. The six weeks since her abduction sped by; she didn't have much time. Erla and Otha expected her to start showing. Having sufficient rations and a canteen, she decided it was time to escape. Although no one before her succeeded, she had an edge. She could live off the land, finding her way night or day. She could protect herself from the elements, thanks to her father.

Evening services provided an easy time to slip away. Gubbin spent an hour or more recounting the sins of the day, bringing his congregation to their knees and haranguing them to repent. He preached a fiery sermon and led the singing of the hymns: *The Old Rugged Cross*, *Jesus Savior Pilot Me*, and *What A Friend We Have in Jesus,* always the same three. Sylvi's enthusiasm during the services increased Gubbin's confidence. Once she had that, she faked laryngitis, and spoke little for more than a day. She did not sing, but she stood through two songs stifling a cough. During the third hymn, she slipped away and was not missed until the service broke up. She was well down trail before Jubal and his two friends closed in on her.

The first, Adam Root, circled ahead once they saw she was headed south. He laughed as he cornered her, telling her he might have some fun with her before dragging her back to the camp. She broke his collarbone. She recognized the next one, Jubal Plunk. He threw a half-inch rope over her neck from behind and pulled her to the ground. He swung the rope over a tree branch and tied it fast as he pulled her to her feet. He failed to tie her arms. She had to support herself on her toes or choke. He approached her from the front and stepped within her circle telling her she couldn't run if she was naked. He placed his hands on her breasts, and she shattered his eardrums with her free hands. Using the rope, she pulled herself up and, in the same motion, kicked Jubal in the face. She freed herself and moved east, the echoes of her victim's crying and cussing fading away.

The third man, Izzy Figg, came up behind her, throwing his weight on her back and finding himself deposited twelve feet in front of her as she used his momentum to toss him over her shoulder. He came up in a rage and charged. She almost drove his testicles into his stomach. He tried to catch himself as he fell back but passed out. She turned from him and found herself facing Little Jug. She wouldn't fight him. He picked her up and carried her back to the campsite placing her before Gubbin. He said nothing.

Sylvi's pursuers made their way back just minutes behind them. When Otha learned what she had done, he was enraged, telling Erla and the women to punish her good. Before they could begin, Erla stepped up and cried, "She's bleeding. she's lost the little ones." Sylvi realized that her period had returned, and she was bleeding heavily. She began to emit a keening cry over her loss. Erla cried, "Oh God, it's the little ones. Forgive us for not keeping her under foot."

Otha did not punish her attackers.

Sylvi spent a week in isolation and every day sat to do penance with Gubbin and Erla. She apologized, claiming that she went into the woods to find herbs for her cold and got lost. When the men came upon her, she was afraid. The first one threatened to rape her. All she could think about was those two babies growing inside of her, and she defended them with all her strength. They accepted her story. Otha placed some of the blame on himself. She cried and swore she would not leave again without asking. Gubbin told her she would have to wait six months before she could be with a man. Sylvi did not question it. It was another bit of nonsense he passed off as wisdom. "I'm sure gonna miss them twins," Otha claimed.

Otha moved Little Jug into her cabin. He wasn't leaving things to chance. Stef Tillis was one thing, but the threat got him to thinking other men in the camp lusted after her. Little Jug's presence, especially after Stef Tillis's carcass was thrown down the hole, would cool their ardor.

Little Jug's move into the cabin was easy. Sylvi built their relationship as he watched over her. They soon bonded. Little Jug's feelings toward this woman, if they were to be understood at all, were akin to what a puppy might feel toward a master. He was devoted. She treated him well, singing lullabies, reading to him from an old Brothers Grimm fairy tale book. He loved the stories but wouldn't look at the pictures. He never lost his fear of them. She kept the shack neat, and she cooked whatever game he brought in, knowing how to clean and cook it, not an easy task. The skinning disemboweling and deboning small animals takes practice. Most young women would shrink in disgust. Sylvi didn't give it a thought; it wasn't new to her, but she seldom ate any meat.

She was allowed outside but not among other prisoners. Security was haphazard. Although the clan members were lax, her earlier attempt convinced her that a lone escapee was an easy search. She focused on building Little Jug's trust while she put together a plan.

*   *   *

Harrington and Maddoc were reviewing a plan that would take them into the most remote communities in the state. Harrington explained.

"I've framed out an area extending north from Berlin northwest to Milan, then east to Stratford and due south to Whitefield. It's about 560 square miles."

"That's half as big as Rhode Island!" Maddoc remarked.

"Not quite, but it's sizeable. This is the area where people most commonly disappear, both men and women but more women. The mountaineers believe they're being kidnapped by aliens. A better explanation is that they get lost and die in these remote areas.

"How are we going to cover the entire area?"

"All the towns within this area have been canvassed by local and state police. They have found nothing. Further, much of the area is mountainous. We'll concentrate on the lower reaches of the mountains where some small unincorporated towns remain. The old lumber camps and quarry stations that survive are uninhabited."

"Where do we begin?"

"We'll work our way through the likely areas. We'll run into hunters and trappers who may have information."

85

Fingering a point on the map, he added, "This plateau is an ideal starting place on which to assemble."

"We're ready to go?"

"Maddoc, we are ready."

* * *

Ludim approached Erla and remarked, "She sure has taken to this new life. Once she's with child again, there's no saying what might follow. You and Otha must be happy. I know that Otha took a shine to her. Her being with Little Jug ends any doubt about her fitting in.

Erla felt that there was something to Ludim's thought. She didn't mind Otha's liking for the woman. He loved all of God's children. She didn't mind his having other wives. They were more like servants. That he shared his bed with them rankled, but on balance it was all right. Otha never did much for her; and she was number one, having almost as much power in the camp as Otha. As for her sexual needs, Zebediah Doody was the better man.

Erla liked Sylvi, or Mary, as she was known in the camp. She was respectful and always greeted Otha and her in a nice way, as though seeing them made her happy. Yet Erla watched Otha with her. She noticed that when he spent time with her, he would bed one of his younger wives. Mary worked hard and proved herself a match for almost any man in camp, which Otha admired. Otha bought her story of getting lost while gathering herbs, but Erla wondered. Jubal claimed she was moving south when they came upon her. It could have happened that way. Erla would not suggest it didn't. She had to look out for herself.

* * *

CHAPTER 18

Having Little Jug live in the cabin was a mistake. Sylvi came to love him. She learned he had a good brain. They hiked and gathered wild edibles, all of which Little Jug knew. When talking to Peter about him she explained, "I've been hunting with him. He's used to traipsing around the woods with me and understands I do not want people sneaking up on us. I trust him with my life."

Peter recalled their early days together a few weeks earlier. She was tough and determined. She won Gubbin over by doing everything required of her. Peter observed, "I suppose you can do whatever you like. You've won the affection of almost everyone in this camp."

Each year Gubbin took teams to the tourist hotspots where they sold, stole and made a pile of money. In his absence, things were easier. Peter and Frank Trotta were planning an escape, and. Peter wanted Sylvi on board. Frank hedged. Peter prevailed. "Do we have anyone else who moves around so freely?"

When they approached Sylvi, they learned she had already worked out a plan, and it included getting every prisoner out of the camp. Success required fooling the clansmen who always went south after prisoners. Sylvi insisted, "We have to go south when we leave."

Frank said, "That is brilliant. We're going to go exactly in the direction they expect."

"They have to believe we are moving south Sylvi argued. Once we're far enough down trail, we'll swing northwest, but this is where I have some uncertainty."

What's that? Peter asked.

"We need to find a town where we can get help."

Frank jumped in. "Northwest is the way to go. Gannett, the closest town, has a constable, but to outrun the scroats, we'll have to get half day lead from the start."

"Frank, you have hiked and hunted in these mountains. Can you lay out route?"

"I'll get on it. Peter, you work out the supplies. We'll run in pairs. Set that up, also. We'll need to earn everyone's trust so that they'll come along without hesitating."

",,, but we tell no one until we are ready to go. Agreed?"

"Agreed!"

"What about Little Jug? "We won't fool him which means we won't fool them."

"Little Jug will be with us."

"That's crazy. He'll tip them off."

Sylvi smiled. "No need to worry about Little Jug. He won't go any-where without me. I have come to love him and he loves me."

Evenings and mornings were chilled, and the leaves were promising the extraordinary colors that characterized the north woods. On the plus side, it was the last tourist glut. Gubbin and his cronies would be so busy hustling they would give no thought to the camp. They thrived on the unsuspecting, swindling some, duping others, and selling anything they could. Some of the junk found in old villages, old lamps, kitchen utensils dating back decades, and tools sold well. The younger girls entertained in rooms pro-vided by Gubbin's friends.

Meetings were held in Sylvi's cabin. Within four days after Gubbin left, everything was ready. They had to choose the right moment.

Sylvi was confident. "The timing couldn't be better. Frank, the map is great. It should not be difficult for me and Little Jug to have them chasing their tails."

Frank answered, "We'll get a big lead on them as they fall behind run-ning south. We shoot for Gannett about 20 miles away. The terrain will not slow us down much. In the early going we'll be on well-worn trails. These are not easy to read. At times, we'll be picking through thick underbrush. We can't avoid leaving signs, but we'll backtrack when we break off the trail. It should fool them. As things get easier; we will cover a mile or more an hour. As the crow flies, the trip isn't long; but, as we work to mislead them, we may walk two miles or more to gain one."

"How much time are we talking about?" Sylvi asked.

"Less than two days. We'll cover at least twelve miles a day traveling dawn to dark. As we get closer to Gannett, we'll see more signs of civilization. We can then move in a direct path. Two days will do it."

Sylvi asked, "What if Gubbin's men catch up with us, Frank?"

"If they get a line on us we'll be too far ahead and moving over the fastest leg of the course. To be honest with you Sylvi, I'll fight to the death if they catch up; but we have addressed every contingency."

Peter asked. "Once we're in Gannett, what happens to Little Jug?"

"I'll send him back," Sylvi answered.

"Suppose he won't go back without you?"

"Then I'll go with him."

Frank and Peter both challenged her. "You'll be killed?"

Sylvi turned on them. "Listen, I'm not certain about anything except no one will touch me if Little Jug is at my side. He is as ready as I can make him. That's the best we can do."

"You're putting your life in his hands."

"We are all in his hands, and he likes us. We're okay."

Peter, how're our rations?"

"We have enough for three days."

"When do we shove off?" Frank asked.

Sylvi hesitated before answering. "I'll let you know."

Peter readily accepted Sylvi's answer, but Frank balked. "That is a decision we should make together."

"No, we have to find the right moment, and I'll know that moment," Sylvi said.

Frank nodded and said,

"We will not meet again until the time is right."

Frank asked again. "Sylvi, are you sure about Little Jug? If he refuses to leave you, he could become a problem."

"Perhaps, but, as I said earlier, I'll come back with him."

89

"You can't do that," Peter exclaimed. "Gubbin would know you're behind the escape. Your life won't be worth anything."

"If Gubbin touches me, I'll kill him. If I can't, Little Jug will.

Peter was adamant. "You'll be at risk."

"That's my decision. By then, you will have reached the authorities. Little Jug and I might get back to the camp without being noticed. If we are, anyone who sees me there with Little Jug will figure I didn't join the escape."

"You might be right," Peter said, "but as long as Little Jug is with Sylvi, she's okay."

Frank asked. "He's a dummy. On Otha's command, he'd break all our necks."

"I care," Sylvi snapped, "and you are being a fool. We won't get out of here without him. Little Jug isn't dumb. He might kill on Otha's command; …he will kill on mine."

Frank apologized as the meeting broke up. Sylvi accompanied the two men back to their shacks.

CHAPTER 19

M addoc frowned at the face in the mirror. His pale skin with its leathery creases after months on the street, seemed strange. He cut his hair and shaved. When his grandfather called, Maddoc was pleased beyond explanation. The old man asked that they meet in the St. Patrick's rectory. He last saw him when he, Marie and Sylvi visited Italy. At that time, the patriarch had no plans to return to America. Now he was here, and Maddoc wanted to see him and explain the last few weeks.

When Maddoc returned from Nam, he learned of his grandfather's vocation. He couldn't image him a priest. He grew up knowing his grandfather was into the so-called "Italian" business. His son Carlo, six years younger than Maddoc's father, also was in the business. Father and son did well. The grandfather, with his seminary education before he fell in love and married, moved quickly to capo regime. He was powerful, brainy and seldom seen. All that was known in those days is that he stood at Gambino's elbow.

*   *   *

Maddoc, in an open shirt and a windbreaker, sat on the right side of St. Patrick's following the mass he knew as an acolyte. Sylvi took her Catholic teachings seriously and, until in high school, dragged the family to church each Sunday and on every holy day, allowing no excuses. He saddened as he recalled those days.

The old man sat in the apse, sitting to the left of the young priest conducting the mass. Maddoc recalled his family and memories of early years, becoming melancholy. The service strengthened his resolve. His hardness was not of the heart.

91

The service ended as Maddoc slipped out a rear door and walked the few steps to the parish house. He rang. An elderly sister, whose bright blue eyes and morning cheer insisted she was Irish, opened the door. He smiled, and she responded with a brogue as cheery as a warm spring day, "Good morning sir, I am Sister Mary Catherine. The Monsignor is expecting you."

"Of course you're Mary Catherine," Maddoc responded. "Aren't all Irish nuns named Mary Catherine?"

She chuckled as she conducted him to a large door that opened into an austere but comfortable sitting room. His grandfather sat facing a wingback chair. A gas fireplace gave off the only light. Maddoc walked to the old man, kissed his hand and pulled him to his feet, hugging him. The old man spoke Italian.

"You have not lost your respect for your grandfather."

"Not in this life or the next father. When did we last speak?" Maddoc asked.

"We last spoke in Rome when you, Marie and Sylvi came to Italy. I remember it so well. Sylvi questioned why such good-looking young men were becoming priests. Marie, embarrassed, told Sylvi not to sway the young men's hearts. How she blushed, and I laughed. Today it is my advice that is needed."

"It's always been so, Grandfather."

"Do you remember, my son, what my life was here in America?"

"I had some idea, but I knew little then. I know more now. I never believed you were doing anything wrong."

"You knew early in life not to make easy judgments."

"Yes, through you."

"Anthony, you are a man now. You know the world. You spent your forty days in the wilderness and returned whole. What I am about to say you will understand, because the world that you knew as a young man is the same world you know today. Today your eyes are opened.

"The Madduccino's," he continued, "come from a long line. It is a line that precedes the Medici. It is a line that Machiavelli respected. The blood of Cesaré Borgia and Girolamo Savaronola is Madduccino blood. You understand that long before the city states were united, long before the universities grew from scholars who were of the church, the Papacy was the law. That line has never been broken."

Maddoc interrupted the old man, afraid that he might be wandering off. "You say my eyes are opened, but I do not know what that means."

"It means that good and evil are always with us; you know them well, but allow me to continue.

"Italy was made up of feuding states. During this period, foreign powers dominated. The Church was the sole cohesive force. There were differences within the Church, of course; but the Papacy was supreme. You can understand that the Church's power could not be sustained if her enemies were not known. The Church of that day reached into every country, every level of society and institution; and it struggled against those willful rulers who wished to control the Papacy. Nothing escaped the Papacy's eyes and ears, and so it remains today. At that time, the Madduccino's lived in Palestrina, outside Rome, and held estates in Basilicata and Calabria.

"By the time we Italians began coming to America in the late 19th century, we were dispersed with the main arm of the family in Rosano. La Cosa Nostra was a criminal element in Sicily, and the traditions of 'our thing' came to America with them. The Italian Church came also, and the Church's power in the minds of most immigrants was supreme. La Cosa Nostra grew out of the Mafia. The Mafia were not always criminals. In the Middle Ages they were employed by landlords to protect their estates.

"Sicily and much of Calabria were the poorest sections of Italy. The peasants depended on the landowners whose fields they worked. The population had no hope of anything in the country of their birth. After many years and in spite of the opposition of the Church, Italy was united under Victor Emmanuel. It was not complete, but it was inevitable."

"Do you know of the carabinieri, my son?"

"Yes. Grandfather, I know much of what you speak."

"The carabinieri lit the spark, but it was almost a hundred years after America's independence before Italy became a country in its own right. With the loss of the large estates, which were virtual fiefdoms, the Mafia found other work. They survived on a little business here and a little business there. It wasn't enough and powerful men, criminals, emerged. They were of the same blood as those who now live in the Little Italy's that sprang up in New York, Chicago, and Boston, and later spread to other large American cities. Of course, not all were criminals.

"During these decades, the Church maintained its power by remaining strong in the hearts of its parishioners. On the Sabbath, the criminals were interspersed with their brothers and sisters, cousins and in-laws as God-fearing Roman Catholics. The Church had not given up its watchfulness. Over the Capo de tutti Capo, over the Consigliere, over the Capo régime, the power of the church prevailed and that hand remains.

"In America, I was a powerful man in La Mafia, but my power then, as it does today, devolved from the Church. The power lives in the Church's ability to give strength and to take it away. Girolamo Savaronola was not the first to be assassinated because of a stand against the interest of the Church. Understand, my son, such matters do not reach to the Holy See."

"I believe that, Grandfather," Maddoc said.

"I tell you this because in America today the network that kept me informed when I lived among you remains intact; and it is as effective as any in the world, more perhaps, because much of its information comes from reliable sources who see their duty to our network as no different from their duty to the Church. I am in America today because information reaching me in Rome concerned my grandson and his daughter, and I need to share that with you now."

Maddoc came out of his chair. "Grandfather, how could you know of Sylvi? Do you know where she is?"

"I know she is safe. I know she is protected, but this does not mean she is not in danger. Yet I must talk with you about Marie, God bless her soul. Let me begin where I must so that everything is clear to you."

"Marie was murdered, Grandfather."

"Anthony, what was intended to appear a break-in and robbery and a message to you went out of control. Two men did this, and they are now dead."

"Do you have their names?"

"No, and we may never learn them. Whoever was behind the break-in took no chances. Their heads, hands and feet were removed. Their bodies were burned black, beyond recognition. If we learn anything more, anything that leads to whoever gave the order, we will deal with it. Their bodies were left on a Fresh Kills garbage heap."

"Grandfather their names were Zip Cinto and Mario the Mole Demeola ."

"How do you know this my son?"

I have sources, also, Grandfather."

The old man smiled. "You must get on to other things, but you must allow me to complete my story. You should not think I was a criminal."

"Grandfather, you know I have no such thoughts, but I want to deal with those who killed Marie."

The old man went on, seeming to ignore his grandson.

"Some years back, responsibility for the Church's sub-rosa concerns in America was turned over to a committee of five, all powerful men. One of these men is a corporate leader who remains invisible except to the committee. Another is well placed within city government. A third sits in a place where information flows freely, though not openly, and the fourth, no longer one who wears the robes, plays a role that has existed since medieval times, a role I once filled. The fifth is one who understands the nuances of power and the money that feeds it. I can identify one of these men, and it is not to be known by anyone outside of this room. As for Marie's killers, your concern must now be with the living. Only God exacts justice."

Maddoc's nod was sufficient.

What information I receive, you will receive. The name I now give you is the one man you can trust no matter what you think otherwise.

"The chairman of the group of five is an old family friend, a man who was part of your youth, Edward Cesaré Gilletti. He is as a son to me and must be protected"

Maddoc was stunned. This old man in his late 90's, whom Maddoc knew as a wonderfully loving man but rumored to be part of the underworld, was not a reformed gangster. He did not question, but said, "I know the man and will accept what you say."

He had to ask one question. "Grandfather what of Uncle Carlo?"

"Carlo went back to his birthplace. He is not well although his appetite and sense of humor survive. Much of what you may know or believe about him is manufactured. I placed Carlo where he was and kept him there to exercise my will, when necessary. Carlo had some blood on his hands, but it had to be. Blood cleanses. Carlo is not and was not the man your father believed him to be. Whatever sins I required of him God has forgiven."

"I will be leaving for Rome tomorrow. Through Cesaré Gilletti, you will have whatever financial resources you require. This is what I came here to do, to see you and to help. If you think it wise, post a $50,000.00 reward for information. Such a sum of money will provide ten thousand watchers and listeners."

"That might be a mistake. If Sylvi is being held against her will, it may make her a liability. If she is not, it will make her a target. We have much to learn before we consider offering a reward."

Madduccino nodded. "Yes, you are right, but the money is there for you to use. I have set aside the full sum. There is more should you need it.

"Let's walk to the kitchen and get some refreshment. It's a blessing to see those here trying so hard to please the servants of God. As a guest, I ask nothing of them; but the Bishop has the last word."

They sat at a work table and ate lightly. They talked of Maddoc's parents and his loss of Marie. Maddoc thanked him for the letter bearing the Pope's seal read at the Mass. Maddoc cried as he spoke, and his grandfather cried with him; but all was not sadness. Maddoc listened while the old man reminisced about the days when Maddoc was not allowed to sit with the men. He paused and asked, "Are you up to a walk around the grounds with this old man?"

They both laughed and rose to step outside. The old priest recalled Maddoc's father's ability to intimidate Carlo and yet remain aloof. It was a contrast that puzzled some. The Monsignor explained,

"Carlo never forgot he was the younger brother. Before my arrival, Sylvio was the titular head of the family. I never interfered. Your father respected me and deferred to me. He asked no questions and made no suggestions. It made my work easier."

The two men continued their conversation as they walked back to the sitting room.

"You know I never had to prove anything to your father. My reasons for coming to America were known to him and to Carlo, but only Carlo had the entire story."

"My father would not question what you were doing."

"There would have been no need. You knew your father if you know yourself. You are much like him. I see the same light in your eye, and the turning of your mind as you absorb more than is spoken."

Maddoc held the gate for his grandfather as they circled the church's grounds.

"Anthony, just a few more thoughts. Do you know what Sylvia was studying?"

"She studied psychology and sociology, a double major; I never discussed her studies other than to ask how she was doing."

The old man paused. "She became interested in remote New Hampshire communities. She wrote her honors thesis on them but believed she missed communities deep in the timberlands and believed if she hiked the old logging trails she would come upon them."

"You know where she is?" Maddoc responded.

"No, our people have not got that far along. We know she planned to write a book if she could build on what she had. Now you must go to where she was lost. That is where you will find her."

"That I have decided."

"You are going among strangers. They will not see the world as you see it. They will have no reason to trust or to help you. Money buys many things, information of course, and loyalty so long as more money remains. If any remains, give it to Sylvia as a gift from her grandfather.

"Now you must indulge me. We must walk a bit more, eat the lunch prepared for us, and catch up on family history. Who now runs your father's butcher shop?"

*　　*　　*

CHARTER 20

Midday—Wednesday, August 25, 1991

Buzz Carleton, local state police officer was excited as he spoke to Harrington. "I suspected the connection when I learned of the call from the owner."

"No one else did, and that call is five days old," Harrington replied. "Where was he found?"

"He was lodged between the wall and bed rails. My inspection was cursory, but nothing seems to have been touched. Is the Criminal Investigations Bureau coming on."

"I don't want them there. I've asked Anthony Maddoc to join us as soon as he can. He's driving up. I'll have my man look things over, but I want things to remain as found. The CID can wait.

*   *   *

8:05 A.M.: Friday, August 27, 1991

Maddoc remained intent as he listened to Harrington

"I got the call from the local state police officer who made a connection to the report on Sylvia. In short, a young man was assaulted and left for dead. When found, he was in a coma and is now in Memorial Hospital in North Conway. Everything on the scene suggests there was a woman. We think that woman may have been Sylvia."

"What makes you think that?"

"The camp owner was certain there was a young woman. She was shown Sylvia's picture but couldn't confirm her identity. What I saw in that cabin suggested one helluva a fight. The man was not alone. Nothing will be touched until you arrive."

"Do you have his name?" Maddoc asked again.

"Maddoc, the man can't tell us anything. He's in a coma. We have his prints."

Maddoc answered, "I'm on my way," and hung up.

"You're on your way where?" Bernie asked.

"New Hampshire. Al Harrington has something."

"…have they found Sylvi?"

"No, but they may have found her last location."

"I'm leaving for a town named Eaton this afternoon. We should be able to make it in six hours. Plan to drive."

"I'm leaving Dogbone with Caleb who will follow us and bring the dog along. We have our team. Pick up your things. I'll be at your place in an hour."

"Anthony, I can't be ready in an hour."

"You'll be ready. You're as anxious as I am."

CHAPTER 21

After briefing Abranos, Maddoc gave him an envelope.

"This will allow you to pick up a van at Pier 76 on West 38th and 12th. Give the job to Reuben and have him take a friend along. There should be no problem. Call the number on the receipt if there is."

*   *   *

Reuben reported to Abranos, smiling like a kid who discovered ice cream. Maddoc must have some important friends. It's incredible: field supplies, including pop-open tents. Food and water for a month. Look at these side arms, 9MM's, even machetes. There are shortwave radios and night goggles. We've got tree climbing spikes – man, are they cool, and both flash and fragmentation grenades. Looks like we're going to war."

"We are. We are into the backyard of the people who don't like strangers. They won't want us there; we insist on being there. That's a war, child."

"But Uncle, who's going to stop us? We've got rifles and machine pistols."

"There's no us, hijo. You're here at the store. I want your friends on the street watching over our friends who may not be friendly these days."

"Big Head will take care of things."

"No, no! Big Head's a good friend, but he likes a woman, any woman, better than he likes us. You will be here. Besides, if I get killed, who's going to take care of our business?"

"Our business? If you get killed, it's my business!"

"Buenos, muy buenos. Now you understand."

Maddoc arrived and shared Harrington's report. "I want you to drive up tomorrow? We'll rendezvous midday in Milan as planned. I'm going to Eaton with a quick stop in Portsmouth to review the police report on a confrontation that might have involved Sylvi, perhaps speak with the officer who wrote it."

The arsenal was excessive. He chose a combat knife, night goggles a 9MM pistol and a carbine. Abranos took the same plus flash grenades. Maddoc laughed at the grenades. Abranos reacted,

"Hey, gringo, you never know when your grenade will be your best friend."

"We have our best friend Dogbone. He will greet anyone before we see their eyes."

"We run into a bear or an angry moose, the dog he go at the bear and the grenade save his skin."

"…and kill the dog and everything else within striking distance."

The remaining small arms were separated for team members. The rest went to a secure locker in Abranos's cellar. Not one piece was American made. He suggested Abranos instruct team members to have standard hunting gear. "Harrington and his sidekick Sossa will be in uniforms."

Maddoc turned, saying, "Bernie and I are going together. I'll call you later with details on our meeting and our rendezvous plan."

Abranos held out his hands and shrugged. "What about the dog?"

"He's yours for the night. Buy him a steak and let him roam the neighborhood and he'll be fine. Give him the steak first. Otherwise, he'll go back to Manhattan."

"He'll be all right? What about me? I'm not a dog sitter."

"You don't understand, Caleb. Dogbone will be sitting you. Buy him that steak, and he'll be your friend for life."

"Oy, that crazy mutt may not have much of a life. If he runs these streets, he maybe gets torn up by some loco 'Rican's pit bull."

Maddoc laughed.

* * *

6:51 P. M. Friday, August 27, 1993

Al Harrington met Maddoc and Bernie at an inn on Crystal Lake. He introduced them to Sergeant Lenny Sossa, a CID specialist assigned to the team."

"Sergeant Maddoc, it's a pleasure to meet you. I'm a New Yorker. My uncle, Griffin Ritter, was at the academy with you and said you were the finest police officer he served with."

Maddoc smiled. "I might say the same about Griff. He's a man you want at your back."

Sossa smiled and explained the events at the cabin. "Sgt. Carleton found the young man wedged between the bed rail and the wall. "The assault was brutal and explains the condition in which we found him."

"…and it accounts for the broken furniture," Harrington added."

Maddoc asked. "Did anyone follow the evidence? If Sylvi was here, more than one person was involved."

"The lieutenant wants you to see the room before I go over it."

Lenny responded. "Our concern was to get the victim to a hospital, but the room is sealed and has been under guard."

Harrington broke in. "I delayed doing anything but glancing in. If your daughter was in this cabin, you'll know it. Nothing was disturbed."

"And you believe that Sylvi was here."

"My gut say so, and there's the owner's story. She's sure there was a man and a woman, strangers. Few newcomers come to these small camps. Most are returnees."

Maddoc relaxed. "I shouldn't be second-guessing you."

Ignoring his apology, Harrington went on. "Well, worst case, we find nothing and scratch it off the list, but I don't think so. Maddoc, let's walk to the cabin. I'm anxious for your take."

Maddoc, Bernie, Sossa and Harrington walked in pairs with Sossa leading the way. Once they arrived Maddoc stood just inside the cabin door. He looked around before stepping in. He adjusted to the light, walked through without touching anything, and committed everything to memory. He emerged in less than five minutes.

"Sylvi was in this cabin. I did not handle anything, but I'm certain. It has a familiarity to it. There was a fight, no doubt. Sylvia would not have shied away.

Any chance one of the bed sheets was used to carry the victim out?"

Sossa answered. "No. The medics had a gurney."

"A bed sheet is missing," Maddoc observed.

Harrington said. "Why do you ask?"

"Properly wrapped and tied, bed sheets are effective constraints."

"Sergeant Maddoc," Sossa interrupted. "My team has arrived."

*   *   *

Maddoc, Harrington and Bernie walked the 60 yards to the office.

Maddoc broke the silence. "Strange fellow, this Sossa. He speaks like an English Don. How long will they be?

Harrington laughed. "Maybe 30 minutes or so.

Lenny is okay. He was a teacher before he joined the force. Came up from New York, a John Jay graduate. Did a spell in public broadcasting and bears a strong likeness to an extra in "The Godfather."

"If Sylvi was in that cabin; we'll find her things," Maddoc murmured.

"Has there been any news on the man, lieutenant?"

"It's Al, Ms. Van Eyck. I'll call you Bernie, if you don't mind." Bernie nodded.

"He's stabilized and breathing well. It's a matter of time. He'll wake up."

Maddoc Interrupted when he saw Sossa walking down the trail. "Looks like they're finished. Let's get on with it."

Sossa spoke as he approached. "We've seen everything we need to see. There's blood on the dresser, but not much."

They all walked to the cabin and stepped in.

Maddoc and Bernie began looking through the things around the room.

"Anthony, this is Sylvi's bag. This is a sweater I gave her."

Maddoc didn't speak. Bernie turned and saw that he was holding a well-worn blue and white teddy bear.

"Anthony, that's Sylvi's. She slept with it as a baby."

Maddoc choked up, whispered as he turned away from Bernie, "She didn't go anywhere without it. When she would be away from home it was the first thing she packed. She was here, and this is where she was taken. I've seen enough. Let's get her things together and go find my daughter."

"The odds just got a whole lot better," Harrington beamed.

Maddoc muttered, "Spooner, Jeff Spooner. The young man is Jeff Spooner."

CHAPTER 22

12:45 P.M.: Tuesday, August 24, 1991

Milton looked at his watch. Jonetta should be arriving within minutes. Milton fidgeted. Things were in motion, and he soon would be done with her. He looked back on their years together.

She was quite a woman then. Their relationship had always been wrong, but when her father died, he proposed, despite their age difference and his marriage. She laughed. She remained attractive, but men now found excuses to avoid her. Milton was not one of them. It made little sense that one with so much wealth and success could be so bitter.

* * *

The click of Jonetta's heels announced her arrival. Milton admitted her. He reviewed the position she was in, showing great concern, but Jonetta laughed and lost patience.

"Sit down, Milton! No one's looking over your shoulders. I don't give a shit about anything that Toni or anyone else told you. Those bastards will shit when they see the files I've built up. I didn't fuck Milton Cash on every continent and come away empty. Matterlink can't touch me and will settle for whatever we demand."

Milton stared.

"Don't give me that look. I know that Gilletti and his thugs are the movers and shakers behind Matterlink and use the foundation to launder money. I've been over the books. Those goombas are not as smart as they think. I've got them by the short hairs, including that Toni bitch."

Milton was stunned. He expected her to be frightened; yet she strutted. He asked her to sit. She refused. He insisted.

"Jonetta, listen to me. Matterlink withdrew its severance offer, but you have a far more serious problem, one I cannot help you with. My firm will not take on any additional work for you. The IRS is charging you with tax fraud going back twenty-three years, very unusual. It amounts to millions. We are named as co-conspirators and are seeking a separate hearing. The firm isn't concerned. We have your signature supporting every filing."

She started to speak, but he waved her off, snapping, "Please don't interrupt."

"You are in a precarious position. Special agents are assigned to your case, a bad sign. The IRS is tying up everything you own. Your checking account may be accessible, but that's all. If you are charged and convicted of tax fraud, you may do jail time."

Jonetta began to come apart. She was a closet pessimist staring calamity in the face. She trembled. She had no files on the IRS.

"What should I do?" she whispered. Milton shrugged.

"You have to get an attorney, someone with IRS experience, and work out a deal."

"You can't be serious. It's a joke; tell me it's a joke. I pay my taxes. You're trying to scare me, you bastard. You're softening me up."

Milton was amazed. She was in denial and tried bullying. He frowned. "Listen to me. You cannot wait until you're charged to get an attorney."

"How in fuck am I going to pay for an attorney if all my funds are tied up?" she peeped.

"That's a fair question. I have some thoughts."

"You'll represent me?"

"The Firm cannot be involved with your defense. And I will not give up a partnership that pays me more than a million dollars annually. You've pissed off the wrong people. Arnold Shaw, the firm's chairman and our senior tax litigator, advised that you settle and keep your mouth shut if you expect to come out of this intact."

"What did he mean?"

"I asked the same question. He said he was speculating, but if you make peace with whomever - you would know who- and settle with the IRS, you would avoid the courts."

"They'll take all my money!"

"No! You will be left with the bulk of it, but your access will be limited to a court determined allowance until the IRS back taxes, penalties and whatever else are determined and paid. In recent days, suits were filed against you for hundreds of millions."

"On what basis?"

"There are several claims, including criminal fraud."

"I didn't …."

"Jonetta, it matters not one bit what you did or did not do. What does matter is that it will take years to go through the courts unless you choose to settle."

"You call whoever you're supposed to call and tell them they can go fuck themselves. I want this shit to disappear within the next forty-eight hours or I go to the newspapers and expose that fucking Gilletti gangster and his dyke daughter."

"That isn't wise, Jonetta. Take Shaw's advice."

"You're nuts," she screamed. "Your powerful people can kiss my ass. To hell with them. To hell with you. You fucked me when I was a child." She was on a roll.

Tell Gilletti for me that I have a dossier on his dealings with Otha Gubbin. I know he approved of Rubino's takeover of PLAN. That guinea bastard wouldn't make a move with the great Cesare's nod. Rubino was passing his share to the top.

Ask him, either before or after you kiss his ass, how he would handle a subpoena. He cannot lie in court. Neither can Rubino. He puts up or I'll trot out a basket of files that will bury him.

Halprin was stunned. He knew nothing of these matters, but they might explain Gilletti's edginess.

She needed to get back to her pets. Once Milton made his call, the wheels were in motion. He tried to make things easier for her, but she killed any chance. Every word she said was transmitted.

*   *   *

Jonetta came out of her reverie when she heard the driver cuss. "Shit, there's a tie-up and I'm hemmed in." Ten minutes passed before she reacted.

"What the fuck's holding us up?" she demanded.

"I don't know, but we're not going anywhere. You're better off walking."

She looked at the meter, which showed $12.80, handed the driver a twenty dollar bill and got out at the curb without looking back. Not bad. A hundred to pick her up plus the double sawbuck. The driver turned on his Off Duty light and executed a tough U-turn to a chorus of shouts and curses.

Jonetta fumed as she walked east. The dumb bastard. Why were they on 58th and Broadway? It was the long way to her apartment; it was too late now. She walked east, annoyed by the crowds; everyone seemed to be moving in the same direction.

As she crossed 7th Avenue, she could see lights flashing and traffic standing dead still. People were stuck in their cars. Black smoke reached into the mid-afternoon sky, its billowing arms twisting and embracing roof tops in a macabre dance. Its heaviness blotted out the sun at unpredictable intervals; wind gusts swept shadows across the ground below. One gust lifted the curtain to reveal flames shooting from the upper stories of a building close to her co-op. Then the smoke, cat-like, jumped back, teasing her as it cut off any view of the building. She never considered that the inferno might be her building. It was closer to Fifth Avenue.

As she drew near, the view was blocked by other high-rise buildings. She could hear the glass exploding and raining down. People were streaming toward the fire as the police set out barricades. She felt cheapened by the smallness of New York curiosity-seekers.

Not having eaten since breakfast, she turned around, working her way to the University Club for a light lunch. Her blood sugar was dropping. She would spend an hour or so there, have her meal and catch up on the news. It would still be light when she left; the fire would be under control, and the crowds gone.

* * *

108

The fire started in an apartment on one of the middle floors, the tenth or eleventh, given its progress. It was tough to tell once a fire spreads because it moves down as well as up. If an accelerant were used, it would move faster but leave evidence. In some odd situations, open staircases provided strong counter-drafts creating vortexes that could pull a fire in every direction. Once the fire was under control, assuming anything but ashes remained, experts would figure out its entire history, from the first spark to the path it took as it ate its way through the building.

The building was without sprinklers. Instead of sprinklers, there were standpipes and hoses on every third floor, thought to be sufficient when the building was designed and approved. The firefighters were able to get above the fire and fight from two directions, confining it and bringing it under control within seven hours. Three apartments in the northeast corner were burned out, and more than quarter million gallons of water poured down staircases, through vents, down walls and along raceways. The wall coverings hung, falling over furniture like forgotten drapes, creating an eerie, almost funereal effect on all sides of the spacious lobby, silent testimony to the relentlessness of water.

Odd things happened. Furniture floated and settled in odd locations. Every mailbox in the lobby became a small font, water filling up and then cascading out through the face of each, appearing to be miniature falls springing from a sheer cliff. Wall mirrors broke before crashing to the floor, the weight of the water flexing the walls and snapping the glass, leaving only anchors. The building was vacated while inspectors decided when it could be put back into service.

Jonetta's apartment was destroyed, her pets, records, jewelry, clothing and everything else reduced to ashes and slush. All she had left she wore and carried. The water coursing through the building did most of the damage, but the fire delighted in consuming Jonetta's corner.

Her mailbox contained two letters, one from her casualty insurance and the other from the IRS. Her insurance payment was 30 days late and had lapsed. Of the seven days grace, six had passed. The second gave her fourteen days to meet IRS demands or an arrest warrant would be executed. With the exception the cellophane, they were pulp.

*   *   *

Jonetta's late lunch of fresh fruit, cheese and tea, quieted her. She skimmed through the *Times* and scanned the *Wall Street Journal*. Almost three hours passed, and she was anxious to get home. Having worked things out and confident she had everything under control she stopped at the ladies room, checked her appearance and was on her way and on the sidewalk. As she took a left toward Fifth Avenue, all seemed right with the world. She had the big picture; others were paid to worry about the details.

As she came closer to her apartment building, she found the traffic had cleared, but some of the crowd remained. She could see the stragglers and the police as she approached 63rd, but only as she turned the corner did she realize that the fire had been in her building. As she rushed toward the entrance, she was turned away by a policewoman.

"But I live here! My pets are here."

"I'm sorry ma'am, but no one can enter the building."

Jonetta screamed. "I have to get my pets."

"What apartment are they in, ma'am?"

"12J."

"Please wait a moment."

The policewoman walked over to a captain and spoke to him for a moment, both shaking their heads. He turned and looked toward Jonetta. Confident that her earlier buoyancy was not without reason, she stayed calm.

The captain approached her. "Sorry, ma'am, you can't get into the building at this time. We're inspecting, and there's no chance the building can be occupied until next week the earliest. We're going floor to floor. If your pets are all right, we'll take them to the S.P.C.A. where they'll be cared for. It appears your apartment was in the midst of the worst of it, and you should not be optimistic about the pets. If the fire didn't get them, the smoke did." He turned and walked away, too tired to be concerned about her loss.

As she passed out, Jonetta thought not of her pets but of the files she believed were the key to extricating her from the IRS and regaining her job.

* * *

Halprin's phone woke him at 1:55 A.M. Jonetta was calling from Mt. Sinai where she was taken after she fell. She struck her head on a brass hose connector, requiring seven stitches. Told an hour earlier she could leave, she didn't know where to go. In the confusion, her purse disappeared with her cash, credit cards and ID's. She tried getting help, but no one was taking her calls. Hospital security was courteous but there was no record of her arriving with a purse.

Milton answered her call "Milton, I'm lost. My precious Amarillys, my sweet Tic and Tac, my neon's, my tetras, my swords, all burned up," she whispered. "My purse is gone."

"Jonetta, are you all right?" Milton was not fully awake.

"No, you fucking asshole, I'm not all right. I'm in the hospital. My apartment's gone, and my purse is stolen. I got nothing. This is too much shit to be bad luck. Someone's fucking with me, and I'll get them," she raged.

Milton grew cautious. The idea was to break her will, and she did not seem broken. As quickly as she raged, she dropped back, shaken and unsure. "Please, please, you're my friend; please come and get me."

Milton checked her into the Continental, a suite, and ordered food and wine. He instructed the concierge to bring her a change of clothing and the toiletries and such that she might need and arranged to have a thousand dollars for her in the morning. She showered and wrapped herself in a house robe. She ate lightly accompanied by two glasses of wine and her appearance picked up. She left his office her cocky self and ended in the ER haggard, downcast, and whining. Now she was transformed, almost her normal self. The Sauvignon Blanc was a good year.

"What am I to do, Milton? Who's going to help me now? Who can I trust?"

"I understand. One week you're on top; the next you're flat on your ass. What would you like to do?"

"Can you help me, Milton?"

"My hands are tied."

"Can you get Matterlink to reconsider the severance offer?"

"After your call last night, I made a call. I was authorized to pay for the hotel and to give you a thousand in cash as walking-around money. Five thousand dollars was authorized for wardrobe needs. The man who made that decision is the man who withdrew the severance offer. I think your turning down the severance package offended him and the board. At this point, it may be possible to get something more for you; but I doubt that they're going to give you the full package."

"Those fucking bastards. I have three years left on a five-year contract. They have to pay."

"Jonetta, you are locked out. It's unrealistic for you to expect anything more."

She did not respond. She looked around the room. She got up, walked across the floor and looked at herself in the mirror, and then she spoke. "Milton, why not now? Let me tell you! Not now because those bastards had something to do with the fire and the rest of it. Are you one of the sons of bitches trying to ruin me?"

"Jonetta, you are dealing with powerful people. I was instructed last night to tell you the thousand dollars cash and five thousand clothing allowance are your severance package."

"Do they think they can get away with this?"

"Jonetta, they have a complete dossier on your activities with the Perfect Love Adoption Nexus. Bram Stephens laid out the full story. There's no chance anything will change. Rubino is dead, a motorcycle accident."

Jonetta stared at him. Her face screwed up; her eyes narrowed. She opened her mouth but nothing came out. There was a moment of absolute silence and then she got her voice. "Get out! Get out, you bastard! I still have friends in high places."

Before he left, Milton told her he would do what he could. He would speak to some friends and try to get her some relief as she sorted out the issues and attended to her relocation and the insurance issues.

Halprin contacted Cesaré Gilletti. "Mr. Gilletti, I believe we should provide an attorney. Otherwise, they'll squeeze everything out of her. She claims she has documentation."

"She has nothing. If you want to pay for it, get some young guy fresh out of Brooklyn Law looking to cut his teeth. She'll get good representation." He hung up.

Jonetta was picked up as she left the hotel and taken to the interior of the Federal Building and told she was set up. She could help herself by giving the FBI information. Jonetta's confidence was shot. She called Michael Chen's office, desperate to tell someone where she was. The receptionist, who recognized Jonetta, was very sweet.

"Dr. Chen is not available. Can someone else help, Ms. Van Loos?"

No one at McDonnell would help. She thanked the girl and hung up. Two more calls and two more failures. She would reach no one until the agents were ready to have her reach someone.

Convinced she could get a deal, she shot her mouth off. On her information, Bram Stephens was picked up and held by the Feds. Gilletti's people did not find him, and Neary despite his claims got nowhere. Gilletti was not worried about the Feds. He had prepared Stephens. Nevertheless, he was disappointed that his friends in the local Federal Building could not see their way to release information. He buzzed his secretary who came in with her pad. "Gerri, call Washington for me, dear. I want to speak to the Attorney General."

CHAPTER 23

11:48 P.M.: *Thursday, August 29, 1993*

Sylvi did not underestimate Gubbin. Subtle changes among his prisoners, a more confident step or a smile made him uneasy. He and most of the camp population left three days earlier, and Otha left behind several of his key men with Zebediah Doody in charge.

He warned Zeb Doody, "Things ain't lookin' right. You best stay awake. You'll get your full share of the pickings; just do your job. Ludim and Maximillian will watch our guests."

Now the pair were on night watch duty. The others of the seven left behind, Luke, Matthew, Ish, and Malachi, were more than enough to keep order. Routines held; and within a week, everyone relaxed. Ludim, not one to slack off, reminded Maximillian of their responsibility. "We watch'em at night. Ain't nothing happening when the sun shines."

Sylvi knew it was time. Ludim and Maximilian were angry at being left behind. The annual treks were happy times. They were well positioned to watch the prisoners, but Ludim's mind was on his losses.

"I be doing all right for myself if I got to go. Otha knows it. I always brung in a pile of money. Now I ain't getting no money, an' I can't do any flatland girls."

Maximillian's concerns were more basic. "Otha thinks something funny is going on wit' the prisoners. We gotta watch 'em. If something bad happen, Otha gonna take Naomi from me."

"He's just fretting you. The prisoners ain't doing anything, and Otha ain't taking Naomi from you. I ain't letting no one take Naomi way from you. Otha giv'er to you and that's enough."

"We married; ain't takin'er away."

"I said I won't let him, Maximillian. You get so dumb sometimes. "

Ludim stood in the woods half hoping something would happen to take Maximillian off and he could get to Naomi.

He saw Peter go into Josie's cabin. Maximillian moved forward. Ludim held him back. "It's no matter. The man is poking her. Otha don't care none about that. She's supposed to make babies and can't do it without a man."

Ludim, envying Peter, felt his own stirrings. Otha might kill him, but he got worked up as he pictured Peter doing Josie. With Otha gone, he might chance her. She was so scared she wouldn't say anything. Ludim fumed. Otha left him with the prisoners, but Zebediah was the boss.

Maximillian was nervously watching the cabin. Ludim wasn't over-anxious about the prisoners. They couldn't run. The woods were almost impassable in the light of day; at night, even with a full moon, they were impossible.

Ludim's thought drifted back to Josie. She'd be afraid to tell Otha any-thing, and there is the other young one, Sandy. He could poke her without any resistance. She never said anything.

Concealed under the cabin, Eban Docker lay watching. As Otha decreed, he crawled wherever he went. His broken leg was healing, but the swelling remained. It would not yet support much weight. Little Jug's dam-age to the other leg was less severe but the pain hung on.

He recalled the day he dragged himself to the stream and submerged his legs in the cold water. Once the pain eased a bit, he found two large stones close together and worked the damaged ankle between them. The pain was great, but Eban was tough. Using his arms, he was able to grasp a low hanging tree branch. He pulled on it with every bit of strength he had left, straightening the ankle though imperfectly repositioning it. He left it in place for a time before lifting it out. He lay on his back, the cold water washing over his legs, and rested. He then inched himself onto the grass bordering the stream, shivering with the cold but remaining still. Finally, he slept.

Little Jug saw him lying on the grass and laid down beside him until he began to shiver. He got blankets to cover them both. He remained with Eban for many days, feeding him and making certain no one bothered him.

He wrapped the ankle as Eban told him, first packing mud around it and wrapping it with willow bark strips and then tying them as tightly as he could with rags. The pain almost knocked Eban out, but he knew he had to keep the ankle from moving.

Those coming for water avoided them, not concerned with Little Jug, but afraid to bring Otha's wrath upon themselves. Otha would not interfere with Little Jug. Eban's damaged tendons, healing from within, firmed up. He would heal, but no matter how well he healed, Eban's days were numbered. He marked time and planned for the one opportunity that would allow him to avenge himself. He would destroy Otha or die trying.

He saw Ludim within his reach, but he needed a gun to do what he had in mind. His obsession reinforced his resolve. He acquired a knife and some small tools, including a shovel blade, rusted and bent but serviceable. He had a burrow, a small cave under the cabin where he now lived. He was determined to survive, if only to destroy Gubbin and Ludim. Ludim betrayed him.

Eban and Ludim were friends, almost brothers, and no one but Ludim knew of Eban's plot to kill Gubbin. Eban drew Maximillian into his plot by convincing him that Naomi would marry him once Gubbin was gone. Naomi went along, allowing Maximillian to touch her while promising more. Upon Ludim's discovering Eban and Naomi coupling, he cornered Naomi, telling her what he wanted from her. She laughed; Ludim threatened to tell Otha. "I'll tell Otha you tried to do me, and he gonna do you." Ludim informed Gubbin of the plot.

Eban ate when people threw him scraps. Sometimes he scrounged garbage left in trash. Sylvi gave him real food, but she did not seek him out. If he were nearby when she was cooking, she fed him. He had to be careful. The children beat him with sticks and urinated on him. The few dogs, not fearful of him, attacked and bit him until he got the knife. At first he had to curl up in a ball and hope that someone would call the dogs off. The attacks stopped when he killed a beagle but not before he received serious bites. No one would treat him. He had to work his way to the stream to clean his wounds and make a poultice to thwart infection. His survival kept him occupied full time.

His hatred of Otha did not override his fear. There was the hole, and Eban had things to do before he could face that. No one heard those dropped in the hole hit bottom, but their screams echoed for many seconds.

The hole was discovered before Otha's time. Legend told that a bear came into the camp and was set on by the dogs. The bear did not fear dogs, but there were too many pestering him and nipping at his hind end and lower legs. Some were killed, but they kept coming. The bear backed up, swatting dogs aside as the men ran for their weapons.

The bear came up against a natural hedgerow that impeded his retreat. He turned and crashed through the barrier, followed by several dogs. Everything came to a stop. Some dogs kept up their barking, but there was no bear, and no sign of the dogs that followed. Investigation revealed a hole about eight feet in diameter concealed by a ring of thickets and small trees. Some thought it was an old well. Some thought it a sinkhole, but it was too deep. People thought it was more than a thousand feet deep, but no one knew for sure. Otha attempted to solve the mystery by tying a strong bell on a rope and measuring the rope down the hole ringing the bell as he went. He gave up when he could no longer hear the bell and ran out of rope at 300 feet. Otha surmised it was submerged; but when it was pulled up, it was dry. No one knew how many had disappeared into that hole over the years. Stories became legends, and the hole was seen as the entrance to hell. Some claimed to have seen the light of the fires escaping on the blackest of nights. Otha was not reluctant to throw miscreants into the hole.

Eban was a fastidious man; but Otha had him living in filth on his belly. At night, with little chance of his being seen, he was able to accept the pain and move about foraging using his hands and legs, but progress was slow. Within time, he could get to his feet and practice walking but not erect and very slowly.

Under the circumstances, his life expectancy, unless he could get some blankets, was a few weeks at best. Once winter set in, the stream would freeze, leaving pools in the deeper sections, but Eban could not bathe. Of course, no one would be pissing on him either. The cold and lack of food and water meant he would not survive without help, and helping him was a crime. Sylvi and Little Jug were not afraid to help, and in Otha's absence others helped. Eban got blankets enough to allow him to sleep peacefully unless interrupted by a critter.

Eban recognized Maximilian's feet as they joined those of Ludim. He was amused by this perspective on life, but it had no value.

Ludim spoke. "Peter's still poking the crazy girl in the shed."

"How do you know?"

"He went in there and ain't come out."

"He takes care of her."

"Only when Otha says so, and Otha ain't said he should be with her tonight."

"Otha ain't here saying if he can of if he can't. What should we do?"

"We ain't doing nothing. He can poke her all he wants. If he knocks her up, it ain't gonna do no harm."

"I heard the' child comes out wit' an extra head if the' woman is poked too early when she's first seeded."

"That happened once, and it was because she was poked by a stranger."

The explanation satisfied Maximilian. Just as Josie's shed opened and Peter and the girl emerged carrying her few things, Maximilian, afraid of losing Naomi, started forward to stop them; but Ludim pulled him back, telling him to be quiet. They watched as the pair entered Sylvi's cabin. Ludim and Maximilian worked their way toward the cabin to get a better view. Maximilian stumbled, his three-hundred-fifty plus pounds driven against the corner of the dilapidated shack. The cabin swayed and then slipped off the second of its three remaining supports, the one holding up the corner above the burrow where Eban made his home. It dropped noise-lessly, emitting little more sound than the cracking of a stiff branch in a strong wind. Eban was not hurt, but he was penned in, unable to reach his tools; he would dig his way out with his hands.

The two men skirted Sylvi's cabin and positioned themselves in a copse slightly above, the place where Ludim stood when Stef Tillis died. They had sufficient light to see movement in the cabin, though not enough to make anyone out. Ludim knew he shouldn't approach the cabin. He figured Sylvi was feeding her friends. The woods were too dark for them to run. If they ran and Little Jug found his woman gone, he'd track them down. Ludim and Maximillian would follow.

*   *   *

12:07 A.M. — Monday, August 30, 1993

Sandy, easy prey to the few men left behind, cowed as her door opened. Being raped and then abducted and raped again, she lived in despair. She had a twenty-eight-inch table leg ready to strike. She practiced with it every morning but wasn't confident she could use it. She recognized Peter's gangly frame.

Peter said, "We are escaping tonight. Pull your things together and let's go." She hesitated. Once Peter explained that they all were leaving, including Josie, she relented.

Vincent was already in Sylvi's cabin playing tic-tac-toe with Little Jug. Vincent and Little Jug became friends early. Sylvi knew Little Jug would not react to Vincent's craziness. Vincent told him where to put his X's. Little Jug won time after time, and Sylvia criticized Vincent for letting Little Jug win, yet after a few games, Little Jug won on his own.

*   *   *

Vincent's story was like Peter's with Sylvi, but Sandy was younger. Vincent was locked in a shack with the terrified 15-year-old. His directness was the first understanding she had of why she was there.

"Look Sandy, I don't like this anymore than you do, but I have to get you pregnant.

She became unhinged as he explained.

"But I was raped. In God's eyes I'm still a virgin. I promised my mom I would wait until I was married. You can't ever touch me!" She shook edging her way into a corner as though death stood over her.

He became angry, but not with her. He didn't touch her but spoke with her for hours. As she relaxed, he learned that she and her girlfriend had been passed on by two boys who held them for two days, assaulting and raping them. They were then passed on to two older men who dragged them into a truck. Her friend got away. Once in Gubbin's hands, she spent most of the

119

time crying. Marlene and Josie helped her along, and she got herself together. Then Gubbin decided it was time for her to produce.

Raised by a hidebound Baptist father and an ascetic mother, flatland counterparts of Otha and Erla Gubbin, Sandy was terrified of sex. Her parents' death in an auto accident two years earlier changed her life, but she remained true to her upbringing. Her aunt and uncle brought her and her brother into their Christian home but not her parents' straitjacketed bigoted world. With them, Sandy lived a life of Christian celebration.

Vincent was determined to protect her. At the end of the third day, Gubbin and Erla appeared. Vincent believed that once they realized the depths of the girl's conviction, reason would prevail. He explained Sandy was a virgin and had made a commitment to God to live as a Christian and remain celibate until she married. Otha himself had made such a big thing of living through the scriptures Vincent thought he would accept the argument. But Otha had no interest in her chastity and avowed faith. They were no argument when considering the babies she would produce. In his mind she was common street girl. Otha asked, "If she is such a good Christian girl, what for was she running around dressed like a common street whore with her tight pants showing her privates?"

"Well," Erla declared, "I just think she's a-fooled the boy. If you're afraid to poke her because the gate's at the door, we can fix that." Erla told Vincent to hold her down and keep her legs apart so that she "could poke her with a stick and open things up."

Vincent stepped in to protect her, and Erla came at him with the stick. Vincent, his combat instincts taking over, deflected the stick and smashed her nose flat and to the left of her face with the heel of his hand. She passed out. Gubbin pushed a 45-caliber revolver into Vincent's face, stepping back and telling him, "I ought to kill you right now, but that won't give Erla no pleasure."

Gubbin stood with the gun leveled. He directed Vincent outside. He summoned Luke and told him to lock up Vincent under guard.

Otha sent for Esther to attend to Erla, who was laid up for two days before she showed her face. It was a mess, one side black and blue, both eyes blackened and her nose twisted to one side. Gubbin didn't call in a doctor, although either on hand would have reset her nose and minimized the bruising.

Vincent was brought out and spread-eagled upright between two saplings. Debilitated, having been beaten severely, he seemed dead. Gubbin told the entire story. He was quite explicit about the law and reminded all of the consequences of breaking it. He spoke directly to Vincent, "Boy, you got to thinking you were the judge, and you ain't. You got to thinking you could strike your betters; that was a bad thing. You got to thinking you could protect this whore, but you can't."

Gubbin then nodded to the men holding the girl, and Vincent, hanging and helpless, in excruciating pain, was forced to watch while Sandy was pulled into the circle in front of the saplings to which he was tied. She was stripped of her miserable flour sack, spread-eagled on a log bench and raped by any man who had the stomach for it. Few had. Vincent cried, not because of his pain and hunger but because he was helpless. After the spectacle was underway, the women, Erla leading, beat Vincent with their water-soaked hickory and willow switches. Sylvi, standing to one side with Little Jug, added the moment to the list for which Otha Gubbin would answer.

Erla was hell-bent on castrating Vincent and letting him bleed to death, but Otha would have no part of it.

"Woman, you are an abomination afore God, damned to suffer for your mother's evil in leading man into sin. You ain't the even of this man or any man God put on the ground. You ain't gonna bring him to your sinful state."

Before Erla could respond, Gubbin walked to Vincent and cut him down.

Sandy, now unconscious, was carried off to her cabin. If she got pregnant, she would be treated like the others. The baby would be turned over to a clan woman no matter how normal it might appear. Gubbin was particular about his breeding stock. He was also ignorant about it, believing once a woman had a defective child because of a 'mongrel pregnancy,' as he termed it, she could not have a normal child unless she was cleansed by her own blood. This was necessary in order to 'purify the well where the babies growed.' Gubbin claimed she must wait through six 'moon times' before 'being seeded'.

Vincent was left in the dirt, bleeding and unconscious. He was then returned to the cabin and held for a week, almost dying for lack of food and water. When he was freed, he was emaciated. His friends brought water and what little food he could ingest. He had been a little crazy and given to outbursts, but this experience left him morose, and his outbursts lessened.

*   *   *

As Ludim and Maximillian worked out what was going on with the prisoners, they saw Frank and Marlene arrive with two burlap bags. Ludim thought they were planning to run. "That's it. Them bags got vittles in them."

Sylvi prepared a warm meal for everyone, pleased that they were running ahead of schedule. She had rabbit stew, turnips mashed with cranberries, warm cider and unleavened bread. Having a huge appetite and no sense of decorum, Little Jug ate about a third of everything she cooked, but there was enough. While they ate, Sylvi laid out the plan.

"We leave within the next half hour and move toward a good-sized town where we'll get help from the authorities. It'll be tough, but we intend to travel twelve hours a day, taking ten-minute stops every two hours, and sleeping at least six hours. To succeed, we need a six or seven hour lead. We'll have some advantage. Little Jug and I will travel behind, setting false trails."

Peter said, "They'll go around in circles without Little Jug."

"Don't fool yourself," Sylvi responded. "Every man and most women in this camp are born to these woods. They are skilled in tracking and hunting. Although none has Jug's gifts, they may have taught him much of what he knows. Our advantage is in the few people Otha left behind. Their advantage is they have guns and dogs. We will fool the dogs a whole lot easier than we'll fool the trackers. As dimwitted as they seem, their instincts are sound. I learned that when I tried to get away. We plan to reach our destination no less than an hour before them. That will give us enough time to speak to the authorities."

"We can't rehearse this trip, and so, during the first few hours, there are absolute rules we must follow. We have to be quiet. We'll speak to each other using signs. We're paired up for a reason" – here Frank explained the pairings, which made sense." I'll be with Josie, Peter with Sandy, and Vincent with Arthur. Marlene and June will be at point. If they run into strangers, they won't seem a threat. Arthur, I'm counting on you to keep Vincent calm. If he acts out, Sandy will switch with you. We'll stay within sight of each other at fifteen-yard intervals. Stay aware of those in front of you. The terrain and dense brush will slow us down. During such times, our ranks will close. Once we break out into open country, we pick up the pace. If the scroats catch up with us, we scatter and travel northwest; someone is bound to get through."

With this, Frank asked Peter and Josie to hold up a rough map he had sketched on a plain cloth. Peter explained, pointing out key spots, "We start here and gather over here. There's almost no chance we'll be separated; but should we be, follow the sun. You will cross well-traveled trails heading east to west. Go west. Sylvi and Little Jug will remain at our backs and may find you, but do not wait for them. Keep moving.

Peter will carry messages up and down the line. Little Jug and Sylvi are our first line of defense. Anyone who gets by them will face Vincent and Arthur. Both are combat veterans, and Vincent is an ex-fighter. They can raise hell." He looked toward the pair. "Sylvi says they're almost as tough as she is." Everyone chuckled; Sylvi shook her head in denial.

"Once we're on our way, we'll travel south about a mile, the usual and easiest route out of here. We then swing northwest. At some distance, perhaps 300 yards, we'll pass the camp where we expect everyone to be sleeping, including the dogs. Sylvi and Little Jug will travel another mile to pull our trackers further south.

When we turn northwest, we'll come upon a stream. We'll walk the streambed for more than a mile. It takes us off our line of travel, but also creates real problems for the trackers. The stream is shallow most of the way, but the water, coming from the mountain, will be cold. We have to stay with it. If we stay the full distance, it'll be impossible for anyone, even with dogs, to track us.

"Once we're far enough upstream, we'll come to the pilings of an old bridge. The bridge itself is gone. An overgrown but visible road leads to it.

We'll follow this road for a quarter mile or so. We will come to a rock formation rising about 100 feet. The old timers call it Skag's Leap. We'll climb to the top where we'll find a grassy plateau concealed by a natural rock enclosure. We'll rest there. Sylvi and Little Jug may be waiting for us. If not, we'll wait for them. It is a perfect resting place. Peter, would you continue?"

"Okay. When we stop to eat and drink, we'll eat small portions. This will sustain us without taxing our systems. Each pair of you will have enough food and water. Food scraps are to be thrown into the deep grass or woods where the critters will get them. Any other waste you put in your pockets. If you lose your food or run out, we'll make up your losses."

With this, Peter raised his arms above his head and crossed them. "This is the sign that you will use to show distress. It is to be used only when necessary.

"If you have to relieve yourself, find a place where you can dig a deep hole and cover your waste. Try to be at least ten yards off your path when you do. Just think about what animals do in the woods. You have to be a veteran woodsman to find animal scat. Does everyone understand?"

There were nods all around. Little Jug had fallen asleep, his full meal taking its toll. No one else was sleepy. What lay ahead made them more alert than they had been since being abducted. Each couple was handed a backpack containing food and water.

Peter spoke, "We're as ready as we can be. We'll leave in two minutes. Get your things together. Those who wish may join me by the stove for a brief prayer." Everyone but Sylvi, who was waking Little Jug, kneeled.

* * *

12:33 A.M. — Monday, August 30, 1993

Ludim and Maximilian watched Frank and Josie leave the cabin and waited to see who came next. Peter and Sandy emerged and took the same route. Ludim watched for the others in the cabin. Vincent and Josie followed.

"I'll be whupped," Ludim remarked just as they came from the back cabin and followed the same line. "That's all of 'em. Let's go get 'um, Maximilian. Our eight prisoners has flew the coop."

Maximilian pulled himself from where he was sitting. As he fell in with Ludim, the cabin door opened again, and Sylvi and Little Jug stepped out. Ludim smiled. He would tell Otha when he got back, and Ludim would have his revenge. He didn't expect Little Jug to be with Sylvi, although, after Stef Tillis died, wherever Sylvi was Little Jug would be nearby. Ludim wouldn't challenge Sylvi with Little Jug at her side.

"Hold on, Maximilian! We ain't gonna mess with Little Jug. You follow them and see where they go. I'm gonna round up the others. I'm not wanting to cross Little Jug, but if we have to, we gonna shoot him dead afore we let them prisoners get away. Otha would do the same."

Maximilian stared at Ludim. "I ain't going. You shoot Little Jug and Otha gonna kill you. I ain't going."

"We have to stop them. We take the dogs and the other mutts an' Li'l Jug be happy to see us. It be like old times, them running and us a-chasing. Li'l Jug will go along if we don't do nothing to that woman."

Maximilian nodded. A fine woodsman himself, he followed the two of them at a distance. Little Jug knew someone was behind him, but that wasn't part of the game. Maximilian trailed forty feet behind them when they came to the assembly point. They did not speak to each other, just nodded and started down trail in pairs. They traveled south. Maximilian stayed where he was, waiting for Ludim and the others. They would catch up and cut them off.

Ludim was having problems. No one in the camp jumped for anyone except Otha. Otha put Ludim in charge of security, but answerable to Zeb. Ludim awoke Zeb's children. The oldest, a nubile thirteen-year-old in a threadbare shift, told Ludim she didn't know where her dad was. Ludim kept asking her questions. He left when the baby started to fuss. He next went to Luke's door. Luke answered. Ludim explained things, and Luke thought they could wait until morning to fetch them. Ludim convinced him they shouldn't, and Luke agreed to get the others while Ludim found Zeb.

Luke gathered them together, but Ludim had not found Zeb. No one would make a move without him. Ludim went from cabin to cabin and came upon Zeb in Maximilian's cabin with Naomi. Ludim pushed the door in and Zeb came to his feet, his rifle in hand.

"Luddy, you get your ass out of here and keep that big dumb ox busy or I'll shoot you both."

"Can't. We got the prisoners running, and Little Jug is with 'em."

"That's your worry. Otha left you in charge of the prisoners."

"My worry, but it's gonna take all of us to get 'em back. You explain to Otha you're not helping."

"You explain. You're supposed to be watching them."

Ludim barked, "They gone, and we have to get them back. If we lose them 'cause you're a-diddling, you got some explaining to do. If Maximillian had come instead of me, you'd be a dead man."

"Hell, Ludim. You find out what way they gone. Keep that dummy away from here. Makes no difference if we start now or in the morning. They ain't going far in the dark, even with Little Jug. We'll set out at sunrise."

Ludim resented Zeb's characterization of Maximilian although he also called him a dummy. Part of the resentment came from his wanting Naomi, but she paid him no mind. He thought about Zeb's thirteen-year-old Martha. She was at the curious age that might take her partway down the trail. There wasn't time for anything more. He followed the path back to where he found Maximilian. He explained the prisoners took the usual route south. That gave Ludim some comfort. He told Maximilian to wait until he got back with the others. Maximilian objected, but Ludim barked, "stay or lose the prisoners and Naomi."

Unable to reason it out, Maximilian stayed.

"They might get too far ahead. We need the dogs."

"We don't need no dogs. We know right where to find them." In truth Ludim didn't want to get the dogs because it would have eaten into his plan to position to Zeb's thirteen-year-old enough for his purposes. When he got to the cabin, Zeb was there, waiting outside with the rest of the posse. Ludim silently cursed him. He reported they went south. Zeb decided that they could leave at first light. They'd bring the dogs and have them back by midday.

Zeb and Ludim made the same mistake. The logical course was south. It was where the runners would find towns they knew. Hell, it was the direction that every escapee took. Any other direction was close to impassable. Traveling south would put them on a serviceable mill road. The southerly route, if they swung eastward, would bring them to Berlin, but they might die in the mountains before they reached Berlin. Zeb was sure they'd catch the prisoners before they were halfway up the first hill they ran into.

Ludim argued against waiting until morning, but backed off when Zeb glared at him. Ludim was unarmed, and Zeb was holding his rifle. He might use the butt of the rifle on his head. Ludim had no idea that Zeb was waiting for an excuse to punish him. Ludim had been ogling his daughter.

He spoke to Ludim. "When I left Naomi, she was fidgeting, wanting more than I had time to give her. I can't go back. She asked me to ask you to do her a favor." Ludim couldn't believe his luck. Zeb was telling him he could poke Maximilian's wife. Zeb continued speaking, "She wants you to go find Maximilian and tell him to bring his big self home. I left that woman with a terrible hankering."

CHAPTER 24

5:15 A.M.: *Monday, August 30, 1993*

Zebediah Doody slept fitfully, awakening off and on with Ludim's fears on his mind. He decided to do what Otha would do. He awoke everyone just before sun-up and dragged the men south moving fast with the aim of getting ahead of the escapees. Of the seven beside himself, he didn't trust Ludim and Maximillian. He knew Luke was reliable but had doubts about Matthew, Ish and Malachi. Though close to Ludim, they would follow Luke. Zeb was confident that he had sufficient numbers even without the support of Ludim and Maximillian.

Working in the shadows of the early light, they missed the point where their quarry broke off the trail and headed northward upstream. They passed the point where Sylvi and Little Jug entered the woods to lay a false trail. They were now almost six miles south of where they should have caught up, and everyone but Zeb was ready to admit it. The sun was up and gave no evidence of anyone coming that far. Zeb was not able to acknowledge he was stumped. He rationalized.

"They're running, trying to get way ahead; may have a few hours lead on us. The wind that blew through here earlier wiped out any sign. We'll split up. Ludim you, and Ish stay after them. Me, Maximillian, Luke, Malachi and Matthew will go back, get the truck and drive down below Deacon's Crossing and pick up the trail in front of them. There's no way they be out of the wood before we find them."

Ludim, still smarting from Zeb's bullying, disagreed. "We gotta backtrack off trail and find some sign."

Zeb was not one to take insubordination. He brought his rifle up and slammed Ludim across the side of his head with the butt, knocking him

128

down and splitting the top of his ear where it joined his head. Ludim went down to his knees, his hand coming away from his head soaked with his own blood. He was stunned by the surprise and by the blow. Zeb then kicked him in the sternum driving the breath and remaining consciousness from him. Then he swung his gun on Maximilian as he stepped forward to help his friend.

"Just hold on! Leave him there. He ain't gonna bleed much. No little shit-faced chicken-boned horn toad gonna tell me what we ought to be doing. Ish, you and Maximilian get moving. We are going back for the truck. We'll pick Ludim up on our way back up trail. He just learned he don't tell me nothing."

Ludim wasn't thinking when he confronted Zeb. Smarter than Zeb, he could do what was necessary without Zeb's being any wiser. He should have undertaken the pursuit without him. The others had to come along, but he was afraid. If he failed, both Otha and Zeb would blame him. Now the failure rested on Zeb, unless Zeb could find a way to shift the blame. It would not be easy. Maximilian would support Ludim, as would Luke; but there was no knowing what the others would do, tactical lies being close enough to the truth to them.

Ludim's frustration and resentment had the same effect upon him it has on anyone, even the brightest of people. It prevented him from looking ahead and understanding his options. He was certain that even with the help of Little Jug, the runaways would not find their way to safety.

*　　*　　*

6:27 A.M. — Monday, August 30, 1993

Eban was aware of the preparations around him. His friends Sylvi and Little Jug had run off, and a hunt was getting underway. When he saw every man gathering their weapons, a plan he was working became possible. He had prayed about it. He knew that what he was about to do would condemn him to Hell, but he had been in a living Hell for many weeks. Their pursuers were off down trail without a thought to their women and children. Eban felt no remorse. He thought of them alone and asleep and became intoxicated with the joy of destroying their black-hearted souls.

129

Eban didn't consider himself and could afford no thoughts to the few who had been kindly. He was no longer a man. He lived like a grub, scavenging and living in dirt, always at risk of being stepped on and fighting off biters and snappers. Few helped him; most ignored him. The children threw rocks at him; no one intervened. The older boys pissed on him; he was forced to cover his face. He came to accept it, not yelling but plotting his revenge. After each day's sacrilege, he dragged his body to the stream to be cleansed. While no better than an animal, his rage was a jagged-edged knife waiting to rip out their souls. His burning hate became his will, and he relished the vengeance to come.

While Zeb and Ludim were trying to get their expedition underway, he dug himself free. His purpose and its workings were simple. He dragged an old wash pan and rudimentary tools as he worked his way across the rock-strewn grounds.

Scattered around the camp were vehicles of every description and every generation, some little more than rust piles, though still recognizable. The oldest was a rust-blackened 1920 vintage flatbed with a heavy chain drive, its crushing threat long gone. It had been Otha's grandfathers. Zeb's 1956 Ford pickup, one he stole eight or ten years back, was the only one that ran. Otha's entourage had the other serviceable vehicles.

Once Eban was certain the men were far enough down trail and not likely to be back soon, he scurried to Zeb's truck and pulled himself into position under the gas tank. His tools, a shallow pan and iron rod, would not unseat the fitting that held the gas line to the tank. Nor could he open the drain plug, but he was resourceful. He couldn't get much leverage; but after weeks of dragging himself around with his arms, his upper body strength was sufficient to enable him to support his body at the angle he required.

His working tool was a three foot piece of half-inch rebar. Eban was able to force the rod between the steel gas line and the undercarriage. Once in place, he forced the gas line away from the frame, extending the line fractionally each time he worked the rod to pull it further down. The line was not stronger than the rod and it wasn't very pliable. It wasn't long before the line gave at the fitting entering the gas tank, and gasoline ran out in a steady stream. Eban placed his pan under the stream and filled it with enough gasoline for his purposes. Almost an hour had passed since the men left, and it would be another 30 minutes before the sleepers would awake.

Eban pulled himself from under the truck and worked himself upwind to the point where the line of cabins began. He rationalized what he was about to do was just. Since his crippling, he fantasized that the Lord had something special in mind for him. He brought him through a terrible physical ordeal broken but mentally intact. God willed him to overcome the abuse, cold, hunger and hateful loneliness.

God loved him. God had ordained him to be an avenging angel in a nest of sinners. Like Nebuchadnezzar, he was driven from the people and ate grass. He was scourged by the elements; his hair grew long and unkempt, and his nails grew like the claws of the eagle. He would be delivered as Nebuchadnezzar was delivered. He knew it.

Anyone looking in would see what appeared to be a ghost town, a collection of ramshackle buildings in a setting that showed some organization but was neglected. A muffled snore and the smell of the previous night's cooking were the few signs of life. The buildings were placed in a circle. The circle was broken where a hardscrabble road separated the residents' cabin from those of the prisoners. No more than ten feet wide, it entered from the southwest, hard as iron from years of quarry stone pressed down over generations.

The cold wind beating on his back reminded Eban that the weather was turning, fall dropping early with winter's discomfort trailing behind. The breeze became a companion to Eban's plan. He was doing God's work, and God was providing. He looked at the shacks, fourteen of them. He didn't know how many slept in them. Some contained seven or eight women and children, some contained fewer, and several were unoccupied. If the number were known, it would make no difference to Eban. Even the fact that the wives and children of some of his former friends resided in the cabins made no difference. He had no friends.

Eban pulled himself along the ground to the side of the first cabin. It was a difficult journey, but he covered the distance quickly. The ground was stony and scraped away his skin as he pushed the clumsy tin along the ground. He ignored the pain as he moved along the side of the first cabin and played out the gasoline. He paid no attention to the gasoline that splashed on the rags he wore. Some splashed into open cuts and burned like the fire it would soon become. Once the gasoline was exhausted, he pulled himself back, dragging the pan with him.

It took him several seconds to find the matches he tucked into an open seam of his well-worn leather belt. The wind took the first match. The second flared and fizzled out and the third died as he tossed it toward the side of the cabin. He was getting anxious. Everything had gone according to plan, and now he couldn't light a damn match. He was down to the final match. He hunched over, turning his back to the wind, too close to the flash point. Shielding the match in his cupped hand, he brought it to full life and flipped it at the base of the cabin. It arched, showing a trail of orange and yellow flame fading as it dropped, bringing a moment's anxiety. It struck the ground, sparked and ignited the gasoline.

The fire raced alongside the cabin and up its walls, the dried bark quickly igniting. A back flash reached the gasoline traces in the pan, throwing a flame that ate at the ragged edges of Eban's trousers. They were so caked with mud they should not have ignited; yet mud burns when soaked with gasoline.

Eban's pants ignited; the gasoline now very evident as the fire raced upward. Eban did an amazing thing. Ordinarily, when he used his legs, one of which was a half-extended frog's kick, the other was able to propel him as he walked half-crouched. In this situation, driven by the fear and pain of the fire, he rose as high as he could and began running in a jerky, tilting dash toward the stream thirty feet away. He was a running torch. He made no sound, intent so on his objective as he skirted dense underbrush to reach the stream. He tripped on a root, falling onto the path. The gasoline flowing from the truck had followed the path creating a vapor cloud that enveloped an area about thirty feet as it rose into the night sky. It ignited. The silent explosion consumed every atom of life-giving oxygen. Eban drew the vapor and the fire into his lungs, and his system closed down.

The whoosh of the igniting gasoline was followed by the baying of the hounds and the crackling of wood as the fire ate each cabin in turn, sparing no one. Ironically, had the prisoners been in the back cabins, they would have survived. Eban did not hear the screams of the victims. The sight of Samson and Mariah, blistered and screaming as they emerged from their shack, went unseen. Ruth, the younger, one of the few children who ever showed Eban any pity, stood at the threshold behind the young lovers, her nightgown aflame and a piercing scream coming from her weakened lungs. This was the wrath of God; this was Eban's revenge. Twenty-seven people slept, and the few of the twenty-seven who did not suffocate in their sleep died in agony, crying that they, too, might be among the lucky dead who had evaded the fire's touch.

The hounds, kept in a pen on the far side of the living quarters survived. The few residents who got out were pulling at their burning night clothes and screaming with pain while breathing in the dense smoke. They collapsed. Zeb's truck burned but did not explode, and the fire, after it had burned fourteen cabins to the ground, weakened, licked at the underbrush but did not spread into the dense woods. The wind had swung around, pushing it back toward the camp center where it survived on dry grass and the little clothing remaining on the bodies. It burned itself out. The smoke lay heavy among the trees and in the gullies seeming to invite the early morning drizzle that fell just long enough to clear the air. It may have soothed those lying outside the cabins. Their dying moans seeming to be expressions of gratitude, but they were beyond help.

*   *   *

Little Jug and Sylvi were just minutes behind the rest of the party. Their pursuers, hours behind them and losing ground, tried to pick up their trail but were not uncovering any sign.

The escapees would arrive in Gannett, which Frank estimated as the closest town, well ahead of them. Although Gannett did not appear on most maps, Frank had been through it several times when hiking.

Sylvi and Little Jug climbed Skag's Leap to the table rock where their friends were concealed in shadows. They stepped out when the pair appeared, anxious for Sylvi's assessment. Their plan was working; they were elated. Even Sandy and Josie were smiling.

"Anyone behind us?" Frank asked.

"Yes but moving in the wrong direction," Sylvi responded.

"They're lost," Peter volunteered.

"Not for long," Sylvi observed; "but we will reach Gannett well ahead of them."

CHAPTER 25

August 27, 1993

Once Maddoc had the information from the Eaton cabin, he and Harrington sat down to plan the search. Maddoc contacted Caleb and filled him in. Star Engstrom. G. K. Jones, and Dave DeCarlo were standing by. With Maddoc, Abranos, Harrington and Sossa, they had three teams to work the target areas. Bernie would maintain communications. Harrington and Sossa would go to adjoining towns. "We're not going to find Sylvia in one of them, but we may get information. These folks cooperate with authorities. Lenny and I will cover all of them in one day. If there's anything to find, we'll find it."

Maddoc contacted Abranos with the details; reminding him to bring Dogbone. Abranos laughed saying, "You would have no friends at all without that mutt."

Harrington arranged for Maddoc and Bernie to spend the week end at Glynn House in Ashland just south of Little Squam Lake and not far from their jump off site. It was a time for them to relax and refuel.

They arrived just before check-in and had a late breakfast in the first New England dining room Bernie or Maddoc had seen. Bernie loved its storybook atmosphere, finding the double hung multi-paned windows and quaint chintz curtains sweet. She could not contain herself as other guests and locals smiled at her.

"Anthony, isn't this place beautiful? The window glass distorts everything outside. It must be very old. The rag rugs are just like they were in colonial time; these chandeliers must be worth a fortune. This is another world. Let's move here. It was so thoughtful of Lt. Harrington to find it for us."

"It where he comes with his girlfriend."

"Oh, he isn't married?"

"I don't know. I didn't ask him. What difference would it make?"

Bernie wanted to say something, but all she could come up with was "You men!"

They finished their eggs, sausage, pancakes and coffee just as the owner signaled their room was ready. Maddoc rose and remarked, "Did you notice how everything tastes better with pure maple syrup?"

*   *   *

Engstrom picked up Route 95 out of the city and cut over to Route 15 north in Greenwich to the Charter Oak Bridge and proceeded 84W to the Mass. Turnpike. They stayed on the Pike and picked up 93N just below Lawrence. It was a straight line to Lincoln. Dogbone slept away the six hour ride. Abranos complained about his coccyx, his hemorrhoids and anything else he could imagine. Engstrom wouldn't let him drive. G. K. laughed at him. Starr Engstrom slept with Dogbone.

"Caleb, you are a legend in the department. Cruisers sit outside of East Harlem waiting for you to cross 97th Street going south. Most hope you turn right on 1st Avenue so they can pick up what's left of you."

"Oy, another of Maddoc's friends has heard his stories. I drove a three-Q in Nam without a hitch. I am a very fine driver."

"Maddoc told us of Nam. The most peaceful days were those days when you drove. All Vietnamese, men, women and children got off the streets and all hostilities were suspended. The birds sang for they could fly, and livestock were herded into dead end streets for their safety."

"Eh, you listen to Maddoc, you become a fool. I once hit a chicken; chickens are not so smart, and Maddoc got a drumstick and a breast."

Both men laughed. Engstrom chuckled. "…and it cost the army $100 to compensate for the eggs it would never produce. The peasants threw their chickens in front of the convoys."

Engstom confirmed it. "Caleb Abranos, you are a good driver, but better we keep you under wraps. Then G. K. and I have no reason to show both our badges."

"Oy, I'm outnumbered by gringos who believe the lies of a gringo. Latinos get no justice, and we are not all drug dealers."

G. K. laughed and changed the subject. "Caleb, I thought Reuben would be along."

Caleb thought back to his last conversation with Reuben on that subject.

"Hey, Tio. I do all the work, you have all the fun. What use am I if I can't go hunting with you?"

"Sobrino. You are here to help. Next time, after I have taught you all you must know to survive among men, you will be with us."

"Uncle Caleb, I am a man. I fight and live like a man. In El Barrio, men respect me."

"Es verdad en El Barrio. It is not true in the woods. In the woods you are a puppy. Be thankful. You are young and free of worry. As I grow old I have no son to worry me. I have you, and you do not go into war as long as I am alive. We do not speak of this again. You stay with the store."

Reuben, understanding his uncle was the only real father he ever had, said nothing more.

Caleb answered, "He's minding the store."

Engstrom said, "The next exit is ours. Anyone have any idea how to get to the hotel? Maddoc gave me directions, but I handed them to Reuben when I thought he was driving."

*　　*　　*

Maddoc and Bernie arrived in Lincoln early. Caleb, not far behind them, arrived with Dogbone, Engstrom and G. K. within the hour.

Maddoc walked out to meet him just as Dogbone jumped from the van. The dog looked at Maddoc, brushed against him and gave a low growl.

After inspecting the connecting rooms, Maddoc checked in. He offered cash in advance, but the clerk required a credit card.

"Sorry, young lady; I don't use them."

"But I can't register you without a card."

"Cash is not as good as a card?"

"I'll have to call my supervisor."

With these words, a young man appeared at the desk. He stood as straight and as tall as his sixty-seven inches would allow.

"Sir, I'm Mr. Guilfoil, the Assistant Manager. I understand we have a problem."

"It's not a problem. I don't use credit cards. I believe cash is still legal."

"Of course it is Sir, but you are a walk-in and we require a credit card on file in the event of damage to the property or theft from the room."

"I understand, but you need not worry about it. They'll be no damage, and they'll be no theft. If you check, you'll see that Lt. Al Harrington of the New Hampshire State Police made the reservation."

"Oh! Please accept my apologies. Everything is ready for you."

"I'll be keeping my dog in my room."

"Sir, dogs are not allowed in the rooms. The sign is posted at the entryway."

Dogbone, standing at Maddoc's side at the registration desks, gave a low growl. Maddoc assured the young man he need not worry about the dog.

"Sir, the sign is clear, and we do have a kennel.

Maddoc turned to Dogbone. "How's the kennel sound to you dog?"

Dogbone emitted a growl, a low rumble that started deep from within and drove forward like a locomotive at somewhat fewer decibels. He then gave off several sharp, very loud barks followed by an intemperate resonant howl as he moved toward the retreating assistant manager.

Maddoc called the dog to his side. "He does that all night in a kennel. In the room he sleeps."

Collecting his wits, Mr. Guilfoil conceded, "Well so long as he does no damage, you can have your dog in the room."

"Thank you." Dogbone, thank the man."

Dogbone gave two soft barks.

By the time Al Harrington and Lenny Sossa arrived, their meeting room was set up. By 3:45 P.M., the maps and schedules were posted and the weapons were on the floor for a final check and distribution. No one worried about being stopped. There were enough badges to satisfy any trooper. The rundown on operations would take place once everyone settled in.

Harrington, Maddoc, and Bernie sat talking. "We've checked every small town hospital," Harrington explained, "and can't tie your daughter or her friend to any visits. We also had local constables report on anything unusual in the smaller drive-through communities."

"Where are these towns?" Maddoc asked.

"They're scattered near the White Mountains, some deeper in the mountains, large enough to subsist. They're sparsely populated. Few are close to hospitals."

"What kind of people live there?"

"Old timers, descendants of early settlers. They work at hunting and trapping and, in season, produce syrup. They collect firewood for their own use and to sell at roadside for campers and occasional tourists."

"There's nothing unusual?"

"Hell, there's plenty that's unusual. These are very clannish people. You tread lightly around them. They all carry guns and have a right to. They're not troublesome, but they don't accept anyone, including the law, telling them how to live. They're inbred. It's a situation that seems worse to outsiders than it is."

"What can we expect from them?"

"You should expect trouble. There may be none, but it's something you have to anticipate. State policemen serve as constables and cruise through the towns regularly but won't make arrests unless necessary."

"Are the citizens lawless?"

"Not really. Not much illegal could go on there without our knowing. Some have stills, but that's a Fed problem. We have occasional thefts of sugar-maple buckets. There are bad apples among them who will take a townie girl into the woods for a time, but few of the girls complain. They may have scrapes with the law but only one, as I recall, has done hard time."

"No trouble with the tourists?" Maddoc asked.

"Occasionally an outsider finds himself at the wrong end of a gun. We had a truck driver stop in one of the towns looking for help. He reacted badly to some of the youngsters climbing on his truck. He got no help and beat up."

"There should be no trouble simply moving around," Maddoc said.

"That's right. If they think you're hunters, they'll ignore you. Hell, they make money off hunters."

"How's that?"

"They're guides and damn good and welcome new hunters. They also sell moonshine and home preserves. They'll provide any man with a woman. They thrive by bringing settlers into the community. A girl will find a young man who fits in and wants to stay. More likely, one of the men will bring someone who has a life that can only be improved by a move. They're standoffish. Many fear being outside their community unless in a group. This keeps them in place and, in part, explains the inbreeding, which largely is exaggerated."

Harrington insisted they know what they were getting into. Men like Maddoc survived in Nam because they thought like the enemy, coming to know him well enough to anticipate his moves. They would not have that advantage in this case, but the information Harrington gave was useful. They would depend on it.

Two hours passed during which the studied maps, especially the terrain, got acquainted with local law enforcement resources, identified emergency medical sources, and so forth. Sossa proved to be a good listener, contributing only when appropriate. He was a city boy, having grown up in New York. This territory was almost as strange to him as it was to Maddoc and Abranos. He had camped in the White Mountains in his youth, but that was it.

At four o'clock, Maddoc and Harrington were ready to begin the orientation. Maddoc made the initial statement.

"We know something of what we're facing. We'll be ready when we leave here. Each of you has material to review; study it. You have to rely on it. In addition, you have your pick of weapons. We have no license to be here; but we're working on that —or so Harrington tells me.

Harrington smiled. "I spoke with Colonel Smith just before I left. He expects to be kept informed and has authorized me to deputize you."

"That's great," Maddoc acknowledged. "Personal weapons remain in the van. Those you receive are sufficient. They're in good order and cannot be traced back to anyone but the manufacturer. If you have to get rid of a weapon for any reason, disable and discard it.

Harrington interrupted. "They should be buried or concealed under the low lying branches of a remote evergreen. The weather will destroy them. We can't have them falling into anyone's hands."

"We have three teams. Abranos and I will make up the primary team. G. K. and Harrington will work to our north. DeCarlo and Engstrom will make up the third, working the area to the south. Bernie will man the command center tracking and informing us of anything new. Sossa will move among us and also keep us informed and updated."

Maddoc continued. "You keep in touch by radio when necessary and remain within easy distance of each other, if possible. Bernie can track you as long as your transceivers are open. We'll work north to south, east to west, meaning we start in the first three sectors in our targeted areas." Here Maddoc pointed to the map to make it clear. "We'll have open ground much of the time. Be vigilant. Questions anyone?"

Sossa raised his hand.

"Yes, detective?"

"How much ground do you think you can cover?"

"Good question. There are twenty-three possibilities, some are remote communities. The unincorporated towns are inhabited by mountain people.

Five communities meet our profile. Lt. Harrington will talk of them and give you the specifics."

"Suppose we find nothing for four days?"

"Harrington is optimistic, but he'll address that question."

The lieutenant stepped forward. "It is a good question. If we do not have any leads within four days, we will have to reconsider our approach. We know Sylvia Maddoc was abducted, probably by mountain men. We do not know why. From what I have learned, she is a resourceful woman, yet she has not been seen or heard from. Our analysis tells us she likely is among people who will not assist her. Everything points to one of these communities. The first three, each in Lancaster County are Anson, Hopkins, and Gannett. Each has small populations, 300 inhabitants, more or less. Each is self-sufficient although for some, the poverty line would be a step up."

A chuckle followed. "Bernie will be coordinating our movements and feeding information into the computer to insure we do not waste any effort. She'll receive emergency signals if anyone gets into trouble. Each of you has a transceiver. The small devices on the table are easily concealed signal generators. Carry one. If you're hurt or taken prisoner, turn it on. We will find you."

He turned the floor over to Abranos.

Maddoc and I will work independently shadowing each other. We used this method in Nam to clear out snipers. Those of you who served know the drill.

Abranos reviewed the cover stories. "Less is best. My nephew has provided credentials. You will behave like hunters, but if challenged, you're either part of a geological survey team or business people looking to revive local industry. You answer no questions beyond that.

"While aware of our purpose, the authorities do not endorse it. Deputizing us is a practical matter. Chief Withers and Colonel David 'Deadass' Smith, state superintendent, came on board after being briefed by Harrington and Maddoc and conferring with NYPD Commissioner Byrne. The rules are simple: meet force with force but no killing unless in self-defense. Remember, although deputized we have no authority."

"No badges?" Coombs asked.

"You have ID's. Badges are not consistent with our cover stories."

Engstrom reviewed communications. Harrington reviewed the terrain and its difficulties. He left no doubt the natives would shoot if skeptical. Everyone in the party will be wearing normal hiking garb and carrying side arms. He suggested body armor.

Harrington warned, "You can die in these woods if you underestimate the weather or think the natives are quaint. These people might kill you for your boots. To them killing has no meaning; they believe they are the law."

"Just like New York," Abranos added.

"Not quite," Harrington advised. These people move around these woods without making a sound. They'll be on top of you before you see them. Don't use anything perfumed and sleep in your clothes. They may still smell you from a hundred feet away, but let's not make it easy. They do not travel alone. Where there is one, there are others. They'll approach you openly. If they think you're poachers or revenuers, they will try to run you off. Though seemingly friendly, they are veterans of clan clashes and run-ins with city folk. We lose people in these mountains, … not always to the terrain.

"They will not fear you, even if you get the drop on them. If you take prisoners, call in and have them picked up."

"What if we have to kill anyone?" Engstrom asked.

"It's a legitimate question. Avoid killing unless there's no alternative. They are citizens, and we have to account for them, dead or alive. Prep your companion if you have no witness. "

"What does that mean?" Caleb asked.

"If we arrest one of the scroats for killing one of you, he will have a slew of witnesses testifying you tried to molest a child. They will have family, twenty friends and their preacher supporting whatever story they tell. If you do not have a solid story with a corroborating witness, you be facing a phalanx of liars making you out a stone cold criminal."

Maddoc distributed pictures of Sylvi. "If you see her with others, call it in. Do not approach her but keep her in sight. There is no room for mistakes."

Harrington stepped in.

"Our purpose is to find Sylvi and get out. I believe Maddoc's daughter is looking for a way out."

"Buenos," Caleb declared. "We are ready, amigos."

*　*　*

Maddoc looked toward Abranos and motioned to him to step outside. They walked out into the hall together and found the nearest exit, which placed them in the cool evening air.

"Caleb, Do you remember William Battison?"

"Willy the Spook. Man, he was one scary dude. He must be locked up for life."

"Not really. His lawyer proved he was not involved with that street killing and got him released."

"How did he do that?"

"You might say that I found the real killer. It's a long story I'll share it another time."

"You sunovabith. Whoever he was, he didn't need prison as much as Willy."

"Willie visited me shortly after he got out. He named Marie's killers."

"Weren't they already found?"

"Yes, but not identified, no feet, no hands, and no heads."

"Madre de Dios. That's insane!"

"Willy claims they were Neary's guys, wanna-be's who did odd jobs for him."

"Sunuvabitch; I am the wisest man you know. When we get back to New York, we kill Neary."

"We cannot be part of that." Maddoc answered.

*   *   *

CHAPTER 26

U pon leaving the camp, Otha's entourage of nine men and five women returned to Gannett to pick up others and gather whatever they needed during the two weeks they'd be exploiting the tourists. They had funds to buy treats, something they craved. Largely, they would live in their vans and trucks. Rooms were rented for the young women. Without the privacy of a bedroom, substantial income would be lost.

Of the males in the group, aside from Otha, two were unique, Edom Zink, a bright man by clan standards who was very good with a rifle. He was Otha's lieutenant. The second was Otha and Esther's fifteen-year-old son, Noah, a precocious boy with physical gifts unlike those of any other.

Noah size suggested he was ten or eleven. He was very quick, his movements almost monkey-like; and he was the clan's best fingersmith. Put him in a crowd with two or three drops, and he would reap wallets, jewelry and purses without creating a stir. On one occasion, he cleaned out a rival's drop without her being the wiser. He then seduced her in the back of a random van. He was insanely lecherous, held in check by severe discipline until Otha arranged with his doctor for something that quieted him down.

He had other odd gifts. With eyes that seemed placed at the corners of his head, he had 230 degree peripheral vision, an edge when he worked jewelry shops. He would go in with nothing and come out with watches, rings, bracelets, and more. Like the monkey, his strength compared to his body weight was equally unusual. His fingers enabled him to climb a brick building like a cat. Otha used him late nights to get into buildings with open windows. Noah took anything of value he could carry and left no sign of having been there.

145

Finally, he had a natural gift for beating combination locks; his touch and hearing enabled him to feel his way through the mechanisms.

Edom and Noah were seldom far away from each other, but no one recalled their speaking to each other.

Otha's teams traveled the hundred plus miles to cities like Manchester, Keene, and Portsmouth. One team went to Rochester, another to Lebanon, and the neophytes, under Esther Gubbin's direction, to Berlin. Otha's group, four men and eight women, went to Laconia's Lake Winnipesauke, an area rich in tourists and a magnate for boaters and campers. With four experienced men, Otha could average almost $2,000 a day in cash thefts. Campers were easy. The summer was ending, schools would soon open, and the first hint of fall had crept in. Tourists considered New Hampshire natives to be rugged individuals and honest. Precautions they took in any other busy urban community were overlooked when they traveled through the rustic small towns of New England. People didn't say much, but they were courteous.

Hard goods begged to be stolen. Otha preferred jewelry – watches were aplenty – cameras, camcorders, small radios and televisions, binoculars and expensive footwear. He didn't worry about dumping the stuff. He had a dealer in Portsmouth who took everything and gave him a decent price. Otha insisted on 30 percent, a figure the fence gave willingly. Otha's booty turned over quickly. In recent years, Otha had been grabbing off laptop computers. He got $50 for every one in working condition, enough for something he couldn't see being of any use.

Not all the teams were set up to steal. Some carried home-canned goods, crafts, and old furniture to sell near the entrances of state parks, campgrounds and other places where tourists were drawn. They didn't have much problem with the police because they were respectful, and they moved on when told to move on, although they were usually back the next day. Some team members took temporary jobs that allowed them to pass on goods or steal cash from their employers. Most of the women who came along were younger, and turned tricks with men camped in the fishing areas. Something about the smell of a campfire, the open air, and a willing, full-breasted, for-a-price woman that made even Bible-thumping Sunday-go-to-church males randy. An aggressive girl could make $500-$600 a night, some more.

146

Lest one think this prostitution was at odds with Otha's religious fervor, it should be noted that Otha counted his money more often than he read his Bible. Further, with any of the girls there was the possibility of a marketable infant. In the final analysis, Otha considered women, all women, the tools of the Devil. He conceded that he could not out-wrestle the Devil, so he gave in to the women's wanting and saw no downside.

*   *   *

2:47: Friday, September 1, 1993 — Late Afternoon

So it was when each of the teams, except that in Berlin, started home. The Berlin team would meet them in Ashland before traveling to Conway, selling, picking, and tricking as they made their way toward Gannett. Otha liked the route because there were a couple of campgrounds off of Route 16 that were easy pickings for the girls. Otha only allowed selective stealing in these campgrounds because he had come to know some of the campers over the years. Many of them used him and his men for guides when fishing and hunting.

The city slickers making their first, perhaps their last visit, were fair game. Everyone was feeling good. It was rare when they didn't return with $180,000 or more in good years for their work, not spectacular for 54 people bent on finding money any way they could, but a solid return from every one of them. Otha set aside $500 for each man in the community, adding $250 if he had a woman and $100 for each child. It mattered not that some families got more than others. Five hundred dollars went a long way in Gannett. The balance went into the town coffers. It wasn't all they earned in the course of the year, but it was the second largest source of income. They realized more from their maple sugar industry, common to Gannett for generations. Earnings from the baby business were exclusively Otha's, but he was known to hand out cash gifts on impulse.

Otha stopped every year for a night or two at the Concord campgrounds. The past two weeks had been highly profitable but less eventful than most. Their stay at the campground was a customary respite that generated more couplings and allowed the girls to pocket much of their earnings.

147

The ride from Concord to Gannet took somewhat more than an hour, and Otha would arrive in Gannett with everyone in tow between 8:00 and 9:00 A.M., depending how the time it took to round up his women. He wanted to be there before the sun climbed too high. Usually when they arrived, the only people to welcome them were a deputy and the security people at the maternity house. Unless there was a problem, the nurses didn't come on duty before 9:00 A.M. Otha stayed in touch with the constable each day by telephone. Except for births and an occasional stranger drifting in, including a ride-through by the state police, there was nothing to report.

*   *   *

4:14 P. M: Monday, August 30, 1993

Zeb, Luke, and Matthew heard the dogs howling before they neared the camp. As they got closer, they were assaulted by the stench of burned flesh. Fear replaced revulsion and was followed by denial as they attempted to grasp the sight before them. Luke ran ahead and wandered from one burned-out cabin to the next crying and moaning. Upon seeing the black and blistered bodies lying about, Zeb went into a rage.

"They come back and "kilt our families." They fooled Ludim and came back once we got to chasing 'em.

"Ludim's got some 'splaining to do. This weren't no accident."

He wanted to strike out in pursuit, but Luke, carrying the remains of a child, cried without shame and said,

"We gonna bury our dead, Zeb. We ain't leaving them like this. I'll kill you first."

"Me too! I'm putting my family in their last resting place," Matthew declared as he broke into sobs."

Zeb put the threats aside, but not his rage. "When catch them what did this, Otha or no Otha, we'll kill them."

If he thought at all, he might realize the escapees did not set the fire. He reasoned they fooled Ludim into drawing them from the camp so they could get revenge. He didn't ask why the fire had not been set while they all slept. His thought was of the twenty-seven bodies he had to get into the ground as quickly as possible.

He spoke up. "We need to get them murdering bastards. We treated them like family, and they brought the fires of hell on us. We got to move. We got to put our dead where they be safe from the varmints. We can drop the bodies into the hole as their final home."

Luke raged. "You ain't gonna put my wife an' babes into the Devil's hole. They drop in the fires of hell and they burn forever. They burned enough. I'll kill you with my bare hand afore I let you drop my family into damnation."

Matthew advanced on Zeb with the blade of a shovel in front of him. "Zeb, we be friends so long I can't say how much, but I won't wait for Luke to kill you, I'll do it myself. We bury them in the pit until we get back for a right an' proper place. You going down that hole before any of our kin do."

Zeb hedged. "I ain't putting mine down there neither, but I got to thinking' if it was what you might want to do and I didn't want to get in your way. Malachai got no kin. He can set off and find their trail and get back to us."

That was enough for Malachai. He was off, having no desire to handle the dead.

The old charcoal pit was deep enough to accommodate the bodies. Water remained at its bottom year around. The three men lined the bottom with logs and added a cushion of pine branches. They carried the bodies to the pit and placed them in, young ones first and kin together. Once the bodies were dragged to the side of the pit, Luke climbed down and, standing on a log sitting just above the water line, caught the bodies as the men pushed them in. The water was putrid; the bodies were hard to handle and odorous. Luke, who said nothing but whose tears flowed steadily, was dealing with his own losses as he tenderly placed his wife, with their baby girl in her arms, his two young boys flanking them. It took hours to move the bodies, set them in place, and carry enough dirt from the top of the rise to cover them. The smell of damp ashes and death would remain with them always.

Malachai showed up just before they were finished. It was mid-afternoon, and he had been scouring the trail and the underbrush on both sides for hours. He approached Zeb.

"Found the trail. Looks pretty old to me."

"Can't be more than eight, maybe ten hours old. What time you find it?"

"About an hour ago. Followed it for a ways to be certain I didn't miss nothing. It was twelve hours or more old."

"Can't be, unless you missed the trail where they doubled back."

"No sign of any of'em doubling back."

"They doubled back, all right, or at least a couple of 'em did. This fire didn't set itself."

"Might be a couple of 'em doubled back. I didn't see no sign of it."

"You done good, Malachai. You run down the trail and hurry the other's back. We're gonna need to take the dogs, but we don't have anything for 'em to sniff at. Once they gets the trail and we push 'em, they'll catch on. We'll be able to travel fast. Can't wait too long, gonna have to travel through some dark. We be out of here in half hour. Once Ludim's himself and Malachai gives him the message, you have him bring the rest of 'em to meet us at Devil's Root Hollow. Bring the lanterns."

Malachai nodded and was off saying, "Can't be sure it was the right trail."

Zeb picked up a hoe with a scorched handle and, working alongside of Matthew and Luke, pulled dirt over the pile of bodies, none of which were exposed any longer but all requiring a substantial covering or earth to keep the scavengers at bay. They worked for another forty minutes, at which point Zeb decided it was enough. They pulled their things together, picked up their rifles, put the dogs on lines and started down the trail to meet the others. Zeb no longer had a truck.

The dogs were pulling and yipping, but their noses were filled with smoke. Zeb, angered by the noise cut them loose and let them run. He was thinking through Ludim's role in letting the prisoners' burn their families.

*   *   *

4:30 P.M. — Tuesday, August 31,

Frank was pleased. They were moving fast with no complaints. Sylvi and Little Jug checked the back trail and found no one following. Frank modified the course, moving up their schedule. He was in control and confident.

They had reached Skag's Leap at 7:30 P.M. It was a crisp evening, the warmth of the late August day replaced by cool evenings heralding the start of the foliage season. They planned to eat and rest, taking sufficient hours to recoup. None of them, except Sylvi and Little Jug, were in the best of health, but they were buoyed by their progress.

During the back trailing, Little Jug had set snares, netting eight rabbits and two woodchucks. Woodchucks walk easily into traps. Only one trapper in a hundred, even in these parts, had much interest in hunting or eating them; but Little Jug liked watching and eating the critters. He had the ability to get the dirt taste out of chuck. More fat than meat, properly cooked they were sweet. The rabbits were plump and had to be fully cooked. Sylvi made a small cooking fire. A hot meal would lift their spirits.

Little Jug and Sylvi built the fire in a deep hollow dug out of the earth. All brush and other combustibles within a four-foot radius were removed, to be returned once the fire was buried. It was built with twigs and shavings until it burned steadily and smoke free. One would almost have to stumble on the fire to notice it.

The fire grew hot enough to cook the ten carcasses, all looking pretty much the same except for size. Little Jug skewered them on a strong green birch stick resting on birch forks set in the ground about eight inches from the rim. The chucks were easy to see, their plump bodies shrinking more than half as the fat cooked off and flared where they hung. It was a woodsman's fire, one that could only be seen from above. Sylvi had gathered herbs for seasoning, and the meat was ambrosia to everyone. Even Josie, known to be finicky, ate.

They spoke of their progress. Frank spoke confidently. "It looks like we might be in the clear. Sylvi and Little Jug have backtracked four times and found no indication they're on to us. They're chasing ghosts."

"Let's not get too confident," Peter cautioned. "They might be far behind us; but if they figure out our course, they'll race to overtake us. How far behind do you think they are, Sylvi?"

"We know they didn't pick up our trail by noon today. Little Jug checked almost to the point of our departure. That places them at least ten hours behind us. We've been traveling for twelve hours. We'll rest for the next three. Assuming they found and entered our trail half a day behind us and can travel half again as fast as we can, they can close the gap in ten hours …, if we stand still. We can rest for the time we allotted without worry, but we have to assume they'll be about four hours behind when we start moving again. If we pick up our pace, as Frank suggested, we can be three hours or more ahead of them when they reach this point. By then, Little Jug will be circling back to slow them down."

"And if he doesn't slow them down?" Frank worried, "they might be on us before we reach Gannett. Someone should go ahead to alert the authorities in case they do catch us."

"That's a good thought," Peter chimed in. "Who do we send?"

After some discussion, the group agreed that Little Jug and Sylvi should go together. Peter wasn't convinced. "We're this far ahead because Little Jug and Sylvi have them running in circles. Can we give that up?

Vincent, stable since they left the camp, volunteered. "I'll do it. I survived the jungles of Viet Nam and I'm an experienced combat veteran."

Sandy objected. "If they catch us, who's going to fight them off? Why can't Sylvi go ahead and Little Jug stay here? Why does Vincent have to go?"

Sylvi understood the teenager's fear. "Sandy, Vincent will mislead them and slow their progress. They are never going to see him. We may not need him to do it, but it is sensible. Vincent needs to help. You notice how much easier things have been for him since we left?"

The girl nodded.

"Some of it comes from being your friend and protecting you. That will not change. If he thinks you're at risk, he'll be back in a flash. The other comes from his being useful again. We have to let him be useful."

"Supposing he gets caught?"

"When he was in the army, enemy soldiers couldn't catch him. He always found his way home, and he'll find his way back to you."

Sylvi's explanation reassured her.

Vincent, who didn't speak much, suggested he rest two hours before leaving. Sylvi felt they wouldn't get more than two hours' rest during the three-hour break at best. Frank wanted time with Vincent to review the map and landmarks.

He agreed. "Let's stick to three hours."

Vincent was confident. "You can be sure that if they reach this point, they'll keep moving, assuming we're not holed up. They'll send one man to check while they try to close the gap. I can force all of them to climb"

"How?"

"I'll get far enough ahead of them to set a fire. Leave it set up. An open fire with some damp wood will give off smoke. Given this terrain, they'll see it about a quarter mile out and be convinced we're still up here. They'll climb up in force. At that point, I'll be moving to catch up with you."

Frank reviewed the strategy with Sylvi. "It will work. We can rely on that. Vincent's instincts are solid."

"In some ways he reminds me of my father. They are not much different in age although my father looks younger and is bigger. I grew up knowing that Anthony Maddoc was an important man."

"Anthony Maddoc? Your last name is Maddoc? I knew of your father when I was in Nam. We never met, but he was a legend."

Sylvi smiled, liking Vincent even more.

"Let's review your route. We aren't more than six miles from the West Branch River. When you hit the banks, find a shallow crossing and mark it. You'll be close to Gannett at that point and should be seeing more activity. We'll follow your path across the river."

Sylvi interjected, "I'll have Little Jug could put large rock as a marker, something that no one's going to find odd."

Frank smiled. "Good. As you cross the river, you'll see two elevations, The Bulge to your left and The Horn in front of you. There's a good trail running between them. The Horn leads to unmarked fishing areas. You may meet locals who are no better than the people we just left, unpredictable and a law unto themselves. If they see strangers, especially a woman, there's no predicting what they'll do."

"Little Jug will know them or they'll know him," Sylvi responded.

"You're right. He must be a legend in these parts. Once across the river, move inland an eighth of a mile; it's a worn trail. Bear northeast staying to the east of The Horn. You should hit the river again just where it feeds into a large pond. Follow the pond's perimeter, at the end of which you'll be northwest of Gannett. The only road you come to leads into Gannett. You may be seeing people at this time, but don't talk to anyone until you're closing in on Gannett. Assuming we don't run into trouble, we'll be no more than three hours behind you."

Everyone was relieved to have a fix on the final leg of their journey. It bolstered their determination and gave them strength. They would need both in the coming hours.

*　*　*

CHAPTER 27

I t would be after some time before everyone was assembled for the mile and a half walk to where Malachai picked up the trail. They would meet at Devil's Root Hollow before the sun was down. Once Zeb set a rough plan in place, they would move out quickly.

Devil's Root Hollow was believed cursed once night fell. It got its name from an uncommon root of the nightshade family that grew in a low-lying area. The Indians used the root as a hallucinogen. When drank as tea, it induced visions and fantasies. Indians believed that the visions were spirit ancestors and the fantasies were the stories that they told of their new life with the Earth Mother. It fell out of favor long before the area was settled by the white man, but remained in use by shamans. The root was poisonous if not prepared properly, a secret the Indians never shared.

As far the clan was concerned, the place was called Devil's Root Hollow 'cause that was the name for it.

The dogs, six mongrels of the beagle class, were excited and yelping to get to the chase. The largest of them, a basset and mastiff mix, called Brown, weighed a muscular hundred pounds, and stood more than a foot at the shoulder. Some larger dogs drifted into the population, but none of them, except Bear, stayed or were much use in the hunt. Otha reasoned the strays were lost or abandoned by campers and saw no harm in their staying.

After the fire, the dogs were set free to fend for themselves. Bear was undisciplined. He was known to run off for days and then return without any sign of where he might have been. He seldom ran with the pack and was often left behind. At last sighting, Bear, was squat on the ground about twenty feet from the burial plot, his eyes fixed on the point where Luke's two boys were buried.

Zeb claimed they were about eight hours behind the murderers who burned their wives and babes while they slept. Luke, Matthew and Ludim remained silent, but Maximilian cried openly over his loss. Ish had lost his wife and a son and two daughters. He grieved in silence, fearing to do otherwise would unman them.

Zeb said all that he could about the murders and then commanded, "We leave this place to the angels that sleep here, but we are Devils, with blood in our bellies waiting to avenge the doings of them what kilt our families. Malachai picked up their trail, an' they can't get away from us now. We gonna find 'em and kill 'em."

The dogs would prove their undoing.

Ludim, still feeling the pain from his split ear and bruised head, jumped in. "We ain't killing any one. We get 'em. We punish 'em, and then we take 'em to Otha for trial. If we don't, Otha gonna punish us."

Zeb glared at him. "I'm thinking they fooled you, Ludim. I'm thinking they made you think they was running and they didn't run at all. I'm thinking they made a circle and burnt our families once we were traipsing after 'em."

Ludim did not respond, but Malachai was clear about that idea, "That didn't happen, Zeb. I told' you once, and I'm saying it again. Ludim been more right than wrong about everything he done."

Given the events of the past few hours, Zeb did not respond. He was losing ground.

Malachai led them to the place where Sylvi and Little Jug had entered the woods. It was difficult to find because there was no clear sign until they were off the trail about 300 yards. The sign then took them in the wrong direction for a half mile before it swung north and west again and became a clear course. Malachai, one of the best trackers in the community, though not a Little Jug, was not fooled by the early diversions because they did not make much sense to him. Yet he had to check them out. Zeb praised him, reasoning that it saved them a lot of time. They would be diverted several times before they realized that gaining ground on the escapees would demand more than they expected.

Zeb made it clear how they would proceed. "We got six dogs and seven guns. They ain't got nothing except sticks. Li'l Jug ain't never had no gun. The dogs will run 'em down and they'll scatter and run in circles. I figure we go fast as we can, and we catch 'em before dark. We ain't brung no vittles so we eat from the land – you all done that before. That's why we're a-gonna spread out. We kin stretch almost' a quarter mile wide. Ain't no one slipping through that."

Ludim, grown bolder with the earlier support from Malachai, once again challenged Zeb.

"We best be careful. They can set traps. Some of them fellas trained for the army. They get behind us and raise a ruckus. It's best not to run fast when walking steady might keep us at their backs."

Luke echoed Ludim's thoughts. "Supposing we get surrounded? How we gonna shoot 'em all?"

"There ain't enough of them to surround anyone. You shoot the first one and all of 'em stops coming at you. Once you get a round off, you got help coming from both sides. We're chasing rabbits, and they ain't gonna change to wolves 'cause there in the woods."

"What about Little Jug?" Ludim asked offhand.

"Shit. Ain't nothing to worry 'bout with Little Jug. He's family."

CHAPTER 28

J ack Neary and Joseph Reinholds sat in a Route 110 motel room near Berlin, reviewing the Gannett operations. Walsh, Kincher and Figueroa hit a local bar for a nightcap. Reinholds suggested they might strike up conversations with local people and pick up useful bits of information. He neglected to mention Figueroa couldn't be anywhere without having a woman within reach. Neary was speaking,

""You should have cleared it with me. When we walk in there tomorrow, we ain't going to be dragging ass, not one of us. Figueroa does not look like their kind of people; we can't have him hung over and sloppy." Neary looked around the room expecting a protest. He continued,

"Gannett is the hub from which Gubbin does business. His records will be there. He will seem amiable enough. He'll let us walk in. We kill him and the constable first, and the rest is easy. If Sylvia Maddoc is there, we have a problem. We are to keep her safe, but she knows too much. We'll blame her dying on one of those freaks."

"Hold on Jack," Reinholds challenged. "If she is there, we isolate her. We're not killing her."

"Who the hell is running this show?" Neary challenged. "I want to protect the Maddoc girl, too, but we can't risk it."

"Gilletti is running it, and we know what he wants. He'll see through any excuses. Would you recognize her?"

Neary shrugged. "We got her picture."

Neary's insistence bordered on bullying, a mistake with this crew. Reinholds and his battle-tested warriors, each one ruthless in his own way were accustomed to killing. Their experiences of Viet Nam hardened them, but they were private security who served as bodyguards, investigators, spies or assassins, whatever paid. Each was proficient with every killing weapon known, and each could recall Cong prisoners they killed with their hands for sport.

Neary thought of them much in the same way he thought of his police officers, but he was wrong. Put twenty-five like these four in New York's worst neighborhoods, and street crime would disappear. The bodies would pile up; the press would be in an outrage; the feds would send in a task force, but in the end there would be a dramatic drop in drugs, thefts, muggings, murders and anything else built into the Big Apple's underground economy.

Yet, each had a gentle side, the side that enabled them to live normal daily lives. Neary asked for a show of hands, "Who's up for killing Sylvia Maddoc."

No hands showed. Neary, irked by Reinholds, remarked,

"No need to be reluctant." Maddoc will learn nothing from us.

Reinholds reacted. "Not one of my men is afraid to face Anthony Maddoc. Who knows, any one of them might be able to handle him, but none, including me, is interested in trying. The man is dangerous."

"I'm not afraid of Maddoc. I took care of one matter with him."

"You killed his wife?"

Neary, realizing he misspoke, denied it. "Are you crazy? She was killed in a home invasion. I had my best men on the investigation. We got the perps."

"You found the perps, but they were dead and couldn't be identified. If you had anything to do with it and Maddoc figures it out, you are a dead man walking.

Reinholds continued speaking. "We're about fourteen miles from Gannett. We'll be outmanned. I would like you to go in alone. We can observe and come in at the right moment."

Neary's response irked Reinholds. "Gubbin might wonder, but he won't suspect a thing once he sees me. We'll take him and anyone else we choose out of the picture, and then you go to Portsmouth and do Knielex. Catch her in her office. Get her files, and then break her neck. Throw her down a flight of stairs."

As Reinholds listened to Neary, his thoughts turned to villages in Nam where crack U. S. infantrymen walked in without resistance, chuckling to themselves at the smallness of the people and the meagerness of their assets. They quickly found themselves outmanned and outgunned. Most didn't get out alive. He spoke firmly, "Inspector, confidence kills. You cannot rely on anything but the unexpected."

Neary did not yield. "We do it my way!"

Neary continued talking, "Once we retire the old man, we kill the constable and his people. We hit fast and take care of them all in one pass. No chance to run. No chance to give an alarm. After we sweep up any resistance, we burn down the town. It's an old place, dry as leaves; and the one fire apparatus in town is a turn-of-the-century hand-pumper. Any help has to come from Lancaster. By the time they arrive, the town will be ashes."

Reinholds listened, knowing Neary to be a man who would accept credit for a fart if he thought anyone enjoyed it. He wanted to kill him, but Gannett did not appear on any maps. Neary had to lead them in. Reinholds would follow, but he was there to sanitize the place, not murder civilians.

He spoke up. "We will look for the Maddoc girl and bring her home if we find her."

"I didn't come here to do any favors for Maddoc," Neary answered. "I'd like to get him in my sights, also."

Reinholds reacted, "Stay clear of Maddoc. You don't know the man."

"I know him, and I should have killed him when I had the chance."

Neary knew all about the chance and its outcome. He knew Maddoc, as well. Twenty- years had intervened since he encountered him in Nam, years that made Maddoc wiser and more dangerous. Holy hell, Maddoc seemed so innocuous. He appeared to be The Thinker who, having solved the world's problems, stepped off the rock to stretch. He was layer upon layer of hardscrabble and a stone-cold killer.

Reinholds thought about their first meeting.

Reinholds, no angel, kept a bar and bordello in an isolated area on the outskirts of Saigon, one avoided by the authorities. It was managed by a local wise guy who could handle any situation that might arise and was well paid to keep the business operating. Caleb Abranos learned they pimped children. Some were war orphans. Abranos called upon Maddoc and a few of his friends to clean the place up. The manager, bigger than most Vietnamese and a skilled fighter, confronted them as they came in the door. They were not his usual clientele. Reinholds stepped to his side. He did not know anything of Abranos or Maddoc at that time. Abranos was direct,

"You must be Reinholds. We hear you employ children, serve cheap liquor, roll American servicemen and treat women like pigs. We're closing you down. You have two choices: to remove your personal belongings and avoid bad feelings or to watch us trash the place and kick your ass before we burn it down."

Reinholds barked, "Get the fuck out of my place or I'll kick your teeth in."

His manager stepped toward Abranos, his left leg in flight. Maddoc intercepted the kick and broke the man's standing leg with a well place kick of his own. Reinholds, enraged, came at Maddoc. Maddoc sidestepped, and slammed his assailant into the door with a crack. Though dazed, Reinholds came up with a roar. Maddoc hooked his thumb under Reinholds jaw , walked him outside and turned him over to the Military Police.

The business was closed. Reinholds lost many thousands of dollars, and the children, many of whom went to group homes, were placed in shelters. Some returned to the streets and were lost .

Reinholds was assigned to the demilitarized zone, considered a death sentence by many. He did not return to Saigon.

Abranos vowed to kill him if they crossed paths again.

Reinholds challenged Neary. "You should forget Maddoc. He's not a sleeping dog; he's a sleeping cobra. You go after him and miss, and he'll kill you quicker than you can spit. You won't show up one day, and no one will bother to look for you."

Neary was stung by Reinholds' comments. "You don't believe that I became Maddoc's superior because I was his inferior, eh? I can outshoot, outthink and, if necessary, outfight Maddoc at any time on any terms. I taught hand-to-hand combat at the academy for three years, took down some big men, all younger than me. Maddoc was there. He avoided me."

Although knowing the truth, Reinholds responded, "Maybe. After all, Maddoc's not a young man anymore."

Neary responded "Damn right."

Kincher and Walsh came in without Figueroa.

"What's up? Got everything worked out?"

Reinholds' response was non-committal. "The Inspector has a plan. Where's Ernie?"

"He was hustling a broad. We may not see him until morning. He walked out with her just before we left."

"That's not smart. People up here notice strangers, especially if they're hustling."

"You know Ernie. When he gets away from his old lady, he's got to climb on the first woman he finds. This one's a real looker."

Neary couldn't restrain himself. "He's not taking care of business. We leave at 8:00 A.M. If he's not with us, it's the unemployment line for him."

Kincher didn't know Neary well. Walsh did, and Walsh opted to remain silent. "It's not that bad, sir," Kincher said. "He'll show up in a couple of hours with nothing to say."

Neary exploded. "I don't give a shit what he has to say. We're here on serious business. We don't need a loose prick banging around thinking he's the big gun. I'm the big gun, and I want his ass here."

As if on cue, the door knob rattled. The door wouldn't open. Reinholds screwed the silencer on to his 9MM. He nodded to Walsh and stood off to one side. As Walsh opened the door, it was pushed from the outside and Figueroa stumbled in holding his bloodied hand to his face. He fell to the carpet.

Kincher was at him in a split second. Rolling him over, he could see his faced had been slashed, the eye itself sliced through the cornea. His hands were cut. Figueroa was not an easy man to get the drop on. Yet here he was bleeding heavily and maybe blind as well. Walsh came over with a wet compress. Neary was on the phone arranging for a private ambulance. Neary's response was quicker than expected.

They found Figueroa's wallet empty. Walsh put in a driver's license, odd photos and some small bills. Mrs. Michael Perez would find him at the hospital, settle accounts, and get him back to a New York hospital. They were now a man short.

Neary spoke to Reinholds. "Take Walsh and find out who did this. Take them into the woods and leave their remains for the dogs. That includes the broad who set him up."

The two men went back to the bar. Walsh overhead the girl's name earlier. He spoke to the bartender. "Where's Penny? I was supposed to meet her here. I've got papers she needs." Walsh pulled out an envelope and offered it to the man. "Maybe you'll give it to her."

"No thanks. I don't take anyone's stuff."

"This is important. She's been waiting for this, and I'm just passing through. If she doesn't get it tonight, it's gonna cost her. Take it! She told me to drop it here."

"Mister, this ain't a post office. She lives within walking distance. Her last name is Dennison, but the name on the mailbox is Mitchell. It's the next road up, or you can take the path leading from the back door. It's her shortcut."

The two men got into a Blazer and located the house that was set back and unlit. It stood alone, somewhat off the road. Reinholds suggested that they do nothing. Their being at the bar would be recalled. The last thing they needed was cops looking for them. "We'll send a couple of the boys up next month. The girl and whoever she's working with will still be here."

"Neary won't like it."

"You're wrong. He will, but we're not explaining anything. We'll tell him it's done. Let's find another bar and relax. I need time away from him."

Neary was waiting when they got back. Figueroa had arrived at the hospital. There was real concern for his eye, but there was no nerve damage. The doctor believed it would be saved. "Okay, Joseph. Let's go over the details one more time. We'll have to make adjustments now that that fool is gone."

*   *   *

Maddoc slipped out of his room with Dogbone alongside. Bernie was asleep, and the dog needed to run a bit. He was deep in thought when Abranos sidled up.

"Hey, amigo, what's up?

"Don't ask me why, but I'm back in Nam. It took years to forget it and only minutes to get it back. Everything is blackness. My daughter could be dead."

"Oh my friend, you forget what you shared with me. You forget the faith that got us here."

I don't forget. I didn't forget in the jungles of Nam. There I killed without anger, without remorse. Now I want to kill.

Hey, booboo, it is a good thing. We have you here at your best, ready to kill, filled with anger, filled with guilt. What better edge could we ask for?

*   *   *

CHAPTER 29

7:33 P.M. August 31, 1993

The dogs drove everyone crazy. Zeb expected them to pick up the fugitives' trail, but the fire left nothing to fix on. It hadn't destroyed the prisoners' cabins Matthew ran the dogs through them; they sniffed about, but the smoke and gas, permeated everything. Once loose they were chasing rabbits, coons, woodchucks, field mice and anything else that moved in the underbrush instead of leading a rush up the trail. Ludim wanted to abandon them. "Hell, we can move along without dogs."

Zeb rebuked him.

"You can't abandon dogs that run faster than you. They stick around us whether we're awanting 'em or not. That big dumb Bear dog been trailing behind not helping much either. I'd put a bullet in him if I could get him to set long enough. He's pestering the trackers and making the dogs crazy."

Ludim, confident that Zeb wouldn't blindside him again, joined in, "These dogs ain't people chasers. Bear making no difference. I knowed we couldn't leave them setting in their cages after all our kin was gone, but we'd be better if we did. Someone should have stayed back for a spell and took care of them until we got far enough along."

"That make no difference to that damn Bear dog," Zeb snapped back.

Bear celebrated the woods. He was a stampede breaking through the underbrush and mindless of any efforts to bring him to heel. He didn't hunt with the men. He didn't hunt with other dogs. He hunted on his own and had been known to bring badgers and small deer down, not an easy feat for a dog. Badgers are fierce fighters able to disembowel a dog faster than a bobcat. They didn't fight like bobcats, and that sometimes gave the edge to the dog. Bear was scarred from years of running pell-mell through the woods, once almost losing an ear to a rundown barbed wire fence. Luke stitched it back in place.

Stories had grown up around Bear, most not true. He chased off a bear, fought a wolverine to a standstill, and dragged down a moose. They were nonsense. Big and mean as he was, he would not survive a bear or a wolverine and would not approach a moose.

The dogs were the least of Zeb's problems. The others had doubts about being spread out so far; they might be ambushed or picked off one by one. It didn't seem likely; the escapees had no guns. Now the dogs were out of sight and noisy, yapping and running ahead tipping off anyone in earshot and destroying what little sign was left. The men were closing the gap and getting Zeb angry. Zeb was confused but wouldn't admit it. They were moving along, but he couldn't rely on their path.

Zeb convinced himself the fugitives had swung west looking to reach Jefferson. Gannett was closer, but it was out of the question. If he could keep his men in line, he would catch the whole sorry bunch. The route to Jefferson required a whole lot of climbing. Except for the girl and Little Jug, the escapees would be slowed by it. They would have to rest, would be hungry and would lose their nerve. He'd go most of the night. He was certain to catch up with them.

Ludim was hurting. He had not rested since Zeb butt-stroked him. He head ached fiercely. Ordinarily, he could hike all day without losing a step; but he'd lost blood and hadn't eaten in almost twenty hours. His legs hurt, he felt dizzy; and there was no end in sight. He needed to rest and eat. Zeb, 200 yards to his right, kept calling and checking everyone. When the group began to bunch, Zeb foolishly threatened them.

Ludim figured he had to kill Zeb to get even ten minutes rest, and the others were becoming as confused and as lost as the dogs. They were hungry and would willingly eat one for dinner. Driven by his fear, Zeb could not see the others were down. They had suffered losses, also, and needed food and rest. Zeb, always cocksure, was over his head. Ludim had a viable plan, but Zeb would not hear it. Ludim drove himself through his pain and hunger as the men grew rebellious.

Ishmael's grief had turned to anger. He could focus it on Zeb, but it was not his nature to challenge him. He heard Ludim call out,

"We need to rest and eat."

Zeb screamed back, "We're too far behind. We gotta get a sure fix on 'em; then we can stop."

"You can keep on going Zeb. Me an' Maximillian are gonna get some food and rest. We'll catch up with you."

Zeb started back toward Ludim. "You forget what happen last' time you went against me?"

"I ain't forgot, but you suckered me last time. Ain't gonna happen again"

Ish spoke up. "I want to rest and eat."

Luke, Matthew, and Malachi chimed in, and Zeb answered," I was thinkin' we could stop in a bit, but if you want to stop now, I'm agreeing. Let's find grub an' take a rest.

Zeb was fuming, but he could face down all of them. He'd let Otha handle Ludim. He just didn't understand Ish. He usually could depend on him, but Ish admired Ludim. Ludim had gone to jail and come back. Ludim went off in his van for a few days and come back with girls. Ludim was in Otha's inner circle, and Ludim wasn't afraid of anyone, including Zeb. Ishmael wished Ludim was in charge.

Zeb believed Ludim was a threat and would be less trouble if off somewhere.

Ish wasn't alone in his thinking. All the men were angry. They needed to catch the murderers and bring them to Otha. Otha would not hold them responsible for murders committed by someone else, but if Zeb didn't hold the team together, there would be no reasoning with Otha.

Zeb was losing his grip.

*   *   *

7:12 P.M.: Friday, September 1, 1993

Frank would need to move things along. He had relied on Sylvi and Little Jug's command of the back trail. He now had to trust Vincent's ability to do the same. Vincent could set false trails, but he might get caught. Depending on him was something of a risk.

167

Sylvi knew he was wrong. Vincent was much like her father. While he did not have as much time in the jungle as Maddoc, enemy patrols did not catch up with him, either. He and Maddoc were members of an elite corps. The clansmen knew the woods as well as anyone might. The Cong knew the jungles as well as anyone might. Vincent, like her father, could master any terrain.

CHAPTER 30

2:05 A.M.: *Friday, September 1, 1993*

The helicopter touched down in a clearing that rose about thirty feet to a stone outcropping with a grassy flat just beneath. The knoll was less than a mile from the remains of the camp. It might seem fortunate that the drop occurred at this particular spot, but it was almost inevitable.

The planning identified this square as the nearest of three "high probable's." It was at the base line of the three, one south and the other off to the west. The next grouping contained two "high probables," old logging camps located further south and west still operating seasonally. Another "probable" was located southeast at the foot of Mount Crescent, and there were possibles north of the western slope of Black Crescent Mountain. When the helicopter searched for a place to perch, the knoll came into view. Not much else was visible from the air.

Maddoc, Abranos, Harrington, and G. K. deplaned and stood back as Engstrom and DeCarlo jumped out when the helicopter lifted off. Dogbone, who had jumped out with Maddoc, howled.

The six of them checked their watches, checked each other's gear and went over, for the last time, the procedures and codes they would use in carrying out the search. Other than Maddoc and Abranos, who preferred to travel light, each man carried food, emergency medical supplies, a compass, a map, two flash grenades, and a machine pistol. Their supplies were rounded out with field rations and canteens, a 100-foot length of nylon rope, a field knife with a high carbon steel blade designed to cut wire fences.

169

Their intent was to split up and fan north and south to look for anything suggesting human habitation. Before they took their first step, they noticed something not apparent when they touched down. Once the copter swung southeast and its wake settled down, the air stilled and an odor of wood ash and gasoline was apparent. Abranos raised the obvious question. "Fire, Maddoc?"

"Remains of a fire; nothing's burning now."

"It's coming from the northwest," Harrington observed.

"Might be," Abranos agreed. "The wind is drifting down from that direction, but the stink might be coming from anywhere."

"We had no reports of a fire in these woods," Harrington observed. Let's check it out."

It was just after 1:15 A.M., but the stars provided sufficient light.

Harrington took the lead with Maddoc and Dogbone at his heels. The other five strung out behind. They stayed about five yards apart, limited targets ready to respond to any show of hostility. In the jungles of Nam, this procedure, requiring strict discipline, saved many lives.

The odor grew stronger as they progressed. The path they followed was a well-worn trail. Within a quarter-mile, they came to a pond where the smell of the stale ashes was very strong. The pond appeared to be man-made and was fed by a stream at the far end. A path traveled the edge of the bank and along the stream. They followed it to where the stream widened and ran through a shallow pool and proceeded west. The forest broke just beyond Abranos who, at the point, held up his hand to stop all movement."

"Looks like others were here before us."

"I saw that, also, but look to the other side of the tree." Maddoc stood at the edge of the remains of a total conflagration.

As though of one mind, they spread out and checked the entire perimeter. They then entered cautiously, Maddoc and Abranos checking the four intact cabins outside of the circle. They'd been occupied, but there was nothing in them except rags and rough-hewn furniture.

Dogbone had covered every inch of ground, leaving his mark where other dogs had been. G. K.'s attention was drawn to a rise where Dogbone issued a low rumble, more related to a complaint than a threat. There was no question it was a mass grave. Who was buried there? How many died? Could Sylvi be under the dirt and mud? It was a possibility none would voice.

They studied the area, discovering where the fire started and convinced gasoline was used. It was over-fueled. Maddoc closed his eyes, trying to think, perhaps to divine what might lay before him: the burned-out cabins, the burned truck, the burial pit, the stone foundations where larger buildings once stood told a story. Was his daughter part of it?

Dogbone moved into the brush close to the fire's starting point. He growled as he circled the remains of a victim. Harrington stepped toward the dog and called to Maddoc. "Appears we have a victim who was overlooked by whoever buried the other remains."

Maddoc looked at Eban Docker's charred remains. "This is the fellow who started the fire. Seems he didn't know much about fires and gasoline. There was an explosion. Notice the dispersion around him. The lower leaves of the trees have been curled and scorched by immense heat. An examination will show a concentration of gasoline in his clothing and his lungs.

All was quiet. The clearing with its pattern of burned-out building sites was bathed in the light of a three-quarter moon and a star-filled sky. Maddoc appeared to enter a cerebral state, one that Star and El Gato had seen often enough. He concentrated only on charred earth, allowing the desolation to engulf him. He heard a voice: "Daddy, Daddy, come find me, Daddy, peek-a-boo," words he had heard almost every day from Sylvi before she entered kindergarten. He did not deny hearing her small voice. It came as out of a dream, but he was awake. He knew Sylvi had been in this place and the dream was an echo of a past moment very near where Maddoc sat. Dogbone whimpered.

Maddoc heard a sharp intake of breath and raised his head. The others were staring at the charcoal pit where there hovered a glow, an uncertain shape, an almost yellow translucent cloud, not to be mistaken for smoke and too bright to be fog. It took shape, the shape of a woman, a ghostly face, a radiant face, not quite distinct but with warmth and strength. The men were rooted in place. Maddoc approached the apparition. Its mouth opened and its lips moved, but no sound came from it. The words that were mouthed came through with absolute clarity, but they came through the speakers of the transceivers each had clipped to his gear. "Sylvi is waiting. She's lost, Anthony. Find her and bring her back."

The apparition swept northwest, pausing before it disappeared into the trees. Those who previously heard Maddoc tell of Marie's coming to him in a dream would no longer doubt him. They heard Sylvi's voice and saw Marie. The words that came through their receivers had no discernible source other than what they saw. They would never again feel the same about dying.

*   *   *

7:14 P.M.: Friday, September 1, 1993

Sylvi had absolute confidence in Little Jug. They left the camp after resting for less than an hour and followed the course Frank laid out for them. She was optimistic, certain they would run into no obstacles. Sylvi found Frank's recall remarkable. He was working from memory on distances, locations and terrain and was accurate. If they followed his directions, they would arrive in Gannett early. She was not concerned about her friends being intercepted, but she made it clear they couldn't dawdle.

*   *   *

Zeb sat watching as the men ate the stew they had put together with the wild vegetables and few squirrels they had shot. He knew the prisoners were bound for Jefferson and wasn't concerned about their lead. While they were struggling to find their way, his men would travel full speed to cut them off. He did not consider he might be wrong. They're flatlanders. It had to be Jefferson.

It did not occur to him the people he was chasing might be traveling a very different route; but given all the signs, their course took them to Jefferson. Zeb was not as optimistic as he tried to appear, but he would not give up, could not. There was too much at stake. Once he decided Jefferson was their destination, his confidence grew. Within hours he would realize his mistake.

He had considered other possibilities. If they had chosen to strike out for Gorham, they would have been caught by now. He also considered Berlin, but there was no sign of that. Early on, when they seemed to be traveling north, Ludim suggested Milan as a possibility. Zeb rejected Milan. Later markings indicated they swung west. West took them to Gannett, a possibility no one would consider. That left a southwest passage between Mt. Waumbek and Mt. King. His crew knew this country well.

As Zeb and the group got underway, altering their path to an almost direct route to Jefferson, Sylvi and Little Jug were working their way south and west of Skag's Leap to reach Gannett. Not having any need for caution, they moved quickly.

After food and their first night's rest, the clansmen were moving with equal ease and greater speed. The dogs scared up several rabbits that Luke took down with his rifle. Malachi gutted and skinned them, skewering them on stout green willow branches for later roasting.

They camped near a swift brook. Zeb, now confident, was more agreeable. He watched the fire as the fat from the rabbits, plump and ready for their winter's rest, shot up flashes. The men would move ahead easier with meat under their ribs. They relaxed now, believing Zeb had them on the right track.

Ludim sat next to Luke. "Luke, I'm thinking Jefferson is wrong. Whatever trail we had, we lost. That weren't smart."

"You're right, but where are they?"

"They headed the shortest distance they could go. Little Jug's taking them to Gannett."

"That's crazy. Otha be waiting for them."

"Maybe not. If they get to the Constable, they'll get help. Jacob Calin ain't going against Otha."

"No, but he ain't going against the law either. He don't know nothing about Otha's business."

"Well, they ain't fool enough to go to Gannett. They're wandering about looking for help. I'm talking to Zeb."

"Don't mention me," Ludim warned.

7:22 P.M.: *Friday, September 1, 1993*

Zeb was almost relieved when Luke confronted him. With every step, he brooded over the confused state in which they found themselves. The dogs had been no help, causing even more confusion. He found no proof to support his guess as to where the escapees were headed. They followed the route they should have taken; but there was no sign they did. Zeb decided the best thing was go home and try to work things out. With the destruction of the camp, home was Gannett.

He knew the risks. Ludim would turn aggressive again and might get the others' support when it came time to explain to Otha. In the morning he would discuss the option with everyone.

Zeb took one more precaution. Shortly after they were settled by the stream, he took Ludim aside. "Ludim, we ain't seen much sign. I want you to take Maximilian and swing northeast back where we started to see if you could pick up a trail. We need to make up time. If you find their trail, follow along until you know where they are headed and hustle over to Gannett. We'll be there by then. Otha be there, and you can lead us to them."

Ludim repressed his pleasure. He felt he might be the one to herd the escapees into Gannett. Zeb would look bad. This didn't occur to Zeb. What did occur to him was that if Ludim was elsewhere when he explained things to Otha, Ludim would take the fall for the escape and the fire. With the loss of his family, Zeb figured he could shift blame on sympathy alone. Ludim hadn't lost anyone. This had occurred to Ludim, but he wasn't concerned. With Otha, the truth would come out. Getting to the truth was one of Otha's devilish skills. Ludim might not look so good, but he would look a whole lot better than Zeb once the truth settled in.

Ludim got some rations, and Maximilian picked up the rifles. Concealed in the low growing foliage, Vincent, who had picked up their trail, observed every move.

CHAPTER 31

2:51 A.M.: Friday, September 1, 1993

Maddoc abandoned the original plan, and no one put up an argument. Of the six, he was the only one who wasn't stunned by Sylvi's words and Marie's appearance. Even El Gato, who loved the paranormal, took time to digest what he had seen.

"Amigo, we go straight behind her?" Abranos asked.

"Did you not see her? I believe we're on a straight line to Sylvi, and Marie will guide us."

"Hell," said Harrington, "She could be in any of several small towns, each of which would take hours to reach. Caleb, you know Maddoc better than any of us, and we know what we saw. Tell me we're not crazy."

Abranos laughed. "He's crazy, but we're all right. In Nam we learned that he sensed things we did not. He was gone for months. We were sure he was not coming back. We all believed he was dead, but then he walked in with a helicopter pilot. There's no explaining him."

"I don't think she's anywhere but ahead of us," Maddoc said. "You've driven through every small town within a hundred miles – unless what you've been telling me is not true."

"No, you're right. But not seeing any sign of her proves nothing."

Maddoc smiled. "My friend, we have had our sign."

"Supposing she is out of sight?" Engstrom asked, a doubter in keeping with his Scandinavian roots.

"Not this long, Star. By now Sylvi is working the system."

"Or dead" the Swede observed.

"What's your point?" Maddoc spat. "We know she's alive, and we know she's waiting; Marie made that clear enough."

175

"Yes, my friend, but you're charging ahead on the word a ghost."

"Yes, I have the word of a ghost."

Harrington called after him. "What do you want to do, Maddoc?"

Maddoc turned, walking back to where they were grouped. "First we call Bernie and alert her and Sossa to the revised plan. Then we break into teams. Abranos and I will follow the line taken by Marie. Harrington, you and G.K. go about a quarter mile west and start working northwest. Star, you and Sossa take the south flank. Follow pretty much the same strategy. If Sylvi's on the move, we may intercept her."

"What about the others?" Caleb asked.

"Harrington, you know this country. Can you have Bernie and Sossa intersect us at some point west?"

"You're that confident in what you're doing, Maddoc?"

"Al, I'm very confident. I'm being pulled along by a force that allows me no choice other than this."

"It's your call. I just hope we don't regret it."

"Not going to happen, Al. Marie will show herself again."

Harrington shrugged. "She's got me believing. I'm not sure how much of this business I can take without going to church. I want the bastards who took her as much as you do."

"Hey, compadre," Abranos barked, "No sweat. We chase las cucarachas, and you're right at home El Gecko. You'll eat them up."

"Maddoc, what's he talking about?"

"You don't want to know. Abranos has a pet name for everyone. He kills cockroaches to prove they're not better developed to survive on this planet than we are."

Harrington chuckled, "Let's start moving before we lose the moon. "

"Oy muchachito, the moon, she stays."

G.K. asked Maddoc, "If we find run into any belligerents, how should we respond?".

"Ask Harrington. It's his call."

"Talk through it. When talk isn't enough," Harrington said. "Your ID's settles most questions unless you are belligerent."

176

Maddoc interrupted. "Al, it's almost 2:00 A.M.; you and the others should move to your positions now. Let's sync our watches and move out 3:00 A.M. Is this okay?"

"Hell," Harrington exclaimed. "There ain't no choice. The heavens have decided our course, and the heavens will conclude it."

* * *

8:07 P.M.: Friday, September 1, 1993

Maddoc and Abranos, following their routine, made good time crossing the line Zeb and the others had crossed earlier.

They were moving along when Dogbone showed up.

"¿Oye, perro, como tu ladras?" Dogbone responded to Abranos with a short bark. "Man, that damn dog understands Spanish, too?"

"Nah, he just barks at cats."

"Ah, very witty, my friend, double your usual self."

"But not as smart as you, El Gato."

"Hey, you learned over the years. I'm going to stop and water this tree if it's okay with Dogbone. You go ahead. I'll catch you."

Maddoc nodded and whistled for Dogbone as he continued on his course. Dogbone alerted him to something ahead. Maddoc stopped in place using the light of the moon to see what caught the dog's attention. He was greeted by the silhouette of a person who stepped out from a small stand of trees and leveled a rifle on Maddoc. Dogbone gave a low growl. Maddoc gestured to him to remain quiet. The man had the edge and was confident. Maddoc relaxed.

"Who you be and what you here in these parts for?"

"I'm with the United States geophysical survey team measuring the continental drift by triangulating on the mountain peaks around these parts."

"What?"

"I'm studying the land for the government."

"Well, mister, you ain't lookin' to study nothing in the dark. You just turn 'round and get back where you come from."

At this point, El Gato stepped beside the little man and relieved him of his rifle. Almost instantly, Abranos, the cat, was picked off his feet by a man who seemed twice El Gato's size. He grabbed Abranos at the neck and had both of his huge hands cutting off Abranos's air supply. The smaller man attempted to retrieve his rifle, which Abranos had dropped, but Dogbone straddled it.

Maddoc was moving quickly to Abranos's aid but needn't have. Abranos had grabbed the giant's wrists and leveraging himself as his last bit of air was quickly burning up, he brought the boot heel smack against his assailant's groin. Maximillian released Abranos who landed on his feet, coughing and gasping for breath but still having the presence to turn upon his assailant. He caught the man as he was bending over with another vicious kick, this time with the point of his boot. He hit him cleanly in the throat and sent him choking and reeling, finally stumbling over his own feet and losing consciousness though continuing to gasp. Abranos decided the man was not in serious trouble, although he probably wouldn't be able to speak for a few days. His muscular neck saved his life.

Ludim saw it but didn't believe it. The man who had just wiped out Maximilian in less than ten seconds was not much bigger than Ludim, himself. He had overwhelmed Maximilian. It wasn't possible.

Maddoc gently reproved Abranos. "The cat circles his prey, Gato. He plays with it. He closes in, cutting off every avenue of escape. He does not walk up, tap on the shoulder and say, 'Excuse me la rata, por favor.' "

"Oye, ingrato; I take this man's gun so he does not shoot you."

"Sí, Gatito. I was frightened to death. My skirt was trembling at its hem. Thank you for risking your neck. That big man was too gentle for you. Next time, you might run into someone who just breaks your neck instead of giving it a gentle squeeze."

Abranos didn't respond to Maddoc's sarcasm. He knew Maddoc was right. There was no danger, but Maddoc had been careless, also. They both survived in Nam because they had learned to assume nothing and expect anything. This unexpected lesson alerted them to the effects of the intervening years. Time softened them. Both knew it, and neither would make the same mistake again.

"Okay, Anthony" – Abranos used Anthony only when he was peeved – "we were careless. We've been walking around these woods as if we were distributing Salvation Army tracts in Central Park; except in Central Park we would be careful. There was no reason to believe anyone would throw down on us, but it happened. Let's get it together."

"We just did, my friend. Now let's see what we have here."

Maximilian had not moved. Ludim thought Abranos killed him. He was worried for himself but liked Maximilian. He had handled gov'ment people before. He'd talk his way through them.

Maddoc challenged. "Why are you in the woods at night?"

"I'm looking for escaped prisoners. I'm the law in these parts."

"Who are the prisoners you're chasing?"

Ludim found it difficult to bluff looking up from the ground with a big dog standing over him. "Can you get this hound off me?"

"Who are the prisoners you're chasing?"

"Well, I ain't got no reason to tell you 'bout my prisoners."

"Dogbone, release!"

Dogbone stepped away but as Ludim tried to get up, Dogbone growled.

Maddoc continued. "Take those clothes off!"

"What for?"

"Take your clothes off or I'll cut them off you," Maddoc threatened while drawing his field knife.

Ludim couldn't run, and he couldn't afford to have his only clothes cut to ribbons. He removed and folded each piece, piling them at the base of a sapling. He got to his union suit and stopped.

"All of them," Maddoc snapped.

"It's cold, an' I ain't standing here buck naked for anyone."

Maddoc moved toward him with knife extended. Ludim almost jumped out of his underwear, leaving everything where it lay as he scuttled ass-backwards away from the advancing man.

There was nothing amusing about Ludim's appearance. He was a slight man, wiry but without enough weight to give his strength much meaning against a bigger man. He got to his feet and stood shivering, his hands covering his genitals.

"You tell me the truth," Maddoc threatened. "You pointed your rifle and told me to skedaddle. I'm here on business, and you are no lawman. Maybe you can help me with my business, but you must tell me the truth. Anything else, and the dog will be on you. He knows a lie. Maybe you set the fire some miles back and murdered an entire community. One more lie, and I leave you to the dog."

Ludim was thinking as fast as he could. The man knew about the fire. There was no reason not to tell him the truth, but there was no good reason to tell him, either. He decided to feel his way through.

"I didn't set no fire. The fire was set by the prisoners I'm chasing. They were poachers up here stealing our sap buckets. We caught 'em and was planning to bring 'em to the constable when they got loose and set the fire. Me and Maximilian set out after 'em with the dogs."

"Where are the dogs?"

"Something scared 'em off, maybe him," Ludim nodded toward Dogbone.

"There are problems with that story. If they were poachers stealing your sap buckets, you would have caught them in the spring. That means you had to be holding them for months. The dogs would not have been scared off by Dogbone. He doesn't threaten other dogs except on command. If he came among your dogs, he would be friendly. He would not scatter them. Finally, if you're what you claim, why are you chasing fugitives alone? I want an honest answer. Dogbone, hold!"

Ludim was afraid to breathe. Dogbone stood to the left of him, his demeanor more threatening as he bared his fangs showing a cavernous expanse of teeth.

Maddoc warned him of what he might expect. "On my command, the dog will take a firm hold on your testicles. Once he has his teeth into them, don't move. If you move, he'll misunderstand and bite down. Now I am going to ask you once more. If I suspect even the smallest of lies, I'll snap my finger, and he'll clamp down and tear away your scrotum. He'll taste blood at which point I can't stop him. Let me ask you one more time: Why are you in these woods tonight?"

He spoke quickly. "There was a fire, and our prisoners escaped. Zeb, a dumb sonuvabitch who ain't never wrong, got in his head to chasing 'em west toward Jefferson. I come this way 'cause I figure he's wrong. I think they're heading for Milan."

"And?" Maddoc asked.

"That's it. We're chasing down poachers who stole a deer we had hanging."

"Dogbone, release!"

The dog released Ludim and stepped back six feet.

"Mister, you understand that lying to me includes lies of omission."

"I didn't say nothing 'bout no mission."

"You were telling the truth as far as it went, but you did not tell me the full story. I'll give you one more opportunity. If I hear anything but the whole story, the dog will use his teeth. Now I'm going to ask Dogbone to help you remember. I will have the entire story. If not from you then from your friend once he wakes up and buries you. Dogbone, hold! Dogbone, again, took a hold on Ludim's scrotum.

After that, the rest was easy. Ludim started talking as fast as he could, and Maddoc commanded Dogbone to release him. Ludim had no reason to protect Zeb, but he still didn't tell Maddoc everything. Maddoc learned that the prisoners Zeb was chasing included several women. Ludim didn't know their names, but his crude descriptions included one that fit Sylvi. Maddoc showed him Sylvi's picture and got a "She could be Mary, one of 'em, but I ain't certain. I stayed away from the women prisoners. Otha kill any man he found with 'em."

Maddoc then learned about Otha's enterprise and the women he held. His favorite girl had lost her babies from running in the woods. "Otha was sure counting on them babies."

He didn't tell Maddoc about Little Jug but did say there were four men among those who had fled the camp. With prodding, he told him women were brought to the camp to have babies. The babies were sent away after they were strong enough.

While they were talking, Maximilian came awake. Abranos stood over him, and he was afraid to get up. Maddoc called Harrington who arrived within 20 minutes with G.K.

After checking the back trail, Maddoc had Ludim tell his story to Harrington and G.K. Harrington just nodded, understanding that if Ludim were to be believed, the suspicions regarding Gubbin's enterprise were true.

Harrington said, "We'll hold the prisoner until I can get someone in here to take them off our hands. You and Caleb should move ahead."

Maddoc corrected him. "You mean prisoners."

At this point, Maximilian was getting to his feet, holding his throat and coughing as he winced with pain.

"Maximilian Cobb?" Harrington asked. "I shouldn't be surprised." Then he looked more closely at Ludim, "…and Mr. Potter? I didn't recognize you without your clothes on. Well, we have a fine pair here, the original George and Lenny, except Potter's not as smart as George and Cobb is a tad smarter than Lenny. Maddoc, you just took down two of Otha Gubbin's best men. How'd you handle Maximilian?"

"I left that to Abranos. He gets the easy ones."

"Ha," Abranos laughed. "If I had not come to save you, we'd be saying mass."

Harrington laughed. "I'm not going to get anything straight from either of you, am I?"

"Whatever story you get, amigo, es nada. You get more from these dummies than from my friend. We are chasing a ghost."

Harrington shrugged. "We all are. We'll take these two in."

G.K. Jones, no small man himself, was six or more inches shorter and a hundred pounds lighter than Maximilian. He walked over to the big man. Frightened, Maximilian backed away.

Ludim looked at him and laughed, "He got beat up by a nigger as a kid and has been scared of 'em ever since." Jones did not laugh.

"You say 'nigger' again, and we'll have one less prisoner to worry about."

Harrington stepped in. "He doesn't know any better, G.K."

"He knows now."

Harrington tied and hobbled Ludim and Maximillian. They could walk, but neither would be able to run. They were told if they tried, Dogbone would pull them down.

Maddoc shared Ludim's information with Harrington.

"I'm surprised you got anything but lies from him," he said. "These people are liars at birth; it's genetic."

"Once Dogbone had his balls, he talked fast enough, Maddoc replied.

*   *   *

9:34 P.M.: Friday, September 1, 1993

Abranos was moving about 200 yards to the left of Maddoc. Harrington, G.K. trailed a half-minute behind. Abranos heard a bark followed by a chorus. These were the dogs Ludim mentioned. He worked his way back toward Maddoc.

"What do you think, my friend? You think they're coming this way?"

"I doubt it." Abranos said. "They seemed to be moving away."

"It's the people the weasel talked about."

"Probably. We're upwind of them; the dogs can't pick up our scent. I'll run Dogbone downwind of them as a distraction."

Abranos shrugged. "Que significación de downwind y upwind. Yo no comprendo."

"Foolish friend. You knew in Nam, and you know now. It means that should Dogbone eat garbage, you don't want to be upwind of him."

"Aha. Yo ve! And if you eat enough of those bean sprouts you cultivate, I want to be upwind of you, also."

"Now you understand very well."

"Si, but what is downwind?"

"That's where I want you to be, cucaracha."

With this, Maddoc gave a command to the dog. Abranos recognized it. Dogbone was off to find other people. Whoever they might be, Dogbone would remain passive with anyone he came upon.

"The dog's not going to get shot by a gun-happy hunter?"

"He's too smart for that. Dogbone avoids guns, but he'll attack if one is leveled on him."

"Once a gun is leveled on him, he gets shot."

"You would think so, but Dogbone would retreat, circle and take the gun man down."

"They might turn the dogs loose on him."

"...and the dogs would have more chance against a bear."

Maddoc snapped his finger, and Dogbone was off. The echo of the dogs was fading.

* * *

7:19 P.M.: Friday, September 1, 1993

Zeb couldn't manage Bear, but Bear scored points this day. Just after they settled in, Bear showed up in camp with bloodied jowls. The dogs set up a chorus. Zeb released Romeo, the basset, who, despite the difference in size, showed no fear of the bigger dog. They growled at each other as the basset went off into the woods with Zeb trailing behind. Bear meant to follow but got a crack on the head. Within a hundred yards, Romeo led Zeb to the Bear's kill, a doe. Her throat was ripped open, and meat was torn from her forequarter. Bear feasted and left the animal where he dropped it.

Zeb picked it up and carried it back to the camp where he gutted it and hung it to bleed. Bear slept. While wild by city standards, Bear had no instinct to protect a kill. Zeb threw the entrails to the dogs, which fought for them. Zeb included the organs. The old timers ate the organs, but Luke and his friends did not favor them. With the addition of the doe, there was more than enough meat.

Zeb looked at Bear sleeping. He was not a dog for the hunt, but he was a killer and could be useful. He was able to pull down a deer, no small thing in a dog. Zeb walked over and threw a loop over his head, deciding he would keep him in sight and under control. Bear didn't stir.

* * *

CHAPTER 32

9:28 P.M.: Friday, September 1, 1993

Dogbone moved quietly. In the woods, calling on the instincts of his ancestors, Dogbone was a hunter, although unlike his ancestors, he was trained.

A mile away, Zeb rose to see what troubled the dogs. They awoke everyone. He considered loosening them, but he'd be damned if he would let them run around in the woods all night. It was a night critter stirring them up, no doubt. Bringing the dogs was a mistake. They were of no help, and now they woke him.

He was jumpy; changing direction toward Gannett was unavoidable. He still hoped they would pick up the trail, unnerved by the thought of explaining to Otha without having the prisoners in tow.

Though most hadn't slept enough, Zeb wanted to get a two-hour jump on the day. The others rejected it, moving to their bed roles. Zeb couldn't force it; they were already edgy. They would be hungry when they woke. He built a fire. Luke joined him and they cut and hung meat over the fire to feed them. Their moods would improve with the smell of the cooking.

Zeb knew that Otha would interrogate everyone. He would have to explain. He had forged ahead helter-skelter, believing he was closing in on his quarry. They burned the cabins no doubt; but there was nothing to do about it. How would he explain that to Otha? He spoke to Luke, unaware of Luke's distrust. Of the men who remained with him, Luke was the most dangerous.

"I'm worried we will be in trouble with Otha if we don't get them, Luke. They're in these woods somewhere, and we ain't far behind 'em. Soon as we get to Gannett, we'll get help. Then we'll get the slayers of our families."

"Yep, we're gonna get 'em all."

Zeb looked around. Everyone slept. The dogs again began to bark, pulling at their ropes to get loose. Zeb quieted them but they remained edgy. He looked around expecting to see a night critter; but nothing caught his eye.

Nothing had gone as he thought. Zeb thought about the fire. Otha Gubbin would go into a blood lust once he learned of it. He would know Zeb failed them. Zeb had no chance without their support. He couldn't claim Ludim spooked them into the chase. Otha knew Ludim was no fool and Zeb's thinking ability was not his long suit. The more Zeb thought, the more confused he became; the more sleep he lost and the worse things seemed. He was growing certain Otha would kill him.

The dogs started again as Dogbone limped into the clearing and acting cowed as he moved toward Zeb and Luke. "What in hell," Luke remarked, leveling his rifle in surprise.

"It's a dog!" Zeb warned, "an' he's hurt an' scared. Don't shoot him. He looks like a good one." Zeb approached Dogbone, who cowered before him. Zeb got down to pet him. Dogbone licked his hand, although he might have torn it from his wrist. Dogbone turned toward the challenge of the other dogs and gave a low rumbling chest-deep growl. They quieted. Zeb attempted to check his leg to determine why he was limping, but Dogbone snarled and showed his teeth. He didn't snap; the warning was enough. He got to his feet and limped around the campsite, allowing several of the men, now sitting up where they had been sleeping, to pat him on his head. He stopped short of Bear who was tied and didn't stir. Dogbone turned and limped off into the woods. Luke wanted to go after him, thinking to make Dogbone his own; but after a few steps into the woods Luke turned back. "Damn dog was a ghost," Luke muttered. "Sure wish I mighta kept him."

"Well, let's rest," Zeb said. "At least we know what stirred up the dogs. Don't know where that dog came from, but won't last in these woods if he don't know how to hunt. Looked like he hadn't ate in a spell. Whoever lost him gave up looking sometime back."

Luke thought about his losses. He had lost both family and friends, some almost kin since birth. Thinking of all those people being dead unmanned him. He shook off his tears and pretended it never happened while silently crying within.

*   *   *

9:36 P.M.: Friday, September 1, 1993

Maddoc and Abranos were close enough to hear every word between Zeb and Luke. Maddoc counted five men. One sat and was awake. The other remained on guard but inattentive while attending to a fire. He occasionally turned his head but nothing more. Maddoc was not concerned about the dogs, although he and Abranos might have to get close to them. They took steps to cover their man-smell.

The dogs whined, a strange turn in behavior. Luke checked and was pleased to see the big dog had returned. He stayed back from the tethered pack. The dogs sensed he was not a threat and gave way to sleep.

Abranos tapped Maddoc's hand. Maddoc angled toward him and read his lips, a skill acquired in Nam. He asked whether Maddoc wanted to take them down. Maddoc shook his head no. He needed to know their purpose and destination; their knowledge of the area might be useful. He directed Abranos to go back to brief Harrington.

Dogbone watched Abranos move away, raising his head long enough to see the direction he traveled. His head snapped up as he saw Bear slip his rope and move off behind Abranos. Until this point, Dogbone and Bear were at a standoff, neither paying particular attention to the other but conscious of their space. Dogbone darted swiftly through the brush, upwind of Bear and passing silently about twenty yards to his left. He angled over to where Abranos was moving, placing him about sixty feet but within sight of Bear. The bigger dog gave out a threatening growl, lowered his head and began loping toward El Gato.

Abranos heard the growl and turned, seeing only a large animal coming toward him. His first thought was that it was a bear, but this animal wasn't big enough. Abranos pulled out his knife and stood ready to meet the charge. He did not see Dogbone.

What he saw was something knock the animal off its feet. Vicious growls and yelps filled the air. Abranos realized Dogbone was fighting a bigger and heavier animal. He could not see much as the two animals fought their way deeper into the brush.

The attack came from Bear's blind side. Bear turned just as Dogbone struck him, the force of the charge carrying both into the brush. Dogbone took a killing hold on Bear's neck. Bear tried to shake Dogbone loose, spinning about an effort to break free. Dogbone was locked on and would not release. Bear's rage was expressed in his roaring growls and a frenzied dance. Dogbone was a strong animal with great endurance and biting power. The terrier in him assured tenacity and strength. Further, Dogbone was working as little as possible expending only enough energy to keep his legs under him.

Abranos cautiously tried to get close to the two animals, but they eluded him. Their thrashing and growling, especially the loud rumblings emanating from Bear, unnerved Abranos, who feared Dogbone might be getting the worst of it.

Maddoc stepped up alongside Abranos and barked a command to Dogbone. Dogbone released the bigger dog and moved to a defensive position just in front of his master. Bear was exhausted and shaky on his feet but still growling, though he didn't have much left. The smaller dog showed no sign of stepping back. Bear had no sense of size and no experience in which he did not dominate. He saw a large animal and two men, and the fight left him. He dropped down, placing his huge head between his front paws and stared at Dogbone. Maddoc walked to him, under the watchful eye of Dogbone, squatted and patted Bear's head. The bigger animal pulled himself closer to Maddoc.

"Fine animal, this one. We would have done wonders with him in the corps. He's a little too big for the streets, but a fine animal nevertheless."

Maddoc, Abranos, and Dogbone moved on to meet G.K. and Harrington. The dogfight might have impelled the clansmen to come nosing about. Maddoc did not want to chance that. Better they believe they were alone.

Their two prisoners were enough of a pain in the ass.

CHAPTER 33

5:16 A.M.: *Sunday, September 3, 1993*

S ylvi could not contain her excitement as she moved along with Little Jug. They stopped to rest and both fell asleep for about half an hour during which Sylvi dreamed her dad was near. When she awoke, she was certain it had not been a dream. She believed he would walk over the next hill. A mantle had been thrown over her and nothing more could hurt her. As she grew more awake, she remembered as a child standing and reaching toward her dad to be lifted. The dream lifted her. She had been sleeping yet did not believe she was hallucinating. She felt as though she were home and he was about to walk through the door. Her stress eased. She accepted her intuition. There was happiness in her talk as she explained to Little Jug.

"When I was a child and afraid, I thought of my father. He was my best friend just like you are now."

Little Jug smiled. He was happy at that moment because she was.

"My dad is nearby Little Jug. I'm sure; and he'll like you." Impulsively, she walked to where he was sitting and hugged his big head. It wasn't the first time, and Little Jug always giggled when she did it.

Her voice trailed off as she spoke, ...he'll be here. I'm sure."

*   *   *

6:04 A.M.: *Sunday, September 3, 1993*

Otha was checking on the entourage, making certain they'd be a ready to start within the hour. It was almost fifty miles to reach Gannett, some over unpaved roads. The heavy mountain rains had inundated Higgins

Creek and left the road toward Gannett a mess of ruts and gullies. Otha planned to be on the road by 6:30 A.M., but the young ones were paired up with locals; he was having a time finding them. The girls had been turning more action than common. He brought as many of the younger girls along as he could. Zeb would regret not sending his daughter, as Otha suggested, and missing out on the extra money the Johns gave out.

Otha was troubled. Three days earlier, he had hired out Eve Sprill for two days to four men outside of Laconia who claimed to be hunters, but it would be weeks before they could hunt. Otha had settled on a price of $1,600 for her services, getting his money up front. It was about double what she might have done soliciting. Eve was overdue, but he wasn't too worried about her absence. He and Edom went to the hunter's camp to fetch her and were told she had gone.

"Well, she ain't come back to her kin; and that means she still be here."

The spokesman for the group said, "Well, hell. She's run off. Young girl like that, good looking, nice tits, satisfy four men all night long – she have her pick of men. She probably got wise to your pimping her and went off somewhere to go into business for herself."

"Nope, no chance that'd happen. She's here somewhere."

"Hey, man, I told you she's not here. You got your fuckin' money. Get out of my face or I'll kick your skinny ass back to the fuckin' hole you crawled out of."

Otha didn't react. Neither did Edom, although Edom would have killed the man had Otha nodded. "Ain't got no need to be unfriendly. The girl wouldn't go off. She may be asleep in one of your trucks and you just lost sight o' her. I'd sure appreciate your looking."

"Well, we don't want to be unfriendly. Sure we'll look. Gary, check the vans and the trailer 'n' see if she might be sleeping somewhere."

"Edom, you help with the lookin'. We don' want to miss her."

Ray interjected. "Gary will look and won't miss a thing. You stay put, boy," Ray warned as he dropped his hand next to the butt of his side arm, a long-barreled 44 magnum. Edom would have put two rounds in him before his hand closed on the grip.

"Get looking, Gary," he said.

Gary checked the vans and trailer and came back. "The girl's not around.'

Otha saw the lie and assumed the worst. He asked, "Who was she with last? Who was the one what saw her leave?"

All eyes turned on Ray, who said, "We had a good time last night, and she left here very happy. I gave her $50.00. Saw her walking right down that path with her money and whistling. She's off somewhere with that fifty. I guess I made a mistake in giving it to her."

"I suppose' you're right."

People in the clan believed that Otha could see a lie falling from anyone's lips even before the words reached his ears. Otha read the eyes, body language and voice inflections. He was not an easy man to fool even with a simple lie. He knew Ray was lying; whistling was a sin.

He relaxed, "She probably went to Portsmouth to visit friends. We'll pick her up when we're down there next. Sorry to doubt you. I usually know when a man is being truthful with me."

Ray didn't notice Otha's switch to the vernacular.

"Hey, no trouble," Ray sang out. "I'm sorry I was so unpleasant. Where I come from, people don't usually question my word, but I understand your concern. Tell you what. We'll cruise around. If we see her, we'll make certain the authorities get her back to you."

"Well, thank you. Her ma and pa will appreciate it." As they walked away, he said to Edom, "You best stay around and watch them. If she turns up, bring her home, but they may have killed her. When those boys go out hunting that Ray fellow going to have an accident. You stay around to see to it. If he dies, that's all right. If he spends his life in a chair, that's better. I'll send Joseph to give a hand."

Edom nodded. Edom could shoot the eye out of a one-eyed jack hanging from a string at 100 yards. He hunted with a Remington 22 and was known to drop a deer in place with one shot. He once brought in a marauding black bear, a big male that threatened campers, sources of Otha's income. When the bear was cut up and the meat distributed among the clan, three slugs had shredded its heart. Few men will hunt bear with 22-longs; but Edom gave that no thought.

"We're going off without Eve, something that shames me. Her ma and pa trusted me, and I got to tell them she ain't coming back. I expect to see you in Gannett late tomorrow. If you find Eve, I'll be a glad liar for what I'm thinking. If you find her body, bring her home for a Christian burial, but get that Ray fella and remember the faces of the others. They be back next year, and we'll meet them up with Little Jug in the woods. I'm awanting to tell her ma and pa something to ease their hurting." With this, Otha left Edom to work things out.

CHAPTER 34

R einholds was doing his best to hold the Bronco on the road. He cussed trying to figure out what was road and what wasn't. Neary wasn't making it any easier. From the moment Neary knew Anthony Maddoc was on his way to New Hampshire, he complained about every problem.

Neary had no idea where Sylvi was. He didn't know if she was alive, and if alive, did Otha take her. He had to get rid of Otha and whatever evidence was lying around. Gilletti was sure that among Otha's records would be information on Matterlink that could be damaging. Unknowingly, Neary acknowledged that the girl at Carter Notch was Sylvia Maddoc. If she were found and well, that would be confirmed. There was no explaining Neary's lie.

Reinholds was concerned. With Figueroa gone, he was down to Walsh, Kincher, Neary and himself. He was counting on Neary to gain the old man's confidence; but given Neary's state, Otha would see through him. Hell, a six-year-old would see through him.

The operation would not be easy. Gubbin had them outgunned. There was no counting on Neary. Given the roads, they wouldn't arrive on time; and arriving early was important if they were to neutralize the constable and his deputies and get Gubbin as well.

Neary's earlier exchange had been bravado, with Neary a strutting rooster and Reinholds subdued. Neary expounded on what he would do with Maddoc if he crossed their path. Reinholds laughed to himself. He feared almost no one, but he didn't forget Maddoc's shutting down his business. At 230 pounds, the same weight he carried twenty years earlier, Reinholds, in his reveries, figured that he could handle Maddoc. He didn't underestimate Maddoc. The man earned a reputation in Viet Nam after returning from behind enemy lines for months. Then there was Maddoc's encounter with Chou Eng, a huge Mongolian who owned a bar in Saigon.

Chou Eng was sixty pounds heavier than Reinholds and several inches taller. He taunted smaller Vietnamese men, holding them off their feet by their collars with one hand and squeezing their balls with the other, laughing at their screams. It was known as Eng's Ecstasy.

One Sunday afternoon an American country boy who'd been drinking too much spit on one of Eng's whores. As Chou Eng reached for the American, Maddoc slapped his arm down. The crack of the slap and the expression on Eng's face shocked everyone. Eng turned and rushed at Maddoc, throwing his full weight at the smaller man. Maddoc dropped under Eng, threw his arms up to take the weight as it came over him, and then lifted Eng off his feet and using Eng's momentum tossed him into a Koi pond. As the big man climbed out, raging and shaking off water and fish, Maddoc brought the side of his hand across his throat, smashing but not crushing his trachea. Eng, choking and gasping, was stunned by the pain. Maddoc then brought him down with a crushing kick to the side of his knee joint, blowing apart cartilage, muscle and sinew with amazing force. As Eng caved to the floor, his shattered tibia and fibula broke through the skin and muscle of his leg like two ill-placed splints. The Mongolian passed out. He went to a Vietnamese hospital and never returned. Sometime later, Reinholds heard tell that a small Vietnamese man came into the same bar months later and nailed an oversized scrotum and balls to a beam running above the bar.

Reinholds thought it best to avoid Maddoc. Neary certainly had to know he should do the same.

Reinholds knew Maddoc was now in New Hampshire, but he did not expect to cross paths. If he found Maddoc's daughter, he would get her back to New York as Gilletti required; but his was job was to wipe out all connections between the Samuel Trust Foundation and Matterlink. Although it was Neary's assignment, Reinholds was to insure it happened.

* * *

4:29 A.M.: *Sunday, September 3, 1993*

Sylvi and Little Jug arrived in Gannett at 4:29 A.M. exhausted but relieved. The streets were dark and empty but there was light enough to distinguish one building from another. They headed for the only fully lighted building and walked in on Constable Jacob Calin and his deputy, Hezzie Simpson, Erla's sister's son.

While Calin and Gubbin were cousins, Jacob did not grow up in Gannett. He was the first of his line in three generations to live in Gannett. Jacob's grandfather, a stonecutter, settled in Vermont and worked the quarries.

Jacob, a retired Vermont State Police Inspector, came to visit one summer after his wife died and stayed. He had no children and no desire to remarry. Few knew much about him. Otha wanted it that way.

Sylvi and Little Jug were tired and hungry. The constable sent his deputy to get breakfast while he fixed Sylvi a cup of coffee and, to Little Jug's delight, handed him a Yoo Hoo. The man was a generous host and gifted listener.

When Calin greeted Little Jug, Sylvi realized there was a problem. Her first impulse was to run, to get back to the others and warn them. This was replaced by anger; Frank had set them up. Her despair led her to believe her optimism was idiocy. She contained herself, working through each reaction with the same calm that kept her from striking out when Gubbin humiliated her. This was different and she would find a way to exploit it.

While her mind raced, Sylvi played her role well, showing deference to the constable, his deputy and Little Jug. She said that Little Jug got it into his mind to find Otha and thought he was in Gannett. Calin did not believe Little Jug would have any such impulse but remained gracious.

Hezzie brought them a breakfast of toast with butter, oatmeal with walnuts and maple syrup, slabs of cheese, coffee and fresh apple cider. Sylvi ate too much and became nauseous and exhausted as her body worked to digest the meal.

Little Jug ate for an army and was unaffected. Calin suggested, "Let's get you both some rest. Afterwards, we'll arrange for clothes and a bath for you, missy."

He promised to wake them within an hour. Sylvi was too beat to resist. She could not ask Calin for help.

As the word traveled through town, no one in Gannett gave any thought to Sylvi and Little Jug's coming. It was curious that Little Jug was there without Otha. Calin gave little thought to Sylvi. It was rumored that Little Jug had a woman, a source of ribald speculation, but here she was.

Both the constable and his deputy showed great regard for Little Jug. He never refused to help when asked. He might look to Otha for approval unless it was a common chore. Jacob was tickled by the relationship with Sylvi. He was chuckling at the thought of telling Otha that his lapdog was in someone else's kennel.

Jacob was Otha's true friend. He challenged Otha with impunity. He mocked his pretenses and was one of the few people who could draw a laugh from him at any time. Despite the friendship and loyalty existing between them, Jacob Calin knew where to draw the line. Although it wasn't apparent, he admired Otha who brought prosperity to Gannett. Most of this was concealed, hidden from the agencies that provided community relief funds and school system support.

True to his word, Calin woke them both to have baths and receive fresh clothes. Little Jug resisted bathing but obeyed Sylvi when she told him he had to. By 7:45 A.M. they met with Calin, Hezzie, and Mort Clagger, the third deputy. It didn't seem possible they had emerged from the woods, breakfasted, rested, bathed and dressed in little more than two hours, but here they were. Now Sylvi fussed about getting out of Gannett and intercepting her friends. While suspicious, Calin and the deputies were struck by her manner with Little Jug. She showed great regard for him, and Little Jug loved her. The last time he took a bath, Otha had to stand away from him with a whip as he was hosed down. Now Little Jug had bathed at her command, no small accomplishment; he hated water.

Calin spoke to Sylvi, "It's still a bit early. Once people see you and Little Jug, they'll be a big stir. It might be a good time for you both to sleep a bit more. Another hour would do you good. Ain't much else goin' on."

Feeling the effects of the trek and her reaction to breakfast, Sylvi agreed.

* * *

196

CHAPTER 35

Abranos fretted about the men ahead of them. He wanted to lift their weapons, but Maddoc saw no need. The fact that they were armed was not a threat. Their disagreement led to laughter.

"Hey mano, these people have guns. We need to take them down."

Maddoc laughed. "Hey, piojo, everyone in your neighborhood has guns. You don't take them down."

"They are my friends, and they do not carry guns into my store."

"Of course, Caleb. They check them into that little booth with the sign 'Check your guns here.' "

Abranos realized the absurdity of his defense and laughed, but he was not one to give up.

"What's wrong with you? They could turn on us."

"In that case we will take away their guns."

"You gonna do that yourself?"

"No, no my friend. I leave such easy tasks to you."

"All right. I know you too well. Why are you not taking me seriously."

"Caleb, our weasel friend says they are looking for escaped prisoners. We are looking for Sylvi. Is she among those they are after? I'm asking you, Caleb."

"I don't know."

"Nor do I, but the weasel suggested there were women among them and one of them, in his words, looked like Sylvi."

"And you believe him? The man was so close to being dog food he would have said anything."

"Yes, but did you read a lie? I did not. He had good reason not to lie. He told the truth, and that means Sylvi may be among them."

"Ah ha. So you believe these hillbillies find her for us?"

"Not quite, Caleb. I let them show us where she might be. They have an understanding of the territory that we do not. Our weasel is content with the path we take. If they find Sylvi, given what they believe, we need to be there to protect her."

Meanwhile, Harrington's patience was wearing thin. He'd been traveling with the prisoners for the better part of a day and wanted to be rid of them. They were a distraction. Abranos heard the letdown in Harrington's voice as he sought someone to pick up his prisoners.

"Hey boss!" El Gato called to Maddoc. "I can't make out what Harrington's pissed about."

"He hasn't been able to get rid of the prisoners."

"We can leave them with Dogbone."

"That would be true if Harrington can get assurance of a pickup."

"Ah, I get it." Abranos looked at Bear walking close to the prisoners.

"That big dog like those two donkeys."

"He knows them, but he is friendly only to the big one."

"Best we not leave Dogbone with them. They may set that big dog go on your rag bone again."

"Not in this lifetime, Gatito. His fear of Dogbone is branded on his brain. He's a bully dog who will not bully again, at least not while Dogbone is around."

"So amigo, your mutt has ruined this fine animal."

No more was said. Abranos knew as much about dogs as Maddoc, and he knew Bear would not have passed muster in the K-9 corps. He was a tough dog, but he was not attentive. A terrier, almost any terrier, would fight to the death, one of the reasons that pit bulls are so dangerous, but many dog breeds are not inherently fearless. Abranos knew Bear was not the equal of Dogbone.

The events of the past several hours were bringing them closer to finding Sylvi. Ludim said enough to convince Maddoc they were on track. It began with the apparition. Maddoc accepted much that was well beyond his understanding. He trusted his instincts, believing instincts were passed on from one generation to the next or were inferred through subconscious retrieval of past experience. Yet he didn't bend himself into a pretzel trying to explain. He let common sense decide.

Abranos interrupted him. "Look likes Harrington has reached some-one."

Maddoc looked ahead and saw Harrington gesturing, a chopping motion savagely renting the air. He pulled the instrument from his ear and started walking back toward Maddoc, leaving the prisoners where they stood.

"Sonuvabitch! Smith is assembling a troop to join us. Wants us to stay put. He's directed Sossa and his team to return to the ranch, but they won't move without your instructions. What do we tell Sossa?"

"To join us. There's no reason for him and Bernie to wait for Smith. What about the prisoners?"

"We have to hold onto them."

"He's not so dumb. He's trying to slow us down."

*   *   *

6:28 A.M.: Sunday, September 3, 1993

Reinholds, Neary, Walsh and Kincher drove into Gannett an hour later than planned. They stopped in front of the constable's office, exiting their vehicle nonchalantly, stretching and walking and lighting up. Neary waved as Calin stepped outside. Confident in their membership in the same fraternal organization, Neary felt they were friends of a sort. He was mistaken. Neary's asking Calin to keep an eye on Otha short-circuited any chance of gaining the man's trust.

Calin took the measure of the three other men standing alongside the vehicle. He didn't trust strangers. Unless everything said "not a threat," any stranger was suspect. These three looked like hired guns. Neary didn't worry him. Otha classified him as a man "with little sand in his craw," a fair assessment. Neary had no legitimate business in Gannett.

He would take no chances with the others. He had Mort Clagger break out a shotgun and sent Hezzie out the back door with matched side arms and a modified Mossberg shot gun, telling him, "put yourself where you won't be seen. First sign of trouble, you come at them from the backside shooting first."

Jacob stayed close to the door as Neary walked toward the building. The station housed a few retention rooms but was not built for that purpose. It was a storefront with windows looking out on the main street. Almost thirty years earlier, after problems with tourists, the windows were covered with heavy inch and a half mesh that could stop a small car. The glass panel on the front was also screened. Neary saw none of the positioning Calin undertook. He approached aiming to take Calin out. The rest would be easy.

"Hello, Constable Jake. I don't know if you remember me, but I'm Jack Neary, New York City Police Inspector. I bring greetings from the Big Apple."

"I remember' you, Neary," Calin replied flatly. "Otha's not in town. Who are your friends?"

These might have been the last words that Jacob Calin ever uttered were he not a suspicious man. He read Kincher's thousand-yard stare and was moving before anyone knew what was happening. To Neary's shock, a bone-handled Bowie knife hurdled toward Calin and whacked sharply against the screening on the door as Calin whipped it closed. The force of the throw rang off the plate glass window as it drove the wire mesh back against it.

Harvey Kincher let out air and an almost unheard grunt as he fell forward, banging against the fender. A bullet had grazed his scalp and knocked him down before anyone heard the report. Reacting quickly, Walsh circled around the back of the 4X4 and tossed a gas grenade toward the door as it bounced open. The grenade rolled within inches of the opening; upon its explosion door open another foot. Carried by a breeze flowing through the building the gas poured in.

Within seconds Mort, coughing and trying to clear his eyes, came through the door, his shotgun held waist high pointing toward adversaries he could not see. He took a 9MM slug through his right eye from a pistol that gave almost no report. He was dead before he hit the ground, the slug meeting no serious resistance until it tore through back of his skull carrying much of his cerebral cortex with it.

Walsh had gone to Kincher's aid as Reinholds killed Mort. He motioned Reinholds to circle around to establish a position behind the building now housing Calin, Little Jug and Sylvi. Neary, who seemed rooted to his position, realized that the fight had been joined and scrambled for the shelter of the vehicle. He went down after his first step, a bullet from Calin's carbine striking his foot, cutting through his heel and passing across the arch without touching any bones as it exited through the sole just below the third toe. It bled heavily.

Hezzie was not positioned in time to witness any of the fight, which lasted less than fifteen seconds. His misfortune was in not getting there before Reinholds came around back. Hezekiah was barely in place when he heard the report of the bullet that shaved Neary's foot. Reinholds had already spotted Hezekiah. He came up behind noiselessly and dropped a nylon loop over his head which he pulled tight and quickly knotted so that it could not be pulled loose. Hezekiah died while struggling to break the heavy filament. His panic blinded him to the blade strapped to his leg.

Neary, who dragged himself to a sitting position against the wheel of the Bronco, was stunned at being hit and not able to rest his foot on the ground. From his sitting position, he turned toward Walsh, who was behind the Bronco, tending to Kincher.

Neary screamed, "What the fuck do you think you're doing? I had everything under control."

"You had shit. That hayseed constable had a man moving around to get us in a cross fire."

"I didn't see anyone behind us. It was the gas that drove the deputy out. Calin didn't make one gesture, not one threat toward us."

"You're not thinking, Neary. That old fox wasn't worried about you. His eyes said so. He made two mistakes, however. He left the door open, and he looked beyond us to see if his man was in position. I saved your life Neary. You would have been the first to fall if that old thief had decided to start shooting sooner."

"We had a plan, damn it, and you messed it up."

"Wake up, Neary. That smiling old man had killer eyes. You weren't going to fool him, and he was setting us up while he danced with you. Let's get off the street. I'll check with Reinholds to see how he made out with the other one."

"What other one?" Neary sputtered.

"The one who was gonna put a bullet in your back if the old man missed you."

Walsh spit in Neary's direction.

* * *

6:41 A.M.: *Sunday, September 3, 1993*

Sylvi welcomed the opportunity to rest, needing time to work things out. She planned to slip out once the constable and his deputies were busy. That she was alone did not trouble her. The room, normally used as a jail cell, was small with only a cot. She went to the door with the idea of checking out the surroundings. It was locked. This troubled her. Was it possible that news of the escape reached Gannett? She remained calm, knowing she would know soon enough if there was a bigger problem than finding her friends. She would rely on the advantage that Little Jug gave her.

Little Jug found himself alone and grew anxious. The space was too small. There were things he didn't recognize and a faint, distasteful odor. He turned the doorknob, but the door wouldn't open. While the door was of heavy hand-hewn oak in an equally heavy frame; it wasn't something that could stop him. He placed his hands flat against the door and, using his weight, pushed it free of its frame, tearing the screws that held the hinges out of the frame and shattering the wood around the plate that secured the lock.

Sylvi heard the shooting. She had to get out of the room. She yelled and began kicking at the door. Without warning, door and frame crashed into the room so quickly that she barely got out of the way. Little Jug heard her scream, and nothing would stop him from reaching her. He stumbled headlong into the room, arms akimbo and fell into the debris he scattered.

Jacob Calin heard the sound of the building being torn apart and thought Neary and his cronies were breaking in from the back. He sidled quickly to the front door, kicked it shut and threw the dead bolt. There was no reaction, further convincing Calin they were trying to get in through the back. He wasn't worried. Hezzie, second to almost none with a carbine or pistol, was in position outside. Jacob had a 45 on his hip and a shotgun under his arm as he moved to the back to see how well the door held. He saw Little Jug and Sylvi as they left Sylvi's cell. The shattered doors explained the noise.

"Hey, now, you're not going anywhere. There are strangers out there with guns. They already killed Mort. Hezzie's covering out back, but we are outmanned. You step outside and you're likely to be shot."

"Why'd you lock us in?" Sylvi asked. "What's going on?"

"Locking doors here is a habit. Mort wasn't much of a thinker. He locked them without a thought, like pulling up a zipper. As for the attack, I figure someone thinks we have money here. They're strangers driving a New York vehicle."

Sylvi didn't believe Calin but did not challenge him. Calin directed Little Jug to stay at the back door and not let anyone in. He went back to covering the front of the building.

Once he was gone, Sylvi went to the door. Little Jug stood in front of her, unwilling to move. She gently pushed him aside and pushed open the heavy oak-planked door. As she leaned out, she was grabbed from outside and pulled through the door. Reinholds had a hold on her and was shocked to find himself with a woman in his hands. He held a knife poised but stopped short, recognizing Sylvi from her picture. He released her. She stepped back and drove a kick into his midsection, knocking him backwards but not off his feet. Reinholds was about to address her by name but deciding she needed a lesson. Her sheathed his knife, and came directly at her. She ducked under his arms as he reached for her and drove her knee between his legs. He anticipated the move and grabbed her around the waist, lifting her off her feet.

"You're a tough one, eh? I'm gonna break you the same way I'd break a mean-spirited horse. You're a chip off the old block. We'll find time to get acquainted, but I got business first."

Sylvi struggled, but Reinholds was a powerful man. She knew he could kill her with ease, but she knew, also, she could not let him separate her from Little Jug. She continued to struggle and scream. Reinholds dropped her. She fell forward and landed hard on her right shoulder, banging her head on the packed ground. She was dazed.

Reinholds was lifted off his feet. His head was held in a crushing grip, two huge hands squeezing against his temples. He grabbed at a point behind his head, trying to get a hold that would allow him a counterblow. He knew he was in trouble. He was 230 pounds and very strong, yet whatever held him was frighteningly powerful.

Reinholds felt he was being pressed in a vise. He felt the forearms, amazed that his large hands were unable to fully grasp their bulk. He was being shaken, his body dancing and bouncing, dislodging his limbs and organs to the point that he lost control of his bodily functions. He couldn't help himself, couldn't understand the full horror of his situation. He lost consciousness. Still, the body-breaking punishment continued until Sylvi screamed "Stop!"

Little Jug let go, and Reinholds dropped to the ground.

CHAPTER 36

7:51 A.M. *Sunday, September 3, 1993*

O tha knew something was amiss when he hit the edge of town. The 4X4 parked in front of the constable's office didn't belong there. Otha had no intention of driving into town to see what or who it was. He pulled the caravan out of sight.

The constable's office door was shut. Most in town might be curious about the truck but not read much into it. To Otha, the truck told its own story. It had New York plates. It was very new and, despite its recent rough passage, was cleaner than most trucks in these parts. One of its doors was open; it had been exited in a hurry, and there was no sign of the constable or his deputies. Customarily, one or more would be out front, expecting the caravan. Who would come to Gannett from New York? This was not a hunter looking for directions.

"Esther, take Noah and stroll over 'hind the constable's office and see what you see. There's something peculiar going on."

Noah and Esther seemed no more than a harmless woman with a boy in tow. As they approached the building, Noah saw Little Jug shake and drop someone and then move toward a fallen woman and pick her up. He then turned and stepped toward the woods line. Esther saw the situation almost simultaneously and was about to call Little Jug when Noah shushed and pulled her back. Out of Little Jug's line of sight but clearly within Noah's, a man was crouched and moving steadily toward Little Jug and his burden. The man was carrying a gun.

Noah pushed Esther down and scurried to the left and above the man so that he could come at him from the blind side. It did not occur to him that he was at risk. He was a creature of appetite and instinct seemingly

205

incapable of fear and sensing what he had to do. His were the instincts and savagery of his prehistory ancestors .

Noah bore down on Walsh, at this point the only member of Neary's team not injured. Walsh was in a state of shock over Reinholds and convinced the giant killed him. He never saw anyone so big, never imagined it. He had to shoot him to bring him down. Hadn't Neary known about this man? Dumb question, Walsh thought to himself. There was a whole lot about this situation Neary didn't understand. They were in trouble and had to get out of Gannett. The enraged man was going to kill Little Jug and then take out Neary. He and Kincher might get back to the Bronco and get out of this fuckin' town.

As Walsh bore forward, intent on getting close enough to shoot the giant, Noah jumped on his back and locked his arms around his neck and clamped his teeth at the point where the neck curved into the shoulder. Walsh was shocked. The sonuvabitch was gnawing through muscle and was choking him with arms locked as tight as barrel hoops.

Walsh reached to get a hold on his assailant. His pistol fell from his hands but remained swinging on the lariat attached to his belt. There was surprisingly little noise. Walsh was unable to yell despite his growing desperation. His was operating on the oxygen that remained in his lungs with only seconds before he blacked out.

Had the carotid artery been shut off, Walsh would have been finished. He finally got a handful of hair, dropped forward and attempted to pull his assailant off his back. As he rolled, the assailant's arms loosened enough to enable Walsh to breathe fully, but the bite held. Walsh was now on his back with his assailant beneath him. The arms closed and the strangle grip once again began doing their work. Walsh was in trouble.

In desperation, he placed his hands against the ground and lifted his body, slamming it back hoping that the force of the drop and his weight would dislodge the attacker. It did not. Walsh tried the tactic again out of sheer rage. He knew it was his last chance to break away. In the struggle, both bodies shifted somewhat, and when Walsh raised himself once more, the angle of the drop changed just enough to bring Noah's back down onto a large stone sharp enough to break skin and bruise muscle. Noah loosened his hold.

That was all Walsh needed. He shook the boy loose and broke free. Scurrying to the side, coughing and gasping, ignoring the pain, he focused only on dealing with his assailant before he recovered. He tried getting a hold on his gun while attempting to stand but he placed his foot on the gun, pulling him forward and once again to the ground. The lariat holding the gun tore loose. He instinctively rolled, pulling himself to his hands and knees and moving crab-like to the side as he again attempted to stand. At this point, Noah barreled into him, knocking him over on his back. Noah went for the eyes with his fingernails, but Walsh blocked his arms and threw the boy off to the side.

Noah came back almost as quickly as he was thrown aside, but Walsh, now on his back, unsheathed his knife and drove the blade into the boy's abdomen. The shock totally finished Noah, who dropped across Walsh, his blood and the contents of his bladder spilling on the bigger man.

Walsh pushed him off and got weakly to his feet. He looked around. Little Jug and the girl were out of sight. Walsh, so pumped with adrenalin that he felt no pain, picked up the gun and looked toward the spot he last saw Reinholds. He saw a woman moving away rapidly as Reinholds struggled to his feet.

Reinholds was unsteady and hurting. When he moved, the pain turned into a raging flood crashing against his joints, teeth and head, producing white flashes of agony. He toppled to the ground, then struggled up and stood rooted, unable to move. Walsh, unsteady himself, moved toward Reinholds, happy he was alive. Both were seriously injured. Walsh then felt the pain in his neck and reached back. The movement stretched the bruised tissue around his throat and neck nauseating him as the pain burned into his shoulders. Nothing prepared him for the cavity he found. Noah had torn a sizable chunk of flesh from Walsh's neck. It was bleeding heavily. He needed immediate care, but he had to help his friend first.

Esther was stunned when she realized the bigger man had a knife. She started forward screaming and trying to distract Noah's assailant, but as the knife opened her son's gut, Walsh turned toward her and picked up his gun. Esther turned and ran to find Otha who stood at the jailhouse door with Edom and Joseph. She spoke to him, her voice trembling.

"I fear our little monkey-boy is gone, Otha. He went for a stranger who was fixin' to shoot Little Jug."

"Little Jug in town?"

"Yep, he's toting a woman. Must be his or he nary would bother."

Otha was not one for sentiment. He was preoccupied with the invasion of his town and the losses accompanying it. He lost a son, but he could wait to mourn for him. Esther explained as simply as she could. Otha didn't need details. His job was to get the murdering bastards. "What happened?"

Esther was joined by two women, Erla and Leah, and went through the entire story, including the account of the two strangers and Little Jug's man-handling one of them. She spoke with pride of Noah's saving Little Jug. "I sure did love my little monkey boy. He brought me grief, but he made me laugh mostly.

He had his way with almost every woman in the community. How many times did Otha talk about putting him away? I wouldn't let him. Otha gonna give me the man who killed him."

Otha spoke with the men as the women moved out of sight.

"Well, I don't know who they are, but Jacob Calin would have stopped them if he could. Once I find him, we'll fetch them strangers."

Otha called his men to join him. He quickly formed two armed groups and began the sweep through town. He instructed Esther and Ruth to bring Little Jug and the girl into town. "Them strangers ain't going anywhere without their truck."

CHAPTER 37

5:21 P.M. *Saturday, September 2, 1993*

Abranos and Maddoc gave no thought to anyone being behind them. Dogbone was circling as they moved. The command, "circle" would send the animal off several hundred yards from which he would criss cross the entire area before returning.

Zeb's party was on the move. Maddoc and Abranos remained behind them. There was risk, but with Dogbone along, Zeb and his crew could not circle back on them.

Zeb, Luke, Matthew, Ishmael and Malachai were working their way northwest toward Gannett with Zeb still looking for signs. He couldn't figure the brindle dog, but Bear was gone. If Bear ran into Little Jug and his companions, he would have stayed with them. Zeb continued to deceive himself. He was determined to capture the escapees.

"I knowed they was out here, Luke, and I'm prayin' they stumble into us. They almost did when we was asleep. First I got mad 'cause I figured that you weren't paying enough attention on your watch. Then I got mad 'cause that damned Bear dog run off. I think Bear is with 'em. We find that dog, and we get our prisoners back. Otha's gonna fill with gladness when we bring 'em in. He'll make them pay for killing our kin."

"We ain't got 'em yet. What was the fighting and the growling we heard in the woods?"

"I figure Bear run into that brindle dog and killed him before going on with the others."

"That brindle dog showed no fear of Bear."

Zeb snapped back, "Luke, you don't know nothing. That brindle dog is a flatlander's dog. That dog been sitting around for years. Can't hunt. Can't fight, and is living off his fat. Bear killed him, and the critters are leaving what's left to the worms and bugs."

Usually quiet and uncommunicative, Luke was frustrated. He wanted to strike out at Zeb. The man always had to be right. Luke brooded. He knew Zeb to be a mean sonuvabitch. What he didn't understand was that Zeb was a creature of conditioning. Every beating he got from his pa, every rejection he ever felt and every rebuke Otha and Sam Gubbin laid on him over the years still smoldered within the furnace of his hate.

Zeb was busily cutting and shaping a piece of hickory as he walked along, working it to a width that fit easily in his hand. He let the shavings fall mindful he was marking the trail, remarking they might lure the escapees to follow their path. Luke laughed.

*　　*　　*

7:19 A.M.: Sunday, September 3, 1993

Little Jug moved quickly into the woods carrying Sylvi until she told him to put her down. They covered almost a half mile on the heavily trampled path before she fully recovered. She got her bearings, realizing she was on the wrong side of town and could not intercept her friends. They would lose half an hour circling.

Sylvi didn't know what to do, but it wasn't going to be a fool's journey to intercept Frank. The day was clean and crisp, and Sylvi had no difficulty striking out in another direction. Little Jug, calm now that he realized Sylvi was all right, followed along. Sylvi reasoned she'd not be able to get help from Calin if they fell into Otha's hands.

*　　*　　*

5:37 P.M.: Saturday, September 2, 1993

Zeb was as nervous as a canary in a coal mine. He hurried everyone along, hoping to find the escapees. He promised that when they caught the murderers, he would give them the women to do with as they wished. Despite their recent loses, getting the women got them moving. Zeb was convinced, but Luke saw no promise in it. The others now paid little attention to Zeb, believing he was crazy. So much went bad since they took up pursuit. As to Zeb, he couldn't think straight.

"Starr King Mountain's over there; that make it east and south, so we got to be traveling north," Malachai explained. "If we gonna hit straight on Gannett, we gonna have to bear a mite east. We're more than a mile from Mather's Road, and Zeb ain't gonna walk through that swamp to get there, not after the day him and Jubal got pulled into quick sand. We got climbing head of us."

"We ain't climbing." Luke observed. We ain't catching no one today."

"Why, hell, Luke, that's Zeb's problem. He's wouldn't take old Ludim's word. Ludim would a had them in no time if Zeb weren't so dumb."

"Best not let Zeb hear that. He's already half cracked with fear of what Otha gonna think. If Ludim gets to say his piece first, Zeb be dining with the Devil."

"If we ketch them women, I gonna take one to wife," Ishmael observed. "I lost Letti and the little one in that fire and I gotta claim."

"Yep, Zeb got you thinking as dumb as him. We ain't catching them; and if we do, it'll be a fight. Family or not, Little Jug ain't letting no one touch his woman, and she ain't letting us touch the others. Anyone wanting to shoot Little Jug?"

Luke's reasoning sobered them. Zeb might shoot Little Jug, but Otha would surely kill him if he did. The five of them might bring Little Jug down, but with Sylvi and Little Jug together, they would lose. She had a history that told them what she could do. Their fantasy waned. They asked Luke to talk to Zeb about heading directly to Gannett. Luke refused, but Malachai agreed and went directly to Zeb.

"Zeb, ain't we fixing to run straight to Gannett."

"Can't head straight to Gannett yet. That's the way I was thinking 'til it was them passed near to our camp. We'll circle on our way to Gannett and catch'em."

"You ain't gonna catch them. They too far ahead. If we don't get to Gannett before Ludim, Ludim's story will be the first one Otha hears, and that story ain't about Zeb in any of the good parts."

Zeb could see they had made up their minds, and he needed their support, especially with the story telling. Having initially traveled too far south, they were now five hours from Gannett. If things went as usual, Otha would be there.

"Well, you right about Ludim. Him and Maximillian ain't catched up with us, but they should have. We got light left. We'll fan out but stay in sight. We can meet at the old camp near the fork at Great Brook. If we find no sign, we'll stay the night and swing direct for Gannett in the morning"

*   *   *

7:37 A.M.: Sunday, September 3, 1993

Reinholds needed a doctor. Neary sat in a corner, his shoulders shaking. Walsh functioned, but the pain at the back of his neck was crippling. Kincher, the first of the quartet to go down, was the only fit one. They were concealed in a shed a hundred yards north of the constable's station. The smell of the putrefying remnants of gutted carcasses hung to bleed was nauseating. The shed was dark, foul, and populated with parasites that thrived on the carrion and blood-soaked earth.

The four had stumbled into the best possible refuge. The men searching for them would not open its doors. Hanging and bleeding the kill was women's work. In the woods, the man might gut and bleed a carcass, but when game was brought home intact the women took it to the shed, hung it, removed the innards and the head, and let the carcass bleed.

The men sat on a soft spongy surface sticky with rotting waste. The same insects that would strip an abandoned carcass in a few short days now emerged to feast on living flesh. The men, who were well clothed and booted, found themselves brushing the bugs from their heads, faces and necks, an annoyance but little more. The half-inch black and white carrion beetles were unseen in the dark, but they were felt. They gathered quickly, finding their way in through the cracks that provided the little light. The smaller black beetles were worse but less apparent as the men were preoccupied with their larger kin.

Reinholds lay on the filthy earth and barely had the strength to brush them off, but he had no open wounds. Walsh, who could swipe them easily, could do nothing about those that found their way into his open wound. It was too painful to touch, and the invaders could not be dislodged. Kincher would cauterize the wound once he could build a fire.

Neither Kincher nor Walsh knew what to do with Reinholds. Neary was nominally in charge, but, Reinholds was their leader. Neary did not object to Kincher's taking charge. He examined Reinholds and found that his joints were seriously distended, and he stunk of his own waste. They could do nothing about that. They had to wait until dark to leave the shed. Walsh doubted Neary would be of any use.

Kincher said. "I'll slip out and raise hell with the searchers. I want to get that constable."

Walsh objected. "If we can get the Bronco, we can get to a safe house and a doctor within an hour."

Reinholds spoke. "There no getting the Bronco. They've already disabled it."

Ignoring his pain, Walsh argued, "We got both deputies and aren't better off for it. Right now, everyone is looking, and each one is a threat. We can't get them all."

Kincher answered quickly. "I did more than that on nights in Nam."

"but not in the middle of Hanoi," Walsh shot back at him. "We wait until they stop looking. We aren't getting the Bronco. It's bait now. Not having a back-up was stupid."

"Neary insisted it wasn't necessary," Kincher spit out. "Maybe we steal one of their trucks."

Neary heard his name mentioned and forced himself to listen.

"We can't steal anything. Hell, we have to fight our way out." Kincher remembered the radio. "Neary, you got the transceiver?"

Neary looked up and shook his head 'no.'

"Is it in the truck?"

Neary shrugged.

"Hell, Walsh, that pasty bastard can't help!"

Kincher rejoined, "He can handle a gun."

"This isn't New York. He is out of his element."

*　*　*

9:58 A.M.: Sunday, September 3, 1993

Otha sat with Jacob Calin. "We didn't find a one of 'em. There's four of 'em, you say, Jacob?"

"Four come in, but I ain't certain how many are alive. Mort hit one of 'em afore he died. Neary was hit, but he was still moving when I saw him last. Could be they are down to three. I lost Hezekiah and Mort, and I want these murdering bastards."

"They are in the Lord's hands now. When we get them, we'll see what judgment the Lord has for 'em."

"Otha, What's Neary looking for?"

"Only the Lord knows, Jacob. Sometimes you know so much about your friends they get nervous, thinking about who's telling who what. Revenuers were nosing around in Portsmouth asking about the Van Loos woman, but there weren't nothing to find. They been handling our babies. I don't see no problem. They come to us. Ain't nothing to get nervous about."

"The bastards," Jacob interjected. "I thought Neary's wanting reports was just business and you thought so, too."

"Appears so, but no need for profanity, Jacob. It's something else. Our business with'em been going good. The fight is not of our making, but we'll wait to hear their story before we try and execute them."

*   *   *

4:11 P.M.: Sunday, September 3, 1993

The four were lucky. Otha's men passed the butchering shed. They could be heard looking through the brush and cussing. They had circled the shack several times without stepping in. One opened the door but closed it once the stench hit him. It was the smell of death. That the dead were animals made no difference. Old stories were told of men being locked inside and going mad. Being locked in the butchering shed was a fearsome threat. No clan male would enter it, especially at night. The women had no choice but the butchering was done at daytime.

Kincher returned and announced the search was suspended. It was time to move on. Neary's insisted he lead. He would not have them think him a coward. There seemed no other choice considering that Walsh was the only one who could handle Reinholds' weight and needed Kincher to spell him.

Shaking with pain but able to walk, Neary skulked through the brush fearing an ambush. Kincher was twenty feet behind him while Walsh, assisting Reinholds, trailed an equal distance. Neary was not an outdoors- man. He came into the New Hampshire wilds thinking it would be a holi- day compared to New York. In his years with the NYPD, except for the early years, he went from desk to desk.

To him, New England was a vacationland. The *Times* supplements printed nothing about the bugs and the briars and dangerous law-unto- themselves backwoodsmen. He drove himself forward thinking only of get- ting back to Manhattan. There was no thought of accomplishing what they came to do. He'd rather face Gilletti.

Kincher startled Neary as he sidled up and whispered to him. "There seems to be movement ahead of us." Neary listened carefully. Were Otha's people were still searching? Were they waiting for them to walk into a trap? Neary didn't know but felt he had to speak up.

"Maybe they gave up?"

"Not for long," Kincher replied. "They believe we're lost and are wait- ing for daylight."

"How did they miss us while we hunkered down in that pest hole?"

"The stink was too much. I can't wait to dive into water."

Neary answered, "Oh God, neither can I."

"We all need a bath. I'll move ahead to see if things are clear."

"That's good." Neary, anxious to gain Kincher's trust, approved.

Kincher looked back on his years in Nam, most in the jungle. Walsh, Reinholds and Figueroa had been in different units, but each had reputa- tions. Reinholds was a legend. If he were not injured and Walsh hadn't been hurt, they would get out. Now Kincher had doubts.

He thought about Maddoc and Abranos. Were they on the team, they wouldn't be running. He moved through the woods skillfully. He focused on every oddity, seeking any hint of a trap. By the time he was a quarter mile north of Gannett, there was no activity. Within another quarter mile and they could swing east and find a phone. They had friends and fire power.

But for Neary's stupidity, they could have a helicopter and another six men. Yet he knew each of them failed. No point in blaming Neary. He never served in Nam.

He worked his way back and found Reinholds improved. With support, they were able to move faster. Reinholds believed they could fight their way out.

Walsh's pain didn't slow him down, testimony to his grit; but he was having a bad time with the infection. It was increasingly painful. The beetles added to his discomfort. There was nothing to be done until Kincher could cut away the infected tissue and cauterize the wound. He could not yet build a fire.

It took them thirty minutes to reach the point where Kincher thought they could swing east. Neary believed the search for them was over. Kincher knew better. While reconnoitering earlier, he moved closer to the town. He saw the buildings were being searched. He also saw the Bronco, still sitting, with its door open. Calin was waiting for them to take the bait.

Kincher considered all the dumb moves they made. Neary's ties to Calin were a fantasy. Further, he vetoed routine precautions. Reinholds' failure to challenge him was out of character. They should have replaced Figueroa. As combat veterans under a seasoned commander, they would have entered Gannett after dark, taken over the jail and grabbed control before anyone was awake. Driving into town based upon Neary's egocentricity was stupid.

*　*　*

When the assault broke down and they were on the run, there was no serious pursuit. Once Otha arrived he needed to deal with the families of the dead and the apparent death of his son. The boy was now in the birthing center, not quite as dead as Esther thought.

Otha was confident Calin would get them. "You go ahead and check out the places they might hole up Jacob."

During the confusion, Edom returned to camp with Eve. The girl was in sorry shape, having been severely beaten. Edom knew the entire story, an alcohol-induced rape by three drunken hunters who beat her as she fought.

Ray, their spokesman, stayed out of it, and it fell to him to call in the authorities when the three became murderous over who was next. Two died, and the third was in custody. Edom found the girl hiding in a culvert. He was disappointed that he couldn't exact his own justice. Once the police cleared out, it took Edom less than ten minutes to find Eve. She had broken ribs and was cut and bruised. The townswomen would clean her up before taking her home.

Once Otha knew the girl was alive, his attention turned to the late model Chrysler Edom stole to return to Gannett.

"We'll get something for it in Jefferson" Otha observed. "We can take care of any unfinished business with that Ray fellow come next year." The girl's parents would be compensated and a marriage arranged. She can't be serving men no more. No matter, we got a passel of good ones back in camp."

Less than thirty minutes had passed when Calin reported that Neary and the murderers were a quarter mile north of town. Calin wanted to go after them. Let's think on it, Jacob. They can't run far. Don't know this country well 'nuff. You need to help with cleaning up. There are bodies to bury and people to console." He turned away and spoke to Edom.

"Edom, I need you to go hunting with me. We be getting on with it at dawn. Get some eating and sleep a spell. Then you and me go catch them varmints what killed Mort and Hezzie and cut up my boy Noah. Doubt if he will live through the night. We'll take Little Jug."

Edom, who didn't miss much, commented, "Little Jug's gone."

CHAPTER 38

5:37 P.M. *Saturday, September 2, 1993*

Major Calvin Cadwell Withers thought through his most recent call from Harrington. The man wanted to be rid of the prisoners. Withers told him to let them go, which he knew Harrington would not do. He called in Lip Caruthers, a gnarly old bastard who should have retired fifteen years earlier but was grandfathered in. Lip always got in the last word, even with Colonel Smith; thus, his name. He was cantankerous but not contentious. As a sergeant major with forty-plus years, few challenged him, even when he behaved in ways that would give anyone else a quick exit. The years showed in his face, but he had not grayed and at 66 was physically tough.

"Shirl," – Lip's given name was Shirley, one reason why everyone else called him Lip, "I want you to take a car north and report what you see." He shuffled papers around, pulling out a brief report. "Apparently those three hunters were fighting over a woman. Two died, one's charged. The woman disappeared. She might have been one of Otha Gubbin's people. Drive through and take a look-see. Take a couple of men along."

"Okay, Cad. Anything specific you're looking for?"

"If you run into Harrington, he has a couple of prisoners you can take off his hands."

"What's that about?"

"He'll explain. Tell him I'll call him once I bring the colonel up to date."

"On what?"

"Talk to Harrington."

"You're not getting me in trouble are you, Cad?"

218

"Nothing you can't do for yourself."

Withers didn't like being addressed as Cad any more than Lip liked being addressed as Shirl. It was a running jest. The major waved him off.

Withers had an interest in Gubbin's operation. The people from New York contracted him to keep sight of their interests. Things were going well. Once the Maddoc girl disappeared, everything changed. He called his commander, Colonel Smith, to let him know what he should have revealed months earlier.

"You're telling me you were being compensated by people in New York?"

"That's about it. It was a part time job. It did not involve my normal working hours."

"Bull shit. It involved your office and its influence. You break that off immediately! It's time you sit down and write your resignation. You have enough time in."

You made a mistake that could have you facing charges. I don't want you facing charges. You are to say nothing more about it. Have your papers to me tomorrow." He hung up the phone.

Withers called him back. "I'll have my papers to you as soon as we resolve this Maddoc business."

"It better be resolved damn soon." Smith hung up.

Withers planned to quit anyway. The job wasn't fun anymore. Early in his career, he thought he might make it to the top, but Smith was younger.

Withers called Harrington. "I'm retiring Al.

"When?"

After we finish this current business. I'm ready to hang it up. I have the time in and Jean wants me home. The grand kids are in New Mexico, and she wants to see the Grand Canyon."

"I'd like to see the Grand Canyon, myself."

* * *

8:57 A.M.: Sunday, September 3, 1993

Frank, Marlene, Josie, Peter and Sandy emerged from the woods and saw Gannett with its roofs and outbuildings. They sang as they entered Gannett.

Almost immediately, they found themselves in Otha Gubbin's custody. Otha spoke to Peter and got the full story, including the roles played by Little Jug and Sylvi. Otha, wanting to see Zeb and the others, sent a runner to the camp. Sylvi and Little Jug couldn't be far away.

Otha called Erla. "I want you and Joseph to put these folks where they'll be comfortable. No need to have Jacob nosing around."

The runaways were locked in rooms in the infirmary cellar. As Marlene's eyes adjusted to the light, she saw a toilet bowl, small sink, a cot and blanket, and a single chair. The cellar was dry and warm. In the early days, these rooms served as the community lockup.

Within an hour, Otha and Erla showed up. Erla told Marlene to disrobe. She balked. Erla displayed a riding crop and said, "I kin whip'em off, and you be naked either way." She disrobed, glad for the dim light though she knew both were examining her closely. Marlene had lost weight and firmed up since Otha and Erla had last seen her.

She ain't pregnant," Erla remarked.

"Didn't 'spect she would be. "We have to decide whether we keep her or ship her off."

Erla voted to ship her off. Otha hedged. "We expected good stock from this one." We'll wait a bit. We be out of new babies real quick if we don't keep our breeders."

Irked, suspecting Otha's real intentions Erla raised the crop to strike Marlene. Otha anticipate Erla's intent and blocked her arm just as she swung, diverting the blow but not preventing it from striking a glancing blow off Marlene's breast. Marlene struck back, knocking the older woman to the cell floor. Otha shoved Marlene aside, but he didn't offer Erla any help. She struggled to her feet, holding her hand to her cheek, which was showing signs of bruising and swelling.

"Otha, I gonna teach this bitch not to strike her betters."

"Nay, Erla, nay. If I leave you with her, she'll kill you. She hit you because you hit her. You had no cause."

Erla believed Otha was thinking about taking Marlene to wife. He didn't say so, but she was the first of seven, and now that the seventh, Naomi, was with Maximillian, he wanted a younger woman.

Otha's wives answered to Erla and, but for Esther, were intimidated. Esther was the only friend Erla had. None of Otha's wives had been able to give him an heir. Esther's boy, Noah, wasn't right in the head.

Marlene would not submit to Erla. She was a city girl with her city ways. If she had a normal boy-child, Erla would not simply fall a notch; she would drown in the neglect that followed. Of all Otha's wives, Erla was the thinker, but she was no match for Marlene. Marlene was standoffish and could be a problem.

Marlene believed she and her friends would be marched back to the camp. She wondered about Sylvi and Little Jug. Wherever they were, they were the last chance. This was no time to be anything but contrite.

She spoke, head lowered, voice very subdued and respectful. "I'm sorry, Miss Gubbin; I didn't mean to hit you. I'm sorry. I reacted wrongly. I'm sorry."

Otha was pleased. Erla remained cool, but her anxiety eased. She believed she could maneuver Marlene and create doubt in Otha. When it came to the flesh, Otha was a fool, but he was a suspicious fool. Erla would use that.

Otha spoke next. "If you agree to stay put, you can move into the house."

Marlene had no idea what he meant by the house, but she knew it meant something better. It might get her to a telephone.

*   *   *

5:12 P.M.: Sunday, September 3, 1993

Sylvi was flagging. She was moving for hours with no sign of civilization. Little Jug, who was following behind, stepped to her side so quietly she was startled. She was deep in thought, fretting over her friends. He looked down on her with as big a grin as he could muster. He laughed, something she seldom heard from him. She felt his love and loved him, knowing he would protect her with his life.

Her friends were now in Gannett. She had to reach the authorities. She retraced her steps to a worn path she crossed earlier. Little Jug followed her.

They found a trail and followed it for little more than an hour. Dusk was falling, and she urged Little Jug along. Inexplicably, Little Jug stopped moving. He heard something and seemed transfixed. It was seconds before Sylvi heard the noise, too. It was a distant barking breaking the silence of the falling night.

The unmistakable sound of dogs was directly in front of them. Once he heard it, Little Jug began to race forward, the call of the dogs a joy to him, as alluring as sirens enticing men to watery graves. Sylvi followed behind him.

The barking drew closer. Little Jug, well ahead of her, stopped and held out his arms. In the now dim light, a small animal hurled itself into Little Jug's arms, and Little Jug sat right where he stopped. Sylvi reached him in seconds. When she saw the dog on Little Jug's lap, she understood.

Sylvi had not counted on Cha, Little Jug's name for this still frisky beagle. Little Jug's earliest pet, they were inseparable until she was taken from him to be trained. He was allowed to visit her every day. Sylvi had to get Little Jug to his feet, even if he had to take the dog with him.

Sylvi could see her pursuers racing toward them. She was checkmated. The conditioning she turned to her advantage, now worked against her. Little Jug was allowed to hold Cha only while sitting. She was unable to get him to his feet.

She tried talking as she tried to take the dog from him; but he sat. As she turned to leave, Ishmael Corday and Zebediah Doody faced her. She turned to Little Jug. He saw no threat. These were his friends. Cha was his friend. Sylvi was his friend.

"Don't ask Li'l Jug for help!" Zeb barked. "If he tries to help you, we'll kill him on the spot."

Sylvi said nothing.

"Maybe we should kill him anyway," Ishmael interjected. "He's trouble if he thinks she's being hurt, and I'm awanting to own this one."

"I might let you try, but there be rules. You take her off into the woods without your rifle and your knife and if you both come back with smiles, she's yours."

Ishmael had no intention of dealing with Sylvi alone, even with a knife in his waistband. He knew what happened to Eban. Micah was almost deaf since she beat on him. She was a devil. Otha said that the 'Devil' would have helped her beat Little Jug, too, if Little Jug hadn't been pure in heart.

"Shit, I ain't gonna fight her for it. The woman ain't human, but when we're all sitting around the fire thinking of what to do with ourselves, we vote."

"Ain't gonna be no vote. This bitch burnt up all our families; and she's gonna pay. She'll tell us where the rest of 'em are, and we get them and head for Gannett. Otha's there now. When he knows what she done, he'll let us do whatever we want with her. Then you and the others can pleasure yourselves with her long as you want, but Otha gonna put the torch to her. While you're diddling, I be stacking wood."

"Li'l Jug will kill you if you touch her."

"Li'l Jug ain't gonna be around. He'll be off in the woods doing exactly what Otha says while the rest of us roast the bitch."

Deep in thought, Sylvi heard only part of Zeb's accusations. Had she heard, she would not have absorbed it. Zeb's lies and fantasies were commonplace.

She did not react visibly, even as Ish sidled up and cupped her breast. She ignored him. She could not afford to set Little Jug off. She needed time to work out her next move. She did not fear being assaulted. She had bigger concerns.

They cursed her, claiming she set a fire. She did not deny it. She was too deep in thought.

"Tomorrow we get the others and make our way to Gannett with prisoners" We'll give them and this she-Devil to Otha."

Sylvi's chances were not much better with Otha than with Zeb, but Otha would listen.

*   *   *

CHAPTER 39

9:21 A.M.: *Saturday, September 2, 1993*

Maddoc and his party were moving, increasingly confident after the first full sleep they had since touching down.

They planned to enter Gannett late Sunday afternoon in force. Colonel Smith and his troop would intercept them within the hour.

Maddoc was on point when he crossed Zeb's well-marked trail. Scattered wood shavings and other signs were a composition waiting to be read. "'Ey, Gato, what do you think?

"Our friends and their dogs, perhaps?"

"How far ahead of us?"

"Caleb, you've been reading the same sign I have." Maddoc snapped. "

He answered, "Of course, amigo, but how I am to know you haven't lost your touch. You are no longer *le fantôme de diable.*"

Maddoc's mood lightened. "No, Caleb, not by a long shot; and you are not El Gato either. Could either of us do today what we did in Nam? I guess I'm losing patience. One moment I'm sure Sylvi's nearby, another moment I think I'm fooling myself. Dispénsame, por favor."

Abranos laughed loudly. "Excuse you? Ciertamente. None know what is ahead. Que será, será, but I am confident that Sylvia Maddoc sleeps easy tonight."

"Thanks," Maddoc responded offhandedly. "Those we chase may have stopped for the night."

"Do we care?"

"My guess is they're headed for Gannett. Let's hear what Harrington thinks. If so, we come in directly behind them. That suits me."

"They could be following us"

"And squirrels grow roses. Our little rat has not said much, but his mood has shifted. He's expecting his friends to step in and save his ass."

Abranos looked toward Dogbone. "They cannot surprise us with Flea Bite here."

"Do not insult Dogbone. He gets testy."

Abranos laughed. Dogbone growled softly.

*   *   *

8:47 A.M.: *Sunday, September 3, 1993*

Walsh was feverish. Neary's leg was swelling and itching. Kincher would not let him remove his boot. Neary, not knowing that parasitic beetles found their way into his boot, insisted something was eating his foot. Kincher didn't care. His concern was with his friends. He doubted Walsh would survive without help. Reinholds was improving. A few weeks in bed and physical therapy would bring him back.

After they traveled little more than a half mile, Kincher let them rest, a decision he regretted as he tried to get Neary to move. He and his friends called upon the grit they built in the South Asian jungles. Neary had nothing.

He threatened Neary, "We left two or three people dead back there. If they catch up with us, we're dead."

"I can't move, you sonuvabitch. You screwed us when you attacked my friend Jacob."

Neary hadn't seen a thing. He did not understand that Calin caught on as soon as he saw them.

"Okay, Inspector. You stay here. We'll come back for you."

"Wait! You can't leave me here alone!"

"We are going for help. We'll reach someone within an hour. Once we do, we'll call in a 'copter and get you to a hospital."

"All right, but if you fuck it up, Kincher, I'll have your ass."

Walsh and Kincher moved Neary to a knoll where he was comfortably set up with a clear view of the trail. He was armed with an Uzi and his knife.

They moved back. Reinholds was completely concealed beneath a large spruce, its lower branches touching the ground. They climbed under its canopy. Kincher explained that Neary was sitting on a knoll, exposed but confident he was safe.

After hearing Walsh's explanation, Reinholds said. "Put a gun to Neary's head and tell him to move. If he's taken he'll run his mouth off."

Walsh didn't argue. Failing was one thing. Exposing the client was another.

If necessary, Walsh would carry Neary.

They found him asleep, and Kincher stepped on his swollen foot.

Neary awoke with a scream, attempting to rise but tripping over himself. He sputtered,

"Who the fuck stepped on me?"

"You were asleep. You didn't cover for us, you bastard."

"I was awake. I was awake!" I closed my eyes for a second to clear my head. I knew you were here. I knew you were here! I'll have your ass for this Kincher!"

We need to rethink our plan. Reinholds wants you back."

"My plan is the plan. " Neary insisted.

"No problem, Inspector; that's why we need you. You, Walsh, and Reinholds can rest while I clear the back trail and find help."

The two men pulled Neary to his feet and pushed him along despite his complaints. He made no attempt to help himself. When they got back to the tree, Reinholds was gone.

* * *

9:44 A.M.: Sunday, September 3, 1993

Harrington kept Ludim and Maximilian under tight security. Ludim's situation was desperate. He could not explain anything away. He and Eban raped Josie, and Josie's girlfriend got away. If charged and convicted, he would spend the rest of his life in prison.

226

They were on a direct line to Gannett. Otha will be there, and these city slickers will get a proper welcoming. He laughed at Zeb's arriving there first. How would he explain the escape. How would he explain not catching them and leaving the women and children unprotected. He thought, *I have the answers, and Zeb doesn't have one friend.*

When questioned by Harrington, Ludim was fully cooperative as he laid everything at Zeb's feet. Ludim hoped to gain Harrington's confidence.

He also hoped for a chance to break away; but with that dog around, it seemed impossible. When Bear first appeared, his hopes climbed. He'd kill the smaller dog, but Bear disappeared.

The flatlanders had no idea of what they were walking into. If luck was on Ludim's side and he played his cards right, he might come out of the mess looking good.

CHAPTER 40

Kincher felt the hair rising on the back of his neck. Walsh's head turned in every direction. Neary's reaction was maddening.

"Reinholds ran off and took his guns. I knew he would cut out the first time things got rough. All of you are no fuckin' good. If I had brought three of my finest up here, we would be dining on Otha Gubbin's dumb ass tonight. Instead, that guinea bastard Gilletti sends you clowns."

Sick as he was, Walsh would have killed Neary on the spot, but as Neary slowed down, Gubbin sidled up to him soundlessly and remarked, "Dine on my ass, eh? I thought about it and thought, 'My ass's too tough for you, Mr. Inspector.'"

Neary blanched, turned toward Gubbin and wet his pants. He started blubbering, claiming he was Otha's friend and tried to prevent the others from invading Gannett. He named Gilletti, claiming the man feared Otha would implicate him in the baby business. Gubbin listened. Neary wound down to a whisper, as though Gubbin's confidante, drawing him out of earshot of Walsh and Kincher

"These men came to subvert you. When I tried to tip off Jacob Calin, one of them shot me. I am their prisoner."

Finally, he stopped talking. Otha was amused.

"Subbbverrrt," he sang, drawing out each syllable. "That's a real fancy word for a dumb bastard like old Otha to understand. I sure appreciate you looking out for my interests, Mr. Policeman. You came back and showed your true self to this ignorant mountain man, but I ain't no fool. You made me a prophet.

228

Neary fell and lay on the ground sobbing, his anguish taking over. It is doubtful he heard anything more; his last desperate lie failed.

Walsh and Kincher remained silent, neither fearing Otha's arrival. They experienced equally tight situations in Nam. They would act with one mind, but Edom's rifle hung easily in his hand.

* * *

Gilletti looked back upon the moment he failed. His meeting with Gubbin a year earlier was happenstance. He liked the man, respected his native intelligence and his fundamental Christian values.

"Bram, as I recall, the initial contact with the man was during our holiday in New Hampshire some time back. When he claimed he had a "baby farm," as he characterized it, you encouraged him to get into the business."

"I was humoring him. It seemed a pipe dream. Who could have anticipated what he has achieved? He does not seem to be in it for the money. He solemnly claims "We are in it for our souls.""

"Remaining silent, Gilletti thought back, ...*my mistake was approving the hiring of Jonetta Van Loos. We had a blue chip board overseeing our operations. Van Loos marginalized them. What led me to agree to Michael Chen's nomination to replace Phillips? I knew of her and Chen's history. That should have been enough. That was enough to reject her nomination but courtesy prevailed. Back in the day I would have smelled a rat."*

Breaking the silence, he responded, "Bram, who gave it any thought? It seemed a pipe dream under those circumstances. The idea of an uneducated backwoodsman doing such is absurd, but history tells us that we must not dismiss the thoughts of a man who has a vision."

"Now I see that I made the mistake of disregarding Rubino's involvement. That was the pivotal moment, a moment I now regret, but I had no hint of Van Loos and Rubino's treachery."

I'm getting too old for all of this, he mused. *It will soon be past us.*

* * *

Gubbin looked down at Neary's leg and intoned,
"Look's like you have a problem."

He reached down and cut the laces on Neary's boot. The boot spread open from the press of the swollen flesh, and Gubbin kicked it off, drawing a scream. Neary's foot and leg were swollen to almost twice normal size, the sock soaked with blood and the skin red, yellow and purple.

Gubbin cut off the sock. He took his blade and made a quick cut in the heel, opening a wound that burst with yellow and green pus, the accumulation unusual considering the few hours that had passed since Neary was hurt. Neary cries diminished to whimpers as the expulsion of pus relieved his pain.

Gubbin pointed to a pronounced bump midway between the injured heel and the ball of Neary's foot. Another flick of Gubbin's razor-sharp blade and the bump opened. A little coaxing from Otha, and a beetle, about three-sixteenths of an inch climbed out of the opening. It was fattened and slow, enabling Otha to pick it up and pinch it between his fingers..

"Yep, these little suckers sure take holt. Eat a deer carcass in a day and a half, more or less. Favor carrion, but they pretty happy with any open wound, 'specially one that's festering. My guess, Mr. Commander, is that you got more than a dozen of these little suckers eating your foot, and there ain't nothing you can do."

Turning away, he looked at Walsh. "That hole my boy Noah bit in your shoulder ain't much better. My guess is them bugs will get into your innards long afore they hit the Inspector's. It ain't a nice way to die, but we all die one way or t'other."

Otha didn't understand much about the carrion beetles. They seldom went after living flesh, the body's own defenses usually were enough to keep them at bay. Walsh's situation, despite Otha's predictions, was better than Neary's. His wound was closer to vital organs; the body's management system understood this and launched a vigorous defense.

Neary's case was one of the exceptions. The strain of the past 30 hours burdened his immune system. Further, they all were exposed to infectious bacteria. Neary's foot was not a high priority. When Otha Gubbin teased out the beetle dining under Neary's skin, he exposed its level of morbidity. Without treatment soon, Neary could lose his leg. He might die.

As Otha motioned to Walsh and Kincher to move down the trail, Joseph asked about Neary. "What about that one? He gonna run?"

"Can't run far with that foot, but I suppose there's no need to take the chance. Of course, we could let him go. He would die in the woods, but that won't bring no satisfaction." At this, Joseph leaned over Neary and quickly cut through his healthy Achilles heel; the blade cut cleanly through the tendons. Neary passed out.

Edom looked to the others. "Want to hobble them, Otha?"

"Think not. They can't run anywhere now. They'll come to judgment when they're fit enough."

They moved to a clearing. Walsh and Kincher then realized that Otha and his two killers had anticipated their moves and were waiting.

Reinholds was tied at legs and knees, arms and elbows, unnecessary given his condition. Four ropes swayed easily from a heavy branch, its further end having bridged and bonded to an opposing tree.

Kincher and Walsh were on their knees. Joseph stood back training his gun on them while Edom secured them as he had Reinholds. Walsh was the first to be hanged. His shoes were removed, and his feet were allowed to touch the ground. Yanking him up brought a perceptible moan but no scream in spite of the pull on his damaged shoulder.

"Tough one," Otha commented with respect.

Kincher was next, followed by Reinholds. Neither made a sound although Reinholds experienced a renewal of the pain inflicted by Little Jug. Edom emptied their pockets and removed their shoes. He turned over a money belt taken from Reinholds.

"Shame we have to get rid of you fellows," Otha said. "You being so generous, but we lost two of our men and a fine boy may follow. You have to pay for that. But I thank you for this heap of money. It'll go to their kinfolks."

Edom fetched Neary, who screamed as he was dragged over the broken terrain. He was strung up alongside the others, though tied only at the wrists. His feet also touched the ground, causing excruciating pain. He evacuated, adding to everyone's discomfort. Otha chuckled.

"Now, Mr. Inspector, need not get all heated up. We ain't gonna leave you here. Me and Joseph gonna get back to Gannett and send the women, kinfolks of them what you killed. They're fine women. They'll bring what-

231

ever is left when they done with you back to Gannett for a trial and a Christian burial."

Edom remarked "Looks to me this one's gonna bleed to death afore the women get back for them."

"Could be, I suppose, but it should slow down a bit."

*   *   *

12:03 P.M.: Sunday, September 3, 1993

Marlene grew confident during her first hours in Gannett. She had company wherever she went, and was seldom free of Erla's scrutiny; but she made friends. When she met Rebekah she learned that the girl believed that following Otha was what God wanted of her. She explained the larger picture.

"Otha's gonna marry me but I know he is bound to you. He says we have to wait a decent time after you get pregnant with his son."

"Otha told you he and I are going to be married?" Marlene asked.

"Not in words, but when I asked him if it was you, he smiled. You know Otha. Are you so surprised he'd tell me?"

Marlene thought it wasn't the right moment for a disclaimer.

"Well, I'm not surprised really," I thought Otha was still trying to decide whether he would marry you or me first."

"That's what he said. He said it was more proper to marry you first because you're older and you came first. Otha likes to keep everything proper. I don't mind. I'm already part of the family."

"Well, if you want to marry him first," Marlene offered, "I'll release him from his promise to me."

"No, no. I don't think Otha would like it if he knew we'd talked it over. I shouldn't have said anything," she responded nervously.

"No need to worry. It's between you and me; but Otha isn't telling me much. I hate surprises, don't you?"

"I sure do. All the surprises in my life was painful." My mom died, and I was left with my pap and my brothers. After that, well, you know."

Marlene didn't know, but she could imagine. "I can guess. I hope you'll keep talking to me though, especially about Otha's plans. Like every man, he can't appreciate what a girl has to do to get ready for her wedding."

232

"Ain't that the truth. He thinks getting married isn't much to fuss about. It's what follows that's important, and I already know what follows with Otha. I know I have to share him with his other wives, but I don't mind."

Marlene smiled, increasing the intimacy between them. She learned much from the talkative Rebekah. She was now sixteen years old and had come to idolize Otha as God's prophet. Until Otha, every man she met beginning with her father when she was eleven and her three brothers had beat her and passed her around.

At thirteen, Rebekah found herself in a small house outside of Portsmouth servicing men. Her father hit upon the idea after her mother died. He stopped letting her go to school. The men she satisfied thought she was older.

Rebekah broke away one night with a young man who, after his first sexual experience, was smitten. He had a car, and Rebekah convinced him to take her north. They ended up in Laconia and spent a week in a fleabag hotel. Then he ran out of money and went back to work, professing his love and promising that he'd come back in a week. Within a nine days, she was on the streets that brought her to Otha.

It was not surprising that Rebekah clung to Otha. He was a father who cared for his child.

The insight Marlene gained through Rebekah should have told her enough, but her sighting of Frank emphasized it. It looked to Marlene that Frank was their Judas, and Sylvi's precautions, which Marlene had considered overly dramatic, now were clear.

Here was Frank, recognized by everyone, and seemingly at home. He knew the geography. Had he led them to Gannett by design? Yet, Marlene reasoned, I am free to move around, also. I could be wrong. He spoke of having hiked throughout this part of the state for many years. He had been to Gannett, the closest community to their impound. He led them directly into Gubbin's stronghold.

Yet he didn't expose their escape plans. Marlene didn't know what to believe.

* * *

233

CHAPTER 41

6:17 P.M.: *Sunday, September 3, 1993*

Once within Zeb's hands, Little Jug and Sylvi were trussed up. Zeb worried about Little Jug and told Sylvi that she either directed Little Jug to accept the ropes or they would shoot his legs out from under him. With Ish and Matthew positioned to do so she agreed, not knowing that neither would shoot Little Jug.

For Little Jug, there was no issue of submission. Sylvi herself put the ropes around his wrists and ankles, tying them as directed. He was disturbed more by Zeb's demeanor than Sylvi's tying him. She calmed him, not showing any discomfort with Zeb. Zeb then secured her as Matthew turned Little Jug out of sight. Little Jug's arms were pinned to his side with quarter inch hemp rope and the ropes were removed from his ankles, freeing him to walk. Within a short time, they were concealed in a wooded camp, smaller but not unlike the one they had escaped. Only the pilings reflecting former cabins remained. Zeb was ready to move on but met resistance. His men needed to rest and eat. He asked their opinions and they agreed the morning would be soon enough to face Otha.

Sylvi and Little Jug were held close together, Sylvi, uncomfortably bound hand and foot, sat without any back support. She lay down, hoping to work into a comfortable position to give her back a rest. She was tired and anxious. As a child whenever she was upset she coped by crying quietly before falling to sleep which still served her well. Little Jug, just as he had ever since she came into his life, worked his way over to get closer to her.

*   *   *

4:28 P.M.: *Sunday, September 3, 1993*

Caleb Abranos and Anthony Maddoc were talking when Harrington joined them.

He complained, "The plan was to have the prisoners picked up, but I'm losing hope. They should be gone by now.

Maddoc responded. "We're not far from those fellows whose trail we crossed yesterday."

Abranos chimed in, "I'm thinking I should circle and get ahead of them. It may not mean much, but it can't hurt."

"Why now?" Maddoc asked. "We have less than three hours of daylight."

"That is true, my friend, but we have not gained an edge, and I got that thing happening."

Maddoc got it. He understood it in the jungles of Nam. He experienced it on the streets of New York. Abranos had to move on, and there was no reason to deny him. They decided he should reconnoiter Gannett, instead. Before he left, Maddoc took out a worn and tattered stuffed animal from his pack.

"¿Que es eso?" Caleb asked.

Maddoc was silent for a moment. Caleb knew the raggedy toy Maddoc held was important. Harrington watched.

"When Sylvi was a little girl," he replied, "this was her sleepy toy. She wouldn't go to bed without it and didn't allow her mother to wash it. It was hers. She didn't chew on it. She wouldn't take it outdoors, except on long trips. She simply held it when she was going to sleep. She took it with her when she left for college. It has many years of her touch incorporated in its threads. Marie kept it well repaired, including the odd button eye, and handed it to her when she left for college.

"Before Marie returned to the hospital, she looked everywhere for it, forgetting that Sylvi had it. She cried once she realized it was gone. She wanted a small piece of her baby with her should she pass on. I thought the therapy had taken her mind, but now I understand. This was, in its way, as much a part of Sylvi's life as we were, and Marie wanted a bit of it back."

"How's there to know, amigo?"

"Through faith, my friend. Intelligence and faith."

Maddoc called Dogbone to him. He placed the bear to the dog's nose and then dropped it on the ground. There was no way to know what was going on in this remarkable dog's mind. He probed the bear with his nose, stepped back, circled it, and then came at it from another direction. He sniffed every inch of it again, imprinting in whatever coding system nature gave him, every pheromone embedded in its threads. He then picked it up and dropped it at Maddoc's feet. Maddoc placed it carefully in his backpack.

The dog stepped away and began crisscrossing the trail that Zeb and his bunch had traveled, checking every sign until he was satisfied. He then came back, sniffed at the ground where the bear had been, and wandered away.

This was evidence enough to assure Maddoc that Sylvi was not with that bunch.

"You believe that dog could get a scent off a rag?

Maddoc laughed, something not recently heard from this dour man. "You know he can, Caleb."

Abranos struck out northwest intending to see Gannett early afternoon and return after nightfall. He traveled fast, the woods of New Hampshire not so challenging as the jungles of Nam. There was little chance he would run into anything he couldn't handle. He was armed and with his night googles could see in the dark.

Harrington and Maddoc continued their course with Harrington pushing his prisoners along but slowed. Once an hour along, Maddoc stopped to let Harrington catch up. He gave little thought to the dog; he would show up when he chose. Maddoc was confident there would be no surprises. El Gato would study Gannett and return with ideas on how to take over. Dogbone would ensure that Maddoc and Harrington could sleep without any chance of being surprised. Their comrades were closing the distance, planning to assemble for the meeting with Colonel Smith. They would camp before nightfall and get some sleep before meeting Smith in the morning ... if he remained on schedule.

*   *   *

236

6:49 P.M.: *Sunday, September 3, 1993*

Dogbone moved noiselessly through the woods seeking a scent unique to Sylvia Maddoc. Somehow he knew he was to find Sylvia.

His behavior was based upon two simple facts: the first is that as dogs go, Dogbone was high on the intelligence scale, a mongrel whose intelligence was derived from animals bred over the years to work and fight. The second is that Dogbone was marvelously well trained. Once with Maddoc, he took to the training easily and showed no sign, during the progressively more difficult program, of reaching any limits. Add sound instincts, and as dogs go Dogbone was near perfect.

Less than an hour into his search, Dogbone came upon the camp occupied by Zeb, Luke, Matthew, Ishmael and Malachai. As he grew close, he grew excited, a response to a scent very new to him. He circled the encampment, the cooking of the remaining deer meat a mild distraction. He came upon Sylvi and Little Jug. He grew excited and began to lick her face. Sylvi was immediately awake, initially startled by the slimy assault but recognizing it as a dog. Without questioning what she felt, Sylvi was calmed by the dog's gentleness.

Usually young women adore their fathers; Sylvi was no exception. He was a good man. He let her mother worry about the female things, not talking to her about what she did as a girl or young woman. He challenged her behavior, but he did not challenge her thoughts or ideas. Her thoughts and ideas represented a developing mind; her behavior reflected her values. Her father didn't interfere. He taught her to use her hands. He involved her in strength training assuring she would be the equal of most men, capacity that she never demonstrated. Having it was sufficient in itself. Marie complained that he was treating her like a boy but demurred when he said simply that his daughter should know who she was and what she could do as an adult. It had nothing to do with her gender.

Marie taught her about the birds and the bees and the behavior of excitable young men toward women. She taught her to cook, as well. Maddoc taught her how to control a male in any situation. She learned more about fighting than about cooking.

Although she adored her mother, she thought of her father when she was stressed. His teaching enabled her to survive. Her mother's love allowed her to accept and love others. The dog was a mystery; but when it pushed her and looked at her, it was her father who came to mind. At that moment her fear left.

*　　*　　*

7:07 P.M.: *Sunday, September 3, 1993*

They found no sign of anyone else, but Zeb was sure once they had Little Jug and Sylvi the others were nearby. Earlier, Zeb was anxious to get his team moving toward Gannett. He wasn't as anxious to face Otha, and feared Ludim's getting to Otha before he did. Not fully familiar with the area, he could not know Gannett was less than three hours away. Now encamped he accepted that arriving there with Sylvi and Little Jug would have to do.

Dogbone trotted through the camp passing Zeb and the others as they sat eating. "It's that big brindle dog again. I guess Bear didn't get him," Luke said with satisfaction. Luke called to him, but he kept moving.

"Still a bone skinny dog," Zeb countered. "No match for Bear. Probably been following us hoping to get some vittles; he's too late now. He'll follow right into Gannett, Luke, and you can have him."

Dogbone was out of sight by the time they finished their little exchange. Luke fancied what it would be like to have such a dog in good fighting trim. Ten pounds on him and a little exercise to muscle him up, and he'd be fine. Probably too old to train as a hunter, but he would be a good pet. Luke took comfort in the thought of having that dog.

The dog circled back to where Sylvi lay thinking about him. He dropped next to her and placed his head on his paws. The night was beginning to chill, and the heat of the dog's body provided warmth. They both slept. More than an hour passed before the dog quietly slipped away.

Dogbone raced toward Maddoc, reaching him just as he emerged from his sleeping bag, dressed and readied for the trail. "We must be getting close, Harrington. He wouldn't be so nervous otherwise."

Maddoc's inference was correct. Dogbone came back to alert him. He went to Maddoc and blocked his movement. He leaped several times,

238

impeding Maddoc's progress, and then rapidly circled him, as if to turn him around. Maddoc never had seen such behavior from Dogbone and didn't know how to respond. He called him to heel, a command the dog never ignored but now refused. He told him to stay, but the dog kept moving around him. Maddoc couldn't understand.

Finally, Dogbone crashed into the back of Maddoc's legs at his knees, knocking Maddoc forward on to the ground. He went after Maddoc's backpack, grabbing it in his great jaws and not releasing it, forcing Maddoc to slip it off as he got to his feet.

"What is it, you crazy dog? What are you trying to tell me?"

Dogbone was worrying that pack to death, shaking it, dropping it and picking it up to shake again. Maddoc pulled it from him and dumped the contents in front of the dog. In the next instant, too fast to be anticipated, Dogbone had Sylvi's tired bear in his teeth. He took two steps to Maddoc and dropped it at his feet. Maddoc was stunned, the breath caught in his throat, his senses reeling with what the dog had just told him. Sylvi was alive, and Dogbone had found her.

CHAPTER 42

1:09 P.M.: *Sunday, September 3, 1993*

E dom led the women to Neary and the others. The entourage included Esther, Martha Clagger, and Maud Simpson, the nearest kin to the victims and three other women who were related.

The ritual was well-established. Each man would be beaten in turn, the closest relatives having the first round. They would not be beaten to death. Otha wanted them to stand trial in Gannett for their crimes, something not seen since Reverend Manzlicher, an itinerant preacher, murdered Jobidiah Dick. That trial lasted almost twenty minutes with Otha as the judge and Jacob Calin as the prosecutor and chief witness.

Reverend Manzlicher was found guilty and pleaded for his life claiming, "the Devil came upon me and made of me a sinner. He stole my faith. I have prayed for absolution. The Lord has forgiven me. I beg you to do the same."

Otha, as judge, said, "I prayed, also, Reverend, and an angel came and said you are a lying, fornicating, murdering bastard who serves Ole Beelzebub."

The reverend was hanged.

The women were in no hurry. They talked of what they could or could not do short of killing the men. Esther suggested they take the time to cut hickory branches. "If you look around, you should find a felled oak or pine that'll provide fine barbs for the sticking." The women soon had everything they needed, and they broke into pairs, each of which took turns beating the men. They had no idea who was guilty of the killings.

They started with Neary who was stripped naked to the delight of the women. They made certain he was conscious by jabbing him with a sharp stick. He grunted with pain, and when they began beating him, he cried, his carefully cultivated persona reduced to mush. They added to his humiliation by belittling his manhood. Esther had the first opportunity to punish him because she had lost a son. She wanted to emasculate him, but Edom stopped her.

"He can't live through' that," Edom said. "He would bleed to death. He bled enough already."

She settled for sticking sharpened sticks into his inner thighs, testicles, breasts, and other soft tissue, perversion that elicited a high-pitched wail. She then invited the other women to do join her.

Neary screamed and passed out, but he would be revived several times before his ordeal ended. The women took delight and time in avenging their losses and Edom was in no hurry.

They found less satisfaction with the others who accepted their brutality and perversions without a sound.

*   *   *

3:39 P.M.: Sunday, September 3, 1993

Caleb 'El Gato' made good time. He arrived at a point he believed put him north and west of and close to Gannett. He crossed a well-worn trail and stayed upwind of it, not wanting to meet anyone.

Abranos survived in Nam by trusting his instincts. He also trusted his nose. In Viet Nam, he worked the tunnels, looking for Cong who might pop out anywhere to ambush American troops. Survival in the unlit tunnels required moving soundlessly in the dark and sensing what was ahead. Abranos had the reputation of being able to smell the Cong, not a great feat considering that most were as grubby as any soldier in combat. What differentiated El Gato, was his ability to sense changes in the vibrations of the air, even his own echoing back to him. The tunnels were impenetrable blackness, a place where only those who had no fear and no regard for their lives survived. The Cong developed ingenious traps and diversions, but none fooled Abranos. In the tunnel, El Gato, The Cat became El Topo, The Mole.

Abranos moved parallel to the path for a half-mile or so when he smelled a familiar odor, an odor recent in his memory but different somehow. It was the smell of blood, and the prevailing wind told him it was southeast of him, probably on the trail. He couldn't ignore it. It probably was animal blood, but his nose couldn't make that distinction.

He angled his approach to the path, taking every opportunity for concealment. He backtracked a hundred yards to be certain no one discovered his passing. He moved forward cautiously, quite certain he'd see anyone coming toward him.

Neary's screams, growing louder, enabling Abranos to move in their direction.

It didn't take long to discover the source of the screams. One hundred feet ahead of him, there echoed a penetrating scream followed by dull thwacks and more cries. Abranos moved above the trail, staying with the cover as he approached the sounds. El Gato was back in the jungles, doing what he knew best, moving through underbrush silently, crawling and edging his way to his prey. He was stimulated and ready for whatever he might encounter, but he could not have anticipated the scene that opened to him.

Abranos was positioned above a clearing. It was horrific, a scene that in future telling would need no elaboration. Seven or eight people, one a man holding a rifle, the others, women. Two of them beat a naked man with truncheons. The victim was one of four men, all appearing to be unconscious as they hanged by single ropes from a tree limb. One man cried out each time he was struck. The other men were silent, although they, too, were being abused.

El Gato had seen similar scenes in Nam. Men were hanged from trees or posts, sometimes feet up, while spectators watched a tormentor insert bamboo slivers into sensitive parts of the body or use knives to remove small patches of skin, opening wounds that would be rubbed with astringents, giving pain but stemming the flow of blood to ensure a slow painful death. Sometimes, the only thing El Gato could do was to send a cyanide-laced dart into the victim in the hope that he would not be seen. The silent missile never missed, and he always got away.

Today he had no cyanide darts, but the odds were okay. He knew he couldn't walk away. He was determined, the rush of combat easily remembered.

There was only one rifle in this group. El Gato scanned the area, focusing on details in a wide swath around the clearing. He waited many seconds to ensure there were no others lurking beyond sight. The women, in turn, moved from victim to victim on their brutal mission. Abranos was satisfied there were no others nearby. He removed a grenade from his belt, a grenade that would make a deafening noise and create a blinding light, potentially causing permanent loss of sight to anyone looking directly into it. El Gato slipped on his ear protectors, knowing he'd have time to pull down his visor once he lofted the grenade. He checked the visor to make sure it would swing as designed. Then he pulled the pin and tossed the grenade up and forward.

It detonated about five feet off the ground. The captives would be temporarily deafened; but as long as their eyes were closed, there would be little effect on their sight, shielded by the shadow of their downcast heads, also.

Only Edom, rifle in hand, was left standing; and Abranos, having raised his visor, could see him moving the gun seeking a target. He was helpless. He couldn't see and he couldn't hear. It took El Gato, moving with modest caution, only seconds to reach him and relieve him of his rifle. Edom, the man Otha had sent along to watch the women to ensure they didn't kill anyone, went for his knife only to find that Caleb Abranos had removed it and his sidearm. Abranos then knocked Edom unconscious with a blow to the side of his neck. The women were getting to their feet, dazed, confused and wailing. Abranos ignored them, opting instead to ease down the hanging men. They would take time to recover their sight and hearing.

He recognized Neary immediately, initially amazed and unable to fathom what he was doing in the New Hampshire woods. Though unconscious, Neary moaned as Abranos eased his weight came down on his legs. Abranos could see that Neary's Achilles tendon had been cut. The other injury looked more serious. Unless the man got to a doctor in a hurry, he would lose his foot, perhaps his leg. He eased Walsh down and Kincher, finding Kincher familiar before he came upon Reinholds. He stepped back, felt the revulsion had for this man in VietNam. Reinholds was helpless. Abranos eased him down only to find that he couldn't stand either. Once on the ground, the broken man whispered a moan that seemed to express relief.

Abranos then took the coil of rope that Otha left earlier and used it to tie the women. They were a surly bunch, initially vicious until he turned their attempts to gouge him into self-inflicted wounds. Kincher, recognizing Abranos, was on his feet and helped. The women screamed and cursed. They called to Edom. Though still blind, a couple tried to run. One ran into a tree. In less than five minutes, Edom and the women were bound and tethered.

Kincher gave Abranos a quick rundown, omitting incriminating facts and turning their behavior into defensive actions. He agreed with Caleb's assessment of Walsh and Neary. The latter was now completely delirious and both needed immediate medical care. He explained what happened to Reinholds, knowing nothing of Abranos's sentiments. Kincher remembered enough about this man, whom he hadn't seen in 20 years, to trust him.

"We'll get help as fast as we can," Abranos said, and then moved off, leaving Kincher with Edom's rifle.

Before he moved to skirt Gannett, Abranos called Bernie and gave her the approximate location where the men could be picked up. The only clearing sufficient for a copter was about 100 yards south. They would arrive prepared to pick up the wounded. El Gato decided to forget his hatred of Reinholds and let him live with his pain.

Kincher checked the prisoners, and working through his pain, he cut down saplings using Edom's knife and fashioned a field stretcher to move the injured men to an open area. The copter arrived locating the clearing within minutes. Engstrom and DeCarlo jumped out and took charge. The women and male prisoner, tied securely to a tree were taken into custody to await transport over land.

* * *

6:26 A.M.: Monday, September 4, 1993

Maddoc worked his way to the tree line of a swale where Zeb and the others were readying to break for Gannett. He wasn't quite alone. Dogbone was in the midst of the camp, eluding Luke's efforts to get a rope around him. Maddoc could see two figures lying next to each other, one so much larger that he thought the smaller might be a child.

The smaller figure stirred, giving out a low moan. Maddoc froze. He had heard that sound a thousand times. He was absolutely certain, and he felt an emotional heave driving up through his stomach and into his head, constricting his breathing. Tears leaked down his face.

A faint yellowish wisp hovered above Sylvi, a filmy veil barely visible against the trees in the morning light. Maddoc was close to hyperventilating. Marie had achieved in death what she could not achieve in life. She protected Sylvi, and he understood. How she knew he did not understand, but he was convinced that dead opened windows the living could not. He thought back to her own mother's admonition when Marie had received word that Maddoc was missing in action and presumed dead. "Ragazza del bambino, you must never believe you man is dead, never; justa believe he's coming back to you. If he was dead, he come in your sleep and tell you. That's amore."

Star Engstrom, despite Maddoc's earlier request for everyone to stay back, sidled in and watched the scene unfold. Maddoc caught sight of the motion and waved him away, but Engstrom ignored him and worked his way alongside Maddoc. He touched Maddoc's arm. Maddoc caught himself just as his blade cleared its sheath..

As they both watched, Luke stood transfixed by the airy shape that seemed to hover over Sylvi. He moved toward it, waving his hand in front of him and then threatening with his rifle, jerking it like a baton with his right hand and pushing the air in front of him with his left. He came within six feet of Sylvi's position, and the filmy shape suddenly exploded, filling the entire area around Luke and silently expanding into a flash of light and flame.

Maddoc thought someone had tossed a grenade. He was momentarily blinded but no noise accompanied the explosion. The spectral light and hellish flames were spreading out before him. Luke turned and ran, clutching his rifle while escaping the clearing, fear having taken away any ability to warn his associates. He believed he saw the face of the Alpha and the Omega who, Otha said, would herald the end of the world. He remembered Otha preached fearsomely of the great light accompanying the Day of Judgment.

The dogs quieted. Almost as quickly as the flames came, they disappeared. The shape, a roughly drawn figure that from below looked much like a manta ray floating above, remained briefly and disappeared.

The scene remained exactly as it had been. The quiet of the moment, the awe and restrained breathing of the men, suggested that something incredible just happened. Luke was not in sight, the noise of his thrashing through the woods snapping Zeb out of his trance. Zeb believed for a few seconds that they were under attack. The noise was fading, and Zeb looked around for Luke.

Maddoc mouthed instructions to Engstrom, who moved back silently while Maddoc crouched, keeping his eyes on his adversaries. He edged his way to Sylvi. Once out of cover of the brush and trees, he dropped to the ground and worked his way on his stomach. Luck was with him. No one checked her. Securely tied, she slept. As soon as he could, he looked at her face. The face that looked back at him elicited absolute love. He saw her and understood for the first time how much sadness he had been repressing. The angelic beauty that was Sylvi from the moment of her birth, that was Sylvi when she slept in her crib, that was Sylvi when she announced for the first time that she was in love, still painted her face. Maddoc wanted to shake her awake and just hold her, but now he had to wake her, keep her quiet and remove her from this place before anyone noticed.

Throughout her life, both at home and during their camping trips, Maddoc had awakened Sylvi by placing two fingers against her temple. She learned to awake instantly without moving or speaking, just opening her eyes. Maddoc placed his fingers on her temple; the conditioning held. Sylvi opened her eyes, looked into the darkened visage that was Maddoc's face, and did not move. Maddoc whispered to her. "Sylvi, it is your Dad." Her mouth opened, but she did not speak. Tears came without constraint. He cut her binds, and she reached up, touching her father's face and crawling forward to put her cheek against his.

"We have to get out now," he whispered. "Everyone's distracted but not for long. I'm going to pull you on to my back and carry you outside the perimeter, and then we'll move out."

Zeb muttered, "What the hell," certain that someone was diddling with the girl and started to step toward them. Before he took his first step, Star

Engstrom had him wrapped in a grip that cut off the blood flow. Zeb strug-gled silently, passing out within seconds. His brain, devoid of oxygen, closed down but not before he squeezed off a round, the explosion crashing into the silence. Engstrom eased him to the ground, and threw his rifle aside.

Matthew, Ishmael, and Malachi were on their feet almost simultane-ously. Maddoc and Sylvi rose together. Engstrom reached Ishmael just as he was about to bring up his rifle, taking him down with a sweep across the right side of his leg that briefly incapacitated him, insult to a leg previously damaged. As Ish got out a scream, G.K. appeared and disarmed Matthew as he swung his rifle around. Matthew was quick, able to avoid G.K.'s first blow and drive into him, knocking the bigger man off his feet. Malachi was moving to Matthew's assistance when Sylvi stepped forward and hammered Malachai with a well-placed kick to his solar plexus, knocking him out.

Sylvi saw G.K. squeezing Matthew's breath out of him. She turned to where she had last seen her father and to her horror, saw that Little Jug, free of his bonds was holding Maddoc off the ground by his hair.

She screamed, "Little Jug, put him down!"

Little Jug paid no attention, not knowing the man he held aloft and afraid for Sylvi. She started toward him, afraid he would hurt her father. Before she reached him, Maddoc took a hold on his wrists, as though grasping a parallel bar, and swung himself into an arc that brought his legs up over Little Jug's arms and enabled him to clip Little Jug in the face with his boot, just at the bridge of his nose. The blow hurt Little Jug so much that he dropped Maddoc on his back, sat down and began to bawl, his sobs those of five-year-old who was more surprised than hurt. He had never been pun-ished in his life, and he now sat, terribly confused and frightened.

Maddoc turned, ready to dispatch this dangerous giant who had picked him off his feet so easily. His next blow would have crushed his trachea and killed him, but Sylvi yelled to him to stop. He stopped, a bit startled by the fear in her voice, and stepped back. Sylvi went to Little Jug and cradled his head, comforting him and telling him everything was all right. She rocked his upper body while he sat, the cries slowing down as her voice calmed him. She examined his face, understanding the force of her father's blow as she watched a large lump continue to grow just above the bridge of his nose. He would have a headache and two black eyes, but he would be all right.

Maddoc said, "I was approaching him when he broke free."

"He's my friend, Dad; but he's dangerous when he feels I'm in trouble."

"I've never seen a bigger man," he said. "Why is he crying?"

"He's probably never been hurt before. He's confused."

"Sorry. I didn't have any choice. How did anyone ever get a rope around him?"

"He accepted the ropes in order to protect me."

At this point, G.K., so preoccupied with gathering up weapons that he failed to notice Little Jug, interrupted. "What do you want to do with these?"

"Secure them," Maddoc responded, annoyed to be asked.

Engstrom searched every prisoner, including their meager personal belongings. Only Zeb and Malachi had side arms, both safely in their packs. G.K. tied the clansman, cross-legged so they couldn't stand once awake. Harrington emerged from a copse with prisoners in tow. He cheered on seeing Maddoc with his daughter. She was attending to a seated man.

Harrington thought Maximilian was a giant; but the man who sat on the ground was almost as tall as Sylvi, and she was standing. He had to be seven and a half feet tall, and massive. He stepped toward them, stopping when Sylvi waved him away.

She said something quietly to her dad, and he also stepped away. Al Harrington moved next to him. Sylvi stood next to Little Jug and sang "Bye, Baby Bunting." Little Jug seemed a caricature, but the scene conveyed the love that Sylvi had for him. She then kneeled beside him and spoke quietly, too quietly to be heard. His face was very calm, almost suggesting a smile. She took his hand, as though lifting him, and he rose as silently as a ghost.

Before them was the biggest man that any of them had ever seen, bigger than Andre the Giant, and not as bizarre. Anyone impressed with Maximilian's size would be astonished by Little Jug. He stood nearly a foot above Maximilian. Harrington's estimate of the man's size was shy of eight feet by inches.

He remarked to Maddoc, "There've been stories about this man coming out of these parts for years, but no one believed them. How could anyone get this big?"

Sylvi walked from the clearing with Little Jug behind her, gesturing to her father to follow. She wanted time for Little Jug to get used to their being together. G.K waited a couple of seconds before moving out to meet DeCarlo coming at an angle with three prisoners, Luke now included.

Maddoc walked with Sylvi explaining the events of the many weeks that passed. It was the side of the story she could not have imagined. Sadness settled on her as her father told her of her mother's dying but withheld the details. She held back her tears. He then spoke of her mother's coming to him, guiding him and his friends toward finding her daughter. Sylvi then cried, alarming Little Jug. She couldn't absorb the loss of her mother. Her tears of joy and sadness conflicted. Her father had come for her. She could not bring her mother back.

When Maddoc shared Marie's coming to him, Sylvi understood. She got a full description of the scene that had terrified Luke and driven him from the camp. She had to smile. She accepted the story. Her mother had come for her, also.

Sylvi gave a quick overview of her experience in the camp and her feigned pregnancy. She explained her first escape attempt and Little Jug's catching her. Little Jug became her friend when Gubbin put him in place to protect her after three clansmen attempted to rape her.

Within several minutes, the others, totally awed by Little Jug, joined them. Sylvi kept the details to a minimum as she shared the entire story of her abduction and escape.

"Dad, when I was abducted, Jeff Spooner was with me. Do you know what happened to him,?"

"He was seriously injured and is hospitalized in a coma. The doctors are certain he will come out of it and be fine. It could be any day."

"Are you sure he's all right. He tried to protect me."

"I'm as sure as the doctors are, and they are optimistic. His family is with him."

Maddoc paused, waiting for another question that did not come. "Sylvi, did you know about the fire?"

Sylvi was surprised. "What fire?"

"You don't know?"

Zeb, awake and within earshot, yelled, "That little bitch is lying. She and her friends ran away and then came back and burned our families—our wives, our children and our friends. All dead and in Heaven."

"What is he talking about?" she asked.

"Everyone left at the camp is gone. There was a terrible fire. Everything is burned except the outlying cabins."

Sylvi was shocked. "They're all gone? The children, too? Oh my God!"

She broke down in tears, now understanding Zeb's accusations.

Most were friends, people who came to like and trust her as she became one of them. She found value in their innate gifts and extraordinary skills and praised them. They not only taught her but also admired her. They were simple, loving people following the traditions of their ancestors in a life of blind obedience. Sylvi's sobs faded. She wiped her eyes and spoke sincerely of her loss.

"Dad, these people are simple in the way they live and simple in their beliefs. They follow the way of their parents, most believing the world a good place. Otha Gubbin and his thugs, their fathers and brothers, were never challenged because they took care of their own. Once we got away, we never turned back, had no reason to. Might the fire have been an accident?"

"No, it was set with gasoline. The authorities will determine what happened."

She explained the escape and her arrival at Gannett and the events that followed, including her fear that her friends had walked into Gannett and were being held.

Harrington, despite hearing previous rumors, expressed surprise that Gubbin was running a baby farm in this part of New Hampshire. "There were stories, of course, but stories are part of the fascination of their lives. We never had reason to take them seriously. We knew he placed babies for adoption, but we believed they were the progeny of clanswomen who did not want them."

Maddoc told Sylvi, "Your getting caught while attempting to get help for your friends put you within our reach. He told her of Dogbone's heroics."

"Dad, he slept with me, and I thought of you."

"I guess that's a compliment." Maddoc teased. "Fate intervened. The first men we captured believe you and your friends set the fire. These others, as you witnessed, believe you are solely responsible. It may be that no one in Gannett knows of the fire, but we have to assume they do."

Fate or not, Sylvi's behavior under the circumstances was predictable. She didn't anticipate being intercepted by Zeb and taken prisoner.

Sylvi thought of her friends.

Maddoc interrupted her thoughts. "The authorities are ready to occupy Gannett. A task force has been set up, and we're on our way to join them. Care to come along?"

Sylvi smiled; her spirits lifting in spite of her hunger and tiredness.

"In fact," she said, "Little Jug and I may be able to walk into Gannett without any risk. If I can locate my friends, we might avoid problems."

"That's not what I have in mind. Let's take time to eat and rest. We're stuck here for now and we have prisoners to dispose of."

Ludim, insisting he proved his reliability, offered to stand watch over them, drawing a laugh. G.K. stood guard and was amused as Ludim told Zeb what an ass he was.

As they were speaking, Abranos arrived and grumbled because they did not wait for him. Sylvi rushed him and threw her arms around his neck, displaying the love she had for this man whom she knew as her Uncle Cat. Abranos was delighted, picking her off her feet and swinging her until she insisted he put her down as Little Jug started advancing upon them.

"Anthony my friend, while you were here doing the light work, I ran across Neary, Reinholds, Kincher and Walsh hanging from a tree with one man holding a gun on them. They were taking an awful beating from women with switches and clubs. I stopped it and called to have them taken them into custody."

"Caleb, you have a wonderful imagination; but this is beyond any lie you have ever told. How do you explain Neary and the others being here, especially Reinholds?

251

"Oy, my friend, I tell you nothing more, and I need explain nothing. Yet, if you apologize for doubting me, I might tell you that Kincher and Reinholds explained that Gilletti sent them there to find Sylvi and some files, but first you must apologize."

"Caleb, Gilletti knew Sylvi was here?"

"We spoke before you met the Monsignor. He may have suspected, but will we ever know the full story? Perhaps, but it was also the records he was after."

Maddoc said, "We'll learn the truth Caleb,

"The truth, my friend, is that Gilletti followed up on his suspicion for your sake and that of your daughter. The truth, as your grandfather told you, is that Gilletti can be trusted. Remember what Willie wrote. 'There is nothing either good nor bad but thinking makes it so.' "

"So you believe that I must trust Gilletti?"

"Your grandfather answered that question.

"We will see."

Sylvi introduced Little Jug to Abranos as a mother might introduce a fretful child to a friend. Little Jug was finding all the new faces confusing, but he could see Sylvi was happy. He accepted them, any idea of being jealous totally foreign to him.

Abranos said, "I want some of what they feed him."

Harrington, clearly flustered, interrupted the scene telling Maddoc that a report had just come in telling him to bring the prisoners in overland.

* * *

10:01 A.M.: Sunday, September 3, 1993

The helicopter that picked up Walsh, Neary, Reinholds and Kincher left a trooper, Bruce Tambiso to hold Edom and the women. A second would ride in with Bernie. The women were crying, pleading with the trooper to be released. "They killed our husbands and sons. We have children and babies waiting for us."

Edom remained silent, giving no indication who he was or what he thought.

252

Esther, senior in the group, tried to make a case: "One of 'em killed my oldest boy, cut his innards out of him for nothing. I watched my babe's blood spill from his gut; I heard him cry for his momma. I saw him reach to heaven and beg for his life, and that big man cussed me and laughed while my baby tried to put his innards back in place."

Tambiso showed no interest. She shut up. Her hope was that Otha would come for them once he realized they were gone too long, but it would be close to sundown before that thought arrived, and sundown was hours away.

The trooper radioed Smith, "Colonel, I got people in custody here who claim their village was attacked by outsiders. Family members were killed. The men allegedly responsible are severely injured and are on their way to the Woodsville hospital."

"Bruce, you and Evan hold those people until we pick you up. We'll sort it out. Their story doesn't seem right. You think one of them is a New York City Police Department Inspector? That makes no sense."

Bruce shrugged.

*   *   *

Smith's assembly point was approximately three miles southwest of Gannett on Grange Road. The only access from north of the town was the overgrown dirt road that ran off Grange to the south and traveled the perimeter of Gannett to multiple logging trails found throughout the region. A unit was already blocking unauthorized access to Gannett.

CHAPTER 43

3:03 P.M.: *Sunday, September 3, 1993*

It was not turning out to be a good day for the clan. First came the news of the encampment. Titus had driven there as Otha instructed him to learn what happened. Titus knew something bad happened before he got close.

Traffic on the mill road leading to the camp was backed up. He had never seen any vehicle not owned by the clan on that road, not even hunters. He veered off the road, taking a seldom used path that brought him within a fifty yards of the camp. He waited and listened. His wife, sister, son and daughter were there, and he was anxious to see them; but he wouldn't walk into something he didn't understand. He left his truck and worked his way closer upwind, conscious of the dogs nosing around.

He saw it all as he came within sight of the camp. The air was still and the stench was terrible. The fire smell was minor compared to the odor of burnt and decaying flesh. Titus was stunned. Bodies were laid in a row alongside the old charcoal pit, row upon row, as people passed from one to the next writing things and clipping tags to each. The bodies were placed in black plastic bags and sealed shut. Four vans stood, their back gates swinging like the maws of hell stretched wide in unabated hunger.

The conversation was explicit; Titus listened numb with pain.

"Poor bastards. Most probably never knew what hit 'em."

"Yeah, this fire weren't no accident."

"Sure weren't. There's a lot of accelerant spilled where the fire started."

"Any survivors?"

"If there are, they didn't stick around. Looks to me they got it in their sleep, all of 'em."

"Who would do such a thing?"

"Someone who had a grudge, probably other scroats who been fighting over the sugar. Maybe it's an old blood feud."

"Whoever did it is long gone. It's impossible in this country to learn anything. No one says a word, and you can't buy it or drag it out of them. We'll never find out."

"Never find out? Hell, we won't even find out who half these people are. They don't have teeth, and most their of mouths ain't never seen a dentist. We'll take impressions, but the only way we'll identify anyone is through relatives."

"Yeah, well I'll be surprised if any of the scroats show up to find their lost kin. Bunch of fuckin' animals."

"Yeah, but I feel sorry for the kids."

"For what? They would growed up to be animals, too."

Titus moved away, enraged by what he heard but smart enough to remain silent. These were flatlanders, natural enemies. There was no point in listening to them, but he grieved. He scanned the perimeter, looking for his family. He worked his way to the remaining cabins, hoping survivors were hiding in the bush or under the cabins. He eased himself into each of the four remaining cabins. All were empty. He found nothing in the bush, not even a sign. He turned and stumbled back to the woods unconscious of his direction and not caring whether he was seen. His wife, sister, and little one were gone. He wanted them alive; but there was no chance. He wanted to scream. He wanted to strike out. He was frightfully angry, ready to kill, but who? All he could do was work his way back to the truck and turn toward Gannett.

So it was that Titus, grief-stricken, reported to Otha who more than ever wanted to talk with someone about the fire. There were many questions, but they would have to wait. The dead wait without complaint. Now Otha had to deal with Edom and the women's not coming back. They'd been gone more than five hours, and darkness was not far away. He sent Joseph out to fetch them. Joseph soon returned.

"They're gone, Otha, the prisoners, the women, and Edom, all gone, his rope with them."

255

"You see anything?" Otha asked.

"Looks to me like there been a scuffle, fire too. The trees are dried and withered from heat. Found a spot where a helicopter sat no less than three hours ago. Could be the women and Edom hadn't gone on their own."

"What do you mean?" Otha growled.

"Maybe the strangers' friends snuck up on Edom and took everyone off."

Otha didn't speculate. "Ain't no one gonna sneak up on Edom. They must have shot him. We got some 'vestigating to do right quick."

When the prisoners showed up in Gannett, Otha wanted every detail on how they got there. Erla questioned each of them separately. Their stories varied somewhat, but the basics were the same. They planned the escape and fooled their pursuers.

When Otha sent Titus to the camp to learn what happened, he didn't expect to hear much but excuses. Titus's account was staggering. His rage turned to sadness, and his sadness fueled his rage. Someone would pay. He looked first to the prisoners.

"Erla, I'm thinking they set the fire and kilt everyone."

"Well, Pa, that be my thought, too; but they all tell the same story and there ain't no fire in it. Can't explain the fire Otha, but it ain't them that did it."

"That's something to be found out. Let's get them back in the lockup. I ain't thinking on it now. I got things that need fixing."

Gubbin didn't share anything Titus learned. Though told not to, Titus would say enough. Gubbin would pray with the families and distribute the $500 per clan member to the relatives of the dead. That would not lessen their grief, but it was something. The fire meant the loss of labor and of children who would have graduated to the ranks of wage earners, especially the girls. Otha couldn't accept Zeb, Ludim, Maximilian, and the others' still out there looking for people held in Gannett. With three cross-country vehicles, including Reinholds' Bronco, he took Joseph, Titus, Neb, Aaron, Ben, Daniel, Moloch, and Zak, his entire road team, absent Edom and Noah with the aim of working the back trail to the camp. He would find Zeb and the others, and he had to find Edom and the women.

Having disabled the Bronco, it didn't take much for Mule Grady to get it running. If Edom and the women were in trouble, Otha Gubbin was not going to leave them to themselves. He gave no thought to leaving with his most reliable men. The prisoners were locked up, and Jacob had everything in order. Jacob Calin swore Mule Grady in as a deputy. He was enough. Otha would decide on the second one.

"We set off at first light. We fetch Edom and the women and then we tidy up whatever else needs doin'."

* * *

7:47 A.M.: Monday, September 4, 1993

Maddoc's party now consisted of Sylvi, Little Jug, DeCarlo, and Abranos up front. G.K. and Buzz Carleton herded the seven prisoners a hundred yards back. Dogbone moved along Harrington's blind side within sight of the two groups. G.K. kept a shotgun within easy view while Buzz cautioned their captives to remain silent.

They expected to meet Smith and his force within a quarter mile of Gannett. Engstrom dropped back to join Bernie and Lenny Sossa. No one relaxed although sensing the end was near.

* * *

8:14 A.M.: Monday, September 4, 1993

Abranos motioned the dog to his side as he moved to the head of the party. The terrain, largely grass, shrubs and small evergreens, was more open than any they crossed previously. It left them and anyone approaching exposed. Maddoc directed everyone to maintain silence, stay close to the modest wood line, and use the shadows. Abranos usually could sense trouble, and the dog definitely would. There would be no surprises.

Earlier, after ending the women's macabre beating ritual, Abranos circled Gannett's fringe and reported few people in sight. "Whatever is going, people are keeping their heads down. Who knows how much damage Neary and his crew did."

"I thought it was Reinholds team?"

"Neary was the lead according to Kincher. I saw no one although lights were on in one small building."

With as much stealth as they could fashion, the moved steadily across the open area. It was early, 8:38 A.M. by Maddoc's watch, and the day, at 62 degrees Fahrenheit, was clear. There was a line of sight as far as they could see. A quarter mile ahead, the land began to rise. Traveling wasn't difficult. The brush was thinning out, and they would be on a common trail soon. Caleb Abranos drew next to Maddoc and Sylvi. Little Jug and the dog were now a few yards ahead of them.

"¡Compadre! What do you think about those yokels in Gannett? Any chance we run into them?" Abranos asked.

"Yokels? Perhaps, but no less a threat. At this point they don't know we're coming. If they're looking for anyone, it'll be Sylvi and Little Jug."

"Amigo, I found Neary and the women some distance beyond that rise ahead. The women have been missed by now. We can be sure someone's looking for them."

"You're right. It'll be the women they're after."

Maddoc nodded as Abranos started forward.

Little Jug followed Dogbone and was slightly ahead at the top of the ridge. He heard a sharp yelp, as though Dogbone was hurt, followed immediately by the report of a rifle. Dogbone reacted to the click of the hammer being cocked.

Little Jug was over the rise before anyone could stop him. Maddoc handed Sylvi a pistol and told her to go back with the prisoners. DeCarlo and Engstrom joined Sossa and moved the prisoners back about fifty yards, forcing them face down to the ground. Maddoc gestured Harrington and G.K. to circle to the north of the rise. DeCarlo and Engstrom rejoined them.

Maddoc was very conscious of the shooter's position. Whoever was on the hill was more exposed than they. He wanted to avoid a gunfight. The fact that there was no additional gunfire encouraged him. It might have been a poacher mistaking Dogbone for a deer.

As they worked their way around, Maddoc and Abranos gestured to each other, making certain neither would be exposed. If one went down the other would cover, one of several routines learned in Nam.

Maddoc was the first to see the vehicles. Five men stood in front of Little Jug who kneeled next to Dogbone and nodded at them. One man stood slightly to the side holding a rifle in position to shoot, a precaution Maddoc realized was for Dogbone's sake. These people left little to chance. Maddoc dropped behind a laurel bush and alerted Harrington. Abranos and G.K. of the sighting.

"Let's watch," Maddoc suggested. "They know Little Jug. I don't see others, but there are more. Three vehicles, five men doesn't figure. If you see Dogbone attack, you'll know I've signaled him. At that point we take control."

Before anyone could acknowledge it, a high-pitched scream came from Sylvi's direction. Maddoc had no choice. He gave Dogbone the signal to attack followed by the signal to retreat. Dogbone went after the man with the gun and struck so fast that the five men turned only as Joseph screamed when Dogbone shattered his wrist. Little Jug was moving toward Sylvi's scream.

Maddoc, joined by Dogbone, moved quickly toward Sylvi. Little Jug raced past him showing no caution. Coming at an angle, Maddoc could see Sylvi pinned to the ground by a man while another held a rifle on her. He could see Little Jug moving in on them. Maddoc couldn't get off a shot without risk to Sylvi.

Little Jug was upon the two men, tossing aside the man who was holding Sylvi down. The standing man, Otha himself, swung his rifle in Little Jug's direction. At the same moment, a figure came out of the woods and threw himself at Otha, knocking him off his feet. Little Jug responded instinctively.

Confusion reigned, especially for Little Jug. The prisoners were trying to work free. On command, Dogbone swung back and held them in place as G.K. stepped forward with rifle in hand.

Sylvi was now on her feet. Otha was back on his feet trying to bring his rifle to bear upon Maddoc who was closing very fast. Sylvi, seeing the danger to her father, brought her leg around in a sweep pushing Gubbin sideways, the gun flying from his hand as Maddoc reached him.

Little Jug, in an unrelenting child's rage, clutched at the figure who knocked down Otha and might have killed him had the man not shouted. It was Vincent. Little Jug recognized his friend and let go.

Otha steadied himself and met Maddoc's attack with surprising agility. It was clear why Otha was so feared by the clansmen. It was also clear that Otha carried the genes that had given Noah, his monkey-boy son, his uncommon strength and agility. Maddoc felt a sharp pain as Otha knifed him, missing a clean hit, but opened a slit five inches long across Maddoc's hip as Maddoc swept him off his feet.

Little Jug seeing Otha go down, came directly at Maddoc, his reaction meant to protect Otha. As the giant came upon him, Maddoc sidestepped him and brought the side of his hand in a powerful chop to Little Jug's right kidney. The pain of such a blow would have brought an ordinary man to his knees. Little Jug grunted, stumbled a step or two, and turned to renew his attack. Maddoc was already moving. As Little Jug turned, he was met by the smaller man flying through the air. There was nothing Little Jug could do. Maddoc crashed into his chest with both feet, achieving what no man had done before. Little Jug, knocked off his feet, crashed to the ground, not hurt much but completely confused by the position he was in. As Maddoc turned his attention to Otha, it was too late. Otha had picked up his rifle and neatly smacked Maddoc alongside his head, knocking him dizzy before turning to Dogbone who, seeing Maddoc down, charged directly at him. Otha took the dog down with a clean shot.

Abranos, coming forward to help, and G.K witnessed it all, neither able to move quickly enough to help Maddoc. Sylvi was ministering to Little Jug, who was sitting up scared and confused. She heard but did not see the action that took her father and the dog out of the fight.

She did hear the shot, however, and turned toward the sound just as Otha reached her, his knife in hand, grabbed her hair, yanked her head back and brought the blade to her throat. Little Jug grabbed his shoulder and stood up, lifting the smaller man off his feet. Otha swung the knife around to stick Little Jug. The giant took Otha's head with his left hand and corkscrewed it, breaking his neck.

Otha's companion, recovered from his initial fall, hit Sylvi from behind, knocking her down. Little Jug lifted him by his right arm so forcefully that the arm separated at the shoulder. The man shrieked with pain as Little Jug held him aloft by the damaged arm. Sylvi was up immediately yelling at Little Jug to stop. Once he saw she was all right, he dropped the man, generating another scream. Vincent, on his feet and moving to Sylvi's aid stride for stride with Little Jug, helped Sylvi stand up.

Abranos and G.K. got Maddoc to his feet, Abranos not saying a word. He had seen Anthony Maddoc brought down. If Maddoc had not been up against a giant, Gubbin could not have gained the advantage. Yet Maddoc had fallen, and the banter about fading years no longer was amusing.

Maddoc moved to Dogbone, fearing the worst, but relieved when the beast wagged his tail. The shot had struck at an angle at the thickest point on his skull, knocking him out but ricocheting instead of penetrating. A quarter of an inch lower and Maddoc would be burying his friend. Otha's bullet left a furrow in the dog's scalp that would leave a neat, hairless scar. Dogbone got to his feet, looked around and announced all was well in his world by growling at Vincent, a stranger.

The prisoners saw their giant brought down by a smaller adversary. They saw the invincible Otha Gubbin die. They saw Sylvi save Adam Root's life. What dismayed them most was the towering fall of Little Jug, brought down by a David to their Goliath, just as the scriptures said.

Sylvi broke down when she saw the damage to her father's face, not as serious as it looked, and his blood-soaked pants. Maddoc held her as she sobbed, telling her he was fine, "not even a headache," he lied.

She needed the release. Her sobbing upset Little Jug, but he didn't know what to do. He lifted her, cradling her as he did with Cha and providing comic relief. No one other than Abranos and her father understood how Sylvi was able to survive, but a woman crying made sense. Maddoc knew that few men, perhaps none of those assembled, could be as tough and vicious as a woman when her loved ones were threatened. He wanted to hold her but Little Jug did not give her up.

Sylvi quieted, and Little Jug gently placed her on her feet. She looked at the scene, understanding that her ordeal was at an end. The man she abhorred was dead. She felt no satisfaction. She moved to Little Jug who was seated with Dogbone on his lap, seeming more of a puppy. Everything looked small in Little Jug's arms. Dogbone jumped from his arms and stood to the side, wagging his tail. Sylvi spoke to Little Jug. No one heard what she said, but they understood when she placed her arms around his head and hugged him.

Abranos and G.K. had the eight additional prisoners secured in a queue of their own, the injured, Joseph and Adam, bound only at the ankles. Maddoc saw no reason they shouldn't take the vehicles that had been dropped into their laps and move everyone as quickly as possible to the rendezvous point. The prisoners would be herded overland on foot. The addition of Vincent blotted out any possibility of escape.

Sylvi shared a concern with her father.

"Little Jug won't want to part with that dog, Dad," Sylvi observed. "He's never been allowed to play with dogs, except as puppies. For him, Dogbone is a dream."

"Dogbone is a good-natured slob, but he's also a killer. I can have him turn on Little Jug when we separate them."

"That's cruel, Dad, and risky. Little Jug will get over losing him. If you have the dog threaten him, it will break his heart."

"I prefer not to have Dogbone stay here, although the mutt would stay. He has no loyalties."

"That dog worships you!"

"Looks to me that he worships Little Jug."

"I want to take Little Jug back home with us."

"We'll talk about it but not now.

CHAPTER 44

10:36 A.M.: *Monday, September 4, 1993*

D ead-Eye Smith had a command station set up with radios, first aid support, a table and chairs for six, and some small creature comforts. Maddoc, Harrington, Engstrom, and Lip Caruthers, looked over the schedule and a map as Smith spoke. Sylvi sat with Dogbone.

"The situation has changed, gentlemen. With Otha Gubbin out and Jacob Calin likely in charge, we will meet no resistance in Gannett."

"The local lawman?" Maddoc interjected.

Smith read the question.

"Calin's a good cop. We respect the man's record. There's no hint he conspired with Gubbin. He might have looked away from things he didn't like, but not if they were unlawful. He will not oppose our entering Gannett."

Maddoc nodded.

Smith continued his briefing on the taking of Gannett. "We can walk into Gannett and take complete control. My people will secure the village before we undertake any investigation. I'm proposing we let our advance team go in at 3:00 P.M., and the main force follow us at 3:10.

"Headquarters believes there are records in Gannett bearing on illicit child trafficking. They want our team to handle things from this point forward. I told them to butt out. I leave the records to you, Lieutenant Harrington."

Sylvi spoke up. "I'm going in with Little Jug and Dogbone. I have to find my friends. The people know and accept me."

Smith reluctantly agreed. "We want them out of harm's way. Whatever records you may find, you will turn over. After we have examined them thoroughly, we'll decide their worth."

Harrington spoke up. "Sir, Maddoc and I would like to go in with Sylvi and Little Jug."

Smith, who had already been thoroughly briefed on the events before his arrival, understood the necessity of having Sylvi and Little Jug in the vanguard, responded. "That's what I had in mind, lieutenant. "I'll go in a few minutes earlier to meet Calin. I'll take Caruthers, an old friend of Jacob Calin, along."

Before Harrington could comment, Maddoc raised the question that had been nagging him. "We know that people are being held by Calin against their will, but we still think he's a good cop? It doesn't wash."

"You discovered the fire at the camp, Maddoc. We have twenty-seven dead women and children, presumably murdered. Calin believes he's has the perpetrators. He's holding them for cause."

Maddoc accepted Smith's explanation.

"The plan is simple," Harrington went on. "The six of us, Maddoc, Dogbone, Sylvi, Little Jug, Sossa and I, will enter Gannett from the rear. The Colonel and Sergeant Major Caruthers will go directly to Calin and bring him up to date. The main force will move in behind them."

Colonel Smith broke in.

"However you enter, you follow us by ten minutes. Given Lip's relationship with Calin, I'll let him do the talking. It's his forte." Caruthers looked at Smith on hearing that reference. Smith winked. "Lip and Jacob Calin go back to Jacob's days as a Vermont State Trooper. They understand each other."

Smith continued. "Calin will know where Miss Maddoc's friends are held. He also may know where the records are kept. I doubt he knew anything about the activities in the camp."

Maddoc found this difficult to accept. How could he not know?

*   *   *

When Smith and Caruthers stepped from the Ram, they were met by Rolly Newton and Thomas Ek, both with rifles pointed at them. Rolly and young Tom were Turks, hotheads who were smarting over being left in town by Otha. They were boys as far as Gubbin was concerned, but they were dangerous, especially when holding guns.

"Badge or no, get back in that truck and haul ass out of here. Ain't no good reason for you poking about."

Rolly, a cocky fifteen-year old who couldn't back down from a challenge, was the spokesman. He was little more than half the size of Tom, who mistook Rolly's craziness for courage. He wanted to be like his friend.

"Boys, you put your guns aside. We come to see Constable Calin as friends."

"Hell, I don't know nothing about you being friends. He didn't tell us about no friends coming."

Hearing the exchange, Jacob Calin stepped out of his office and acknowledged Smith. He looked at the boys and said, "Rolly, Tom, this is Colonel David Smith of the New Hampshire State Police."

He paused, seeing no recognition in the boys' faces until he said 'Dead-Ass Smith.

With that, Tom lowered his gun and retreated, apologizing each step of the way. Rolly was transfixed, still holding his gun but not pointing it at any particular direction, his hand off the trigger. He looked at Smith and then at his matching side arms. Dead-Ass Smith, the name Rolly knew well, was his hero, not because he was a lawman but because he could kill in a blink. It was a scene Caruthers had witnessed a dozen times or more. Smith's reputation was mythical; his abilities were not. Few tested him. Rolly, after several seconds of staring, mumbled an apology and joined his friend. Calin invited Smith and Caruthers into his office.

Smith's reputation grew out of one incident. He was driving across country and stopped at a gas station north of Cheyenne, near Yoder. He walked in on two men holding the owner and an attendant at gun point. Smith, wearing a sidearm, asked them to put their guns down. They turned their guns on him, and he drew and killed both of them before either got off a shot.

After hearing a quick outline of events during the previous several hours, Calin took a few minutes to digest it. He was comfortable as he spoke to the two men. "I'm sure sorry about cousin Otha. He loved that Little Jug; raised him from a pup. Never let anyone abuse him. 'Course once he growed up, weren't much chance of him being abused. The boy never knew his own strength. Wouldn't hurt a fly. He loved Otha, but he worships that woman.

Calin didn't understand Sylvi's relationship with Little Jug until he saw them together. As far as he knew, Sylvi was family. He knew of Otha's baby business but figured it did no harm. Did a lot of good as far as he could tell. All the arrangements were by the book. Calin on a visit with Otha had met his lawyer. Sometimes the girls didn't want to give up their babies, but they knew their options. They grew so dependent on their situation they did not imagine being anywhere else. Otha was good about it. If a girl was too upset, he let her leave with her baby and that was the end of it. If she was attached to a clan member, they married and she kept her baby.

"We have people in custody," said Calin. "We believe they burned down Otha's maple syrup camp and killed everyone in it. They come into town, and Otha welcomed them. Kept them apart for a time 'cause we didn't know what to make of them. Otha let some of 'em roam about, and was ready to let the others until he found out about the burning."

"Bad day for Otha," he went on as the others heard him out. "He nearly loses a son, two of my men get killed, and family and friends are lost to the fire. When he left here, he was looking for women who hadn't returned from a walk. His attack on your people is not hard to understand given his losses."

No one gave him any further information.

"About the records, if there are any they'd be in the infirmary. Otha kept an office there and his own telephone. Everything's there. The prisoners are in the basement. I expect you're planning to charge 'em. Can't let 'em get away with burning up women and children in their sleep."

"There will be a full investigation," Smith assured the constable.

Calin, who largely trusted Smith, accepted the entrance of Maddoc and Harrington and was happy to see Little Jug and Sylvi. Once he knew Sylvi was Maddoc's daughter and had been kidnapped, everything became clearer to him. "Otha would never have kidnapped anyone, certainly not a police officer's daughter. He could not have known."

Harrington replied. "His men did the kidnapping, but he had to know. He fostered it, but the victims are clear about it. We may never know how many women fell into Gubbin's hands and disappeared."

Calin, concerned about the implications, was unable to defend his cousin. He nodded and escorted them directly to the infirmary.

"I still don't believe Otha would have kidnapped anyone and surely not a policeman's daughter," he repeated.

* * *

After going through the infirmary, Maddoc and Harrington, given the nod by Smith, were working building to building making certain everything was secured. It was quiet. Most people in Gannett were at supper, the rest with their TV sets. Little Jug and Sylvi stayed in sight. Sylvi and Little Jug spoke to Marlene and the others. Harrington spoke to community members with Calin at their side. When the main force entered Gannett, no one would object.

The entire operation took less than forty-five minutes. There was no resistance. Grady, a slow stubborn man, was more than surprised when Little Jug and Sylvi showed up to free the prisoners. Sylvi explained, and Grady called Calin. That was enough. The seven women and five babies in their quarters were left undisturbed..

Maddoc and G.K. joined Sylvi, going from room to room and pulling the bolts. Maddoc introduced himself. Marlene began to cry, the first time she had allowed herself to show any stress. "You're Sylvi's dad! Is Sylvi here? Is she all right?"

Sylvi heard her and called, "I'm fine, Marlene. Sure happy to see you."

At this, Frank stepped in and talked nonstop to Sylvi. "I'm sorry I didn't tell you about Gannett, but I was sure Jacob Calin was on the up and up. Things didn't turn out as I thought. I was wrong about Little Jug. Do you know about the fire? They think we set it."

"Yes, I know. Whether they know it or not, we had friends there. They simply were powerless to help. Now they're gone."

Frank nodded. "Yes, they're gone, but we didn't set the fire. It had to be an accident."

Maddoc interrupted. "It was not an accident."

"How do you know it wasn't an accident?"

"Someone made an attempt to bury the bodies, but we found one that wasn't buried. I think it was a man who got caught up completely in the conflagration. He was lying close to a pool, his body blackened and both legs nearly burned off."

Sylva broke in. "It had to be Eban. Eban's hate would have driven him to it."

Frank agreed and explained. If we had not left, we might all be dead."

Maddoc asked. "How did you know so much about Gannett and Jacob Calin?"

"I've been hiking and fishing in New Hampshire since I was a boy."

"That doesn't answer my question. Tell me, does the name Caesare Gilletti mean anything to you, perhaps someone you met on one of these trips?"

Frank said nothing. He simply looked at Maddoc.

They were interrupted by Harrington, who was joined by Len Sossa. Lenny found old letters, children's drawings, unopened government tax queries, enough documents to fill an attaché case, but there was little of any use. Gubbin didn't seem to keep business records in Gannett.

The lieutenant said, "I think we're finished here. No secret stash. No concealed hiding places. No ledgers. Gubbin's authority was all the security he needed."

Sossa interjected, "There is a file cabinet with birth documents, most blank.

They returned to the deputy's office. Still disposed to believe the prisoners set the fire, Calin, nevertheless, was cooperative. At Caruthers' request, the detainees were given snacks and drinks, but Calin wasn't completely gracious. Someone murdered twenty-seven people, and he knew nothing about Eban.

Jacob Calin wanted assurances they'd be investigated. Smith had a preliminary report on the fire. The previous day's investigation concluded the fire was planned and methodically carried out.

Smith put his hand on Calin's shoulder and said, "The truth will be known, Jacob. Make no mistake about that. Our findings are pointing elsewhere, and we will get to the truth. I am leaving six of my best men, including two women, with you until we have everything sorted out."

Jacob Calin trusted Smith but still doubted.

* * *

5:41 P.M.: Monday, September 4, 1993

Except for Bernie and Sylvi, the reunion was anticlimactic. It was a relief; but they all knew they'd have to put their lives back together. Sandy had a very tearful telephone conversation with her aunt who assured her that everything was all right. They would drive up to get her. Her brother would be thrilled.

Josie's mother collapsed when she heard her daughter's voice on the telephone. Her father was equally affected but remained coherent through his sobs. Both parents had given up on ever finding her after the body of her friend Calvina was recovered from the Piscataquis River at the mouth of Little Bay. She had been strangled and in the water for about a week although missing for months.

Peter, Vincent and Frank reached their families and friends and explained, as succinctly as possible, that they'd been incommunicado and would bring them up to date on the details. Peter was concerned about getting back to work, a thought conspicuously absent with Frank and irrelevant to Vincent who was on permanent disability. Vincent emerged from the ordeal seemingly more sane than he went in.

Marlene's family was accustomed to her travels and not being in touch for weeks at a time. They didn't know that she was missing, and she didn't tell them anything other than that she would see them in a few days and would be bringing a friend. She invited Peter to go home with her. The strength of their relationship had grown quietly. Peter's parents were gone, and his two sisters and brother had their own families. There would be time to tell them the story. For now, he wanted to be with Marlene. Vincent caught hell from his dad for not calling his mother; he chose not to explain what happened. He spoke with his mother and promised to see her in a week.

Bernie stood with her arms engulfing Sylvi as both women sobbed uncontrollably. They held each other for several minutes before breaking away and seeking out tissues to wipe their eyes. Both laughed as they used their sleeves.

"Oh, Bernie, how did you get here? Dad didn't tell me." She paused and then said, "He told me about Mom. Was it the cancer?"

Bernie explained the break-in, the fire and Marie's dying as a result. With this, both women again began crying, reliving the bond that existed among mother, daughter and best friend. Sylvi caught her breath and said, "Thank God that Mom kept you for me." At this, the gates opened and the flood of tears continued.

It stopped and both women laughed out of exhaustion. Bernie held Sylvi as she again cried quietly. The crying eased and Bernie said, "Would you like to see the clothes and things I brought along for you."

Sylvi screamed, "Yes, Yes, I haven't a thing to wear."

Smith relayed Calin's account of Neary's attack; their vehicle and other testimony were enough. There were three separate murder charges pending. Kincher was charged and in custody. The others were confined in a Woodsville hospital. Neary's foot had become gangrenous. It was amputated below the knee. He would spend many weeks in physical therapy.

Reinholds would recover, but the damage to his joints remained a constant reminder of Little Jug's mauling. Walsh's blood poisoning should have killed him. Doctors administered massive doses of antibiotics. They concluded that had he not been so well conditioned he might have died. He would recover to stand trial.

Of the four men who went into Gannett, Neary was the only one to avoid charges. The others exonerated him. It was not in anyone's interest to charge a New York City Police Inspector. They would treat him as a victim, rehabilitate him, and clean up the record. Neary would testify against Gilletti and quietly retire.

All questions were addressed before they all broke up and headed to an inn Smith commandeered. The mom and pop who owned it were delighted. Their last paying customer had left the previous weekend. Now they had fourteen flatlanders and their friends as guests of the State of New Hampshire. There would be meals to cook, gifts to sell, and the bustle of people coming and going. Yes, they could arrange for clothes. Yes, they would provide for additional guests coming in. After all, their business was hospitality; and, as the natives liked to say, 'It's an ill wind that doesn't blow some good.'

CHAPTER 45

2: 09 P.M.: Thursday, March 15, 1994

E dward Cesaré Gilletti sat across from his daughter at the small work-table in his office. Sol Abrams sat to his left. They were facing a crisis. The room had been swept for listening devices. This was no time to be careless.

The elder Gilletti spoke first. "How in hell did we get into this mess, and how do we get out of it?"

Sol spoke up, "You don't think there's any serious chance of an indictment?"

"I don't know. My sources have gone to ground. There's no information coming from anyone."

"What do they have, Dad?"

"They're threatening an indictment, sufficient in itself to effect serious reversals."

"You think you'll lose clients?"

"As long as I remain with the firm, that's a possibility. Sol, what do you think?"

"Cesaré, we deal with governments. We deal with global conglomerates. The publicity is bad enough. We can blame that on the press, but if a grand jury indicts you, serious questions will be raised."

"Why did we let it happen? We broke from the drugs, the prostitution, the gambling, the loan sharking and all the petty shakedowns and extortion. We were not murderers. We avoided the dirty business, this adoption thing, but it never looked dirty."

"It wasn't dirty, Dad, until that Van Loos bitch got onto it."

"No, she was the warning bell, nothing more. Sol, how far are we into it?

"Internationally, we control more than half of that not controlled by governments. The states have been our best market, but now we transfer it to other agencies. We'll maintain our international trade. It's legitimate, a good thing. Here it got muddy before Van Loos came along."

Sol suggested, "We will transfer the agencies that remain clean."

Gilletti shrugged and answered, "That is of no interest to me."

"Kidnapping Anthony Maddoc's daughter, Elio Madduccino's grand-daughter. Insanity!"

"Sol, it was in the stars, a blood feud going back more than twenty years and unresolved. Jack Neary couldn't think beyond his hatred."

"Dad, what do we do?"

"We wait Toni, we wait. What we know at this point is the authorities have Stephen's depositions and those of Van Loos. Neither can hurt us. We believe they have papers from New Hampshire, information that is meaningless without Neary's testimony. Even then, it may not be conclusive. Gubbin was my mistake. I met him through Stephens who introduced him to Van Loos. Supposedly, Gubbin was obsessed with his journal on everything he did and everyone he knew. That may be all they need. Epstein spoke with Faye Knielex who is expecting to be called as a material witness. She says that Gubbin was both meticulous and exacting with details, noting dates, times, and locations. He often confirmed his information with her. There is a journal, and it is quite possible the Feds got their hands on it."

"What about Knielex?" Sol asked.

Gilletti looked at him and shrugged. "I guess you're asking that question for Antoinette's sake. We have nothing to fear from her, just as we should have nothing to fear from the rest of them; but our name makes headlines. The press will be sharks, and the courts cannot look away.

"Gubbin was a fox. Ownership was in his wife's name, and she's not being charged. She is now Knielek's client and privilege holds. Knielex is grateful. She has friends who will remain friends."

He then turned to his daughter. "I need to reach Anthony Maddoc. He might be able to help."

"How's that?" Sol asked.

"With Maddoc, no one ever quite knows. There's nothing specific to ask of him. Nevertheless, Monsignor Elio said I can rely on him. I want Toni to set up a meeting."

"What reason would I give?"

"You simply tell him that Edward Cesaré Gilletti wishes you to extend his apologies. It's an invitation he cannot refuse."

*   *   *

CHAPTER 46

Thirty-four days after returning to New York

They met midday at Rao's, an Eastside New York restaurant known for its cuisine and its patron list. The front door was locked after they entered. After the usual pleasantries, he asked what was on her mind, as he recalled her as a child.

Toni Gilletti said, "My father has decided to retire. Mr. Abrams plans to retire as well."

"Why should that interest me Ms. Gilletti?"

"Please call me Toni. May I call you Anthony?"

"Call me anything you like Ms. Gilletti."

"Look Sgt. Maddoc. My father knew nothing about the goings-on in Gannett. He would not be a part of such a thing."

"Miss Gilletti, like it or not, your father appears to be a part of many things he doesn't acknowledge. Don't patronize me with fluff regarding Edward Cesaré Gilletti's character and high principles."

Maddoc saw no reason to address the relationship shared by Gilletti and his family. If she didn't know, that was her father's wish.

Toni Gilletti struggled with her anger. At her father's request, she was sitting across from a man as dangerous as he. She had to win Maddoc's support.

"I appreciate your perspective, Sgt. Maddoc; but we're talking about my father, a man who has done more good in almost any year of his life than most people do in a lifetime. He is only one voice in a huge business network. He does not control the organization. Be as angry as you like Sgt. Maddoc, but understand my father would not be a part of anything that could hurt you. My father is a childhood friend of the Madduccino's."

274

Maddoc, well-acquainted with family history, both his and hers, understood she wouldn't know the full story, but she knew enough. He simply nodded, neither acknowledging nor denying her information.

"My father is outside counsel for an organization that employs more than 300,000 people in forty-seven countries. The organization and its ability to help people are much stronger as a result of his efforts. He is not involved in anything corrupt. His work is not easy. He operates within the laws and the traditions of the countries in which the organization does business."

"Even though it means that people in those countries suffer?"

"Because it means that many of the people in those countries prosper!" she shot back.

Maddoc didn't argue. "What do you want from me? Your father is out of reach."

"He may be out of reach, but his name is everything to him. He made the mistake of placing his confidence in the wrong people. He met Otha Gubbin on a hunting trip to New Hampshire. Gubbin was a guide. He had no dealings with the man. People taken in by Mr. Gubbin, people on whom my father relied let him down."

She paused, waiting for Maddoc's response, but none came, not even a nod. She couldn't remain silent.

"My father's last resolution before the Matterlink Board of Trustees was to set aside a trust of thirty-five million dollars to provide for those who were so clearly ill-used by PLAN and by Otha Gubbin's racket."

"That's a gesture with little meaning," Maddoc said. "There are many lives to mend, and who knows whether the girls who've been lost and the babies who've been stolen will ever be found. There is little chance of matching the mothers with their babies and less of anyone collecting any part of that $35,000,000."

"That was the Van Loos bitch's doing!" she spat back.

"That probably is true Miss Gilletti, but PLAN was funded by your father before Van Loos ever got involved."

"And it was legitimate until Van Loos got involved."

"So what's his worry?"

"He's concerned that Neary would lie in order to make things easier on himself. He alleges my father arranged for Jonetta Van Loos to front the operation through Matterlink. My fear is that my father will see his reputation and health destroyed fighting this thing."

"He is a lot tougher than that, and he can afford it," Maddoc commented offhandedly, not surprised that Gilletti had so much information on what was a sealed file available only to the prosecutor, a few select others and a senior judge.

"It's not about money," Toni continued. "It's about his good name. He wants to step aside from everything, but an indictment wouldn't allow him to do that."

"He's not indicted yet," Maddoc reminded her, "and no one believes he will be."

"My father learned something he believes would interest you."

"What could your father have to say that would be of any interest to me?"

"He told me to make one simple statement to you. 'Neary suggested Gubbin take Sylvi.'"

Maddoc didn't react. He already knew. Toni was there because Gilletti couldn't do anything about Neary, but Maddoc could.

"He's a little late, isn't he? So much for the old family ties."

"When he suspected, he did what he could."

Maddoc shrugged.

Toni was growing desperate. It was important to bring Maddoc over to her father's side, and she sensed that she was failing.

"Does the name Frank Trotta mean anything to you?"

She knew it did and was eager to make her point.

"When my father first suspected that Sylvi's disappearance was tied to Gubbin, he sent Trotta to Gannett. Trotta is well placed with one of my father's clients. He sent him to New Hampshire to look around and he found himself in the camp with Sylvi. He worked out a plan to break out of the camp and take Sylvi with him."

This information, even with its spin, confirmed his suspicions. Trotta broke contact once everything was over, but he never mentioned Gilletti.

Maddoc nodded, inviting her to continue, "Why did he lead them into Gannett?"

"My father asked the same question. He chose Gannett because it was the last place anyone would look and had an honest police department."

Her story confirmed Trotta's cryptic explanation. Trotta was Gilletti's man. That was Gubbin's mistake. Yet Gilletti underestimated Gubbin, as many did, and Gubbin never saw Frank for what he was.

Maddoc softened as he resumed speaking. "Miss Gilletti, I find your story unconvincing, especially the business of Trotta targeting Gannett."

"You met Trotta!"

Yes, but that doesn't make your claim any stronger; your father lost contact with Frank?"

"He lost contact, but he didn't lose confidence. Frank had orders to find Sylvi, protect her and bring her back. My father did what he thought best for you, for Sylvi and the others."

"What I find interesting, Ms. Gilletti is your father's having concealed his suspicions when telling me would have made a difference."

"He tried to reach out to you, but you rebuffed him."

"I'm surprised your father told you this much."

"He didn't. Elio Madduccino told me."

Maddoc looked at her and said, "You made special arrangements for lunch today. Let's start with the calamari," he said, "before we learn what else the chef has cooked up."

His mood shift surprised her and she bit her lower lip, believing she had broken through.

After lunch, he left her standing on the sidewalk outside of Rao's, not the neighborhood for a unescorted woman dressed in wealth, although the school provided visible security. Before turning away, Maddoc handed her a plain envelope, large and tightly sealed at both ends. He spoke softly, "Forget about Neary. He has nothing to implicate your father. Anything that might is found in this package. Your father can thank my grandfather. There will be no indictment. Your father knows what he has to do."

He handed her a manila envelope. Your father should not open this; he should burn it.

He walked away not saying another word.

Epilogue

They met at the Howard Johnson's just off Interstate 91 in Greenfield. They found the lodge and restaurant a delightful experience. Mr. B., the proprietor at the time, brought his own flair to the décor and service. It was a favorite haunt of young people and maintained a bar, jazz quartet and dance floor.

They were settled in – Maddoc, Abranos, Harrington, Engstrom, Sossa and DeCarlo. G.K. was back at the academy ready to greet his first class as superintendent.

"Hard to believe what came tumbling out of the cracks," Harrington observed. "I still have the feeling we missed something in Gannett."

"Do not insult us. Maddoc checked it out, and Maddoc misses nothing."

"Overreacting a bit, aren't you? Neary's been granted immunity in exchange for his testimony."

"A little bureau influence in that decision, no doubt," Engstrom interjected. "The bureau is going for Gilletti's throat through Neary, but Neary is not charged with anything."

Abranos laughed. "Que burocrático buffoons. They want to tie him to the mob, but we know there *is* no mob. It's an ugly rumor. Maddoc, you know the streets. You think there's a mob out there?"

Maddoc shrugged. "If there is, it does the simplest of things. Selling babies is a dirty business that thrives as long as people want children at any cost."

Engstrom choked, coughing out his thoughts. "You're saying organized crime can't handle the adoption business."

"That's right," Abranos jumped in. "They steal from the peasants."

278

Maddoc responded, "No, my friend, this is serious business, big money business; but you're right. It is about peasants."

Engstrom changed the subject. "What happened after the fire?

The folks in Gannett were devastated. If Calin had not been there, I think everyone would have drifted away. Esther Gubbin took over. Erla didn't have the will once Gubbin died."

"They're being led by a woman now?" Abranos asked.

"Yes, and the baby business is dead. The remaining women and their babies are where they should be, but the wrong that has been done cannot be undone. Some of the women he exploited will die wondering what became of their children in life."

"Lieutenant, you're serious about a woman in charge?"

"Last I knew, and I'd like it to stay that way, but it won't. At some point, one of the men will emerge at the helm, although it's hard to see who. Calin could, but he doesn't want that responsibility. Esther's holding the community together."

"So it's back to normal," Sossa said.

"It'll never be normal. Too many family members and friends died in the fire."

"Twenty-seven, wasn't it?"

"At least in the fire, but let's not forget those killed by Neary's gang and the others who went down with Gubbin."

"So how did the fire really happen?"

"Ironically, it was started by the first person to die in it, Eban Docker. The evidence is conclusive. Docker had motive, he had means. Opportunity was apparent once the chase was on."

Harrington repeated Sylvi's account of Otha's crippling of Eban. "Eban set the fire. His remains had heavy traces of gasoline. The pan used to carry the gas had his prints. Also, Eban Docker lived under one of the cabins that burned down. His remains were found elsewhere? He did it, but no charges are filed against the dead."

"You mean to say that Gubbin crippled him and made him live like an animal simply because he screwed his wife?"

"Simply stated."

"Sonuvabitch," Abranos chimed in. "That old man was one sick dude."

* * *

The truck that hit Neary was carrying three yards of concrete and was left running at the top of the hill. The fifteen year old kid who boosted it understood exactly what he was doing.

Abranos learned that Neary's attorney had set up an appointment to prepare for his grand jury testimony. Neary came down to his car, able to drive with the prosthesis but still using a crutch. He opened the door and pushed his crutch to the passenger's side. He held the door open as he used the armrest for support to swing into the driver's seat.

The kid released the emergency brake, and the truck rolled backwards. He adjusted the mirror so that he could see from an almost prone position. Anyone looking would believe the truck was driverless. Once the truck had enough momentum, the driver slammed on the emergency brakes, but they didn't hold. The truck careened down the incline, bouncing off several parked cars, taking a dry hydrant from its base while knocking two cars aside as it crossed Jerome and veered into a parked car, slamming it across the sidewalk and into a cement wall. While everyone was distracted, the kid slipped out of the truck and joined the crowd.

Neary saw the truck before it hit him' but he couldn't move fast enough. He threw the door wide to serve as a shield. The door closed on him, pinning him against the roof and the rocker panels crushing every ounce of life from his body. He didn't feel a thing beyond the terror of these last seconds.

It was an accident. Police specialists checked the truck, finding no reason for the brakes to fail. The maintenance records stood up. Everyone was relieved. There was only one fatality. A few people were banged up as they scattered.

* * *

"What do you think, Maddoc?"
"Nothing. Accidents happen."
Sossa asked, "what happened to Little Jug."

280

Abranos laughed. "Ha, he's still shadowing Sylvi."

"That only partly true," Maddoc interrupted. "He has proved to be educable and is in school; he's learning to read. Abranos gave him an apartment. He lives there with Cha, his second love, and takes care of the place. He's won the hearts of everyone in the building, and there's no more graffiti. He cleaned up the whole street. Sylvi looks in on him, but he knows she cannot always be around."

"What? Did he break with Dogbone?" Sossa asked.

"No, no!" Abranos responded. "Dogbone comes to the office with Sylvi. He lives a clean life. L.J. takes Dogbone and Cha walking almost every day. The neighborhood's adapted, but early on it was a show. Can you imagine what the neighbor must think when a man eight feet tall is walking toward them. L.J. cannot avoid attention, and Dogbone has every dog in El Barrio at a distance. There no longer are any drug sellers in the neighborhood."

"No thugs either," Maddoc put in, "and no noise in the halls. Caleb, tell them about the heating system."

"Little Jug is a natural mechanic. Tenants complain about the heating system. With Reuben looking on, L.J. reset all the thermostats, and the system's fine now. I'm gonna teach him Spanish."

"Maddoc remarked, "you must do that El Gato. You haven't been smart enough to get the system adjusted in the seven years you owned that building."

Harrington laughed. "Let's have dinner."

As they walked to the restaurant, El Gato remarked, "Hey, piojo, what do you think of cousin Hector? That kid will be driving in Indianapolis someday."

Maddoc did not respond. It was over.

FINI

CPSIA information can be obtained at www.ICGtesting.com
Printed in the USA
BVOW08s1721110116

432455BV00003B/108/P

9 781457 532399